BREAKERS
OF THE
CODE

CB ARCHER

Cover Illustration and Design Copyright © 2015 by CB Archer
Book Design and Production by CB Archer

ISBN-13: 978-0994773708

First Edition: 2015

Wish to learn more? Visit Annals of Gentalia at the following locations.
Website: www.annalsofgentalia.wordpress.com
Facebook: www.facebook.com/annalsofgentalia
Twitter: @CB_Archer
Goodreads: CB Archer

Dedicated to Another Castles everywhere.
(Seriously, those places are full to the brim with nothing but Princesses.
They need our continued support!)

◈ Chapter 1 ◈
CREATION COMPLETE

Zing! A perfectly animated arrow flew through the air and struck true. One of the Green Slimes, a small amorphous gooey creature in this dungeon, was struck somewhere important because it slumped down without much fanfare, quietly flashed three times, and disappeared, leaving only a *Vial of Green Goo* and six experience points in its place.

According to the *Item Description Menu Box*, a *Vial of Green Goo* was handy for dissolving organic materials and was used as an ingredient for *Combi-Fusion*. A single *Vial of Green Goo* could be sold for twenty-nine Gold Pieces, and fortunately the Green Slimes kept it pre-bottled in handy glass vials that they had hidden somewhere in their ambiguous structure. That certainly made collecting them much easier.

Anders was fairly new to this kind of game. There was a lot of game experience under his belt, but this would be the first time he had played a fantasy style game. Secretly, he loved the fantasy genre, but had always kept that part of his personality hidden to avoid being called a geek. He had always played First Person Shooters, better known as FPSs, and sports games for entertainment because that was what was popular. When Anders had thought about actually trying out this fantasy world, his excitement had bubbled up to near bursting levels. It contained all manner of gaming innovations and he had decided to play this Massively Multiplayer Online Role-Playing Game, or MMORPG, even if no one else he knew was going to buy it. He was going to find some fantasy-loving gamer friends here in this world, and enjoy every moment of it. The textures, the atmosphere, the music, and even the fonts felt completely new and amazing. Manoeuvring through a pixelated world was familiar, but the game was also something completely new, and Anders was thrilled to be living his secret fantasy dream.

The adventure had only started a half-cycle ago now and honestly Anders had no idea what in the Flaming Pit a *Combi-Fusion* even was, but he certainly liked the idea of twenty-nine Gold Pieces per drop. Only four more vials left until he had enough money to return to that starting city, with the long name he couldn't remember, to sell his loot; he was fairly certain that the city started with the letter *C*, though. The thirty-two vials already in his *Backpack* didn't weigh much, which was a nice bonus.

Anders jumped down from the miscoloured pixel that he was perched on and grabbed the *Vial of Green Goo*, then quickly *Double Jumped* back up. A little guilt was mixed into his emotions for standing safely on the miscoloured pixel high above the scenery, and killing these creatures that didn't have any ranged attacks to fight back with.

Anders felt the wind against his skin as he jumped. It was exhilarating. He literally felt it as he played, to a degree. A little fan whirred against his face making each movement more life-like. One of the main reasons that he decided to try this particular MMORPG was the shiny new technology that came with it. Even if the TorTech-Headset was still in beta, it was an advanced piece of hardware that could do many little things as you played that matched the game. It could track where your eyes were looking and adjust the camera angle, change the temperature against your neck to give you a chill, and play all manner of sound effects. What it couldn't do was be an actual working headset. Until they released a patch for this thing (which was promised to be in a future update) the mic didn't work, so if you wanted to talk you still needed to type.

Anders was glad he had picked elf and Night Ranger (Ranged Style) as his race and class. Being an elf allowed him to start with a nice bow that was called the *Elf Starting Bow*, and the use of it was familar to Anders with his First Person Shooter skills. It was not the best name for a weapon, but it did come with an endless quiver of arrows and an official laminated *Night Ranger Certificate (Ranged Style)*. Anders had no idea why he was a Night Ranger as opposed to just a Ranger—the name was a bit clunky, but being one focused on Ranged Style allowed him to jump an extra time while already in mid-jump.

The elf Night Ranger had *Double Jumped* right over this dungeon's scenery and could stay out of harm's way if perched on his precious pixel. Anders had accidently discovered this brilliant plan while waiting impatiently for more Green Slimes to spawn. This particular Scenic Pillar was the only one that worked as a jumping off point; none of the others he tried would let him. It was likely because this pillar was slightly askew due to a level designer's placement error. He had foolishly spent nearly all of his starting gold on a flashy *Initiate's Jacket* instead of a melee weapon. Since Night Rangers couldn't equip the jacket due to class restrictions, this miscoloured pixel was a strategy that desperately needed to be used or he risked getting hit back. Even though it probably was cheating, he promised himself that it would only be for now in his very first Text Box. Text Boxing it made it feel more like a promise than just thinking it.

Anders' Text Box: Just until I buy a melee weapon … then I will stop being cheap and using this pixel above the scenic pillar.

Another harmless Green Slime fell to his arrow, and Anders jumped down to collect the *Vial of Green Goo* that had clinked to the floor. He nestled vial number thirty-four in his *Backpack* beside the *Initiate's Jacket* that he could never equip but refused to sell for half the value. It was still pristine; Anders couldn't even put it on, for crying out loud—that shopkeeper was completely unreasonable.

Remembering when he had button mashed in frustration and accidently drew his *Elf Starting Bow* toward the shopkeeper made him *Chuckle Animation*. The *Cower Animation* from the shopkeeper was well animated, but it had made him hit his head on a poorly placed suit of armour when he tried to do it. It might have been worth trying again to get a good laugh at the shopkeeper's expense, even if it wouldn't accomplish anything, but Anders wasn't malicious enough to do that. A Non-Player Character, or NPC, was just code, not a real person, but they still looked like they had feelings. Even if every NPC looked like the same person dressed in different outfits, Anders couldn't even think about harming one on purpose.

When a Green Slime struck Anders, it not only hurt but it also snapped him right out of his thought process, and knocked him onto his *Body Type #2 (Average)* butt. He had completely forgotten to *Double Jump* back onto the pixel above his scenic pillar and almost cursed colourfully at his foolishness. Anders did not like swearing, even when it was socially appropriate. He liked to keep his vocabulary clean, and his new style of MMORPG communication, the Text Box, would be no exception to his personal rules. With a quick step back, he tried to shoot at the Green Slime but missed. Aiming quickly and up close was something Anders had not gotten the hang of yet. With the TorTech-Headset's self-adjusting camera, Anders had a hard time figuring out where he was half the time.

A *Slam* attack from the Green Slime followed Anders' miss, and he was hit on the forearm by the creature. The horrible green acid that the slime had released began to burn Anders' arm, and he wished that he had purchased the *Glass Bracers* instead of the *Leather Armlets* with his last 60 Gold Pieces while in that starting town (Cardamassis or something?), but he was otherwise unharmed. The *Leather Armlets* did look so much better with his starting *Leather Jerkin* and *Leather Tights*, plus they also had "leather" in the name, making them impossible to pass up. Any class could use them. This was great because he already had wasted money on cool stuff that he couldn't equip.

The next arrow found its mark, and the Green Slime exploded from the *Critical Hit* that Anders landed. He had not yet seen that animation—it was awesome, and Anders was secretly thrilled. His excitement only rose when he heard the short trumpet song which meant that he was now Level 4. He snatched up the *Vial of Green Goo* and *Double Jumped* back up to the miscoloured pixel above his scenic pillar, to both check his wound and his new stats. The acid had stopped burning, which was nice. Unfortunately, it had damaged his *Leather Armlets*, and now he would have to pay to repair them, which was bad. Worst of all, he hadn't gained any new abilities at Level 4, which was a bit of a letdown.

With his *Leather Armlets* damaged, the number of *Vials of Green Goo* Anders needed had technically increased, but he was starting to get really sick of this dungeon. He could always kill a few Gray Wolves on his trip back to Colledaramin (or whatever it was called) and sell their *Gray Wolf Pelts*. They were not worth as much money, but at least when the Gray Wolves hit you, they didn't burn your gear with acid and cost you Gold Pieces.

Anders was just getting ready to jump down when he saw the shadow of another Green Slime coming down the corridor.

> Anders' Text Box: Well, one more vial couldn't hurt.

He nocked another arrow onto his *Elf Starting Bow*. As the creature turned the corner, it became clear it was not the same kind of Slime. This one was pinkish in colour and was either a strong mob creature or a boss. It was much larger than the cat-sized Green Slimes (cats existed in this fantasy setting for some reason, and in alarming quantities). This Pink Slime was as large as a horse, (which also existed here but could not be mounted). He was certain it was a random mob, as Anders was still in the entrance of this dungeon and bosses tended to stay near the end of places like this. He instinctively knew this as fact even though he had never technically seen a fantasy boss before.

He quickly checked the Insta-Wiki, the encyclopedia of *Annals of Gentalia*. All players had the chance to enter their findings here, making the Insta-Wiki the knowledge of the masses. There was no entry. Nobody had defeated this creature yet—not surprising, since the MMORPG had just been released today. If Anders was the first one to defeat a Pink Slime, he would be able to write up its description. It would be something that would forever be logged in the Insta-Wiki. Contributing to the Insta-Wiki made Anders feel important, immortal even. Everyone would always know that he had been here, and anything that he wrote down would forever be recorded. He already had added the entry for the Green Slime when he first got here, and he had yet to see anyone else come in this dungeon. The promise of contributing even more everlasting knowledge to the database was just too much for Anders.

The decision was easy: this large pink version of those little green things must be destroyed, no matter the cost. The entirety of *Annals of Gentalia* must know of his awesomeness. Killing this Pink Slime first would give him two different entries in the Insta-Wiki! He knew travelling right instead of left from the starting city C'Jamridrome (or whatever it was called) was a brilliant idea. Let everyone else go left and find the *Reading Stone* for that NPC Narbenock Wizard guy; Anders was busy becoming famous. That NPC was long-winded anyway; all of his plot exposition was just too boring to bother to read. Anders had tried desperately to listen, but he was so used to FPS NPCs that only yelled at him to shoot at things, he had kind of spaced out during the entire thing, focusing more on the fantastic graphics than the speech. Blah, blah, blah, save the world from the Plague of Something, glory for all time, riches and whatnot … but that wasn't real fame. *Real* fame was your name in the Insta-Wiki!

This was also probably why the miscoloured pixel and askew Scenic Pillar existed in the first place. The game had just been released and the developers had probably thought they'd have a little time to find the bugs as the players did the quests in the correct order. Anders didn't care, he just embraced the fantasy elements and didn't want to bother with Start Quests like Target Practice or Catching Mumblebees.

Zing! Anders' arrow flew at the Pink Slime. He was pretty sure it would be worth a lot of Experience Points, maybe even enough to make it to Level 5. Whatever it dropped (likely called a *Vial of Pink Goo*) would definitely be worth more than the *Vials of Green Goo*. The arrow made a peculiar sound as it hit, sort of a *thwick*.

A Game Explanation Text Box popped up on his monitor. This useful bit of game knowledge written in white letters on a blue background was notifying him of useful information, and Anders took notice.

> Game Explanation Text Box: Some monsters are immune to certain kinds of attacks. If one kind of attack – melee, ranged, attack magic, or healing magic – doesn't work, try another! For example, the Pink Slime is immune to ranged attacks.

> Anders' Text Box: Oh crackers!

Being immune to ranged attacks did not prevent this creature from possessing them. That wasn't very sporting of it. Fair or not, it threw a large pink blob of goo at Anders, just missing his *#6 Light Blond Hairstyle* by a single length unit. Another blob flew at Anders before he got his turn. This Pink Slime had two attacks per round. It was definitely a boss. It shouldn't have wandered all the way out here from the boss chamber. This monster had come here with a purpose. The second blob hit Anders square in the chest. Not only did it do damage, but it had an additional effect based on a Constitution Save—naturally. As an elf, he had a negative to Constitution to begin with, and Anders failed the save horribly. The secondary effect was something called *Knockback*. Anders lost his footing and fell backward.

He now began to regret the earlier decision to stand on his miscoloured pixel above the scenic pillar. Anders painfully landed on his back on the nicely textured, yet repetitive floor. While the fall didn't do any additional damage, there was the alarming sound of shattering glass. The thick green acid inside the *Vials of Green Goo* had begun to defy all game logic. Not only had the glass vials broken while in his inventory, they had also began to burn through his *Backpack*. By the time Anders reached his *Backpack* to try to save it, it had already been completely destroyed, along with most of the other items inside. Things in your inventory weren't supposed to break! Everyone knew that. Only the *Initiate's Jacket* had fallen to the floor, apparently immune to the effects of the acid. Anders used the *Scoff Animation* at the survival of the *Initiate's Jackets*, but then felt a burning sensation on his back. The acid was eating away his *Leather Jerkin*. He used the rest of his turn to frantically pull off the *Leather Jerkin* and toss it aside. Just as the Jerkin hit the floor it dissolved away completely. It was his starting gear, and he didn't remember if they sold replacements in Cuppinhagger (or whatever).

The Pink Slime took its two turns. The first was a full movement, getting right next to Anders. The second was called *Slam*, and it hit Anders with impressive force. During the Pink Slime's turn, Anders was painfully aware that the green acid was burning the bare skin on his back and shoulders, and also that much of it had dripped down and was beginning to eat away at his *Leather Tights*.

On Anders' turn, he had to choose between taking off the *Leather Tights* or just running. As he contemplated, the tights thoughtfully dissolved away by themselves, so he bolted, hoping that if he ran fast enough he could escape the dungeon. With acid burning the entire back of his body, Anders braced for the Pink Slime's turns.

The Slime's next clever move was to move toward Anders and attempt to *Slam* him again. A very original tactic, but it missed.

Painful burning struck Anders this turn; the acid was still in full effect. The TorTech-Headset was making a prickly burning feeling down his back, he had no idea what mechanism was causing it, but it felt extremely real. He camera-panned over at his gear, hoping to see if anything survived. To his dismay, he saw that his *Elf Starting Bow* had landed in the acid. While it—thankfully—hadn't dissolved away, its string had melted completely through.

Anders' Text Box: Just great. Now I have two things to fix.

To make matters worse, the acid that had eaten through his *Leather Leggings* was all over his *Standard Issue Undergarments* as well. He watched his character *Grimace Animation* in pain as he interrupted his escape to run back and grab his *Elf Starting Bow*. If he was going to run out of here half-naked and burning from acid, he was not going to leave his *Elf Starting Bow* behind.

He ended his turn, taking more acid damage and looking down to find his *Standard Issue Undergarments* disappear in a pile of random numbers and black pixels. As it dissolved, it made a horrible screeching noise. Anders thought he heard it say a word but he wasn't sure—it was too loud and painful, almost like a "cheer" or a "cheese" or maybe "cheek". Something with a "ch" at least was yelled at him from his vaporized *Standard Issue Undergarments*. The noise was so loud that he heard a fizzle come from his TorTech-Headset, and he could even smell a faint hint of smoke. He made a mental note of how odd it was to have his undergarments yell at him, but he didn't have any explanations as to why they did so.

It was a question to remember for later; right now his mind was preoccupied. This defied all logic. He was certain that nudity was not allowed in this world. According to the box, the game wasn't rated A. It was rated 18+ for graphic violence, language, and strong themes, but there was no mention of nudity on the box. Allowed or not, he was now stark naked, completely exposed, vulnerable, and with all his elf bits just dangling out there in the brisk cave air. They were not even blurred out!

The Pink Slime seemed to stare at Anders' newly revealed nakedness for its first turn, while its jellied, formless face turned on an invisible axis point. Both the staring and the obscure turning of the head were very out of place, and Anders felt a shiver go down his body while he watched. It executed a move called *Morph*, which ended its turn. *Morph* didn't do anything at the moment, which probably meant it would activate something at the beginning of the creature's next turn.

Anders used his next turn to both change his blush settings to *Blush Shade #1* and move toward the exit. Fortunately, changing *Blush Shades* was a free action. With any luck, he would be out of this creature's range next turn. The acid was still burning him, and he didn't have more rounds to really think about what was going on.

On the Pink Slime's turn, it grew slightly taller as it moved toward him.

> Anders' Text Box: Not a very scary *Morph*, Pink Slime.

The creature activated *Morph More* and ended its turn.

Standing there in his broken *Leather Armlets, Leather Boots, Elf Starting Bow, #6 Hairstyle*, and nothing else, Anders could still feel the acid burning at his skin. He was bewildered. It was like his actual skin was getting warm as the green acid damage numbers showed his health points slowly fading away. He had hoped the effect would be temporary, like the acid that hit his arm earlier. Anders decided to use his turn to run. His Hit Points reached *Critical* status halfway to the exit as the acid burned. He had never had that particular status effect happen before. The camera panned in close up and told him that the *Critical* status reduced his movement by half. Even though he felt the dire need to run, he watched as his avatar fell to the ground and began to crawl. Anders grumbled at the game designers and ended his turn impatiently.

The Pink Slime *Morphed More*, which involved it growing some sort of jelly arms. It slid up to Anders and executed *Morph More More*.

Anders rolled his green eyes at the awful move name, and crawled slowly away from the uninspired creature. Anders cringed as the acid burned before his turn end. The Night Ranger nearly crawled right into a scenic pillar that was in the centre of the room.

> Anders' Text Box: Wait, what?

At once, Anders realized what had happened: when the camera panned onto him to show his *Critical* status, it had turned him around as well. The camera angle had confused him, and his turn was just spent crawling back into the cave, ending right back where he had started. He had only three Health Points left—even a simple Start Rat from the starting area could do that much damage in a round, and the acid still was burning. He really did not want to have to restart since he had forgotten to save so far. His options were very limited now that all of his items were destroyed or broken except for the useless *Initiate's Jacket*. He used his turn to hit his arch nemesis (the scenic pillar) with as much force as could be mustered and ended his turn with a *Sigh Animation*.

> Anders' Text Box: That is it, scenic pillar! That was the last straw! You just made me make my list!

Anders opened the Player Pager for his account. It was the personal place for a player to record anything they wished. Most people used it for game-related posts, or created elaborate back stories for their avatars. Not Anders. It was actually barely used so far; the only thing it contained was an uploaded screenshot of him waving for the profile picture a few rounds before this story began. He started a new List File and creatively called it "Anders' List". It was intended to keep track of least favourite things, but even as he typed it, he doubted he would ever use it again.

Anders' List

1. Scenic Pillars

Once that was input, he was forced to focus back on the battle before him. The Pink Slime formed a muscular torso, and its arms and head became more human in shape. Everything was transparent pink, and while it lacked a true face or legs of any kind, its overall model was becoming more humanoid. Anders wondered why that even mattered. The creature came closer, readying itself to *Slam* its arms down onto Anders' mangled body once again.

> Anders' Text Box: What, no *Morph More More More*? That is just lazy.

Anders closed his eyes, bracing for impact—or he would have if he could have remembered the animation that allowed him to close his eyelids under his own volition.

The jellied arms of the creature slammed down hard on Anders, who was confused when the Retry Screen didn't appear after the hit. The creature's arms were covered in a thick slime, but it was not acidic like the Green Slime. It tingled a little. Anders was surprised when the burning acid was neutralized where the creature touched him. He was so relieved his avatar was feeling better that he swore his real skin was feeling pleasantly cool.

It was Anders' turn. He didn't have much time, as acid was still burning most of his body, so he used his action to jump at the creature, back first. He rubbed himself all over it like it was a very comfy jelly pillow. If the Pink Slime's membrane had countered the acid, he was going to use this creature up for all it was worth. His whole body felt cool, and the acid had stopped burning—but now Anders was at a frightening 1/244 Hit Points. This changed his status to *Dire*, which meant he could no longer take actions until healed. Anders used an *Eyeroll Animation* at the lame status effect, which was the only thing he could really do under the *Dire* status effect. Now Anders couldn't heal himself, as his *Health Potions* had dissolved away—and, of course, running away wasn't an option.

The Pink Slime used its turns to grab Anders with its arms. It activated *Enlarge*, the effects of which Anders assumed he would see on its next turn. Touching the skin of the creature made Anders tingle all over. The tingles even felt pretty good. That did not mean that *Enlarge* wouldn't kill him next turn. Anders was in *Dire* status and could only skip his turn through inaction.

It was the Pink Slime's turn again. Anders was sure that *Enlarge* was in full effect, but he couldn't see anything happening. Nestled in the creature's arms, he looked around frantically to see what was going on, but there was nothing. A few more turns of this creature casting *Enlarge* did nothing, and Anders had to skip his turns by doing nothing. Each turn that passed lessened the burning and increased the mint-scented tingles. He could smell mint; he didn't even know smells were a function of the TorTech-Headset.

> Anders' Text Box: Isn't anything going to happen? This is so strange!

During yet another round of tingling, followed by some sort of chime noise, something brushed against Anders' leg. He adjusted his camera angle to look downward and was absolutely spellbound—but not as in *Spellbound* the status effect. The Pink Slime had been *Enlarging* slowly right below its jellied abdomen this whole time. A transparent pink organ was growing out of the creature's groin. This action was taking a lot of effort for the creature, like it was a move intended for a different purpose altogether. The Pink Slime was determined and kept at it. Round after round passed as the *Enlarge* continued, sliding against Anders' inner thigh as it grew up between his legs. The protrusion finally stopped growing at what Anders guessed was about twenty length units long before it began to fill out in girth. Staring down, Anders would have guessed that it became thicker than his arm. It began to take on a more definite shape. Anders was both surprised and not surprised when it grew a bulbous head and jellied veins. He saw it coming certainly, but the fact that it was happening was alarming.

A pair of transparent gonads descended from the creature's newly enlarged member with a *pop*! They were approximately the size of watermelons. (Watermelons existed in this fantasy setting, but for some reason they were called *MelonMelons*.) Thicker, dense gel bubbled inside them, much darker than what made up the rest of the creature.

> Anders' Text Box: Wait ... this isn't that type of game, is it? What is the rating again? Where did I put the game box?

Anders wondered if this creature, certainly not rated *E for Everyone*, had planned this entire scenario from the start. There was nothing he could do but watch as the creature lifted him up in its arms and positioned its jellied member squarely at his anal opening. Anders winced in anticipation of what would surely be the worst way to lose a last Hit Point in recorded gaming history, but instead Anders felt a very strange sensation. The tip of the Pink Slime's conjured member had begun to lick and tease his hole. He could actually feel it. Somehow his TorTech-Headset was functioning out of its normal range.

Perhaps that loud screech had broken it. It was like he was feeling what his avatar was feeling, and it was exquisite. The tingling was entrancing as it played around his opening, and Anders was suddenly in heaven. He completely forgave his headset for yelling at him and relaxed his forced anal death-grip slightly. The creature must have taken it as a sign. It adjusted itself and slipped a very thin tendril, which had just appeared at the end of its penis, into Anders' butt. The tendril was cool and tingled significantly as it entered. Each tingle was unlike anything he had felt before, it was as if his whole self was buzzing and each sent a wave of pleasure through Anders' entire body.

The creature began to pulse, and Anders felt a cool, sticky slime begin to coat his insides. It tingled far beyond the mere touch of the creature … and it was relaxing, soothing even. The tingles rushed through his body, and he felt his own member hardening rapidly. Some rounds later, the jelly coat job stopped. Anders guessed that it had coated him completely. He looked down and saw drops of precum dripping from his member, and he changed to *Blush Shade #2* Anders felt the cool slime inside still tingling, and he donned a *Strangely Happy Grin Animation*. This TorTech-Headset was the best thing to come to gaming since the invention of cheat codes.

At the beginning of its next turn, the creature removed its small tendril with a plop. The little pink thing retreated effortlessly back into the penis. The Pink Slime grabbed Anders' waist and, with one swift, powerful motion, pulled him all the way onto its huge member.

Anders was shocked. The creature grabbed him tightly, and he had braced for the worst. Instead, he felt only pleasure. All twenty length units of the arm-thick cock filled his bottom completely; it was if his bum had stretched magically around the creature's thick member. That must have been why the Pink Slime had coated his insides with its tingly goop. Yes, it was violating him sexually with an impossibly large monster penis, but at least it was being nice about it.

The legless thing began to roll back and forth while holding Anders tightly. It executed a new move, called *Rolling Waves*. This move created a natural thrusting motion that sent waves of intense pleasure rolling down to every portion of Anders' body. *Rolling Waves* was quickly becoming his favourite monster move. The more it pulsed through his avatar, the further it submerged him into the game. He didn't feel like a guy sitting at a desk, playing a computer game anymore. This wasn't some new technology making him feel like this. He felt like he was in this world. This was happening to him and he was begging for it to continue.

The tingly sensation shivered all the way down to his toes and back up to the very tips of his *#6 Hairstyle*. The creature's penis was pulsing and grew even larger as the encounter progressed, and it continued its *Rolling Wave* technique on every turn. Anders began skipping his turns rapidly. The thick thing felt soft and squishy inside and bent in every direction as needed. It was reaching everywhere Anders desperately wanted it to reach.

Anders yearned for direct stimulation to his own member. Being in *Dire* was like being paralyzed, he could do nothing but skip his turns. He gasped in surprise when he felt a sudden firm hand grip his shaft. He let out a moan as the hand began to work his member, his addled brain trying to figure out if the Pink Slime had grown more hands. After all, there were two Pink Slime hands gripping his waist, Green Slimes had no hands, and he hadn't heard the dungeon door opening. Panning the camera around, he was even more surprised to see it was his own hand frantically working his member. His own avatar had grabbed his shaft under the desperate need for stimulation and was pulling on it, but best of all, he could feel every pump.

Confused, he wondered, *How does that work?* He thought he was in *Dire* status. Checking back through the Battle Log, he realized he was no Rocket Sorcerer, so it was a good thing he hadn't picked that class. Apparently the tingling sensation of the Pink Slime's skin had been a healing effect. Scanning the Battle Log, he realized that, from the round directly following his jumping onto this creature, he had stopped being in *Dire* status. The chime noise he'd heard meant that he had been at full Hit Points for sometime now. He could have moved at any time, but he was skipping his turns impatiently. None of this ever needed to have happened! He could have run out ages ago and completely avoided this Pink Slime "encounter".

The Pink Slime used *Rolling Waves* and ended its turn. Now it was Anders' turn, and he did what any sane elf Night Ranger would do. He readied himself for his actions. He firmly placed his *Leather Boots* on the ground. He spread his legs as far apart as he could manage. He grabbed his nemesis, the scenic pillar, and held on for dear life. Finally he bent over to give the Pink Slime complete and total access to his stretched out, gooped-up elvan fuckhole. The creature responded and doubled its efforts; it gripped him firmly on the shoulders and began *Rolling Waves* with reckless abandon. The creature was obviously enjoying itself, maybe even more than Anders was now. This new position was hitting Anders with incredible accuracy, and he could feel himself on the very edge of climax—a few more thrusts and he would cum hard. He squeezed his butt, gripping the giant, slick cock and increasing the stimulation for both parties in the encounter.

The Pink Slime began to buck. It gripped Anders and began to spurt its cold, tingly seed deep within. It was like nothing Anders had ever felt before. The pulsating jelly cock doubled in size, shrank, and doubled again. Wave after wave gushed into him, and it was tingling with such intensity that Anders was temporarily put under the *Blind* status from the pleasure. It was all too much. Anders arched his back and came in his own thick spurts, liberally covering the infuriating Scenic Pillar with his spunk. The jellied penis let out one last gush, and Anders judged that the watermelon-sized balls were now drained completely into his butt, given how much he felt go in. The Battle Log indicated that the Pink Slime had dropped its drop item but in alarming quantities, *Pink Goo* x99. Anders didn't even bother to look for the vials. He knew he wouldn't find them on the ground. This creature's treasure was buried somewhere else.

The creature slid out of Anders' bum with a loud slurping noise. Already, it had began to revert back into its amorphous, non-humanoid shape. As quickly as it had entered the room earlier, it left, obviously satisfied with itself. It turned the corner and was gone—presumably back into the boss chamber to have a cigarette (which existed here even though tobacco didn't).

Anders took a few rounds to collect himself. He had just had an amazing experience thanks to the TorTech-Headset. He wasn't sure how this was happening, but it was functioning at a much higher level than the listed product specifications. He couldn't imagine what sort of fan or electrode was supposed to make it feel so real. All he did know was that it was a pretty great boss battle.

A short song with trumpets sounding let Anders know he was now Level 5. That was unexpected. Well he had "technically" defeated the monster, and it did drop something (a lot of somethings). So, according to the rules, he had won the encounter.

He had gained two abilities at Level 5—an attack called *Double Shot* and a passive ability which was always active called *Stretch*. Why he didn't get one at Level 4 and one at Level 5, he didn't know; it could have been lazy planning on the part of the developers. Anders did not look at his Status Page as he was still enjoying the tingly feeling in his butt a little bit longer before filling out the Insta-Wiki for the Pink Slime.

Creature Name: Pink Slime
Class: Magical
Level: 8
Special Attacks: Lob, Morph, Morph More, Morph More More, Morph More More More, Enlarge, and Rolling Waves
Drops: Pink Goo
First Player Encounter Notes: This monster is a pervert. – Anders

---

Now Anders had a completely different problem. He was naked except for his broken *Leather Armlets* and perfectly fine *Leather Boots*. There was only an *Initiate's Jacket* to wear, but Night Rangers weren't allowed to because of the class restriction. It was at least a cycle's walk to Cheejra-mallor (or whatever it was called), and the bowstring on his *Elf Starting Bow* was gone. Stupid reality logic.

Despite two watermelons full of *Pink Goo*—roughly translated to *Pink Goo* x99—being dropped into Anders, he felt fine, if not a little bit full. That might save him from eating some of the horrible-tasting food he found earlier (which for some reason had the odd quality of tasting like household appliances). Anders had not known what household appliances tasted like until eating one of the horrible food items here—and now, unfortunately, he did.

He let go of the pillar. His legs were a bit shaky still though. He picked up the useless *Initiate's Jacket* and used it to wipe the cum and other juices off himself. He picked up his *Elf Starting Bow* and walked toward the entrance of the dungeon.

Not knowing what else to do, he left the dungeon before any more slimes could show up and went back into the forest area. It was called the Lower Forest of Althair. After looking around for a bit, he spotted a small piece of scenery that wasn't fully attached to the ground due to a level designer's placement error, (more proof that the game was full of glitches). He covered the opening to Slime Cave with this broken little scenic bush. It was a piss-poor hiding job and probably wouldn't fool anyone, but he wasn't sure what had just happened. He wanted to prevent it from possibly happening to others by hiding the entrance.

> Anders' Internal Text Box: Besides, what if I want to come back later to visit?

Chapter 2

THE NEXT LOGICAL ENCOUNTER

Running around looking for chests was tedious at best, and boring at worst. Anders hadn't killed any monsters for some time now, mostly because he had absolutely no weapons. Instead, he was running away from anything that moved. He desperately hoped he would find something useful in one of those Blue Chests that respawned without an explanation—at least not one he'd bothered to listen to. He thought that perhaps there might have been something to listening to the back-story of the world of Gentalia as well, but he had wanted to start playing too badly to just up and listen.

Anders refused to return to Clinzradpeen (or whatever it was called) naked and weaponless. The last thing he wanted was to hear all the other avatars laughing at him. Try as he might, the juice-stained *Initiate's Jacket* would not go on. It was constantly springing off before the buttons would do up.

But it'll be fine, Anders thought with a newfound resilience, *because according to the Insta-Wiki, equipment shows up occasionally in these Blue Chests.*

All of the chests Anders had opened recently had been devoid of anything useful. He now had many items that served no real purpose, and nothing at all to store them in. Since the items were worth Gold Pieces, he was holding them close and refusing to just abandon them in the woods.

Anders guessed that turning this upcoming corner into the shadier part of the Lower Forest of Althair would probably prove to be just as uneventful as the last few. To his delight, a beautiful green glade opened up before him. It was a most welcome change of scenery. At the very centre of the glade surrounded by flowers was a shiny Red Chest. The red enamel caught the sun's rays as it danced through the Altair treetops, making it seem like the chest had been placed there just for him. Without even a second thought, Anders decided that it was indeed just for him.

Anders quickly opened the Insta-Wiki and looked up Red Chests. Reading the comment from the first avatar to open a Red Chest was promising.

> Red Chests are special, fellow adventurers! Be sure to keep a keen eye out for them! They are known as 'equipment chests'. They only contain equipment and never consumables. – Mr. Max

Mr. Max again. Anders couldn't count the number of times he had already seen that name in the Insta-Wiki, and he felt a sudden pang of jealousy toward the famous Max. His explanations always sounded so pompous, but at least they were useful.

There was space for another comment slot that would be awarded to the first avatar to open 50 Red Chests. According to the Insta-Wiki, someone had already opened 27. It didn't say who, but judging by the number of times Anders had seen the name in the Insta-Wiki, it was probably going to be awarded to Mr. Max. Definitely an overachiever, Mr. Max was going to win the Insta-Wiki contest for sure. Anders didn't know why anyone else would even try to beat the guy. After just a few rounds of play, Anders had given up any hope of winning the fabled mystery prize.

Well, whichever avatar's name eventually showed up under 50 Red Chests, it certainly wasn't going to be Anders. This would be his very first one. He didn't really mind because the strangely fulfilling encounter with the Pink Slime had renewed his sense of optimism. He had been the first to record a battle with the Pink Slime, and he was sure that there were a few other things that he could discover first—things that Mr. Max could never even dream of. He let his mind wonder back listlessly to his wonderful fight with the Pink Slime and felt a tingle of pleasure wash over his entire body. Anders happily used a *Fondly Reminisce Animation*. Suddenly hopeful, Anders ran toward the end to the circular glade.

Just as he bent down to open the red bounty, he felt the ground shake. He was forced to postpone the opening of this mysterious Red Chest and claiming the reward contained within.

> Game Explanation Text Box: Some chests are guarded by dangerous monsters. Always be prepared!

> Anders' Text Box: Well, crumbs!

Anders had a strange way of expressing his dissatisfaction. Saying the names of random baked goods instead of the more tried and true curse words was something of a habit. He knew it was because of his aunt, who had always expressed displeasure with the most bizarre and catchy words. He wasn't exactly certain when he had starting emulating her, but it had become such a part of his programming now that he didn't even think about it. It was automatic, and crumbs sometimes just happened.

Anders slowly turned to check behind himself. Standing just a few move units away from him was a horrible mass of vines. The vines slithered and moved on top of each other, and somewhere deep down Anders knew that they were hiding something dark and sinister. In that wiggling mass there may have been a body, but Anders couldn't see any traces of it. Hundreds of the thick, ropey vines were writhing in turn, each ending in a suspicious closed red-and-yellow flower.

The vine creature smelled far more awful than one would have expected from a giant monster bouquet. Anders almost felt the *Nauseated* status effect, but resisted the urge to vomit. For some reason, he felt like he should know what this thing was, even without having seeing one before.

A quick survey of the area did not help Anders. The serene feeling he had originally experienced in the glade had quickly vanished, replaced by an intense feeling of panic. There was only one way out of this glade and this horribly mass of vines, was blocking it.

The vine mass took its first turn to look over Anders' mostly naked body. It had no visible eyes, but Anders could sense that it was giving him the once over and sizing him up. It began to spin in place at an alarming pace, but it abruptly halted. The entire situation was familiar. For the second part of its turn, it lashed out with its tentacle vines. Thankfully, it missed.

> Anders' Text Box: At least this thing can miss, even if it is a boss. Maybe I have a chance to escape if I lure it away from the exit.

Anders spent his turn moving backward in an unnecessary (but cool) barrage of back flips. Then he waited.

The thing followed him on its turn. It was certainly big, but it was not very mobile. Trying to grab the Night Ranger with a mass of vines, it missed again. It was too stupid to realize that he was out of its range. After a few rounds of spectacular back-flipping, Anders carefully lured the thing around the glade.

Anders was pleased with himself. The combatants had successfully switched places! He was at the entrance to the glade, and that thing was right beside the Red Chest—the Red Chest that for certain had equipment in it, which he hadn't remembered to open while he was standing beside it. The very reason that he was wandering around this stupid low level forest area was in that stupid chest. Now the sinister vine creature was between him and the promise of much-needed pants. Anders used a *Facepalm Animation*.

Anders took a round to think. This monster was pretty stupid. He could just shuffle it around again, grab the contents of the chest, keep shuffling, and be right back here in just a few turns. It seemed to be a logical solution to his problem, and Anders set his plan into motion. With just a few rounds of work, he perfectly shuffled the thing back to where it came from. Now he was right beside the Red Chest, and the vine creature was at the entrance. He leaned against the Red Chest and ended his turn triumphantly.

> Game Explanation Text Box: Some chests are guarded by dangerous monsters. Always be prepared!

> Anders' Text Box: Huh?

The vine-writhing monster disappeared in a flash. It fell from the air again as it had done before, landing with a crash just a single move unit from Anders. Anders' face blanched. He had just respawned the damn thing by going back to the chest, and it was the damn thing's turn now! (Darn thing's turn! He meant to think darn!)

This new version was exactly the same in almost all regards. It was a horrible mass of wiggling vines without a visible body. All the vines ended in red-and-yellow flowers. It smelled awful, and looked nightmarish. On its first turn, its body spun around in place at a furious pace. There was only one thing unique about this creature: this horrible mass of vines did not miss. It hit Anders with its first attack. Ropey vines grabbed Anders' right leg and arm and pulled him into the air with surprisingly little effort.

Now it was Anders' turn, but before he could act, something sprang up in front of him.

> Game Explanation Text Box: You are in the *Bound* status. Your only available action is to *Struggle*. When you Struggle, you will make an opposed check based on your Constitution versus your opponent's to escape bondage.

> Anders' Text Box: Constitution again? Are you kidding me? Come on! Wiggling should be Dexterity!

Anders' *Struggle* was unsurprisingly ineffective. He did not win the opposed check, and now his turn was over.

The thing had finally grabbed hold of its prey. The vines covering Anders began to writhe all over his exposed skin. New vines emerged from the creature, thicker, and with purple tipped heads.

Anders used the *Eye Twitch Animation*. Those new vines were not normal vines, those were plant tentacles with dripping white nectar. Anders placed what this monster truly was. He had heard whispers of these creatures existing on the hidden parts of the internet, but he never dared search for them. Searching or not, this one had found him, and Anders knew that there was nothing in all of fiction that could compare to the pure depravity of this creature. It was the sex deviant to end all sex deviants. This was a Tentacle Rape Monster.

This monster executed a move called *Bind More*, which caused vines to cover Anders' entire right arm and the bottom half of his right leg. It used another one of those well-named moves, *Bind More More*, and Anders' left arm also became trapped in its snare. Anders' turn came again, but his only available action was still *Struggle* and he struggled with everything he could muster. The plant had a bonus to this check, as it was *Binding More* as well as *Binding More More*. Anders was aghast when he made the save, and now had his right arm free again. A glimmer of hope in a sea of tentacle rape. He was now only *Bound More* and *Bound* normally. He clung to this ray of hope, faint as it may be.

The tentacle rapist was upset. It redid *Bind More More* and followed up with *Bind More More More*. Despite the obviousness of this move, Anders honestly didn't see it coming. The vines now covered all his arms and legs completely and held them in a firm, writhing grip. A few vines were wrapped around his neck and torso. He feared what would come next; death by strangulation would be less cruel than a tentacle rape, and the creature could do so without much effort. Instead of squeezing harder, one of the flowers gave Anders' nipple a little flick. Anders used a *Heart Sink Animation*.

> Anders' Text Box: Oh, dear Maker! It is as I feared. I need to get out of this horrible tentacle cliché!

Anders gathered up all his might, with a mighty roar of effort, and struggled against the creature. His opposed Constitution check was failed so poorly that the vine rapist was rewarded with the ability to wrap a few more vines around his torso. Constitution was not in Anders' good books right now.

The plant executed *Bind Final* which almost covered Anders completely with vines. Only his eyes and bottom remained exposed. The next move was called *Bloom*, but nothing happened right away.

Anders was now under the status effect *Bound Most*. He could no longer take actions and skipped his turn with a *Heavy Sigh Animation*.

The blooming began on the thing's next turn. Each of the red-and-yellow flowers began to open, exposing hundreds of fully erect red-and-yellow flower cocks. That was pure madness, not only did this tentacle rape monster have twenty or so thick purple tipped members, it also had hundreds of smaller flowers He was going to be gang raped by a perverted flower's hundreds of members. It was horrible. The plant lifted Anders up in the air and spread his legs open with great force. It lined up sixteen of the smaller cocks and two of the larger ones and pointed them squarely at Anders' exposed butt. Other vines were getting into position near Anders' mouth, nostrils, and member. The plant readied itself, and Anders braced for the horrible impact. Then, suddenly, the creature fell completely apart into two equal halves and crashed to the ground, dead.

Anders used the *Confused Blink Animation*. He had to open the Combat Log and go over that last part again. It fell completely apart into two equal halves and crashed to the ground dead? There was not much time to think, however, as he quickly fell to the ground himself. Luckily he was not in two equal parts. He was still completely bound, which was not quite as lucky, but he was happy to be in one piece and free from the horror that would have been tentacle rape monster sex. He heard some avatars, but he wasn't looking in the right direction to see who they were.

> Fournimer's Text Box: well that was easy, a whole boss in just one hit!

Palcath's Text Box: I think you got a Sneak Attack, Fourni lad. It was probably distracted?

Fournimer's Text Box: yeah I think you are right Man. the damage numbers were a different colour than normal.

Roodg's Text Box: hEY! a RED CHEST? nIGHT rANGER ONLY! cRAP!

Anders' Text Box: Mffph mrrr! Bafpturf!

Palcath's Text Box: Well, give them to Fourni, lad … err, lass? Uh … what do I … you know what? I'm just gunna call you lass. Fourni killed the thing in one hit anyway. They really should be his.

Roodg's Text Box: yEAH i GUESS. hERE!

Fournimer's Text Box: awesome guy … or gal … uh … guy right?

Roodg's Text Box: wHY ARE U USING NICKNAMES? tHOSE ARE LAME. jUST USE MY NAME.

Fournimer's Text Box: my thing is nicknames! they have always been my thing.

Roodg's Text Box: oKAY. i WILL LET YOU CONTINUE TO USE THEM FOR NOW, BUT DON'T OVERDO IT OR i WILL TAKE THEM AWAY. LoL!

Ignoring Roodg, Fournimer switched pants in a flash.

Fournimer's Text Box: oh, hey, these things are awesome! finally some good luck.

Anders' Text Box: Merk.

Fournimer was a Night Ranger. It sounded like he had one of the human starting voices, but Anders wasn't completely sure. Palcath was a dwarf most certainly, and Anders could also tell he was overacting. Roodg sounded very loud, and was using either *Male Start Voice #5* or *Female Start Voice #7*; Anders couldn't tell.

Roodg's Text Box: LoL. tHOSE FLOWERS LOOK SORTA NAUGHTY!

Palcath's Text Box: Of course they don't, lass. Let's go.

Roodg's Text Box: fORWARD!

Roodg stormed off, making a loud racket as either he or she ran back into the forest, leaving Anders to hear some private conversation between the likely human and definite dwarf.

> Fournimer's Text Box: are you sure we need a full party, Man? well, I mean all the caps lock and strange comments so far....

> Palcath's Text Box: Despite the fact that you have no grounds to complain about capital letter usage, lad, Roodg is the only one who answered our Looking For Group in the WorldForums. We can always change for someone else later if the … lass … or lad doesn't work out. We do need a healer more, but an attack magic class is also useful. I really would like to play with a healer type.

As Anders heard their footsteps leaving the area, he tried to call out.

> Anders' Text Box: Mrrrph!!

It was to no avail. The adventuring team was gone as quickly as they came, and now Anders was stuck beside an opened Red Chest that had once contained exactly what he wanted in it: pants. Now his prize was draped over Fournimer's butt! That jerk with a friend and an associate that were playing this game probably didn't even look good in them.

> Anders' Text Box: Mmrell, mf meastm he mavfed me ffmorm gettiffm ramed…

While the vines were still causing him to be *Bound Most*, it was only a matter of winning three *Struggles* to get out of these vines; it shouldn't be that hard.

♦ Chapter 3 ♦

ONE OF THOSE
TWO OF THOSE
THREE OF THOSE

nders awoke. He couldn't move, and his senses failed him. He groggily attempted to adjust his camera angle and tried to get his bearings, but all he could concentrate on was the pungent taste of decaying vegetable matter in his mouth. He gagged a little. The taste was revolting, and when he tried to turn his head to spit it out, even that was locked. He blinked. It was all starting to come back to him, the gentle Pink Slime, the temptress Red Chest, the revolting vine creature, and the pants-stealing adventurers. He remembered successfully biting through the vine that had been gagging him, and a brief instant that tasted worse that all the appliance-tasting food he had eaten combined. That must have been what made him pass out. He noted that not everything about the TorTech-Headset helping him share the experience was pleasant.

That was why he couldn't move. He was still bound tightly in vines—the horrible, humiliating vines. The memory of the encounter was almost more than Anders could handle. He needed to suppress a tear from rolling down his face. It was nothing like his first encounter. The vine creature had felt so much more intrusive than the Pink Slime, who had been gentle and kind in comparison. Anders nearly needed to change *Blush Shades* when thinking of the Pink Slime, but his cheeks were bound tightly and no one could see them anyway.

He knew that he couldn't move, but he also knew that he would still be able to move his eyes. No one was around. The marauding party was long gone, and they had taken the red treasure that he had almost been clichéd for with them. This thought made Anders slightly sicker than the taste in his mouth. He would not be able to spit out this thought or the bile, and he was forced to swallow. The self-pity and the leftover bile slicked down his throat; they were both gone. He decided that he was strong. He knew that he could survive this world, alone if he had to. It was time to buck up and get out of these vines.

It took forty-seven tries and the biting of uncountable vines before Anders finally escaped his bondage. He was happily surprised when he noticed that, although the adventuring team had taken his pants, they had forgotten to pick up the boss drop. It was something called an *Allure Petal*. He grabbed it, and tried to balance it in his arms which also contained a full assortment of random stuff. He really wished that he had a bag or something to carry it all in. He left the cursed glade, being extra careful to avoid the abandoned Red Chest, just in case it decided to spawn another pervert.

Anders was determined now. He knew that there had been pants sighted in the area, and he wasn't going to give up. Let Fourni have those *Hard Leather Leggings*. He could find his own—probably even some *Extra-Hard* ones!

> Anders' Text Box: Well, at least I have collected enough random junk to buy some useful junk when I get back to Comeramondrallin or whatever.

He considered trying for one more chest. Just one more and Anders would admit defeat and humbly walk into Chrumbkeller in the buff for all to see and *Point Animation* at.

Five hundred turns eased by uneventfully without a single chest, and Anders was getting very irritated. There had to be something he could do, and he finally remembered that there was a Game Tutorial he had never watched. Well, he "remembered" this by accidently clicking it while looking for something to eat to get the lingering taste of vine creature out of his mouth. While it wasn't a very exciting video, he did learn something about a tenth of the way through, then didn't bother to finish. He could *Kick*! He had never even tried that button, but there it was—a *Kick*! It really wouldn't do very much damage, but at least he could cause some harm to his attackers. He knew that he really should have finished watching the tutorial instead of stopping it so early, but now he was obviously good to go.

He walked up to the next Gray Wolf he saw and *Kicked* it square in the maw, doing an impressive 0 Damage to the White Wolf.

> Anders' Text Box: Wait, White Wolf?

The White Wolf used *White Fang* on him in retaliation and did a much more reasonable 318 damage. Anders ran screaming—that was almost his entire Health Bar.

Finally far away, hiding inside a poorly placed scenic tree and safe from the White Wolf (of death), Anders was curious. He checked the Insta-Wiki, which indicated that a White Wolf was a Level 27 monster. Anders used the *Hard Swallow Animation*. He was now in the Upper Forest of Althair, which was for mid-level characters.

> Anders' Text Box: Level 27? Cookies!

He had ventured into an area far beyond his level. Even if he weren't naked except for his boots and broken bracers and he had functioning weapons, this place was way too dangerous for him. He really thought that someone should have at least put up a warning sign or something. That wolf-thing had nearly ten times the Hit Points that he had. Streaking through the Lower Forest of Althair in a straight line for five hundred turns to search for chests with pants in them had not gone as well as he had planned. He'd stumbled into a much higher level area, and while it looked exactly the same in every way as before, he knew that he should probably head back before things turned ugly.

Anders heard a growl. He glanced up from his Insta-Wiki. A large, four-armed demon bear with horns was blocking the path. It was throwing other poorly placed scenic trees into oblivion. It was ugly, and it was turning. Well, that was ironic. Ugly things had literally just turned.

The bear glowed purple as it began to chant something. Without wasting a round, Anders ran. This was the one thing he had gotten pretty good at it. Hopefully the casting time would keep the bear busy. To Anders' dismay, it didn't take long for a demonic *Flaming-Pitfire* to erupt right behind him. Fortunately, the spell's area didn't cover enough move units to catch up to a naked elf Night Ranger (with proper footwear) as he ran scared. Just to be sure, he ran until his Stamina Bar was depleted. He knew he was even further from the Lower Forest of Althair now. Something in the distance caught his eye, and he used the *Squint Animation.*

It was a flash of light down the path ahead, in a small glade. A treasure chest lay in the open, glinting in the pre-dusk sun. The chest was golden; that had to be good. It was in a high level area, so that had to be even better! Anders walked toward it with high expectations and an underserved sense of accomplishment. Whatever was inside this chest was for someone who had reached Level 27 or so, and it was going to be all his.

He opened the chest in anticipation of something awesome, and was confused with what he saw. It was a silver urn with purple trim and blue jewels.

> Anders' Text Box: Well, whatever this is, it is probably valuable since it is jewel encrusted. Encrusted always means good.

Anders reached inside to get it. A quick and important sounding flute song followed, and he was informed that he had found the quest item *Combi-Fusion Pot.* A quick search into the Insta-Wiki confirmed Anders' suspicion. The first avatar to find a Golden Chest told him what was what.

> Gold chests are quest chests; they contain important quest or special items but never gear or consumables. They are infinitely useful, and it is advised that you collect every Golden Chest that you find. You never know when they will be important for a quest at a later time so be sure to keep track of any items that

> you find within Golden Chests. It might not hurt to make a list of the marv— –
> Caëlahenâilenẇhei.

That was a pretty long description to effectively say, "Get Golden Chests. They are good". The long-winded avatar even ran out of room in the description area. All of that paled in comparison to that avatar name. It was harder to remember than that starting city, which also started with a "C".

> Anders' Text Box: Wait, was Caelahenailenwhei the actual name of the starting city? No, that would be stupid. How could a city find a Golden Chest, open it, and type things into the Insta-Wiki? That is just someone with an unfortunate avatar name.

> Combi-Fusion Pot's Text Box: You can now fuse items together. This will allow you to use the magical science of alchemy to turn two different items into a much more valuable one!

Well, at the very least, Anders could now perform *Combi-Fusion*. Even if it was somehow both scientific and magical, he decided to try it out. He was intrigued by the idea of reducing the amount of items he was carrying around without reducing the value. The *Combi-Fusion* menu was pretty slick: he could insert two items into it and a different one would pop out. The concept was pretty familiar to Anders for some reason, though he wasn't sure exactly why.

Anders noticed a combi that would be useful. He threw in his *Old Twine* (which made sense) with a *Gray Wolf Pelt* (which didn't) to make a *Bowstring*. His *Elf Starting Bow* was now repaired through magical science. It cost 50 Gold Pieces as well, which was really a small price to pay to regain his ranged attack weapon and increase his odds of survival.

> Contest Announcement Text Box: The Insta-Wiki Combi-Fusion contest has been started! May the best avatar win! The first milestone is 10 combis! The second milestone is 50 combis!

That was exciting—the prospect of being the avatar with the write ups for *Combi-Fusion*, which was something that all avatars would probably see eventually. As Anders scrolled down, he was shocked. Some of the pre-revealed recipes cost thousands of Gold Pieces. He didn't have enough money to try out any other combis. This *Combi-Fusion Pot* was a total *Combi-Scam*! So much for a special item just for him! Anders felt a bit let down, but his pity party was interrupted.

> Contest Announcement Text Box: Congratulations! You are the first avatar to gain the Combi-Fusion page of the Insta-Wiki! You have won a special *Combi-Fusion Pot*! This *Combi-Fusion Pot* will not charge you any Gold Pieces to use it!'

The little silver pot became a little golden pot in his hands. With a *Ka-Chink* 50 Gold Pieces came out, a full refund!

> Anders' Text Box: Flaming Pits, yeah!

Now that this was free, he decided to put down all his junk and see if he could reach ten right then and there. He began to notice a pattern as the chart filled out automatically in the *Combi-Fusion Recipe Book* that had popped into existence after he mixed his first recipe.

Combi-Fusion Recipe Chart:

	Something that made sense	Something that didn't make sense	Result	Snarky Thought
1	Old Twine	Gray Wolf Pelt	Bowstring	Pelts are good for all sorts of things, of course.
2	Bottle	Red Flower	Health Potion	Flowers have magical healing powers.
3	Gruff Goat Cheese	Eggshell	Cheese Omelette	Eggshell was pretty close to egg. It almost made sense.
4	Timing Hammer	Strand of Dream	Repair-It	Probably a Strand of Dream about going to high school in only your *Standard Issued Undergarments.*
5	Lake Trout	Magnet	Squid Fruit	Nothing more can be said about this one.
6	Hard Leaf	Chewing Gum	Antidote	Hard Leaf Gum was the most popular brand around.
7	Thunderbolt	Crisp Breeze	Lightning Shard	It makes sense, but I have no idea how I'd been holding them both this long
#	Allure Petal	Perfume	Allure Potion	Wasn't Perfume already an Allure Potion?
8	Glass Gem	Trowel	Initiate's Ring	What part of the Trowel was even used?
9	Old Key	Freedom Rock	Stone Softener	Unlocking the rock did the trick.

Dang! He only made it to 9 combis! That was strange. He was certain he had made 10 things! The *Combi-Fusion Pot* must have glitched. The *Allure Potion* didn't count toward the total, and Anders could not figure out why. He also could not figure out why this potion acted differently than the other potions. *Health Potions* glowed red and contained red liquid, *Mana Potions* blue, *Stamina* yellow, but this *Allure Potion* contained blue liquid, but it glowed a soft pink colour. No kind of potion that Anders knew about was even pink.

The only non-mixed thing he had left that could be used in a *Combi-Fusion* was a *Square of Tanned Hide*. He could combine a *Square of Tanned Hide* (which made sense) with a *Triple Coat* (which didn't) and make an *Ultra-Pack*. The *Ultra-Pack* icon was just like his old *Backpack's* icon, but in a different colour. He had a *Tanned Hide*, but he did not have a *Triple Coat*. He couldn't make the blasted combi that he had wanted the most. He tossed all of his new items into his old *Backpack* and was annoyed when everything fell to the ground because he lacked an old *Backpack*. Anders used a *Facepalm Animation* and picked up his items while feeling foolish. He really wanted a new *Backpack* now, or clothing. Clothing would be better.

The *Repair-It* fixed Anders *Leather Armlets*. They returned to perfect condition with a single hammer smack. Anders was pleased when the *Repair-It* didn't vanish. He could use it multiple times, but wasn't sure how many times it would work. He was able to properly equip the *Leather Armlets* again; that would help him feel less naked.

Now he could use his *Elf Starting Bow* again, and with his *Leather Armlets* repaired, he had gained back 1 Defence. It was a start, and his confidence swelled. It was getting late, and it was probably time to try and head back to the lower level areas. He would be on the lookout for more junk to mix so he could get the first contest spot.

The *Sunset Animation* was nearly over, and he stopped for a moment to watch; it was beautifully rendered. Once the sun finally dipped own, Anders turned around to go back the way he came. When he saw the two hidden Red Chests on short side paths near the entrance to the glade, Anders' eyes nearly exploded. He picked up his *Combi-Fusion Pot* and assorted mixed junk and started toward the entrance.

The sun had set. A wolf howled in the distance; it was officially night.

> Game Explanation Text Box: Some creatures only come out at night. Always be prepared!

> Anders' Text Box: Wait, what?

Crash! A huge beast fell into the glade, blocking what Anders now realized was the only exit. Anders used the *Gasp in Alarm Animation*. He had been tricked again, by the crafty glade.

> Anders' Text Box: Crumpets! Screw you, glades! That's twice. You just made my list!

Anders' List:
1. Scenic Pillars
2. Glades

It was at least Level 30, and there was absolutely no way Anders could defeat this new monster (or survive a single hit from it, for that matter). Three vicious heads were attached to a single body. A lion, a dragon, and a goat stared intently at him. The monster spent its first turn flickering a bit, then sitting down and waiting. Anders guessed that this boss probably had three turns per round, and he was right—it waited once more. This was no ordinary boss; this was a Chimera, and its three heads gave it more moves than regular bosses.

Taking a shot from his newly fixed *Elf Starting Bow*, Anders did an impressive 0 damage. He muttered, "Crumpets" under his breath. The Chimera waited three more times. Anders could see a smugness in its demeanor. It would be impossible for Anders to hurt the Chimera, and the Chimera knew it, it gave him three a shrewd grins.

Anders didn't consider any other options; he quickly formulated a plan. He put all his items safely on the ground in case they decided to defy logic again and break. He turned to face the beast. It was his turn, and he began to run directly at it. The Chimera sat there, blocking the exit as Anders suspected it would. Just as Anders got within range, he *Dodge Rolled* right under the beast's claws, ending the roll deftly under the beast's chest.

Anders had decided that his only hope for survival was to expect that this boss was a pervert, just like the others he had already met. Attacking head on would do no damage; both he and the Chimera knew this. What other choice did he have? His suspicions were correct; three large cocks were hanging hard from the beast's crotch—one of a lion, one of a dragon, and one of a goat. Six heavy testicles hung behind them in a row. Anders ended his turn by frantically grabbing the outer two cocks with his hands, and impulsively sticking the middle lion dick into his mouth.

It was the Chimera's turn now, and Anders hoped that his act of good faith would prevent the vicious heads from attacking. He was pleasantly surprised when the Chimera skipped all three of its turns. It was withholding them, likely to see what Anders was up to. Anders decided it was best to not disappoint. He began to work the three cocks as best as he could, pumping one in each hand and getting as much of the middle one in his mouth as possible. Each was large, but not unusual for a beast of that size. So, while it made Anders gag a bit, he could manage.

The Chimera skipped its turns again, and Anders showed his appreciation by moving his mouth to a different cock. The dragon cock was covered in small red scales and was hot to the touch. Anders did his best to not burn himself as he went down on the hot member. On his following turn, Anders worked the goat. It was the smallest of the three, and he could almost take the whole thing.

Turn-switching by Anders and turn-skipping by the Chimera went on for several rounds, with the beast slowly becoming more aggressive as the encounter continued. It stood up and was pushing its cocks so far into Anders' mouth that he gagged. Anders pushed them away to try to catch his breath. The cocks had begun to twitch, and the balls were tightening; Anders knew that they were close to bursting.

The Chimera did not skip the next round. It spent each of its three turns attempting to get a different penis into Anders' face. The heads were fighting with each other as to which cock would get sucked next turn. This time, Anders skipped his turn to see what would happen. The beast spent its next few turns attacking itself. The resulting winner of the fight was rewarded by presenting his cock in front of Anders. Anders decided to spur the beast on further by using his turn to suck whatever was in front of him, neglecting to even touch the other cocks. Rounds went by, and the beast continued to combat itself, becoming more and more sexually charged.

It was the goat that won. On his turn, Anders had barely even put his mouth on the goat cock when the goat's nuts tightened up and released into his waiting mouth. Anders did his best to avoid it, but he had been taken by surprise and most of the goat spunk ended up on his chest and face, spraying him everywhere. The next round's victor was the lion. Anders had thought he was far more prepared this time, but even though he was expecting it, the lion's cock jerked out of his hand at the last moment. Anders was now covered in Chimera cum, and there was still one that hadn't gone off yet.

> Chimera's Lion's Head's Text Box: Wow. That was a great win, Clyde old buddy. Enjoy yourself!

This monster definitely wasn't just a brainless beast if it could talk; it was programmed with sentience. That made Anders feel better about the game and himself. Even if this was a beast, based on animals it wasn't a mindless beast. It was a thinking creature like all the other bosses here, which would help prevent this entire book series from getting too ethically confusing.

After that congratulations from the lion head, only the dragon head did not exude loud snorning noises, and it was in complete control of the entire beast. Anders got into position near the dragon dick, but the dragon had other ideas. No longer fighting for pleasure, the dragon could take its time. The dragon head dipped down and wrapped its jaws gently around Anders' waist. It took Anders to the side of the glade and was getting ready to take this to a new level.

Anders felt a flicker of panic as he realized that this might not end pleasantly. This creature could flip him over and try to stick that far-too-large burning hot member into his backside. He thought that there wasn't much he could do about stopping it, but he realized how foolish he had been. He had the ultimate power to stop anything truly bad from happening to him at any time. All he had needed to do all along was just logout of the game to stop his encounters. It was almost as though, by simply not logging off and experiencing the erotic events as they happened, he had given his consent. Anders used the *Smile Animation*. Things didn't seem so bad anymore. No matter what this Chimera or any other monster did, Anders had the real power here. He decided to see what the beast was planning to do next … and maybe he would just go along with it. Anders changed to *Blush Shade #1* when a little voice inside his head also commented that this encounter had been pretty hot so far, and he decided to see it through. Besides, how scary could a dragon named Clyde possibly be?

The Chimera reared up and placed its front paws on the cliff side. The large dragon cock was right at Anders' eye level, and wouldn't be forced inside anywhere else. Anders could be persuaded to be okay with that and opened his mouth to welcome Clyde inside. He began to move his hands down the shaft. The dragon let out a roar, bent down its flexible neck, and used the *Wink Animation*. Clyde had other plans.

Clyde started to move its hips slowly, face-fucking Anders. The pace slowly increased over the rounds, and Anders just stood there. He spent his turns doing what he could with his tongue to make this encounter more pleasant. The dragon had originally begun at a slow pace, but soon it was thrusting hard and fast at Anders' face.

Anders was gagging slightly on the dragon dick, and it was getting uncomfortably hot. He couldn't keep this up much longer. On his next turn, he reached forward, grabbed Cylde's heavy balls, and squeezed them hard. The dragon head let out a mighty roar and pushed forward. Wave after wave of dangerously hot cum rushed into Anders' mouth, and he was forced to swallow it to prevent himself from choking. It was almost too hot, and it nearly filled Anders' stomach completely (though much dribbled out the sides of his mouth).

> Clyde's Text Box: Thanks buddy, I needed that!

The beast moved off the wall and curled into a tight ball. Clyde had fallen asleep with a smoky snort. The cum covering Anders hardened, and came off intact in one big, thick skin. Anders was both excited and disgusted to find out that it was a *Triple Coat*. It really should have been a *Double Coat*, as one of the coats was inside him, but Anders didn't file a formal complaint with an Administrator.

The sound of three trumpet songs let Anders know that he had become Level 8 from Level 5. One level per cock was pretty good, Anders decided. He gained a few abilities that involved using melee attacks, which didn't matter right now, seeing as he didn't have a melee weapon.

Anders was asked to fill out the Insta-Wiki. It made sense; no one should have been able to take that beast out yet. It was far too strong without getting lucky—or rather letting it "get lucky".

> **Creature Name:** Chimera
> **Class:** Beast
> **Level:** 30
> **Special Attacks:** Tri-Attack, Tri-Claw, Fire Shot, Goat Ram, Lion Maul
> **Drops:** Triple Coat

First Player Encounter Notes: This monster can be made into a pervert. – Anders

He promptly opened the *Combi-Fusion* menu and made an *Ultra-Pack*. From what he could see, it was just a different coloured *Backpack*. He placed his belongings inside and strapped it on tightly. It was sort of like a jacket.

The Insta-Wiki chimed, and he was allowed to write the first entry for *Combi-Fusion*.

For *Combi-Fusion*, simply take two items—one that makes perfect sense and another that doesn't—then mix them to make something new. – Anders

Anders turned to what was really important, the Red Chests. Inside the first was a *Mithral Vest (s),* and the other was a *Mithral Leggings (s).*

He watched his new items until the Item Description Menu Boxes appeared to explain their statistics. They were identical in everything except for the name.

Mithral Vest (s) / Mithral Leggings (s)

Anders' Text Box: The (s) must stand for special, what luck!

Rating: Epic

Anders' Text Box: Awesome!

Level: 34

Anders' Text Box: Totally awesome!

Defence: 144 (+144 more than current equipped)

Anders' Text Box: Wow, crumpets! My entire outfit before was only 7 Defence!

Class Restriction: Night Ranger only

Anders' Text Box: Oh my Maker!

Special Qualities: Immune to being destroyed.

Anders' Text Box: Sweet!

Level Restriction: Level 20+

Anders' Text Box: Flaming Pit...

◈ Chapter 4 ◈
CROSSING OVER

Anders slept well that night, hidden as best as he could behind one of the opened Red Chests. He dreamed of how awesome the special equipment he just found would look. He couldn't see it yet because he wasn't high enough level to put it on, but the icons were really nice.

The dragon cum in his belly kept him far warmer than any fire could have. The liberated spunk also made it so that he didn't need to eat anything, which Anders appreciated because the *Squid Fruit* he had combied gave off a barbecue smell (not as in a barbecue sauce, but as in the barbecue itself). As soon as the sun rose, the sleeping Chimera disappeared, along with the other nighttime-only wildlife.

Flipping open his Micro-Mini Map, he scanned around. He was northwest from the starting city; he saw it on the edge of his map. All he could see was one letter. Whatever the place was called, it certainly started with a "C".. Heading back the way he came was not going to work; he tried that way a few times and had to run from the demonic bear each time. During his last attempt, the bear did a back flip and smiled with a lewd grin. Anders would have attempted another "encounter", but he had noticed it was a giant demonic she-bear, and he wasn't really into that. Perhaps he could see a different way by using this Micro-Mini Map that he kept forgetting he had.

Darn. If only he had checked his map originally. There had even been a line marking this area as a dangerous "medium level only" spot. He noticed another path out of this Upper Forest of Althair, and it was close. If he followed that path, turned south at the next crossway, and crossed the Rampage River, he could be back in the starting city of

Caelahenailenwhei (or something). He would just be at a different gate. Crossing the Rampage River might be dangerous, but there was a bridge a bit further down that he could cross if it turned ugly. No, not turned ugly, he wasn't going to think that anymore in case of ugly turning demonic bears.

The path there was full of random monsters. He tried shooting one White Wolf, but did very little damage to it. The wolf returned the favour by shooting icicles out of its mouth like a *Gatling Gun*. This fun event and a few others (one involving a small aggressive BitBat monster that he mistook for just a non-combat BatBat and one with a very angry Ultra-Rabbit) led to Anders being completely out of recovery items and at half Hit Points by the time he made it to the end of the path. It was a harrowing journey, but the important thing was that he made it.

Anders inhaled deeply from the low level air. It felt great. He was in Start Area Upper, which he had never been to, but was identical in feeling to Start Area Lower. He quickly shot an arrow at a passing Start Rat, and it exploded violently with only one hit, leaving only its *Start Rat Tail*, two Gold Pieces, and 3 Experience Points behind. This was how things were supposed to be—simple enemies that could be killed without much danger. Easy-to-spot chests. A lack of ugly, demonic, four-armed, horned magical bears. How he had missed this!

Many Start Rats died that cycle. On Anders' trip south toward the Rampage River, he gained two Levels. Level 9 came with just a few Start Rats and a handful of Mumblebees, but Level 10 took a bit of hunting. Anders didn't mind because of his new ability, gained at Level 9, to shoot out a spread of arrows at foes. *Spread Shot* made the experience feel epic even thought it really wasn't. Six chests on the way provided a few more random things to try to *Combi-Fuse*, but he had both ingredients for only one recipe.

Out of a *Hunk of Silver Ore* (which made sense) and a *Mumblebee Feather* (which didn't), Anders made a *Jewel Necklace*. The listed cost of the *Jewel Necklace* was 250 Gold Pieces, which was his true motivation for making the item, but afterward he found out he could equip it in an Accessory Slot and gain +3% Critical Chance. That was great for his bow attacks, and it even showed up on his character. While a necklace wasn't much of a shirt, it was the closest thing that Anders had come to wearing real clothes since his original outfit had dissolved.

The Rampage River was just ahead now, and Anders could hear it flowing. Closer inspection revealed that, while the Rampage River was indeed close, it was also a good 500 Move Units' drop straight down. Well, the Micro-Mini Map was a top down map; it didn't show depth, so that was almost fair. Seeing as how Anders nearly died after falling just 3 Move Units off a miscoloured pixel above a scenic pillar, he decided to not try jumping down. The bridge, which he could now see was called the Triple Bridge, wasn't much further. Besides, it wasn't even midday yet. There were still Start Rats to kill; he wasn't in a hurry.

He arrived at the Triple Bridge some time later, with an *Ultra-Pack* that should have been heavy with *Start Rat Tails* but still felt empty. He had gained a new level. Level 11 had earned him a new melee weapon skill to try out later. It made him one step closer to his new goal of Level 20. He was certain he would find something else before then, but the thought of the special gear excited him anyway.

The Triple Bridge spanned across three different land masses and met in the middle in a small, circular area. All of this was supported by a large, freestanding pillar rising majestically from the water. He would take the south bridge once he got to the centre and go back to Cybinhorshee. He would be back in proper equipment in no rounds flat.

Leather Boots clicking on the stonework of the Triple Bridge, he began to cross. He could see the middle of the bridge's model in the distance, and it had a small garden on it.

Pretty classy stuff for a bridge, triple or not!

The middle circle was nicely kept. Grass grew, and trees quietly swayed gently in the breeze. In the exact centre of the grass circle was a Red Chest. This was out of the way, so a nice chest was appropriate under the circumstances. Anders walked toward it without thinking.

He reached down and tried to open the chest, but it made a rattling noise. It was locked. This was new to Anders; he had never seen a locked chest before.

> Game Explanation Text Box: Be careful when surrounded. Ranged attacks become impossible.

> Anders' Text Box: Beg pardon?

Three large humanoids fell from the sky, each positioned to block one exit. They were roughly human in shape but were easily twice as tall and were packed with muscle. Each had pale brownish skin of a slightly different shade and stringy hair of a different gray, but they were otherwise identical. Three pairs of tiny eyes stared down at Anders for a round too long, and their browns and grays switched around in a blink. They grinned from ear to downward pointy ear. Their smiles took up much of their faces, and the size of their foreheads indicated that they were not good candidates for the Rocket Sorcerer class.

> Anders' Text Box: French loaves, I can't believe I fell for that. This is another glade.

Anders tried to pull out his bow, but the Text Box was indeed correct; he could not use it while under the *Surrounded* status effect.

> Anders' Text Box: That is the last straw! Status effects, you just made my list.

Anders' List:
1. Scenic Pillars

2. Glades
3. Status Effects

> Bridge Ogre 1's Text Box: Well, well, well, what do we have here?

> Bridge Ogre 2's Text Box: Looks to me like a little 'un, without a useful thing to defend himself with.

> Bridge Ogre 1's Text Box: Looks to me like he also forgot to wear anything.

The Ogres all laughed as they shifted closer.

> Bridge Ogre 2's Text Box: That's not true. Look—he has *Leather Boots*.

> Bridge Ogre 1's Text Box: Yeah, and a pretty little sparkly *Jewel Necklace*, too!

> Bridge Ogre 2's Text Box: Don't forget the *Ultra-Pack* and *Leather Armlets!* He is so well prepared!

> Bridge Ogre 3's Text Box: Wait, why are we Bridge Ogres? That doesn't make sense. Shouldn't we be Bridge Trolls?

> Bridge Ogre 1's Text Box: Shut up, Harry. You're ruining it.

> Bridge Ogre Harry's Text Box: Sorry.

> Bridge Ogre 2's Text Box: Do you know what we do to lost naked little 'uns on our bridge?

> Anders' Text Box: Nope, not really, I could probably guess, though.

> Bridge Ogre Harry's Text Box: Can I guess?

> Bridge Ogre 1's Text Box: Why don't you check your Insta-Wiki? We are not going anywhere … and neither can you.

Anders checked the Insta-Wiki as instructed.

Creature Name: Bridge Ogres
Class: Humanoid
Level: 14
Special Attacks: Clobber, Bash, Thrust
Drops: Key to Red Chest on Bridge

> **First Player Encounter Notes:** Known for their tough exteriors and bully tactics, Bridge Ogres use strength above all else. Melee attacks work wonders, fellow adventurers! – Mr. Max
>
> **Additional Comments:** They kept on bragging about their love of hard sex. The avatar that got hit with *Thrust* was raped to death. #SoFuckedUp. – Lissa

Raped to death? That didn't sound pleasant. Anders closed his Insta-Wiki and saw that the Bridge Ogres were no longer identical in all ways but colour. Their tattered loincloths had been pushed aside and revealed three very different erections. All were far larger than a human's would have been if it was as tall as them, and all were already dripping with precum.

Bridge Ogre 1 was the smallest of the bunch, but small was only relative in this case. His was about sixteen length units long and covered with thick veins. It pointed upward slightly, despite its big size. His balls would easily fill up Anders' hands.

Bridge Ogre Harry's member was at least twenty length units long and had a very large head that was rusty coloured. His balls were the biggest of the bunch, easily the size of cantaloupes (which existed in this world, but for some reason were called *Counterloupes*).

Bridge Ogre 2 was the stand out of the group. His thick meat could barely keep itself up under its own weight. It was probably twenty-four length units long. His nuts were barely smaller than Bridge Ogre 1's, but the increased cock size made them puny by comparison.

None of the cocks were terribly thick, though. Anders could have gotten his hand around any of them except maybe for Bridge Ogre 2's. The raping to death must be due to the length and not girth, Anders decided with a *Grim Fascination Animation*.

> Anders' Text Box: Let me guess, hard sex?

> Bridge Ogre 1's Text Box: You got it, Elfboy.

> Anders' Text Box: Well, better luck next time, chumps! Elfboy, my buns!

Anders had a great plan prepared. He'd had lots of rounds to think it up while they had blabbered on earlier about not being Trolls. He tried his secret skill that he had gotten so good at: running scared. He knew he could perform a *Double Jump* that was higher than the Bridge Ogres were tall, and run for it. Delivering a snide remark was pretty much a given; it would make his escape sting even more for the hapless Bridge Ogres. Unfortunately, when he tried to *Double Jump* over Harry, he discovered that the invisible space above the Bridge Ogres that was reserved for their Animations was blocking his way. All he managed to do was smack his head painfully on something that wasn't even there. He fell down on his butt. It didn't make him lose any Hit Points, but it did make the Bridge Ogres laugh at his failed efforts.

> Bridge Ogre 2's Text Box: You heard him, 'Elfboy his buns'! Give him the starter dick, Bridge Ogre 1.

That was not going to be much of a starter dick; the sixteen length units of that alone would probably do him in. Raped to death, what a horrible way to go.

> Bridge Ogre 1's Text Box: Okay, Elfboy, get ready for the ride of the rest of your life.

Bridge Ogre 1 grabbed Anders and easily lifted him up. He grabbed him firmly around the stomach and positioned Anders face-down to be used as his personal (and eventually dead) elf sleeve.

> Bridge Ogre 1's Text Box: I sure love me some hot, tight, screaming Elfboy ass. Get ready, bitch! I'm just gunna start with the tip. Be sure to scream for mercy. I like that. It's hot.

Anders was hastily looking for the logout button to stop this encounter while the Bridge Ogre was positioning his cock right at the elf's hole and pressing toward it. Trying to get a scream out of Anders was his goal, and he started to press hard in an attempt to jam the giant head inside with one painful swoop. However, much to the Bridge Ogre's and Anders' surprise, not the head but all sixteen length units went inside in one smooth, painless motion. Anders, who had been ready to logout to avoid the immense pain and death, instead gasped out in a pleasurable moan of anticipation (and promptly forgot about logging out).

The Bridge Ogres were all confused for a round, as was Anders. Anders' bum tingled as it had before when the Pink Slime had gooped him up, and Bridge Ogre 1 let out a loud moan.

> Bridge Ogre 1's Text Box: Holy Maker, that was fucking awesome. Your ass is as slick and tight as all fuck. Now make it tingle again, Elfboy bitch, or I'll break you in half.

Anders had absolutely no idea how to make it tingle again. He was only just realizing that he had kept the stretching effect from the Pink Slime goop some time ago; he'd thought it was just for that encounter. A quick check of his passive skills confirmed this—his butt had been magically gooped up to *Stretch* by the Pink Slime, and the effect was still active. It was permanent! He had never gained two skills on the same level. He, however, didn't have the rounds to think about that at the moment. He had more pressing Ogres to deal with. He took a shot in the dark and guessed.

> Anders' Text Box: Um ... keep doing it?

The Bridge Ogre did as he was told, and began moving Anders up and down on his member like he was jerking off with a custom Anders sex sleeve. The ass did not disappoint; once it started moving, it began to tingle every now and again. Each tingle sent a wave of pleasure into the Ogre, and Anders could feel the big cock squeeze hard every time it happened.

It only took a few very fast rounds until Bridge Ogre 1 came. He screamed wildly and unloaded many thick ropes of jizz into Anders' hungry hole. The spurting lasted several rounds, almost longer than the thrusting had.

The other Bridge Ogres just watched with tiny, wide open eyes. They had never seen an avatar not only live through being raped, but also enjoy it so much.

Bridge Ogre Harry grabbed Anders next, pulling him off the softening Dick 1 and turning him around in a swift one-turn action. Cum was still oozing out of Bridge Ogre 1 at an alarming rate, but Anders didn't get time to let any of the cum out of his butt before the next one started.

> Bridge Ogre Harry's Text Box: Let's see how you handle a real man … Troll … Ogre … Whatever!

Holding Anders stomach side up this time, Bridge Ogre Harry got his Elfboy positioned and pulled him onto his dick as fast and as hard as he could, as if he were trying to cause as much pain as possible. Anders and the Bridge Ogre both screamed out in pleasure. Anders was stretched more, and he loved it; he could feel every hard length unit of the Ogre inside him. The Ogre began to move him up and down with a great force, giant balls slapping Anders hard with every motion. Harry tried his best to get a reaction, but all Anders could do was moan wildly. A sudden tingle burst brought on by the intense pounding shivered all the way up Bridge Ogre Harry's thick cock and into his massive balls. Only a few rounds into the act, the giant balls began to quiver.

> Bridge Ogre Harry's Text Box: No fucking way, I'm gunna shoot!

Bridge Ogre Harry began what would forever be his biggest cumshot. The first spurt nearly threw Anders off the cock, but he was still being surrounded by Bridge Ogre 2 and couldn't use ranged attacks. Anders lost count of the spurts eventually, but felt at least thirty full-force ones. By the end of it, his belly was noticeably swollen with Ogre cum. He was so full he wasn't going to have to eat appliance-tasting food again today, which was a nice bonus. Anders looked over at Bridge Ogre Harry, who had passed out beside the snoring Bridge Ogre 1, and saw that the brute's balls had decreased from roughly cantaloupe size to about the size of oranges (which existed here only in shades of blue). They were still quivering, and a stream of cum was still flowing from his softening cock.

Surprisingly, Anders loved it. The intense pressure of the cock filling him was beyond measure, and he was certainly relieved to not be dead. He wanted more, and he knew where to find it. Yes, they had started this with the intent to harm him, but he was going to finish this his way. Even thought he was no longer *Surrounded* and could have left, he instead pointed at the stunned Bridge Ogre 2, acting before any cum could pour out from his elfhole. Anders wanted to keep it all.

> Anders' Text Box: You're next. Now lie down and keep quiet.

Without a word, the remaining Bridge Ogre complied. His giant cock was flopping in the air. Anders needed to stand on the Bridge Ogre's hips to make his rump reach the tip of it, and he positioned himself over the meaty head. Slowly, Anders went down on the hard Ogre member, and after a few very nice rounds, he had reached the base. All of that Ogre cock was now somehow in him. He tingled at the thought of it.

Moving up and down on the big thing proved hard, but Anders was trying his best to keep up the movement. The pressure inside him was wonderful, and he didn't want to stop, but he had a hard time keeping his balance.

> Bridge Ogre 2's Text Box: Yeah, ride that cock, you little bitch.

> Anders' Text Box: No, you don't! Call me Elfboy, or so help me, Maker, I will throw your sorry Ogre butt off this bridge.

> Bridge Ogre 2's Text Box: Oh, you little Elfboy fuck slut, I'm going to give it to you hard!

> Anders' Text Box: Darn right you are!

Anders was relieved when the Bridge Ogre grabbed him by the hips and began to jack himself off with the Elfboy. Anders grabbed his own member, now strained with all the pleasure, and began to work it in long, hard strokes.

The Ogre lifted Anders off his cock with a slurp and turned him around. The Ogre got up on his knees and positioned himself over his prey. Anders had to stand to allow this doggy style to work due to the Ogre's height, but he kept himself steady by grabbing the heads of the other two unconscious Ogres firmly (they really didn't seem to mind). This gave Anders the leverage needed to push himself backward onto the giant cock, and it made the pressure on Anders' place very intense. Anders could no longer jerk off; the Bridge Ogre was pushing far too hard, and he needed everything he had just to keep himself from falling. With intense desire, he pushed back onto the cock that was filling him with as much force as he could.

Anders was at his limit, and with one more thrust backward, he came. His bottom tingled with rolling waves of intense pleasure. The waves were felt by the Ogre, who began to twitch inside the magical hole.

> Bridge Ogre 2's Text Box: Oh fuck, Elfboy, yeah!

The Bridge Ogre began to cum in multiple quick spurts. All the Ogre could do before passing out was write a quick Text Box.

> Bridge Ogre 2's Text Box: ... wow ... zzz....

Anders was feeling empowered. He had been bare of equipment for so long that defeating monsters in a physical way was exhillerating.

The head Bridge Ogre had dropped the key to the Red Chest, and the treasure would soon be his.

He had defeated three Bridge Trolls (or Ogres or whatever), and was now Level 12. Anders cleaned the cum off himself as best as he could with the *Initiate's Jacket*, and quickly unlocked the Red Chest. He thought there should be a lot more of the Bridge Ogre seed somewhere, but he couldn't find any. He did feel really full, though.

Just before porting into the next area, Anders realized that he actually had a melee weapon of sorts after all, besides that useless *White Wolf Kick* (a term Anders had just coined) that nearly got him killed. It was close ranged, powerful, super effective, and it was helping him win some boss encounters. Anders couldn't help but use the *Giggle Animation*. The most dangerous melee weapon on the entire map: Elf butt.

Chapter 5

QUEST EXPERIENCE

Anders tightened up his snazzy new accessory with a giggle. This belt, aptly named the Snazzy Belt, hung around his waist, nothing was keeping it in place. He felt a bit ridiculous with a belt on that wasn't holding anything up, and he was still a little swollen up with Ogre. The accessory increased his %HitChance, which would make his attacks more likely to connect.

He got to the south end of the bridge and gazed into the distance. He could scarcely make out the names of avatars, there were so many, but they were still too far away to be visible. They were just starting out in the very first area. Anders recognized it as Start Area Lower. There was Cilantro City in the distance, almost close enough to see the real name. The thought of strolling right into town mostly naked was suddenly more nerve-wracking than anything else. Hundreds of avatars would be able to see him, and he had no animation to cover himself with. The thought made him change *to Blush Shade #2.*

> Anders' Text Box: Perhaps I will just see what is at the end of the west bridge. I'll stay near the Triple Bridge in case anything is too strong. Maybe I will see a chest right nearby that isn't in a stupid glade. That sounds like a great idea!

Retracing his steps (while avoiding the middle of the bridge glade), he made his way down the west bridge. After a round and a half of looking, Anders stepped off the bridge. He was pleased to see that there wasn't an avatar around anywhere. At least that was promising. The air had become hotter at the end of the Triple Bridge, and the grass was singed and smouldering. Surveying the land (and reading the area name that popped up), he realized that this was the Salazarm Desert. Large sand dunes stretched out as far as he could see. The way north was blocked by a large canyon wall called the Canyon of the Crossed Eyes. This Salazarm Desert was a very good place to try to find pants!

Deserts were harsh, unforgiving places, as far as Anders knew. You couldn't survive here without the proper equipment and attire. The thought of perishing while unprepared in this harsh environment sent a somewhat welcomed cold shivered down Anders' spine. Even if he was naked and unprepared, his only other choice was to return to civilization and face certain humiliation. His pride would never allow that. He would pull the pants off the sun-bleached bones of another dead avatar if he had to. He soldiered on.

A dog-sized Desert Scorpion was within sight (dog existed in this world but only as special mounts for small-sized avatars). Testing the sandy waters, Anders aimed his *Elf Starting Bow* and fired. Within three attacks, the Desert Scorpion was dead. The experience gained was about five times greater than the Start Rats he had been fighting earlier. This place was going to be perfect. He could stay over here until night time and try going back to Cheyeteelawtay to buy some new equipment. Fewer avatars would be out at night to see him anyway (well, probably).

The experience was coming quickly here in the Salazarm Desert, and he did not complain at all. As he wandered, following the wall of the Canyon of the Crossed Eyes, he killed anything he could safely snipe from afar. Desert Scorpions, Cactus Brothers, Heat Pigs, and Velocivultures all fell to his *Elf Starting Bow*. The Heat Pigs were the strongest of the bunch, but they did drop *Desert Bacon* which smelled delicious, unlike the other food he had found so far. Anders was wishing that his *Elf Starting Bow* was an *Elf Second Bow*, just to help make the process of exploring faster. He still was making excellent progress; by the time Anders reached the direction-change in the canyon wall, he had become Level 15.76.

The sound of a wolf howling in the distance meant that the sun was beginning to set. Anders had been distracted and hadn't even noticed how late it was getting. He opened his Micro-Mini Map but couldn't even see the Triple Bridge anymore. It would be a very long trip back. Still, there would be experience to gather along the way, as well as more *Desert Bacon*, so Anders was not discouraged.

Anders stood against the wall of the Canyon of the Crossed Eyes, waiting for the sun to set. Although he didn't want any nighttime-only monsters sneaking up on him again, he changed to *Blush Shade #1* when he remembered his last nighttime boss battle. He noticed that where the wall changed direction, there was a small cave inset. He knew it couldn't have been a proper dungeon, however, as it lacked a dungeon door, but it felt like something to check out after the cycle shifted to night.

The time changed officially to night with another wolf's howl, and the monsters reset. During the night, the Heat Pigs were gone and replaced by Molten Blue Lizards. Nothing else dropped from the sky. He shot at a Molten Blue Lizard, and it charged at him. Luckily, it was dead in only a few shots. The Heat Pigs were the strong ones of this area, Anders noticed, not these Molten chumps.

Anders put the small inset cave on the backburner for a moment; the enemies had all reset with nightfall, and the killing was good. After about a tenth of a cycle or so of killing anything that moved in the surrounding area, Anders spotted another Blue Chest. He was expecting to find just another *Bottle* or *Hard Leaf*, but inside this one was something different, a sword—an *Iron Cutlass*, to be precise. Anders had just found his first equipment from a Blue Chest and was overjoyed. It was even for his class, so he could use it.

> Anders' Text Box: Score!

The blade was heavy, but was in a handy little scabbard. Unfortunately, try as he might, he just could not get the thing to attach to his belt. It just hung in the air beside him. While it certainly wasn't the be all and end all of melee weapons (it was only Level 9), it was far better than his current melee weapon of elf booty. It was also much better than his *Elf Starting Bow*, which was only Level 5. After a few practice swings, he was running over to cut a small group of Cactus Brothers into *Cactus Strips*. The *Iron Cutlass* was fun to use, but it did force him to be much closer to the enemies to damage them. He was painfully aware of his low defensive power by the massive amount of Hit Points he lost to the Cactus Brothers. If he had not reached Level 16 halfway through the encounter, he would have been forced to use a *Health Potion*, and he liked to save those for emergencies.

He picked up the remains of his foes and felt a shiver go down his body. It was at that moment when he realized something. He was cold. Really cold. The thrill of battle, the excitement of the *Iron Cutlass*, and the urge to level up had made Anders not take notice. He had dodged the heat of the day by staying in the shade of the wall (plus, he wasn't exactly overdressed for the climate). Now, with the night temperature dropping, he knew that making it back to the Triple Bridge wasn't possible tonight. Temperatures mattered here. Darn logic. He remembered the cave inset into the wall of the Canyon of the Crossed Eyes. That would be a good spot to check. A fire should warm his makeshift shelter, and with any luck it would stay that way through the night. It was only a quick walk and two Molten Blue Lizards away.

The inside of the cave was a little bit deeper than Anders had originally expected. The floor was some kind of oddly smooth textured stone, and there was very little sand near the back of the cave. Stalagmites and stalactites dotted the area, and were the same rusty brown as the walls. A cluster of gray stones was slightly out of place in one corner, but Anders could have sworn he had seen the exact same group of scenic rocks a few times already before. The developers were probably just saving time. He nearly jumped out of his *Leather Boots* when he saw the colour of the group of gray rocks change to a shade of pink, but laughed at himself when he realized it was just a trick of the light. Everything else was flickering and changing colour in the torchlight as well.

He began the *Campfire Making Animation* near the base of the gray rocks and used them to help reflect the heat around the cave. Thank goodness his default backstory had mentioned that he went to Night Ranger Scouts as a child. The campfire was starting to burn nicely, and Anders built it up with an extra *Velocivulture's Fur*. After cooking up some of the *Desert Bacon* and roasting a few *Cactus Strips,* Anders stretched out on the floor and closed his eyes. It took several rounds to get the taste of Toast-R-Ovens out of his mouth, and he wished he had eaten the *Cactus Strips* first. Wishing he had a *Blanket*, he checked out the *Combi-Fuse* menu and saw he could not make one without some *Soft Feathers* (which made sense) even though he already had the *Heavy Shovel* (which made even less sense than normal). He *Combi-Fused* a few Salazarm Desert Area items, and his total recipes were up to 17 now—pretty respectable, and he was still in the lead for making it to 50.

He knew he would probably need to wake up and resupply the fire to prevent from freezing every eighth of a cycle or so. He promptly fell asleep sprawled out on his back and snored exceedingly loud all night instead. It had been a very long cycle. It was that pleasant resting music playing in the background that did him in. That tune always made him so sleepy. He awoke warm and cozy just before dawn the next day. He was happily surprised to see the fire was still going strong. He figured it must not use fuel, but ANders noticed that the pile of wood had depleted during the night and was almost gone. It must just stay on for so many rounds and stop when the supplied wood was finished. Anders guessed this as he never had to make a fire before and could not prove his theory quite yet.

Anders looked around the area again, but nothing else had moved besides the firewood. His eyes lingered on the gray rocks for a round; there was a group of three increasingly larger protrusions sticking up from the ground. He didn't remember them from last night. He honestly hadn't checked closely either, and got up to get closer.

The three rocks were a little bit phallic in shape. Anders used the *Gleeful Giggle Animation*. He felt immature for using it, but he couldn't help himself. More narrow at the top and getting increasingly larger as they went to the ground. Anders touched one, and it felt a bit warm; heat from the fire must have warmed these stones. He remembered his pleasure from last cycle.

Anders had a perverse idea. Ever since his encounter with the Bridge Ogres last cycle, he sort of wondered how much he could stretch his ass out before it stopped feeling nice. He sheepishly stuck a finger inside himself and felt that it was still very slick and wet. However, it still felt a bit tight on his finger.

The first rock protrusion was a little bit shorter than Bridge Ogre 2 had been and wasn't as thick. He didn't want to overdo it and hurt himself. He wanted to do this slowly, so he started there. The rock was dry. Anders thought that he might supply plenty of his own goop, like before. The only way to find out was to try, so Anders positioned himself and slowly inserted the rock inside. He went down a few length units and came off to see what had happened. The tip of the thing was slicked up. Anders had been right; he was somehow self-lubricating. The first protrusion didn't give much of a challenge. While it did feel nice spending a few turns moving up and down on it, he decided to try the next one out.

Not much longer than the first, this protrusion was thicker, and certainly thicker than anything he had ever had inside him before. Anders almost couldn't get his hand around it, but slowly tried lowering himself onto it anyway. There was more pressure this time as it filled him. He moaned and tingled a bit. He had to push back a little this time near the start, but once it started, it went completely in. Anders tingled and enjoyed this rock for longer than the last, but he didn't want to finish his experiment yet, so he slowly stood up and let it out.

Bigger around than the second protrusion by a few width units, the final rock was more of a challenge. When Anders wrapped his hand around the stone, it formed the shape of a "C" Anders lined himself up to straddle it, and took a deep breath. He slowly moved down onto the stone and needed to pause after he felt resistance After a few turns of breathing, however, he could feel himself relax, and the rock slipped inside without any more problems.

He was happily bobbing up and down. His tingling was going crazy and he was rubbing himself gently, when he saw something out of the corner of his eye. There was something he had missed the first time he looked, another protrusion sticking out from the ground a few move units away. It had been in the shadows. Now that the sun was coming up and the fire was burning down, he could see it. Anders slurped himself off the now very slick rock and went over to inspect the new protrusion.

It was sticking out at a low angle and was nearly a full move unit long. Anders could only barely get both of his hands around the very base of it. It tapered gradually until it ended with a nicely rounded tip. Near the tip, Anders' thumbs and index fingers overlapped at the knuckles. This one was far thicker than the last, even just at the tip. He only wanted to challenge himself, not hurt himself, so he gathered up as much of the goop as he could from the other protrusions, and spread it all over this one. The goop was very slick, and it didn't take much of it to fully coat the stone.

The angle of the protrusion meant that Anders could not just lower himself onto it. He'd have to be more creative this time. What worked the best after a few attempts was kneeling on the floor face down with his ass high in the air. If the thing fit, he would be able to rock back and forth on it without much problem.

He pressed his hole up against the rock, but it did not simply slide in like the other pillars. He moved around a bit, and finally the very rounded end went in, though there was still a ways to go. He tried pushing backward and made a little progress, but he was feeling the tightness now. He moved off the rock and instinctively tried relaxing himself with a finger. When he stuck it in, he was surprised to find that he still felt a bit tight. Taking a few moments to explore, he felt inside his slick chamber and began to rub and relax it. As he felt his opening give way to his finger, he added another and began to work it. Whatever his bum could do, it still needed to relax. It was probably good that he started slowly.

After a few more turns of exploring himself, it was time to try this again. He took a few deep, relaxing breaths and slowly pressed himself against the rock. The relaxation paid off; his ass gave way much further this time, and he almost got the rock structure inside. Without moving his bum, he tried to spread his legs a bit further apart and took another long breath. He had begun to sweat now, but the feeling of getting close was intense. He tingled.

The tingles raced inside his butt and rolled through the rest of his body. They had added more slime to his insides. He could even feel the stuff accumulating now. It was an intense feeling as more and more tingles went through his body. He was pressing down and rubbing toward the now-coated stone with a sense of urgency now. He nearly got it inside. There was only another width unit or so around to get in, but Anders knew that it was never going to happen; he was sure this was his limit.

> Anders' Text Box: Aww, I was hoping I would *Stretch More*.

At those words (which for some reason were in italics), a strange feeling washed over Anders. He was suddenly thirsty, as if all the liquid in his body shifted, and he felt his entire body surge. He felt it most on the inside; a new kind of tingle was happening, and he stopped rubbing to feel it. He churned internally, almost as if his insides did a flip. A few spinning balls of light formed around him, and he felt a warm sensation. It was followed by a new wave of goo that flooded from his insides, spilling out on the rock behind. He reached back and almost slipped; this new layer of goop was so slick that he could barely even touch it. The area of the floor that had been gooped was too slick to even attempt to use as a support.

He wasn't sure what had happened to him, but whatever it was, it caused his entrance to relax significantly. He tried to press against the bulbous rock protrusion as a test, and with a satisfying gasp, he took the thing a few length units fully inside with absolutely no problem. The pressure was intense as he slowly lowered himself onto the rock. He finally had taken the entire pillar. It was starting to get tight near the very base of it, and while it should have came out his mouth twelve length units or so ago, he only really felt it inside It was as if it had disappeared deep into his magical elf bottom.

He began rocking himself on the stone. He enjoyed the feeling of it stretching him. He moaned openly as he rocked. His moaning was becoming louder. It even echoed in the cave as if he weren't the only one doing it. Anders heard a moan he knew was not his. He slowed, startled. He saw the cause of the moaning—the rocks behind him were blushing a deep red on what now resembled a face. It was nervous that it had been discovered and shifted. Some of the dirt fell off the construct, giving Anders a much better view of the huge, roughly-humanoid rock creature. Anders returned the blush and used a *Shy Grin Animation*. He noticed that the creature's right hand was what he had used to test himself earlier, and now he was firmly planted with the construct's rocky erection completely up his bottom.

> Rockagin's Text Box: Sorry, I didn't mean to interrupt you, but I couldn't keep from moaning.

Anders was surprised that the creature was not just shouting random rocky things. Its voice was rough and pebbly, but it actually sounded quite intelligent.

> Anders' Text Box: Why didn't you say something earlier? Like ... before I jammed myself onto you, maybe?

> Rockagin's Text Box: I haven't seen an avatar come in here naked before. Usually I just say my lines and give up the Quest Item and sit down again. But when I saw you, I got nervous. I kept the fire going and the monsters away, hid you from the quest-seeking avatars, and then when you woke up and started this, and ... well, I didn't know what to do....

> Anders' Text Box: You did all of that for me?

Anders was taken aback. The thought of this gentle creature, which was now impaling him, taking care of him all night sent a different kind of tingle down his body. It was clear that the golem had felt the tingles as well, since it shuddered.

> Rockagin's Text Box: Yes ... ahhhh! I don't know what to do now.

> Anders' Text Box: You were so nice to me.... Now let me be nice to you.

Anders flashed a *Wicked Smirk Animation* and turned back around. He began rocking back and forth on what he now knew was a huge cock with an accelerated pace. While he could only move a fraction of it in and out, the intense pressure on his insides began to make his butt tingle almost constantly. The creature rested his non-slick hand on Anders' back with an unexpected gentleness. It began to slowly thrust back. When Anders felt that, he *Smile Animationed*.

As the rounds passed, the speed increased. Soon the construct was no longer content to just sit there. With an unnatural swiftness that could only come from a *Reveal Animation* (or possibly some kind of *Serpent Speed* spell), the golem was on his feet. This left Anders dangling several height units up in the air on the huge cock.

> Rockagin's Text Box: Is this okay?

> Anders' Text Box: You bet!

With that, Rockagin grabbed Anders gently with both hands and began to thrust deeply into the elf. Anders could feel the rocky member slide in and out, each time going all the way to the base and almost all the way to the tip. Anders grabbed his own member and began to feverishly pull it. Combined with the thrusting, this pushed him over the edge. With a surge of tingles, Anders started to cum in thick ropes.

The tingles went straight to the golem's very core crystal, and he quickly pulled out, orgasm impending. Anders wasn't sure why at first, but a shower of teardrop-shaped crystals erupted from the construct's rocky member. In short order, the cave floor was coated with them. The crystals made little twinkly noises as they hit the floor. Anders was thankful Rockagin had pulled out. It wouldn't have been very pleasant to have those shot into him.

The golem caught his breath and returned Anders to the floor. With two mighty sweeps of its arms, it gathered all the crystals and pushed them to the edge of the cave and into a hidden NPC-only compartment. Rockagin's camera shifted down at Anders as he blushed shyly. He handed Anders the largest and most brilliant crystal from the load of *Teardrop Crystals*. It was a Quest Item.

> Rockagin's Text Box: Here, you will need one of these for the main storyline. You helped me replenish my stock like never before.

> Anders' Text Box: I will need one of these?

> Rockagin's Text Box: Yes, of course. I'm surprised you didn't know that. This Quest is in the Game Tutorial.

The main storyline? A Quest? Anders now realized that he'd accidently had sex with a very important Quest-giving NPC, one that was even in the Game Tutorial! If Rockagin was part of the main storyline, it was a marvel that no one walked in on them replenishing the Quest Items.

> Anders' Text Box: Thank you, Rockagin. You can give me a quest anytime!

Anders gained some experience, as he had completed this part of the quest. He wasn't sure what to do next in the quest line, or even how it fit chronologically in the story as a whole. He may not have been certain where he was in the storyline, but at least he was further. He was still thirsty and checked his status. All his Magic Points were depleted, which was odd because he didn't even think he could cast spells. After a bit of research in his Passive Skills, he saw it: under *Stretch*, there was a sub-skill called *Stretch More*. It was what had happened when he became ultra slick and saw the bubbles. It was now a spell he could cast at will. What intrigued him more was that under *Stretch*, there was room for three other sub-skills. He wondered what they could possibly be. Finding out, Anders decided, would certainly be interesting.

> Rockagin's Text Box: Some avatars are coming for the quest; I can feel it. You might want to get some pants on.

With that warning, Anders ducked behind the golem's mighty leg, as Rockagin began to play out his integral role in the game.

Rockagin's Text Box: Hail avatar(s) and welcome, I am the Rockagin. You have proven yourself to be of ample worth....

◆ Chapter 6 ◆
ELVESDROPPING

Roodg's Text Box: OMM! cOME ON ALREADY! tHIS IS soooo BORING! gET TO THE POINT ALREADY, WE HAVE OTHER THINGS TO DO!

Anders' elfy ears perked up. Wait—that was Roodg the yeller and perpetual user of caps lock.

Rockagin's Text Box: ...and the flowing river of the crystal ...

Palcath's Text Box: Be quiet, lass. The epic quest is upon us. I need to hear how it will be revealed by the Rockagin.

Lass? That was the dwarf from before; there was no mistaking his role-play style.

Rockagin's Text Box: ...forever will the world be changed if the Cult of the...

Fournimer's Text Box: yeah, Guy, be quiet I want to hear this. this is my first epic quest, so exciting! now I know why you told me to play this, Man.

It was definitely them. He silently flapjaked the adventuring party that stole his pants and stopped the cliché tentacle vine creature encounter earlier.

Rockagin's Text Box: ...through the sleeping mountains shall the ...

> Roodg's Text Box: gIVE US cRYSTAL!

Anders risked peering up over Rockagin's knee, and saw what must be Roodg. The avatar was in *Crimson Robes* and a *Crimson Cowl* that covered his head, making it completely impossible to see what Roodg was. Maybe it was *her* head; Anders wasn't sure of the avatar's gender even after looking at him (or her). There likely was some other equipment under that oversized robe, but all Anders could make out was the bottom of a pair of *Crimson Boots* and the fingertips of some *Crimson Gloves*. He (or she) was set to a little below average height and the shape showing under the robes was not a regular human model. He (or she) was likely *Body Type #1*, and *Slim*. You could see ribs showing even through the robes. Roodg was leaning on his (or her) *Casting Rodstaff* and, therefore, was an attack magic casting class. Judging by his (or her) personality thus far, not the Rocket Sorcerer class, so Roodg must be a Magic Mage. Anders also wondered why the name was not entered as rOODG.

Anders couldn't keep calling Roodg by his or her, so he made a mental note to find out either what this avatar's gender was or, alternately, to look up what a gender neutral term for a living thing was. Calling someone an "it" didn't seem right.

> Rockagin's Text Box: ...eternal visage of the Queen of ...

> Palcath's Text Box: On second thought, this is not particularly interesting, lass and lad. I am going to look at some Player Pagers. I heard that another player's page tells almost everything.

Anders shifted his gaze. Palcath was a dwarf, as he had expected. To Anders' surprise, Palcath had picked *Facial Hair #5*, which was the close-cropped beard. Most dwarves only picked the big, bushy facial hair styles past *#14*. His medium brown hair was set to a *#16 Hairstyle*, which was longer than Anders would have guessed and it framed his face while it draped just past his shoulders. He was *Body Type #6* and *Average*, a little thin when compared to other dwarves Anders had seen before. The dwarf had an almost complete *Steel Armour Set* excluding a helmet. Palcath was holding a *Steel Small Hammer*, and having a shield equipped in the other hand meant he was the Defender Class from the melee group, but his shield was under-leveled compared to the rest of his equipment.

> Rockagin's Text Box: ...and so you must travel to the lands of...

> Fournimer's Text Box: I read about that somewhere, Man. do a search for Mr. Max. He is going to win the Insta-Wiki contest for sure. that Bro is hardcore into this.

Anders finally shifted his eyes toward Fournimer. Darn. He was not as ugly as Anders had imagined—quite the opposite in fact. He was a human, like Anders had suspected, but had definitely spent a lot of rounds on his facial creation process. Hundreds at least.

His face was chiseled and sprouted *Facial Hair #2*, just a small wisp of chin hair and a hint of a five-o'clock shadow. He had picked *Body Type #5* and *Toned*, and was filling out the *Hard Leather Leggings*. Anders' *Body Type #2 (Average)* was much slimmer than the perfectly built human who Anders looked at for longer than necessary to complete the mental description. Fournimer's *#6 Hairstyle* shimmered in the torchlight.

His *#6 Hairstyle?* The colour was different, set to medium brown and not blond, but Fournimer had the same number hairstyle as Anders! This made Anders forget about how nice Fournimer looked—that was Anders' hairstyle number!

> Roodg's Text Box: gIVE US cRYSTAL!

> Palcath's Text Box: Mr. Max … here the lad is. Wow! Look at all this stuff! He is 46.9% complete already? Wow, I'm only at 12.7%. We will never beat him and win the contest. Oh, his latest Insta-Wiki is about getting 50 Red Chests open? We have only seen 4 of those.

> Roodg's Text Box: gIVE US cRYSTAL!

> Rockagin's Text Box: …frozen sceptre of the old gods…

> Fournimer's Text Box: click it, Man, what does it say?

> Palcath's Text Box: Hmm … oh, Red Chests in dungeons are different. They always contain equipment for your class, no matter who opens it. Hey! Any boss chest can be opened by everyone in the party, lad. He even has posted a whole Micro-Mini Map algorithm of them; some have higher chances of containing certain things. I admire all the math he has in this thing.

> Roodg's Text Box: gIVE US cRYSTAL!

Roodg was jumping around the room impatiently while obviously copying and pasting the crystal message. On one jump, they landed directly on the patch of floor that had been covered by Anders' thick goop when his new ability had activated earlier. Nobody but Anders saw a *Body Type #1 (Slim)* avatar covered in oversized robes literally fly across the room and crash into a large pile of scenic crates, virtually destroying them. Anders had to stifle a *Laugh Animation* at the sight of Roodg's pointy-toed shoes and stocking-covered legs sticking out of a pile of destroyed scenery. Palcath and Fournimer were too busy with the Insta-Wiki, and Rockagin was an NPC who didn't matter.

> Roodg's Text Box: hEY! i FOUND 15GP IN THESE CRATES, i AM AWESOME!

> Fournimer's Text Box: really? that info is pretty choice. bookmark that, Man!

Palcath's Text Box: Already done, Fourni. Hey, lads and lasses! In a dungeon just south of here, there is a 99.8% chance of getting a Level 26 (Level 16+ needed to equip) secondary weapon. That would be a shield for me, a ring for Roodg, and a bow for Fourni. It's a place called the Dungeon of the Five Ts.

Rockagin's Text Box: ...then forever shall you be marked down in the...

Roodg's Text Box: lAME NAME! lET'S GO THERE NEXT! mY RING SUX HARD!

Fournimer's Text Box: I agree with Caps Guy, let's go there next. it isn't that far, and we just made Level 17.

Palcath's Text Box: I agree with Caps Lass, too. My shield sucks hard as well. This Rockalad needs to hurry up already.

Rockagin's Text Box: ...and so in conclusion...

Roodg's Text Box: gIVE US cRYSTAL!

Roodg's Text Box: gIVE US cRYSTAL!

Roodg's Text Box: gIVE US cRYSTAL!

Rockagin's Text Box: ...take this *Teardrop*...

Roodg's Text Box: gIVE US cRYSTAL!

Roodg's Text Box: gIVE US cRYSTAL!

Roodg's Text Box: gIVE US cRYSTAL!

Roodg's Text Box: gIVE US cRYSTAL!

Roodg's Text Box: gIVE US cRYSTAL!

Roodg's Text Box: gIVE US cRYSTAL!

Rockagin's Text Box: ...*Crystal.*

Roodg's Text Box: gIVE US cRYSTAL! oH WAIT. tHNX K BYE.

Their *Teardrop Crystals* secure, the trio turned to leave the cave. Anders could not get the idea of a Level 26 bow out of his mind. That would let him slaughter things in this area like nobody's business and reach Level 20 much faster. He had no idea where the Dungeon of the Five Ts was, but he knew three avatars that did.

He gave the Rockagin's leg a hug.

> Anders' Text Box: I need to follow them. I promise to visit if I'm ever in this area again.

> Rockagin's Text Box: Okay, but did you like my speech? Doesn't it help fill in the wonderful background story of the world of Gentalia?

Anders realized that, just like the other avatars that had been here, he really hadn't listened to a word of it.

> Anders' Text Box: My favourite part was the end.

Anders jumped over the Rockagin's leg and headed for the exit.

> Rockagin's Text Box: Shouldn't you put on some pants or something before you go?

> Anders' Text Box: Yes, I should.

Anders couldn't actually follow the advice as he still lacked any pants. With a *Shrug Animation*, Anders left the cave. He hastily hid behind a scenic bush as he saw some avatars coming in his direction to go into the cave. They walked right by him and didn't see him at all. There was more to these scenic bushes than Anders had given them credit for. From inside, he heard the Rockagin's pebbly voice.

> Rockagin's Text Box: Hail avatar(s) and welcome, I am the Rockagin. You have proved yourself to be of ample worth...

Anders left.

◈ Chapter 7 ◈
FOLLOWING FOURNI
AND FRIENDS

The human, the dwarf, and the ambiguous mage were not a hard party to follow. They talked constantly, and the Magic Mage was so loud it was amazing that the human Night Ranger was ever successful at *Sneak Attacks*. Anders tried to stay hidden behind scenery, just in case they turned back.

Within only a few rounds, they had traversed the Canyon of the Crossed Eyes and the Salazarm Desert, still unaware they were being followed by Anders. They had now ventured into the verdant Lushin Jungle. It didn't make any sense to put a jungle area beside a desert one, but at least it was convenient for Anders. Trees, ferns, and tribal statues dotted the landscape, making hiding one's shame particularly easy.

The party he was following worked together as a group, but certainly not very well. Palcath was the only frontline fighter and took pretty much all of the party's damage. Without a Mendicator or Soother, the dwarf had to use a lot of healing items, but his bonus to Constitution prevented him from failing every stupid resistance check, which helped a bit.

In battle, Roodg slung his attack spells from the backline with a harsh fury only reserved for whatever her race was. He preferred using Fire Magic to burn things, even with things she could not attack. Roodg did not give up; he desperately wanted the rocks, trees, rivers, ground, opened chests, sky, and scenic bunnies to burn. She was very persistent. Anders still couldn't decide what to call Roodg; he couldn't even figure out the race of the avatar, let alone the gender.

Fourni (Anders decided that he was going to call him Fourni from now on) stayed back from the melee with his bow. While he was a Night Ranger (Melee Style), judging from his fighting stance, he stayed back like a Ranged Style. Anders, who had picked Night Ranger (Ranged Style), observed him quietly, eventually figuring out the problem. Fourni was still using a *Human Starting Sword* as a weapon, so no wonder he was staying back, it was far too weak for this area. Anders couldn't judge that too harshly, though; he was still using his *Elf Starting Bow* and was basically naked.

After a few twists, a few turns, and a whole bunch of monsters, the party made it to the Dungeon of the Five Ts in fairly good condition. They were near the entrance, but stopped just before entering an obvious jungle glade.

> Palcath's Text Box: Hold up, lads and lasses. Mr. Max's guide says there is a boss out here, and another inside guarding the Red Chest. The outside boss is hard, and the inside one is a complete pushover.

> Fournimer's Text Box: okay, check the Insta-Wiki so we can be prepared, Man, what is it?

> Roodg's Text Box: cHARGE! pUSHOVER!

With that, Roodg pushed Palcath over and into the glade.

> Game Explanation Text Box: Some monsters are strong against certain kinds of magic. If something doesn't work, try another element.

A creature fell from the sky, covered in a nicely done fire effect. It was a female human torso ended at the waist and was followed by a large serpentine tail. She had long, flowing hair of fire and three sets of arms, each holding their own weapon. Six perky breasts were on her body, each set stuffed into a plate bikini top. (The female near-nudity was not out of place in a video game like the male actual nudity had been and Anders was offended on behalf of female gamers everywhere.)

> Palcath's Text Box: Let's see … it is a monster called the Flamealith. Each of her weapons has an attack … blah blah blah … weak to Ice Magic. Hey, Roodg lass, be sure and—

> Roodg's Interruption Text Box: sTOP TALKING! sHE IS SMACKING YOU! gO!

Palcath took four different weapons to the face.

> Palcath's Continued Tex Box: —use your Ice asklfj;laiowjlas;f. Hotkey 4. Hotkey 5. WAAWSWWWWW sakm;lak;lak;lask;l

Anders understood what that was; he had done it before. Palcath was trying to move and attack while still Text Boxing.

> Palcath's Text Box: Roodg, you jerk!

The battle was on.

Anders opened the Insta-Wiki.

> **Creature Name:** Flamealith
> **Class:** She-Demon
> **Level:** 20
> **Special Attacks:** Burn, Burn More, Fires of the Six, Constrict, Sever
> **Drops:** Flame Powder
> **First Player Encounter Notes:** This monster is resistant to both fire and melee attacks, fellow adventurers! Use your ice and ranged attacks. – Mr. Max
> **Additional Comments:** This she demon *Constricted* an avatar and lowered herself onto him. Crazy snake used *Sever* to chop his cock and balls off! #SoFuckedUp! – Lissa

Sever off his bits? That didn't sound fun.

Anders used his turns to both watch the action and to slowly sneak around to get closer to the entrance of the Dungeon of the Five Ts. Roodg tossed around some Fire Magic, which was pissing the others off. Palcath tried to attack with his hammer, but it did very little damage. After getting another three weapons to the face, he switched over to just blocking. Fourni shot with his bow, and was the only one who could cause any decent damage to the Flamealith.

Palcath was losing serious Hit Points; he was defensively using *Health Potions* but could only manage to stay at about half-health.

The Flamealith was next. She attacked the dwarf again and activated her move *Fires of the Six*. This move took instant effect. A huge ring of fire sprang up around her and Palcath, blocking their battle from the other party members. The scenic bush Anders was hiding behind was also within the perimeter, and he was still close enough to have a visual on Palcath. The fire effect was too overdone, so the others were too far away to see what was going on.

It was the next round.

Palcath blocked.

Fourni shot, but missed.

> Fournimer's Text Box: damn. I can't see!

> Roodg's Text Box: i KNOW WHAT 2 DO!

Roodg threw a Fireball and hit! Unfortunately, it hit both the Flamealith and Palcath. This did nothing to the Flamealith but pushed Palcath into *Critical* status, and he was forced to lower his shield and lose his Defense Bonus.

Anders was completely out of view from anyone except Palcath, who was too busy blocking to notice him, so he shot at the She-Demon for good measure.

On the next round the Flamealith used *Constrict* and Palcath failed his save. He was pinned by the She-Demon's tail and held there. She used her next attack and smacked him into *Dire* status. Anders pitied the lad; he knew what that was like.

Palcath's turn was up next, but as he was still *Dire*, he was forced to skip it.

> Palcath's Text Box: Help, Fourni, I am in *Dire* status here! And under Constrict, it says only a certain amount of melee damage to the monster can get an avatar out of it. It says she will *Sever* me next round unless I'm freed.

> Palcath's Text Box: AND FOR THE LOVE OF F*CK, LASS, USE ICE ATTACKS ALREADY!

Fourni presumably moved forward, but Anders could not see him. There was the sound of some missed *Human Starting Sword* attacks.

> Fournimer's Text Box: sorry, missed. I can't see in there.

> Roodg's Text Box: fINE! bUT FIRE IS COOL! iT CAN BURN SCENIC LAMPS!

A *Bolt of Ice* shot through the fire and did a large portion of damage to the Flamealith, but it was not melee damage and *Constrict* still held Palcath tightly.

It was Anders' turn now. He really did not want Palcath to have his junk *Severed* off by a giant flame demon with overstuffed plate mail bikinis. He sort of liked the dwarf's commitment to stay in character, even if he was overacting a bit. Had it been Roodg *Constricted*, Anders would probably just have skipped his turn and watched to see what was under the *Crimson Robes*, but instead he took action. Hidden from view by the flame circle, he *Double Jumped* at the boss. Unleashing his *Iron Cutlass* from the air that was holding it up, he used a special melee attack, *Fury of the Slashing*, which he had gained at Level 14. The move lasted until his Stamina Bar ran out and caused as many melee attacks in one round as he could button mash out. Each hit depleted something called the *Constrict Bar*, and after eighteen furious button mashes, the move ended. Anders saw the *Constrict Bar*: it was still active but 97.4% depleted.

> Anders' Internal Text Box: Son of a pudding! You jerk *Constrict Bar*. You just made my list.

Anders' List:
1. Scenic Pillars
2. Glades
3. Status Effects
4. Constrict Bars

Anders ended his turn feeling horrible. One more slash would have done it, but he wasn't a Night Ranger (Melee Style). He could only watch in horror at what he assumed would happen next.

The Flamealith was set to go. She lifted Palcath up by her tail and looked him square in the eye. She reached into the hammerspace behind her and grabbed a giant meat cleaver, and activated *Sever*. She raised the cleaver and hit Palcath's *Dwarf Starting Shield*, neatly cutting it in two. The shield was destroyed. Anders was relieved that the dwarf was still in one piece, instead of losing his manhood. The Flamealith looked over at Anders, and all of her weapons randomly switched arms in a quick instant. It was as if she re-spawned in the middle of the battle as a different version of the same monster. Anders stopped being relieved.

During the next round of turns, Palcath was forced to skip, Fourni was forced to miss, and Roodg was forced to use ice attacks. Anders used his turn to back the Flaming Pit away from this She-Demon. He didn't get very far. He was too busy watching her perverse glances and ended up backing into a wall.

The Flamealith now targeted Anders. She moved toward him, the flame circle following her. This put Palcath outside of the flames and out of view. She *Slapped* Anders around a few times; with such a low Defense Score, it hurt significantly. The two attacks that had managed to hit him had put him into *Critical* status. She ended her turn, out of actions.

Anders couldn't see what was going on outside of the fire, but heard the sounds of a *Health Potion* and an ice attack hitting the wall, missing the demon. On his turn, he desperately tried to *Double Jump* away but couldn't as he was *Surrounded* thanks to being against the wall. That was irritating.

The Flamealith smiled and activated *Constrict*, and the darn move worked. Anders was now *Constricted*. He received the same message about needing to be freed with melee attacks. He was also informed that, next turn, he would be *Severed*. The She-Demon spent her next action lifting up a set of jeweled waist flaps, showing Anders her snake-like private parts. She stuck a finger inside slightly and moved it against the side. Bringing it out, she showed Anders the gash in her finger and licked the blood off with her forked tongue. Her privates came complete with a razor-sharp, scissor-like interior. She roughly grabbed at Anders' crotch and used a *Smirk Animation*.

Anders' heart sunk. This didn't make any sense. Why had she only *Severed* Palcath's *Dwarf Starting Shield*, but was going to *Sever* him? Sure, he didn't have any pants on, but he'd seen lots of avatars wearing skimpy Armour, and they didn't get gang-raped by the jerk-butt Start Rats or get their Maker-loving crotches snipped off.

The next round, Palcath ran through the fire and attacked the She-Demon. His *Mighty Hammer Bash* move destroyed the Constrict Bar holding Anders in just one hit. He was a primary melee class, making it super effective. The Flamealith took *Sneak Attack* damage and dropped Anders headfirst into some nearby scenic bushes. He landed awkwardly, and when he opened his eyes, he was staring up at his own elf bits—

and had never been more relieved to see them.

An *Arrow Barrage* followed, which also gained *Sneak Attack* damage, and finally a *Bolt of Ice*, which did as well. The *Bolt of Ice* struck the She-Demon right in the back and burst through her chest, neatly dividing a pair of plate mail boobs and breaking the bikini open, sending one pair of bouncing boobs free. She slumped over dead. Trumpet music was heard all around, and new levels gained.

> Roodg's Text Box: wOW! i GOT A SNEAK ATTACK! i AM AWESOME!

> Fournimer's Text Box: I didn't even think you could do Sneak Attacks.

> Roodg's Text Box: OMFM! lOOK YOU CAN SEE HER BOOBS! iCE MAGIC IS AWESOME NOW! bOOBS ARE RAD!

> Fournimer's Text Box: no you can't, shut up Guy. you just wish you could. you are always saying stupid stuff like that. now stop screwing ar—

> Fournimer saw them, the boobs still bouncing out in the open, and he changed to *Blush Shade #2*.

Palcath wasn't really paying attention to the banter about the boobs behind him—which went on for a while. Roodg took a screenshot. The dwarf interrupted with a question.

> Palcath's Text Box: What just happened, lass and lad?

> Roodg's Text Box: dID YOU SEE HER WEAPONS GO ALL CRAZY LIKE?

> Fournimer's Text Box: yeah, the weapons all switched, I think she had a glitch or something.

> Palcath's Text Box: Really? I didn't see that part, a glitch, huh? But there is more than that to it, I think, lads. Why did my *Constrict Bar* go down when Fourni missed? Why did she run over to the wall and start attacking it? Whose *Constrict Bar* did I destroy when I attacked her? Why did Roodg and I get Sneak Attacks when we can't do those? Something else is going on here, methinks.

> Fournimer's Text Box: I think she just glitched out Man, don't take it too seriously. come on, I know where we can find you a new shield.

> Roodg's Text Box: hEHE. bOOBS.

Palcath's Text Box: I guess so, lad.

As the group was entering the Dungeon of the Five Ts, Anders stayed secretly hidden in the scenic bush. He remained undetected, even though he was stark naked and should probably have attracted some attention. Scenic bushes were the best hiding things ever created! They blocked *anything* from view. From his vantage point, he saw Palcath remain outside after his friends entered. Well, his friend and Roodg.

The dwarf was suspicious and thinking about something. Anders resisted the urge to jump out and hug the dwarf for saving his "little Anders", opting instead to stay hidden. Palcath finally did a *Shrugging It Off Animation* and went inside, closing the dungeon door behind him.

Now Anders could only wait and think on what had just happened. Well, that, and check out his new Level 17 abilities.

◈ **Chapter 8** ◈

THE FOURTH T

T he trio returned from inside the dungeon a few rounds later, cheering ecstatically and brandishing fancy new equipment. Roodg came out first, holding a hand up and showing off a new *Truespell Ring*.

> Roodg's Text Box: sO EASY! LoL.

> Palcath's Text Box: That was a breeze compared to outside, lass!

Palcath had a brand new *Trueblock Shield* to replace the one that was *Severed* in place of his dwarf bits.

> Fournimer's Text Box: wow! I can't believe I got the 0.2% better chest! I absolutely NEVER get lucky with anything. this is like the first time ever!

Fournimer was brandishing his brand new *Truestrike Sword*; it was golden and was much more epic than the other *Trueitems*. They all were made of bones, and were truly well-designed. Anders thought they were pretty cool. The *Truestrike Sword* was the standout of the treasures. It was a higher Level item and it showed.

> Palcath's Text Box: Now, Fourni, you have plenty of luck. Personally, I think you just dwell too much on the negative kind.

> Fournimer's Text Box: you wouldn't say that if you were me Man. you

have no idea what bad luck really is. at least we just got to Level 18, or I couldn't use it!

Roodg's Text Box: sO JEALOUS OF YOUR LUCK!

Anders was jealous as well.

Palcath's Text Box: Now you can finally fight up close again with me, lad!

Fournimer's Text Box: I know Man! this stupid bow is not nearly as easy to use. I am much better with melee weapons.

Palcath's Text Box: Hmm … I only counted four Ts now that we got the Truestuff equipment. I think we missed one, lass and lad…. Yep! My records shows we missed number 4. We need to go back inside.

Fournimer's Text Box: you always think too much Man. it was probably just a T for 'The Floor' or something.

Roodg's Text Box: wHERE NOW?

Palcath's Text Box: I'm almost at full Carrying Capacity, lass. Maybe we should go back to … uh….

Carrying Capacity? Anders didn't remember having one of those. His *Ultra-Pack* had 457 Carry Units taken up. In addition he had +100% Carrying Capacity because of the *Ultra-Pack*. He had no idea what his limit was, though. That wasn't listed anywhere.

Roodg's Text Box: cHOGGUNDERHAL?

Fournimer's Text Box: Coiperhenter?

Palcath's Text Box: Closhunfore to sell some things. After that I want to try and finish that Three Vials Of Green Goo Quest for that NPC Valisha lass.

Vials of Green Goo Quest?

Fournimer's Text Box: I'm almost full as well, let's do that. but Man, we already looked for that Slime Cave for like a quarter cycle and couldn't find it. the signs all pointed to nowhere.

That made sense. Anders had cleverly covered the entrance door to that with an impossible-to-see-through scenic bush. They probably were not going to find it.

Palcath's Text Box: Yeah, but we have Mr. Max's guide now to help us out, lad!

Roodg's Text Box: gO!

The trio left the glade, but Palcath hesitated before leaving. He stood there for a while, lost in thought. It was the sound of ice magic being cast that finally snapped the dwarf out of his trance.

Roodg's Text Box: i LOVE ICE MAGIC NOW! fREEZE SCENIC TIKI IDOL! sHOW ME YOUR TITS!

Palcath used the *Sigh Animation* as he left to follow his friend and Roodg.

Stepping out from the scenic bush, Anders approached the Dungeon of the Five Ts.

Anders' Text Box: Okay, so the last T would have been Truestuff. What about the other four? What are they?

Entering the dungeon cautiously, Anders closed the door behind him with a click. This place had taken them only a few rounds to complete, so it must not be very spacious.

There were four paths, so maybe there was one per T? Anders tried the leftmost path. It took only a round to reach the end. A Blue Chest with an *Absorbing Cloth* inside was the only T down there, and none of that actually started with a T.

The next two paths quickly led to similar results, two more chests contained the items needed to *Combi-Fusion* together a *Mana Potion*. Anders mixed a *Bottle* (which made sense) and a *Blue Flower* (which really didn't. Why were flowers from chests so powerful anyways?). Again nothing with a T. He did learn a new *Combi-Fusion* recipe to help cement his lead, but that didn't start with a T either.

Anders' Text Box: Well, all the Ts have to be down that path.

He headed down the last path and came to a circular opening inside.

Special T Text Box: The first T is Treasure.

Anders noticed a Red Chest at the end of the room. Calling it a Treasure instead of a Chest made for a pretty weak T, but still one down. He stepped forward, and abruptly stopped after noticing something.

Anders' Text Box: Oh, the Flaming Pit, no! This is a frickin' rock glade. You are not going to trick me again, you jerk glades.

Sometime later, Anders was ready to start his plan. He was not going to give up on this *Truestuff* chest nor be tricked by a glade again. He was determined and spent many turns setting up his elaborate glade-defeating device.

He had stacked all manner of things near the glade entrance that did not begin with the letter T. These things (the T in things didn't count) created a tunnel (which also didn't count). The tunnel continued all the way from the chest to the exit. When that "easy" boss fell from the sky, it would not be blocking the entrance and Anders could still run out. Further, using some sneaky *Combi-Fusion*, he made some *Thick Thorns* out of *Thyme* and *Thistled Roses* (none of those were any of the Ts either) for the pervert boss to land on and hopefully take damage. The tunnel continued all the way from the opening to the chest, using every crate and barrel in this place. If a boss fell anywhere in his way, he would be able to run under it.

Placing the last of the flower pots down, he finished his blockade around the chest. If something fell from the sky somewhere else and not on his tunnel, he would be safely in here inside the blockade and it would be out there. Anders was thankful that he could push all these things around with his *Block Puzzle Mover* ability.

After thinking of all possible outcomes, Anders moved to the first T, and touched it.

> Special T Text Box: Some treasure chests are trapped.

> Anders' Text Box: Huh?

Two handcuff-like devices, one from each side of the chest, snatched Anders' hands before he could jerk away.

> Special T Text Box: The second T is Trap.

> Anders' Text Box: Oh, muffins!

Anders was now under the *Trapped* status effect. Apparently to get free, all he needed was for someone else to open these handcuffs. He struggled anyway.

> Special T Text Box: The third T is The Titan.

Anders knew that one of the Ts would be the easy boss. That was why he'd secured himself in his own personal crate fort.

> Anders' Text Box: Calling it 'The Titan' is using two Ts! Take that, you stupid glade! I might be trapped, but I still won at counting 'T's!

The glade responded by opening the floor open near the entrance. Up from the very ground itself came a monster. He was only slightly larger than a human and had four small horns on his head. He had ebony skin with a white outline, making him look like he should have been painted on an ancient Roman vase, not be a monster in this game. The Titan was topless but was wearing a long metal kilt. The kilt hit the floor and scraped against it. Anders thought the kilt also was out of place, since it was an incorrect cultural reference. The kilt should have been a gladiator skirt or toga or something.

> Anders' Text Box: From the floor? Really? I so very hate you glades....

The Titan saw Anders and grew two more horns. It reminded Anders of how the Flamealith suddenly changed weapons. The creature changed after simply seeing him, yet again. The Titan started to move. It was very slow, only moving a single move unit a turn. The large metal kilt was slowing him down. No wonder they killed it so quickly; the thing couldn't even walk. Opening his Insta-Wiki, he read the stats and made fun of them as he went. It was a hands-free device, and he had some time to kill waiting for the kilt dragger to get over here so he could *White Wolf Kick* it and win.

Creature Name: The Titan

> Anders' Text Box: That's two Ts. This is the Dungeon of the Six Ts?

Class: Horned Humanoid

> Anders' Text Box: That's a monster type? Horned Humanoid?

Level: 2

> Anders' Text Box: Is that all? It is so in the wrong area.

Special Attacks: Drag, Release

> Anders' Text Box: *Drag* is it slowly dragging its butt around. *Release* must refer to its soul leaving, as this thing would be killed by any avatar in this area.

Drops: Auto-Trap Release x2

> Anders' Text Box: Hmm … those would probably get me out of these cuffs.

First Player Encounter Notes: The Titan should have been called 'The Tits Up'. Any fellow adventurers in this area that can kill the Flamealith can kill this in one hit. – Mr. Max

> Anders' Text Box: My arms are tied up, but I can *White Wolf Kick* the thing when it got closer.

Additional Comments: The Titan told us that he is a very sore loser. That every loss increases its sexual rage and fills him with a bit more rage juice. The avatar that was unlucky enough to be *Released* into exploded. #SoFuckedUp. – Lissa

> Anders' Text Box: Wait, exploded?

The Titan stopped behind Anders, undid a hinge on its kilt, and exposed itself. Anders now realized that the thing had not been moving slowly because of the metal kilt. Two Ts had been moving slowly because his enormous balls were dragging on the ground. They were beyond gigantic—each was about quadruple the size of Anders himself. The Titan had to spread his legs to almost maximum to attempt to walk, so no wonder he couldn't move fast. Countless losses had sexually repressed this horned humanoid and filled its balls to the absolute breaking point. Wait, not balls,…

> The Titan's Text Box: The fourth T is Testicles.

The Titan's ebony erection rose up, previously hidden within its giant Ts. It was not small for a creature its size, but the massive Ts behind it made it appear absolutely diminutive. The Titan started to drag itself over to Anders.

The handcuffs on the chest suddenly moved, forcing Anders to move along with them. In a quick few *ka-chinks*, he was bent over the chest, bum exposed. Two more cuffs rezzed in and grabbed his knees, spreading his legs apart. So much for *White Wolf Kicking*; that was off the list of ideas. He was going to be pounded until he exploded while prostrated against the first T. He agreed with the additional comment; this was so fricked up.

> Anders' Text Box: That's it, Traps. You are so on my mffbl! Mffbl?

Anders did not have time to put Traps on his list. Another device from the chest had sprung out and filled his mouth with a cork. The Titan was upon him. With one thrust, The Titan was inside him, and it had already started cumming. Anders thought for a round. It probably wasn't cumming; this was likely just the precum, given the swollen size of the horned humanoid's balls. There was going to be a lot of it, and with every thrust, Anders felt another shot hit his insides.

Turns went by as the helpless Anders was rocked on the chest, still hopelessly stuck in the *Trapped* status effect. The treasure was making a scuffing noise as it moved back and forth on the floor, which interrupted the otherwise pleasant flute music in the background. With every turn that went by, The Titan used both of its actions to take a long, deliberate thrust and release another shot of his pent-up losing streak. With every round, Anders' belly got more and more full. Painfully glancing back at The Titan, Anders noted that its Ts hadn't really changed in size. They were maybe a little bit smaller, but they still were dragging on the floor. That was most unfortunate. Anders was already starting to feel full and was rising up higher each turn on the Red Chest as his insides filled up. He wiggled uncomfortably, attempting to make something shift, but all that happened was his insides released a few of the tingles, which made Anders freeze.

The tingles egged The Titan on, as Anders had feared. He tried his best to silence them, but now that this perpetual loser had felt them, it reacted like it was tasting victory for the first time. Every turn was now four hard strokes accompanied by four thick spurts of The Titan's T-juice. Every turn, Anders swelled a little more, and it was now officially uncomfortable. He could begin to taste the stuff in the back of his mouth. Spurt after horrible spurt continued, and he was very near his limit.

Just a few more spurts and Anders was going to burst; he could feel his organs painfully expanding inside. He wished he could have cast *Stretch More*, which might have helped him to last longer, but his mouth was full with the cork. He wished he'd had the forethought to cast it before the encounter. He tried this turn anyway, and was surprised when it worked. It must be a free action, which was helpful. After the spell activated, Anders felt better, but he still felt very full.

Looking back at The Titan, its huge balls had only just left the floor. The new and improved slickness of Anders had spurred the horned humanoid on; now it was thrusting at about eight shots a round. *Stretch More* wasn't going to be enough, though; there was easily still three-and-a-half Anders worth of cum in each of those gigantic things. It had obviously lost to a lot of avatars lately. Anders blamed Mr. Overachiever's guide for telling them all to come here.

With more and more of The Titan's cum swelling up inside him, the chest below was getting further and further away, the binds were becoming tight as they kept his arms and legs down. Anders tried to spit out the cork, but to no avail; it was stuck fast and prevented him from getting rid of any of the seed through other means. Anders was beginning to even choke on it, and felt it inside his nose.

Anders knew he was at his limit after the last round of squirts, despite being under *Stretch More*. Even just one more drop of the sticky stuff would probably make his organs rupture. To his surprise, though, The Titan did not thrust on its next turn, skipping its first action. He activated the move *Release*, which was primed to go off next round. Anders panicked and clicked logout as fast as he could, with several extra clicks for good measure so he could stop this. Logout did not work during combat, and he was informed of this via an unhelpful Text Box. Great. He could still stop this, though, if he could find the power switch of his computer in time.

> Anders' Internal Tex Box: He knows I am going to burst with any more. He was waiting for this moment, and I can't reach my power switch because I stacked my strategy books there. Now he is going to explode me all over the damn walls, crates, barrels, and my brand new **Absorb**ing *Cloth*, whatever that is.

Anders made one last valiant effort to turn off the power but missed by a hair. He closed his eyes and braced himself, not thinking about why the *absorb* in *absorbing* had turned to bold. He was too busy hoping that this wasn't going to be as horrible as it sounded.

The Titan pushed forward with a mighty thrust and screamed of final victory. The first burst hit Anders like a train (which existed here as well but only in Trainville). This was the actual cum of The Titan's tremendous Ts, and the first blast alone had about as much volume as fifty of the previous spurts. Anders would have rocketed across the room from the force but could not move because of the traps holding him down. He came back from the blast with a heavy thud, landing back on the chest. He was certain that he saw blue stars circling his head.

The next blast hit. Anders was surprised he had lived long enough to feel it. He blasted high off the captive chest again. He landed down harder this time, his knees even bruising against the floor. The cork gag broke off, and Anders spit it out. He had expected to vomit up huge amounts of the stuff, but nothing happened. Four more gigantic spurts from The Titan later, and Anders was very confused. The blasts felt like they were increasing in strength and volume, but his legs kept on hitting closer to the floor. He thought maybe he was getting bigger or something, but The Titan was the same size, although his testicles now had only about two Anders worth each inside. That meant he had four full Anders worth of Titan cum inside him already. He completely stopped fumbling for the power switch so that he could figure out this mystery.

What had confused Anders more was the expression of absolute horror on the face of the horned humanoid. With a clunk, Anders felt his elbows touch the ground. He realized something. He hadn't been getting bigger to have his legs hit the ground earlier; he'd been getting smaller. He was now back to his original size, not bloated at all anymore. His butt was tingling almost constantly now, and the tingles sent shivers up his spine. The elfbutt held on tightly to The Titan's cock. Waves of The Titan's cum were flowing into Anders, and while he could feel it hitting inside him, it was not filling up anything internally. His entrance had clamped down on The Titan; it would not let go.

The Titan had begun to panic now. The elf bum attached to him wouldn't let go of his cock and had certainly not exploded. It just kept milking his giant testicles for more. He felt lighter, and panicked more when he saw that his Ts were now only about the size of a normal human and just would not stop *Releasing* (that was the size of a normal human, or about 180 weight units, not as in the size of a normal human's balls). That was the smallest he could ever remember them being since he had been placed in this damn T dungeon. Every spurt showed visible shrinkage of his prized testicles, yet the elf only moaned like he wanted more.

Anders did want more. Every shot had made him feel more and more tingly, and he was legitimately enjoying himself now. The tingles made him desire to feel his own relief. He thrust against the key hole of the Red Chest as best as he could for stimulation; it wasn't perfect, but it was doing the trick. Anders watched The Titan's balls shrink to about the size of *Beach Balls* (even though he had never been to Relaxing Calm Beach yet to see the size of one). The Titan screamed in alarm and let out a final giant spurt about a hundred times larger than the precum ones. Anders lost control and couldn't watch anymore. Cumming hard into the Red Chest, Anders heard the item dropping sound behind him and the traps on the chest let him go with a gentle clicking noise.

With much effort, the exhausted Anders straightened up. The Titan stood before him almost frozen in place. Anders noticed that the Titan's once-massive testicles had completely vanished. A trumpeting sound was heard overhead, but Anders didn't feel any stronger. That was odd. Anders noticed The Titan grow quite a few feet taller. His tiny muscles were swelling up, and the six horns on his head grew to the size more expected of a horned humanoid. His big metal kilt now reached down to mid-thigh. The Titan had leveled up. No longer being filled with sex juice would allow him to move better and be a proper challenge for the avatars. The Titan was elated and gave Anders a huge hug, lifting him far off the ground. It was a completely different monster now, in both appearance and attitude.

The Titan gave the Red Chest a swift kick with his new move of *Titan Stomp* and opened it for Anders. Inside were a cool *Trueshot Bow+* and *Truestrike Sword+*. They were both carved from ivory, decorated with spikes and horns, not unlike the one Anders had seen Fourni leave the cave with. These were some serious weapons. The *Trueshot Bow+* was glowing with a light that constantly changed; it didn't have a bowstring at all but instead a string of pure white light. The points of the *Truestrike Sword+* were wavy and somehow solid. This time it was Anders turn to give The Titan a big hug. He liberated the items from the opened chest (that thankfully he had missed hitting with spunk).

> Special T Text Box: The fourth T is Truestuff.

Since the original fourth T was now gone, the dungeon had been renamed to The Dungeon of the Four Ts.

> Titan's Text Box: What I did to you … how could I do that? I'm … I'm … a monster!

> Anders' Text Box: Of course you are a monster! You are a boss monster. It was your original programming, not you. Don't worry about it; you've changed now. You leveled up!

The Titan used a *Smile Animation*.

> Anders' Text Box: Avatars think you are a pushover, though. Anyone who reads Mr. Max's guide is coming here to kick your butt!

The Titan used a *Wicked Smirk Animation*.

> Titan's Text Box: Let them think that. I will deliver them a proper challenge now! I'll take them all by surprise with all of my castrated glory!

Anders turned to leave, but was given a chance to add a comment to the Titan's Insta-Wiki page.

> Additional Comment: This pervert eventually turned out to be an all right guy. – Anders

◈ Chapter 9 ◈
NEW AND IMPROVED

Anders left the Dungeon of the Four Ts smiling—and cleaning himself off as best as he could with the *Initiate's Jacket*. He was smiling because he had not only helped out what eventually had been a pretty nice guy, but now he also had a magical glowing bow and a wavy sword to try out.

Something was bothering him, and he checked his Status Page before walking away from the Flamealith's glade. He had a new passive ability under *Stretch* called *Absorb*. Reading up on the move revealed that he now could absorb essential fluids shot inside himself to regain his Magic Points, even above his normal limits. He almost dropped his hands-free page when he realized that he now had 69,976,809/257 Magic Points remaining. That was 69,976,552 more than his normal limit, and he had been pretty sure that the max limit of his Magic Point stat was 9,999. That was a whole lot of Magic Points, but he did just take eight full Anders worth of absorbed Titan.

Moving to the equipment page, he checked out his new weapons. They had slightly confusing stats.

Trueshot Bow+
Rating: Unique
Level: Unique (Based on Anders)
Damage: Unique (Based on Anders) (+78 more than current equipment)
Class Restriction: Anderses Only
Special Qualities: Immune to being destroyed

> **Level Restriction:** Unique (Based on Anders)
> **Special Ability:** Elemental Strike

> **Truestrike Sword+**
> **Rating:** Unique
> **Level:** Unique (Based on Anders)
> **Damage:** Unique (Based on Anders) (+52 more than current equipment)
> **Class Restriction:** Anderses Only
> **Special Qualities:** Immune to being destroyed
> **Level Restriction:** Unique (Based on Anders)
> **Special Ability:** Critical Strike

They certainly didn't give away much information, and what kind of phrase was "Anderses Only"?

Anders tried them on. He knew he could equip them because he had seen what they had looked like in the chest—not just the icons, as with his epic *Mithral* goodies still waiting in his *Ultra-Pack*. He could now use Magic Points to charge up and make the *Trueshot Bow+* do Elemental Damage and make the *Truestrike Sword+* have a higher critical chance for a time. The Elemental Damage type of the *Trueshot Bow+* was limited depending on what crystals he had equipped in the weapons' special Crystal Slots. He had no idea what in the map that meant, but it did have six Crystal Slots on the Equipment Page, so at least he could probably find one somewhere. The *Teardrop Crystal* would not fit.

He left the glade when he heard some new voices coming. They were talking about a really easy boss in the dungeon up ahead and how they could get *Truestuff* weapons. They were really under-leveled for the new and improved Titan. These avatars were probably going to be very mad at Mr. Max and his guide in short order. Anders felt a tinge of guilt as he disappeared into the Lushin Jungle, using a scenic bush to hide himself from the other avatars.

A quick test of both new weapons revealed that the *Trueshot Bow+* didn't let him charge an arrow without a crystal equipped, and that running up to slashing distance while almost naked was still an exceptionally bad idea. Anders resolved to use the *Trueshot Bow+* for the moment, and leave really trying out the *Truestrike Sword+* until after he put on some pants.

Not really sure what to do next, Anders just sort of wandered around shooting some monsters. He was a good quarter cycle behind the group he followed to get here, and at this point he really had no real reason to follow them anymore—except to stare at Fourni's well-sculpted human butt, and while that was a good reason, it wasn't a real reason.

Anders shot an arrow into a Red Wolf, which was ranked somewhere between a Gray Wolf and a White Wolf, and heard trumpets. Level 18 now, only 2 more until he could use his epic gear. That was a proper goal.

A wolf howled in the distance. This time it was not a Red Wolf; it was the wolf howl that meant it was nearly nighttime. Leveling would have to wait for now. He was not keen on being surprised by a nighttime-only monster again, even if he was a Night Ranger. Finding a resting spot was uneventfully easy, and soon he was enjoying some cooked up *Desert Bacon* with steamed *BetBat Fruits*. Well, he enjoyed the *Bacon*, but the *BetBat Fruits* tasted like a moldy old refrigerator in desperate need of being cleaned.

Sitting there next to the fire made him think about something that had briefly entered his mind earlier. Now that he wasn't under the time constraint of getting his parts chopped off, he could ponder it properly. Why was it that earlier this cycle when Palcath was *Constricted* only his shield was destroyed, but when Anders was *Constricted* the She-Demon was going to scissor screw him? Palcath's little lad should have been in danger as well; that was why Anders jumped in to help, after all. Why had Palcath never been in danger?

Why did all the bosses he encounter glitch out and change into perverts when they saw him? Why couldn't he find any level-appropriate pants? Why didn't Rockagin just start his prepared speech when he walked into the cave right away like with everyone else? Why did this happen to only him? Why was it that everyone else was just running around killing monsters for fun, but every Tom, Dick, and Bridge Ogre #3 (who Anders recalled was named Harry) he ran into decided they wanted to use him for pleasure?

With a *Flash of Insight Animation*, it came to him. It wasn't just him! This had to be happening to someone else. He had read about what horrible things were in store for him in the Insta-Wiki. That was strange. Some of the comments were really off colour. Also, Palcath should have freaked out significantly more while he was *Constricted*, since he'd mentioned he had read the Insta-Wiki entry before entering the battle. The Titan also had an entry warning of its unsavoury abilities. Palcath was the kind of guy who was always prepared. He would have read that entire entry before challenging it.

Anders reviewed his Insta-Wiki. Three monsters he had encountered shared two common threads. Mr. Max was the first to defeat the monster, which wasn't that surprising; his name showed up in almost every single other Insta-Wiki entry. The other thread was much more interesting.

The Additional Comment had always been made by someone named Lissa. He checked all his other pages, but could find the name only four times—in the Bridge Ogre, Flamealith, and The Titan entries under Additional Comments and under Start Rat as the very first comment. The very first Start Rat? Lissa would have to have been out the gate to get the first comment on the very first monster. The name may have been in more places, but Anders' Insta-Wiki was not exactly bursting at the seams; he had only 7.7% game completion.

Reading through the comments on some other monsters proved interesting. Every single one excluding the Pink Slime and Chimera had normal-sounding first comments. Both the Pink Slime and Chimera had comments calling them perverts by someone named Anders, which he remembered distinctly as he was the Anders who had made the comments.

Inappropriate comments otherwise only showed up in the Additional Comments, and a few were from him. Maybe only a few avatars could see and make Additional Comments? That would explain why no one else was freaked out. Most of the Additional Comments Anders could find that were not written by either Lissa or himself were especially grim, describing just barely living through a horrible and confusing attack. Anders never saw any of those avatar names again in the Insta-Wiki. The comments by Lissa were unique, describing how others had been brutally assaulted by sex-crazed monsters. Anders was both relieved and horrified to know at least one other avatar was sharing this strange experience. He was disturbed to realize that there had been several incidents of the game happening this way. With Fourni and his party acting so surprised after seeing the exposed breasts of the Flamealith, he was sure they couldn't possibly be seeing the monsters the same way as he was. If they found *that* unusual, they clearly hadn't been seeing the kinds of things Anders had.

Anders threw another log on the campfire (thankfully, the wood showed up when an avatar built a campfire; otherwise, it would be very annoying to gather). He kept researching the Insta-Wiki. The Chimera now had a Global Defeat Count of two, which meant someone else had killed one and found a *Combi-Fusion Pot*, probably the overachieving Mr. Max. Crud, someone else had already made 46 *Combi-Fusion* recipes! Anders did his best but could only manage to get to 28 recipes. There went his next impressive claim to fame.

Checking up on some other entries, he saw the Pink Slime's Global Defeat Count was still only one, and Green Slimes were at thirty-five. Anders reviewed the combat log from the beginning of Chapter 1 and confirmed that he had killed thirty-five of them in total before things went crazy.

He decided to delve deeper into the mystery of the pervert monsters. He started with the Player Pagers for names he knew from either Additional Comments or by stalking them.

Grandiger, Hellsfight, Wabbino, Cheekera, and Jee Co Nah Rah, the names from Additional Comments with only one entry, were the ones he checked first. These avatars were very likely not important in the grand scheme of things and probably wouldn't prove to be very insightful. Anders was right. All their pages were blank except for a few random boring pictures. Those names were not important at all, and Anders made a mental note to forget each and every one of them.

He opened his own Player Pager (as he was very much a part of this mystery), and it only had two things: his profile picture (a screenshot of himself standing on a miscoloured pixel above a scenic pillar by a Green Slime and executing the *Wave Animation)* and his list. Under the screenshot was the caption, "Hello, my name is Anders, and I love scenic pillars." Anders changed the statement from *love* to *loathe*, and updated his list.

Anders' List:
1. Scenic Pillars
2. Glades
3. Status Effects
4. Construct Bars
5. Traps

Next he accessed Mr. Max's page. Obviously a melee character, his profile picture showed an avatar made at *Body Type #8* and *Muscular*; they literally didn't get any beefier than that. The picture was a shot of him standing over the corpse of a giant dead something Anders had never seen before. The caption read, "My latest conquest, fellow adventurers: a Flork Demon!" He was wearing a complete set of *Diamond Full Plate* Armour which was silver with orange crystal diamond shapes inset within. His huge muscles barely even fit into his Armour, and a very oversized two-handed sword was strapped to his back. Two-handed weapons meant that this was a Warrior class. That was by far the most popular class in the game. The sword was so oversized it really should have been a three-handed sword. Anders soon discovered by reading further that was the actual name of the thing.

The rest of the page was filled with many pictures of the exact same scene, except with different monsters underfoot. Mr. Max was always in the same pose (*Flexing*) with the exact same caption, just a different monster name. His Insta-Wiki was already up to 57.8%! That was crazy. Anders remembered hearing it was under 50% earlier this cycle. Mr. Max did have loads and loads of information, though, about all sorts of things. Consequently, Anders bookmarked it for later use.

By the time Anders was done with Mr. Max, the *Combi-Fusion* 50 recipe challenge was over, as he was alerted by a Text Box. It was won not surprisingly by Mr. Max, who would be the only other avatar at this point with a *Combi-Fusion Pot*. Anders watched as Mr. Max left a comment.

A very good observation regarding the *Combi-Item* recipes, fellow adventurer! But a very bad one about its keeper! Collect everything you can find, friends, and try to mix up everything. You never know what you will need! – Mr. Max

Fair enough. Now that Anders knew not everyone was getting molested at every encounter, his comment about the Chimera was relatively inaccurate. He went in again and noticed that he could change his comments (another part of the game that was probably explained in the ignored Game Tutorial). Now his comment talked about how dangerous the three heads had been and to be careful of the *Fire Spit*. It was funnier to Anders that way, and he liked it better. An Insta-Beep showed that Mr. Max had changed his entry under the *Combi-Fusion* Insta-Wiki as well. The message was just pompous again, as if Mr. Max had forgotten Anders' original comment completely.

This guy was Mr. Ultra-Committed-To-This; Anders had to give him that. There was even a link now to a bunch of Mr. Max's recipes on his Player Pager, many using things Anders had never heard of. There were already 87 and more pouring in; Mr. Max was obviously mixing like crazy this night. It was blatantly obvious that, if your Insta-Wiki was so full, you had a lot more bits to try to mix with.

It was time to move on to others. Although he was beefy, famous, and handsome, Mr. Max did not have the answers to this puzzle.

Roodg's page was confusing and hard to read. It was full of both grammar and spelling mistakes. It was entirely typed in caps lock, excluding the letters that should have been in capitals. It hurt to look at it, but at the top was a profile picture, showing Roodg standing next to the Flamealith with the exposed breasts. The Caption said, "hEY LOOK! bOOBS! nsfw! bOOBS ARE RAD!" Anders didn't even know what NSFW stood for, but his curiosity got the better of him and some research into it told him that it stood for Not Safe For Work.

Palcath's page was just as Anders had expected. It was full of needless pretend back story about his character, artistic shots of places he had visited, lists of dangerous monsters that he, his friend, and Roodg had vanquished, an unflattering screenshot of Roodg mid-*Battle Animation*, and finally a full up-to-date list of their adventures. They had sold items and abandoned their quest to find the *Vials of Green Goo* (for now). Currently, they were licking their wounds at camp after an encounter with a very aggressive four-armed demon bear with horns on their way to complete a Main Story Quest: Teardrop Returned. At least he knew where they were. This page would be very handy if he ever needed to find them again, so Anders bookmarked it.

It took Anders a few tries to find Fourni's page—mostly because he had forgotten that his name was in fact Fournimer and not Fourni. His page was mostly blank; in fact, all that was on it was a profile picture of Fourni standing in the *Thinking Animation* by the Rampage River at the Triple Bridge. Since it was from behind, from a slightly lower camera angle (and that Roodg could be seen in the distance attempting to set a waterfall on fire), Anders guessed that Palcath had taken the picture. Fourni didn't yet have the *Truestrike Sword* but was wearing the snugly fitting *Hard Leather Leggings*. Anders bookmarked the page even though there wasn't any information on it.

Lastly, Anders brought up Lissa's page. The profile picture was of five incredibly happy adventurers all posing together with another that was only somewhat impressed. They were all human and had bright and impossible-coloured hair. Anders didn't remember any of those colours when he picked his hair colour and knew they were definitely non-standard.

Lissa's page started innocently enough. The first entry was her talking about herself killing the first Start Rat ever. That narrowed it down; Lissa was a girl avatar. The photo showed three female avatars, all with non-standard hair colours; Bright red, bubblegum pink, and a vivacious purple. Their hair colours were all different than from earlier pictures. Something had changed as they had adventured together. Maybe hair dye was an item drop? Whatever it was, it made Anders sort of wanted green hair now.

As the page progressed through Lissa's journal, it got more and more forlorn, but it did go into some strange specifics. The journal started to get more interesting and less about random adventure things with a trip over the Triple Bridge. This was the first picture of the entire party with their new hair. It gave details about how Quoona was attacked and violently killed by the Bridge Ogres when she ran ahead to scout. From then on, there was no longer a girl with impossibly red hair in any of the pictures. Lissa talked about how upset and disturbed she was, and sad that she couldn't heal Quoona with her magic. Lissa was a Mendicator or Soother class.

Skipping a bit ahead, Anders got to the part about the Flamealith and The Titan. Apparently, O'Sklorm was *Constricted* during the battle with the Flamealith. In an effort to save him, Nerchiner ran into the cave by himself to find a *Truehack Doublesword*. O'Sklorm was *Severed* and killed, and when the rest of the party went into the cave to find Nerchiner, they arrived just in time to watch him explode while tied to a chest. The boy with green hair and the one with blue stopped being in pictures at that point, and Lissa reported that she was disgusted.

The next encounter was with something called The Feaster. Vendimm was *Feasted* upon, and the bright-yellow-haired boy was now gone from photos. Anders didn't care to find out what *Feasted* upon meant.

Lissa talked about how she and Zal Finn were going to go report all of the horrible events to the NPC King of … Claymetteron (maybe) … and stop the horribleness after reaching Level 20. On the way, they met the Hydra, and Zal Finn, who had the bubblegum hair, was rotate-killed.

The last entry showed a morose girl with bright purple hair, standing alone. She was the one in the original profile picture that wasn't smiling. This latest picture was most likely taken in a mountain area since there was snow in the air. In the distance, there was a strange mechanical clock tower.

Anders used a *Yawn Animation*. He was tired from all the plot exposition and decided to let the sleeping music take effect.

♦ Chapter 10 ♦
OTHER GROUPS AND
BEAR STEAKS

Palcath Ironburrow, son of Gloni and Defender of the Dwarven clans stoked the fire. His companions collapsed all around him, just as exhausted as he was. The previous boss battle had been an absolute nightmare

> Fournimer's Text Box: that was awful Man and Guy. that Feaster thing was scary.

> Palcath's Text Box: Agreed, lad. We should take a quick break.

> Roodg's Text Box: i WANT TO SEE MY lEVEL 20 STUFF, BUT i AM MORE TIRED THAN CURIOUS RIGHT NOW.

> Palcath's Text Box: Yes, lass. How annoying does this game want to be?

> Fournimer's Text Box: I know! why would they do that to Level 20 gear?

> Palcath's Text Box: Well, at least we were already accidently doing this Teardrop Returned Quest when we found out about that, lass and lad. Only a few more steps left now that we have this extra *Puzzle Block* from the Feaster.

> Roodg's Text Box: tHAT fEASTER MADE ME HUNGRY! wHAT

> DO WE GOT?

> Palcath's Text Box: Sorry, lass, we used the last of the *Desert Bacon* last night. All we have left for lunch is these *Demon Bear Steaks* and a single piece of *Mountain Bacon*. Well, those and a bunch of stuff that definitely will taste like appliances.

> Fournimer's Text Box: we can split the *Mountain Bacon*. cook some of the steaks up Man! hopefully they will taste good since they are made of meat.

Palcath used the *Cooking Animation* on the *Demon Bear Steaks*; despite the fact that there was no campfire, it still worked. Six rounds later, the steaks were cooked to a fine demonic brown. These at least smelled good, but all three avatars spit out their first bite.

> Palcath's Text Box: Oh, these are terrible. That bear lass should be ashamed.

> Fournimer's Text Box: I can't get the taste out of my mouth, not even by washing it down with *Bacon*! what is that?

> Palcath's Text Box: I don't know what that is. It is hard to place, lad. Wait, is that … a water softener aftertaste? Yes, these taste like water softeners.

> Roodg's Text Box: yUCK! lET ME COOK NEXT TIME Palcath. i HAVE AN IDEA!

> Palcath's Text Box: Sure thing, lass.

Really, he was thinking, *Not on your life, lass.*

The leader cooked for his troops, and Palcath was the leader. Besides, Palcath was genuinely concerned as to what a Roodg idea was, but not curious enough to use up resources finding out. Lunch was abandoned, and Palcath stood up, again taking the lead.

> Palcath's Text Box: We should just skip lunch for now, lass and lad, and find more *Mountain Bacon* on the way to the Lova Mines.

> Fournimer's Text Box: sure thing Man.

> Roodg's Text Box: hEY, WHO IS THAT?

Palcath shifted his view to down the path and was too dumbfounded to even move. Coming down the path, in all his muscular glory, was Palcath's idol, the very beefy and very famous man himself—Mr. Max.

Mr. Max was walking with determination. He had so many muscles that he could barely even squeeze into his epic Level *Diamond Plate Armour* with orange accents. Palcath had seen the avatar many times on his Player Pager but never in person. He had the no-nonsense short *#2 Hairstyle* set to ginger, coupled with a cleft chin and friendly green eyes. He even had freckles, something Palcath couldn't see in the screenshots. A ludicrously large sword with orange embellishments was hanging in the air behind him. Palcath could not imagine even attempting to pick it up, let alone attack with it. The last thing that Palcath noted about Mr. Max was that, even though the avatar was as beefy as he could possibly be, he wasn't as tall as Palcath had imagined him. Fournimer was much taller than Mr. Max. Palcath himself was a dwarf and was eye level with Max's chest, not a stomach like he was normally used to.

Mr. Max continued to walk toward them, and Palcath continued to stare in amazement. Mr. Max only noticed him after he walked right into Palcath, toppling the dwarf over.

Mr. Max's Text Box: Oh, sorry about that, little girl! I was updating my Player Pager and was not watching where I was going!

Palcath's Text Box: That is okay, lad. I forgive you because your Player Pager and guide are so very helpful.

Mr. Max's Text Box: I know! They are pretty great.

Mr. Max used the *Flex Animation*. Palcath grinned excitedly when he saw his hero use his patented animation. Palcath noticed that both Fournimer and Roodg were also a little faint. Well, Palcath guessed Roodg was, as he couldn't see anything under that hood.

Mr. Max's Text Box: I assume that you fellow adventurers are on your way to Stronghold B! What fun it will be! I am glad so many have answered my call! What a glorious victory it will be when the next Gigas falls!

Palcath's Text Box: No sir, lad, we are about to do the Lova Mines to reach Level 20.

Mr. Max's Text Box: Oh, yes, that quest! What fond memories I have of that place. Well, do hurry up, fellow adventurers! You three gnomes have lots of time to find another gnome and be up to Stronghold B in time to witness another one of my glorious victories! Raids are so exciting! I'll mark the location on your map just in case you can make it.

Palcath's Text Box: We will try and hurry, lad.

> Mr. Max's Text Box: Why do you keep saying 'lad', fellow adventurer?

> Roodg's Text Box: hE IS ROLE-PLAYING i THINK!

> Mr. Max's Text Box: Interesting. I have never tried that before. I would think that gnomes would say 'pip pip' or something, not 'lad'. Well, I should get going!

> Palcath's Text Box: Sure thing, lad, but can we just ask you something? Where are those Green Slimes hiding out? I thought if anyone would know, it would be you.

Mr. Max used the *Eyebrows Furrowed and Face Twitch Animation*.

> Mr. Max's Text Box: I don't know. How many times do I need to tell people that? They are not where they are supposed to be. That is all I know.

Mr. Max changed his expression back into his original carefree smile from earlier. Palcath wasn't sure if Max had forgotten completely about being upset or was just excellent at putting on a phoney smile to hide his frustrations.

> Mr. Max's Text Box: Please tell me if you find them, fellow adventurers. I am offering a reward!

With that, Mr. Max gave them all a *Wink Animation*. He walked away with a sure step, closing the distance between himself and the path of the Lova Mountains. Palcath noticed that both Fournimer and Roodg were staring after Max, checking out the toned and chiseled derrière that only just fit into the orange *Diamond Pants*. Palcath chuckled to himself.

> Palcath's Text Box: Well, that was unexpected, lads, Mr. Max in such a low level area.

> Fournimer's Text Box: wow, in person he is so much more...

> Roodg's Text Box: sHORT!

> Palcath's Text Box: I know, lass. I guess Flork Demons are shorter than we thought as well! Wait ... did he just call us gnomes?

> Roodg's Text Box: yES! hE EVEN CALLED YOU A LITTLE GIRL EARLIER! Palcath, THE MIGHTY LITTLE GIRL GNOME!

> Fournimer's Text Box: Bro was probably just distracted with his Player Pager. did you see him *Wink Animation* at me? wow, just wow.

> Roodg's Text Box: cAN WE GO DO THE RAID INSTEAD OF THE MINES? iT SOUNDS LIKE FUN!

> Palcath's Text Box: No, lass. Raids of that level will certainly kill us. Maybe if we can finish the Lova Mines first. We will have much better equipment. That will give us the needed stat boost, and we could survive. If we hurry, we can probably do both!

> Roodg's Text Box: gO! nO WAIT! sTOP. nOW WHO IS COMING?

Just as the mighty little girl gnome was getting ready to order the party onward toward to Lova Mines, he saw what Roodg had seen. A group was approaching. They were all of high levels, judging by their expensive gear and holier-than-thou attitudes. Palcath was busy attempting to figure them out, and this time a thin, self-assured avatar with black Armour and a jet black *#8 Hairstyle* (known to be called angst emo hair by players; it was cut short and covering up one eye) walked right into Palcath and knocked the dwarf over again.

> Grandiger's Text Box: Hey! Watch it. Do you have any idea who you just walked into? Do you? Because you should. Yes, you should! Apologize. Apologize now. We will do what has to be done if necessary.

This Grandiger was startling. He had two sets of arms, two very fancy hammers, and two shields. Palcath did not remember hearing anything about this Defender class feature, but it certainly would be helpful when it was unlocked.

> Palcath's Text Box: Well, sorry, I guess, lad, but your leader did walk into me.

> Hellsfight's Text Box: Stay put!

Hellsfight also alarmed Palcath. She didn't have any eye features to speak of. No eyelids, no pupils, no eyebrows, nothing. Just a blank slate of a face. Palcath had never met someone of the Soother class. It must just be a part of how they healed others or something. Palcath reminded himself to read the back story of the world later to double check.

> Roodg's Text Box: wHY?

> Hellsfight's Text Box: Just cause!

Hellsfight made a motion to the last member of the party, a tall, silent, and mysterious type that had stepped forward and started to unsheathe his *Katana*. Palcath noted that this fellow was dressed in nothing but gray. Everything he was wearing, which was some sort of Eastern-themed Armour similar to what a samurai would wear, was gray. His socks with sandals, his big pleated pants, his Eastern breastplate with flat sideways shoulder plates, and even his open style helmet with two large sideways spiked horns. His skin was gray, his *#19 Hairstyle* (the Eastern long ponytail), his *#8 Asian Facial Hair*, and even his eyes were gray. Palcath thought for a moment that maybe this guy was from another game completely, like one of those old-school, black-and-white silent video games that his grandfather used to play. Palcath did finally see some colour, a very faded brown and almost gray *Plain Belt* was on the avatar, which was only a Level 3 item. This avatar might have bad luck when it came to finding accessories.

Palcath noticed the name. It was a very bad name, and the dwarf had no idea how it got past the role play filter in this realm. Spelt wrong, uninspired, and no capital letter … pathetic.

> warrier's Text Box: …

warrier used the *Point Animation* directed at Palcath and changed his camera angle over to the man with the emo hair. Palcath almost laughed. This avatar with the bad name was definitely from one of those old-school games. Not only was he in black-and-white, he was also silent.

The man with the emo hair finally stood up after his tumble with Palcath. With a *Stretching of His Arms and Dramatic Hand Flourish Animation*, Breaker called off warrier, and the silent avatar backed down.

> Breaker's Text Box: Now, is that any way to treat a potential client? Sorry for walking into you. I was working on a WorldForums post. Hello, little low levels, how would you like to come to a raid? I will show you the way for just a small 500 Gold Piece fee. A genuine steal, really.

> Grandiger's Text Box: I don't understand why we are even doing this. It confuses me. Who even cares about raids?

> Hellsfight's Text Box: Time waste!

> Breaker's Text Box: Now, now, settle down there, you two. I need this money for my research. We will never complete our holy mission from the Maker unless I have the money to do my research.

> warrier's Text Box: …

warrier used the *Nod Animation*.

> Breaker's Text Box: Now how about it, an epic raid for only 500GP!

> Roodg's Text Box: nO THANKS. Mr. Max ALREADY INVITED US. wE GOOD.

> Breaker's Text Box: Of course that Mr. Overachiever would do

something like that. Come on, lackeys. We are wasting our time with these fools.

warrier's Text Box: ...

warrier used the *Nod Animation*.

Grandiger's Text Box: Fine. We should go! We have a holy mission to complete. For glory! We are going.

Hellsfight's Text Box: Just go!

Palcath scratched his *#5 Facial Hair*.

Palcath's Text Box: Those lads and that lass gave me a chill down my spine. Something was off about them.

Fournimer's Text Box: I agree Man. it feels like you just avoided something really bad.

Roodg's Text Box: oBVIOUSLY THEY ARE IMPORTANT. wELL SOME OF THEM. jUDGING BY THEIR DESCRIPTIONS AT LEAST TWO OF THEM ARE IMPORTANT AND WILL SHOW UP LATER. tHOSE OTHER 2, MEH. yOU WILL LIKELY ONLY HEAR ABOUT THEM AGAIN WHEN IT SAYS THEY ARE DEAD OR SOMETHING.

Palcath wasn't sure which was more unsettling, the feeling he had gotten from the party that just left, or the fact that Roodg had just said something meaningful. He decided that it was the second one.

Palcath's Text Box: Pardon me, lass. What did you just say?

Roodg's Text Box: tHEY WERE IMPORTANT. aT LEAST SOME OF THEM. iT WAS LIKE WE SHOULD HAVE BEEN PAYING ATTENTION TO WHO THEY WERE.

Palcath's Text Box: Crap, lass, I was so startled that I forgot to add them to my list of important avatars met. There are only four on there right now since I included all three of us and just added Mr. Max. What were their names?

Roodg's Text Box: i DUNNO. i WASN'T PAYING ATTENTION! LoL.

That sounded more like the Roodg that Palcath had grown to know.

Fournimer's Text Box: umm ... well we had that emo haired guy,

> Buddy? and Four Arms and Eyeless who were less important. there was that gray guy, um, he was pretty jive so I am going to call him Jive Turkey.

> Palcath's Text Box: I'll have to read the log. I'll just use your nicknames for now, Fourni. Give me a few rounds before going into the Lova Mines while I do the research.

> Roodg's Text Box: nOW WHO IS COMING? aLL OF THEM!

Palcath did not have time to check the battle log for names. The dwarf had to get out of the way of about 60 avatars. They were all very low level and especially green around the horns. The dwarf wisely stepped off of the path this time to avoid the large group of avatars, certain that at least some of them were still getting used to the walking controls. The very last one though, a small-sized gnome, froze mid-step. Instead of turning the path like the others, this gnome floated in the air. As he was continuing forward, he knocked Palcath over before the dwarf could get out of the way. The dwarf had seen this before; it was lag. The poor avatar had a very bad internet connection, and it prevented him from seeing events as they happened.

Gliint used the *Formal Bow Animation* and promptly froze in place.

> Fournimer's Text Box: what is wrong with him?

> Palcath's Text Box: This little lad suffers from acute lag. I have seen this kind of thing before.

> Roodg's Text Box: hE IS SO TINY AND ACUTE!

> Gliint's Lag Text Box: So sorry, my good sir. I suffer from acute lag, and I apologize.

> Gliint's Text Box: Oh, you know that already.

Gliint used the *Embarrassed Animation*.

> Palcath's Text Box: That is all right, little lad. No harm, no foul. You would not be the first this cycle to walk into me.

> Palcath's Text Box: …little lad?

This gnome had lag, and he had it bad. Palcath knew through his detective dwarf reasoning that Gliint, along with the other 60 or so avatars, had paid whatever his name was (Buddy?) for the privilege to go and get killed in the raid. Palcath would not let that happen to his group. He knew of the large stat boost at Level 20 and even again at Level 50 thanks to Mr. Max's guide. Anyone below level 20 who participated would be killed for certain.

> Gliint's Lag Text Box: Really? How horrible!

Gliint used the *Forlorn Animation*.

> Gliint's Text Box: I love how you use 'lad' all the time! It is very good for your character. I was thinking of doing something like that.

> Fournimer's Text Box: like 'pip pip' or something?

> Gliint's Text Box: Yeah, like that! Pip pip!

Gliint used the *Cheer Animation*.

> Palcath's Text Box: I don't know, lad. That is a little too obvious. You know what? Just keep using those animations all the time. I don't know anyone like that!

> Palcath's Text Box: …little lad?

> Roodg's Text Box: i LIKE HIM. wE WERE SUPPOSED TO KEEP A GNOME RIGHT? cAN WE KEEP HIM?

Gliint eventually used the *Salute Animation*.

> Gliint's Text Box: Great idea! I love the animations! I will make that my thing instead of 'pip pip'. Thanks a lot you … uh … guys?

Gliint used the *Wave Animation*, and continued on after the other low levels, lagging all the while.

> Palcath's Text Box: Why would you give him that pip pip idea, Fourni? That is my character trait!

> Fournimer's Text Box: sorry Man. it wasn't my idea, that one was Mr. Max's!

> Palcath's Text Box: That is okay, lad. I fixed it. I am going to make a note of him since my page is already open.

Palcath wrote down Gliint's name on his list of important avatars. Beside it, he wrote down "very animated and laggy gnome".

Roodg used the *Point Animation*.

> Roodg's Text Box: nOW WHO IS COMING?

> Palcath's Text Box: What, more lads and lasses? Seriously? More introductions?

A party of five was coming down the path this time. Palcath checked; they were high level, they had no lag, they didn't look full of themselves, and they were paying attention. All good signs that they would not knock him over on the way by. The troll's big frame had swept more of the area than Palcath (or the troll) had anticipated, knocking the dwarf over. This avatar reached down and helped Palcath up.

Palcath almost vomited. He had seen how ugly a male troll could be during character creation, but seeing one up close and in person was stomach churning. At least this troll was friendly.

> Jorthan the Male Troll Warrior's Text Box: Je suis desoleé about our friend Monsieur dwarf. I am forgetting sometimes of size.

> Palcath's Text Box: That is okay, lad, not the first time it's happened today. We leaders need to stick together, right?

An angry female fight elf (a variety of elf with more strength, and aggression, but less patience, than the standard run-of-the-mill elf) with the same no-nonsense hairstyle and nearly as many muscles as Mr. Max stepped forward. She was not impressed with Palcath. Palcath honestly didn't even know she was a girl until she spoke.

> Hippolyta's Text Box: Typical. Just because he is the man in our party, he must be the leader, right? What a typical male chauvinistic view of the world we play in. I can't even talk about how offensive that is.

> Palcath's Text Box: The lad was in the lead. That is why I thought he was the leader.

A slightly chubby, short male sprite elf (a variety of elf with more constitution, and serenity, but less confidence, than the standard run-of-the-mill elf) stepped forward in a valiant attempt to calm down the situation. He did not do a very good job.

> Trev Terra's Text Box: Hippolyta, he didn't mean to … well, what he probably meant, rather, was that … well, he didn't think you were not the leader. I mean, gosh, he just saw Jorthan first and must have well, you know, just thought he was … well, I mean Jorthan is so big and stuff and, well … oh, you know. I don't think he meant to be a pig, or what I mean was like a male pig instead. He is probably very nice and well nice.

> Palcath's Text Box: Okay, lad, don't hurt yourself.

The two other party members a female light elf (a variety of elf with more wisdom, and perception, but less humour, than the standard run-of-the-mill elf) and a female night elf (a variety of elf with more intelligence, and moxy, but less grace, than the standard run-of-the-mill elf), which were identical in every way except name, race, and class, stepped forward to properly resolve the situation.

> De'vini's Text Box: Don't be too hard on him, Hippy!

In'ferni's Text Box: I know, right? He is a guy after all.

That calmed down the Amazon-sized woman who was glaring at Palcath, and the high level party continued on down the path.

Palcath's Text Box: That was the strangest bunch of lads and lasses yet! Why are there so many different kinds of elf types in this game? There is only one kind of dwarf!

Fournimer's Text Box: what kind of crazy role playing was that troll doing anyway?

Palcath's Text Box: I think that was a French-Canadian lad.

Roodg's Text Box: hE WAS NICE BUT UGLY.

Fournimer's Text Box: What about that Amazon elf? What kind was that?

Palcath's Text Box: Super-liberated, ultra-woman-powered, feminist lass.

Roodg's Text Box: sHE HAD ALMOST NO BOOBS!

Fournimer's Text Box: what about that little shy nervous guy?

Palcath's Text Box: Little shy nervous lad with no confidence.

Roodg's Text Box: sO CUTE! Fournimer, MAKE HIS NICKNAME Stutters!

Fournimer's Text Box: and did you see the twins? what were they?

Palcath's Text Box: Twins, lad.

Roodg's Text Box: tHEY WERE SO CUTE TOGETHER!

Fournimer's Text Box: I haven't heard of any of those role playing styles Man!

Palcath's Text Box: Me either, lad. I don't know if I should put those guys on my list. Were they important or not?

Roodg's Text Box: i DUNNO. tHEIR DESCRIPTIONS WERE PRETTY VAGUE AND THEY ONLY SAID ONE LINE EACH. i SUSPECT THEY MIGHT BE IMPORTANT, BUT i WOULDN'T

> COUNT ON THEM BEING IMPORTANT IN THIS bOOK,
> MAYBE LATER ON? i WOULD ADD THEM TO YOUR NOTES
> AND REMEMBER TO CHECK THEM AGAIN LATER IF ONE
> OF THEM SHOWS UP. tHEY PROBABLY WILL.

Palcath eyed Roodg over again. He scratched his *#5 Facial Hair* and made a new document called "Is Roodg smart or not?" He added a checkmark to the "yes" column.

> Palcath's Text Box: An interesting theory, lass.

> Roodg's Text Box: i KNOW! i DIDN'T EVEN EAT THE SANDWICH YET!

Palcath added a checkmark to the "no" column.

> Fournimer's Text Box: now who is coming down the path?

> Palcath's Text Box: You know what, Fourni lad? I don't care. I've been knocked onto my ass enough for one cycle. Let's just go and finish up the Lova Mines and forget about meeting anyone else for awhile. I am sick of this.

> Roodg's Text Box: hURRY! gO! iF WE GO FASTER WE CAN RAID WHILE i EAT THE PASTRAMI!

Palcath wasn't even sure what column to checkmark after Roodg's comment.

◈ Chapter 11 ◈

LEVELING UP

It was a new cycle—time to put away the Player Pager with Fourni's picture and get back to adventuring. Anders' new *Truestuff Weapons* were going to be very helpful with his goal of becoming Level 20 today! He would finally be putting on pants again. This was a very attainable goal for the cycle. Anders was in a mid-level area, and his weapons were more than a match for anything that dwelled here.

Shooting random monsters and collecting their random junk had never been more invigorating than it was today. With very few problems, he reached Level 19, and there were still many turns until lunchtime. It was hard to not watch his Status Page like a hawk (which apparently lived in the mountain areas), but he watched his level slowly rise over the course of the cycle.

Level 19.02   –   A Red Wolf.

Level 19.08   –   Three more Red Wolves.

Level 19.13   –   Some Psycho Killer Bees guarding a Blue Chest with a *Pretty Rock* in it.

Level 19.22   –   An Undead Swordsman and his Skelemaidens.

Level 19.29   –   A pack of Fish Otters.

Level 19.38   –   A very angry-looking Stump.

Level 19.45   –   Three more Red Wolves.

Level 19.57   –   Some Psycho Killer Bees guarding a Blue Chest with a *Pretty Rock* in it. (He had gotten turned around at some point and had ended up going in a circle.)

Level 19.66 – A trip back to kill some Heat Pigs in the Salazarm Desert for more *Desert Bacon.*

Level 19.75　　–　A few more Heat Pigs couldn't hurt. All the other food except the *Bacon* tasted like appliances here.

Level 19.81　　–　*Desert Bacon* is really good.

Level 19.94　　–　Killed everything all the way back to the Triple Bridge.

Level 19.98　　–　Sniped three Bridge Ogres hanging in the sky before they dropped down above the bridge glade and collected a Red Chest filled with a pair of *Hard Leather Gloves* to wear. Also giggled.

Level 19.98　　–　Start Rat.

Level 19.98　　–　Start Rat.

Level 19.99!　　–　Start Rat.

> Game Explanation Text Box: Level 20 is locked until you complete the Main Story Quest: Teardrop Returned. Experience earned will be saved and applied once completed.

Level 19.99!!　　–　Start Rat shot with bow.

Level 19.99!!!　　–　Start Rat chopped with sword.

Level 19.99!!!!!!　–　Start Rat kicked with *White Wolf Kick.*

> Anders' Text Box: You never cease to amaze me, Text Box.

Level 19.99… – Angrily killed one more Start Rat with an *If Looks Could Kill Animation.*

The Main Story Quest: Teardrop Returned? Anders found it on Mr. Max's guide. It said to go to the Lova Mines within the Lova Mountains with the *Teardrop Crystal.* There was a challenging pushing *Block Puzzle* needed to open a series of tunnels to a labyrinth. Mr. Max did not include a solution or any spoilers. That was pretty stand up of him. Anders had no idea where that was, but he remembered someone that did. The dwarf lad. Palcath's page now talked about how frustrating the Lova Mines were and that the party would continue to try to solve the puzzle after a proper hearty lunch of *Mountain Bacon* without steak.

Anders could even see the Lova Mountains' entrance on the picture of the Micro-Mini Map that Palcath posted. It was right near where that ugly demon bear monster lived.

Anders got excited for five good reasons:

1.　He was close to the Lova Mountains and therefore the Lova Mines.

2.　He knew where to go and all the things to avoid on the way there, ugly demon bears included.

3.　He had a *Teardrop Crystal* sticking to the inside of his *Ultra-Pack* to return to complete that part of the quest.

4.　Palcath, Fourni, and Caps Lock were already there and solving the puzzles.

They appeared to be on a break. If he hurried, they would probably do the stupid *Block Puzzle* for him while he watched from behind a scenic bush.

5.   There was something called *Mountain Bacon*.

Anders straightened up his *Snazzy Belt* and hurried down the path, avoiding everything but chests along the way. He ran right at the four-armed demon bear and used it as a platform. By *Double Jumping* right off its demon head and onto the Lova Mountains' entrance, Anders could skip encountering it entirely. *Double Jump* was awesome. He entered the loading screen before the bear even had a chance to react. Silly old bear.

The Lova Mountains were covered in snow and had a constant snowflake effect. Despite this, it was not cold out, not even with his obvious lack of clothing. The *Cold* status was only reserved for the Salazarm Desert at night. Anders didn't mind not freezing his bits off, but couldn't help but question the logic. He quickly turned away from one split path that led to somewhere called The Lair of The Feaster, and tried the other. He did not want to follow in Vendimm's footsteps.

Specifically killing a Frosty Pig along the way and picking up a *Mountain Bacon* was his only other pit stop before reaching the entrance to the Lova Mines. The entire run from the Triple Bridge had taken only about thirty turns, but he had used up his entire Stamina Bar running the whole way.

The skull of a toothsome creature gaped open, forming the door to the Lova Mines. Anders took a quick screenshot of him smiling in front of it (from the waist up) and added it to his Player Pager before going in. Opening the generic wooden door in the skull's mouth that marked this as a dungeon, he stepped inside, prepared for battle.

The background music was an unsettling mixture of xylophones and trombones. Anders knew that he needed to proceed carefully. There were many paths, but they all kept leading to no-treasure dead ends. Anders tried the last possible path and ended up back at the entrance. Somehow he had gotten himself turned around. He used an *Eyebrows Furrowed and Face Twitch Animation* directed at the camera angles. He took his time on the next attempt and ended up in a large, circular room high above everything else. There was no mistaking it. He knew that this was a mine glade. There wasn't a red box here, but it still had the horrible feeling of a glade. Anders could peer over the edge of this encounter area to survey the scene. Down the path at the far side of the mine glade was the only way to a lower chamber. He saw three familiar avatars below. Palcath and Fourni were staring at the *Puzzle Boxes* intently, and Roodg was attempting to freeze a scenic lamp.

He still had time to avoid doing the puzzle if he hurried. He had never done a *Block Pushing Puzzle* before in this game. However, the whole look of it reminded him of crate pushing puzzles, and he hated those so intently that they would automatically be added to his list if he was forced to do one. The glade would have to have a boss monster; that much was for certain. He checked himself over. He was impressed. He had great weapons, full health, lots of potions, millions of extra Mana Points, epic *(s)* special

Armour to soon wear, and a great attitude this cycle. He was only empty of Stamina after running here, but he was going to kill this boss, not run from it. Having no Stamina this time didn't matter. He readied his bow and stepped forward.

The loud crash of the monster rang through the area. The background music changed into a boss theme. This time, it was not the ordinary boss theme. This was the first officially licensed song that Anders had heard so far—"Hydra-Nated" by The Fergus Finders. Anders would have it unlocked in the Music Player now. This was only getting better!

> Game Explanation Text Box: Some monsters have poison attacks. Be careful of the *Poison* status as it can drain your Stamina. Having completely drained Stamina while poisoned will put you into *Dire* status.

> Anders' Text Box: Seriously?

> Fournimer's Text Box: hey some Dude named Anders is here and fighting the Hydra, want to go help?

> Roodg's Text Box: dIE LAMP DIE!

> Palcath's Text Box: Probably more than just one avatar, lad. No one would be dumb enough to come here without even the starting basics of a full party.

> Anders' Text Box: Hey!

> Palcath's Text Box: Besides, I doubt they need help if they killed the Demon Bear of Kazuul to use it as a step to get up the Lova Mountains and killed The Feaster to get the extra *Puzzle Block* for here lad.

Anders hadn't done either of those things, and without an extra *Puzzle Block*, he wouldn't be able to make it through alone.

> Fournimer's Text Box: yeah I know Man, but this *Block Puzzle* is so annoying and I want another *Hydra Head*. these stupid yellow blocks are impossible to figure out. I want to just destroy them!

> Palcath's Text Box: It only had one head, lad. It wasn't even really a Hydra! It was just a big snake!

> Roodg's Text Box: sO LAME.

Anders didn't know what they were talking about. From his view, wrapped tightly in the serpent's coils in a *Stamina-Drained Dire* status after just one *Poison Spit*, he could see that the Hydra had multiple heads, but they were just the kind of head that occurs below the belt. Counting the one on its shoulders—the only one that wasn't a giant, throbbing serpent penis headed for his bottom—it had eight different prehensile members.

This was going to happen, and those other avatars were going to hear it. They were within Text Box distance since he could read their Text Boxes arguing about the *Puzzle Blocks*. He checked the Insta-Wiki for information about the Hydra.

Creature Name: Eight-Headed Hydra
Class: Serpent
Level: 22
Special Attacks: Bite, Poison Spit, Lance, Sevenfold Fury, Constrict
Drops: Hydra Head
First Player Encounter Notes: This is stupid. That was a one-headed Hydra. What damn idiot named this thing? – Breaker
Additional Comments: This serpent's penises do not get along. They are impatient and cannot wait for their own turn. They all penetrated at once and ripped an avatar in half by fighting inside her. Poor Zal Finn! #SoFuckedUp. – Lissa

Anders had never heard of Breaker, but the avatar sounded bitter. Anders really didn't care, though, because of the more important Additional Comment. Seven fighting serpent penises inside him trying to fuck so desperately it might rip him right open? That sounded right up Anders' alley. Anders cast *Stretch More*, which thankfully he could do in *Dire* status, and readied his alley for this. If he could end this quickly, he might still be able to skip the *Block Puzzle* and the need to go meet The Feaster.

Each of the serpent's cocks was a good twenty-one length units long and about a quarter as thick as Anders' arm. Individually not that bad, all things considered, but the fact that there were seven of them was troubling. The Hydra's cocks spent their first turn fighting each other. Somehow at the end of this, a victor was determined, and the Hydra used *Lance* to forcefully thrust one of the cocks into Anders. It began thrusting into Anders with blazing *Serpent Speed*. Anders could reply only with an *Eyes Crossed Animation*.

The next turn started the same way; the cocks not in Anders fought each other while the one inside continued to thrust. A victor was determined, and with a powerful *Lance,* it was inside. Seeing the other cock inside angered the first cock, and it changed the direction of its thrusting to almost straight up vertically. The other cock was just as upset, but began to thrust downward, trying to get away from the first cock. Anders moaned and tingled from this strange sensation, two serpent cocks pushing in completely different directions.

Two more turns and two more *Lances* later, Anders now also had a cock fucking him extremely left and extremely right. He skipped his turn quietly and waited for the next, and again for the next.

Six of the serpent cocks were now fucking Anders, in a star-like pattern. It gave the impression that a really giant cock with a skinny base was in him. Anders enjoyed the immense pressure, purposely causing himself to tingle, and waited to see what would happen next.

The last cock did not have to fight anyone. It spent its turn penetrating and fucking Anders the only direction it could to avoid the others: straight down the middle. Anders decided that seven cocks fucking inside him was his limit and was glad that this wasn't the fabled Thirteen-Headed Hydra.

On its next turn, the Hydra activated *Sevenfold Fury*.

> Fournimer's Text Box: it sure is using *Lance* a lot, and what is *Sevenfold Fury*? I don't remember it doing that.

> Palcath's Text Box: I don't remember it doing that either. It just kept *Poison Spitting* at us, lad.

> Roodg's Text Box: *sEVENFOLD fURY* SOUNDS LIKE A POWER DRILL OR SOMETHING.

> Fournimer's Text Box: they are certainly loud up there. oh hey, it's spamming *Sevenfold Fury* like crazy! I want to go see what it is. hey Dude up there you okay?

> Anders' Text Box: Ah … yeah! It's good.

> Palcath's Text Box: No, don't move, lad! Otherwise we will have to start this damn *Block Puzzle* again from the start. Stupid fucking yellow blocks! How do we get that red one past you? Why don't they just explode or something?

> Roodg's Text Box: dON'T MOVE! i WANT TO SEE MY lEVEL 20 STUFF!

Fournimer used the *Sigh Animation* and stayed put.

Anders gained some Magic Point reserves and some Experience Points (which would be added later) for defeating the Hydra. He pulled the middle, still-thrusting head out of his ass with a shlunk and threw it in his *Ultra-Pack* (hopefully after giving it a good wash). It had been squeezed off by the other cocks during all the crazy spinning drill moves earlier, but Anders could see that the sleeping serpent had grown back two in its place, as Hydras often do with their heads. It was now called a Nine-Headed Hydra, which would be trouble for the next pantsless avatar to stumble by.

The avatars down the path had stopped arguing and were working together. With that kind of foolishness, they would be done with the *Block Puzzle* in no time. Grabbing his slightly sore butt, he hurried down the path. The door they had been staring at was open, and they had just finished walking through. Anders drank a *Stamina Potion* that he had made earlier out of a *Bottle* (which made sense) and a *Yellow Flower* (which followed the rules of flowers perfectly) and ran for it. As the door lowered, he slid underneath, barely making it through. Panicked, he reached back for his *Leather Hat*, but remembered he had not found anything for his Head Slot yet. The door closed with a satisfying clunk.

◆ **Chapter 12** ◆

THE GREEN PATH

nders had slid in unnoticed under the large, crushing door. He stayed out of sight, watching the party while cleaning the last of the Hydra off with his *Initiate's Jacket*. The others were standing in front of a grandiose scenic stone covered in impossible-to-read text which reminded him of cat scratches. The very centre of the structure had an opening with a path down the middle.

Palcath held up a pulsing red gem that Anders did not recognize. Anders figured it was a Quest Item. It had the same important sheen as the *Teardrop Crystal*. Palcath held the gem to his eye and began to look at the cat scratch symbols carved into the scenic stone. Anders couldn't make heads or tails of what Palcath Text Boxed next, but it was probably clear to avatars that had been completing the story of the game.

> Palcath's Text Box: Let's see, lad and lass…. This is a recap I think…. Because you freed NPC Sergeant Grettit from the hordes of Land Cats, then traded the *Landcat Medallion* for passage across the Rampage River, then got this *Jewel of Danbar* from Danbar's Sack, then collected the *Elemental Dinner Plates* from the Plate Worshipper's Dungeon, then used those to set the Feaster's Table to get the *Extra Puzzle Block*…. Finally. Here is the part to read with new information. Okay, it reads: Enter the Labyrinth, one at a time…

> Roodg's Text Box: k

As if imbued with *Serpent Speed*, Roodg was in the doorway. The entire gigantic structure began to rotate, and Roodg was quickly out of view.

Palcath was still reading through the Quest Item and didn't take notice.

> Palcath's Text Box: ...insert your *Teardrop Crystals* into the podiums and hit all the levers...

> Roodg's Text Box: nEAT! iT'S ALL RED AND STUFF!

> Fournimer's Text Box: no way Guy. let me see!

With that, Fourni went into the door as well, the Labyrinth rotated in a completely different direction this time, and the human had vanished.

> Palcath's Text Box: ...and help to save the land from the Plague of...

> Fournimer's Text Box: wow, this part is all blue, I'm even blue!

> Roodg's Text Box: oH YEAH! i JUST NOTICED CUZ i'M ALREADY ALL RED, BUT NOW i'M MORE REDDER!

> Palcath's Text Box: ...Shadow. Hey! Where did you all go?

> Fournimer's Text Box: Inside, it's all neat!

> Roodg's Text Box: yEAH! i'M ALL REDDER AND STUFF! i TASTE LIKE CHERRY!

> Fournimer's Text Box: you're right Guy! I taste like... oranges? what?

> Palcath's Text Box: Always saving your tails, lass and lad. Always saving your tails.

Palcath walked inside with a little bit of smugness to his step, the structure rotated, and he was gone.

> Palcath's Text Box: Oooh! It is all yellow and banana-flavoured, lass and lad!

> Roodg's Text Box: i KNOW RIGHT?!

> Fournimer's Text Box: uh oh.

> Palcath's Text Box: What do you mean, lad?

> Fournimer's Text Box: it is just that I found the lever Man.

> Roodg's Text Box: i WAS JUST JUMPING AROUND ALL REDDER.

yOU FOUND YOURS?

Palcath's Text Box: Why 'uh oh', lad? Don't keep me in suspense.

Roodg's Text Box: tHERE IT IS! cRAP.

Fournimer's Text Box: I'm going to see if I can go back. nope I'm still stuck here and I'm blue!

Palcath's Text Box: Crap what, lass? Spit it out. Oh. I see it now. Crap, indeed.

Fournimer's Text Box: order of Levers. Fire, Water, Wind, Earth. flip them in order to reveal the way.

Roodg's Text Box: i'M STUCK BEING REDDER! tHE DOOR IS GONE!

Palcath's Text Box: We needed four avatars, lads. Damn! It didn't say anything in Mr. Max's guide.

Fournimer's Text Box: Man … so we are like stuck here or something?

Palcath's Text Box: Guess so, until some other lad or lass shows up.

Roodg's Text Box: dIE LEVER INSTRUCTIONS DIE!

The sound of magic being fired filled the entire area of the Red Maze.

Fournimer's Text Box: well that's just stupid.

Anders thought for the better part of a round, and decided what he would do.

Anders' Text Box: I'll help!

Anders stepped into the doorway, and the entire structure rotated yet again. He was placed in an area that made everything very green and mint-flavoured. He took a screenshot of his face with green hair—although, since his skin was green, he looked like he had contracted the *Poison* status effect again. Still, it was green hair.

Fournimer's Text Box: hey, it's that Hydra Dude and his party! wait… you're a Dude right? or are you a Dudette?

Anders' Text Box: No, I don't have a party. It's just me. Yes, I'm a dude, and I'm all green and minty!

Palcath's Text Box: You defeated the Hydra all by yourself, lad?

Rubbing a hand on his sore, recently septuple serpent multi-fucked, green-tinted butt, Anders smiled.

> Anders' Text Box: Yeah … I guess I did!

> Fournimer's Text Box: awesome, it sounded like a wicked battle up there Dude. you rocked it.

Anders blushed by setting his *Blush Shade* to #2, which given the lighting made him look positively envenomed.

> Anders' Text Box: Thanks, Fourni.

That was a huge relief to Anders. The party had heard the encounter and thought all the screaming, moaning, and battle-named sex moves had just been a normal, run-of-the-mill battle. He toned down his embarrassment and prepared to help.

> Palcath's Text Box: Okay, let's finish this maze, lads and lass, and reach new levels of greatness never before seen by the likes of others! The Halls of Honour will forever remember us, and of this our greatest glory!

> Fournimer's Text Box: uh, what Man?

> Roodg's Text Box: u MEAN GET TO LEVEL 20 RITE?

> Palcath's Text Box: Yeah, that.

The maze was easily defeated. The only difficulty involved having four avatars that could pay attention, and fortunately the new, redder Roodg had brought his or her A-game for this one.

Fire. Water. Wind. Earth.

Roodg pulled the Red Lever.

Fournimer pulled the Blue Lever.

Anders pulled the Green Lever.

Palcath pulled the Yellow Lever.

Nothing happened.

> Palcath's Text Box: Wait, everylad … is Wind Green and Earth Yellow, or is Wind Yellow and Earth Green? It is different in almost every game.

> Fournimer's Text Box: ?

> Roodg's Text Box: ?

> Anders' Text Box: ?

> Palcath's Text Box: All right then.

Fire. Water. Wind. Earth.
Roodg pulled the Red Lever.
Fournimer pulled the Blue Lever.
Palcath pulled the Yellow Lever.
Anders pulled the Green Lever.

The maze rotated all over the place, but the rooms with the levers and avatars stayed put. Finally resting after a few rounds, the labyrinth had changed to a completely different shape; four corners rose up from the ground and made four long, straight paths directly to the centre. It must have had a very high graphics budget due to being part of the Main Storyline Quest because, dang, was it nifty. Anders was in the north corner, and could guess by the colours in the other corners where everyone else was located. Anders saw two new doors slide into view, one behind him and one in front. The door in front would certainly lead down the path to the centre, given the layout.

The pillar that once held a lever now had two crystal insert slots. One was empty, and the other held a green *Earth Crystal*. Anders tried to pick up the *Earth Crystal*, but it was stuck. It didn't take much in the way of problem-solving to finish the last step of the quest called Teardrop Returned. Placing the *Teardrop Crystal* in the empty slot caused the *Earth Crystal* to jump directly into Anders' inventory, and the pretty light effects stopped. One by one, the other lights went out, meaning other crystals were probably taken as well.

> Roodg's Text Box: mY CHERRY POPPED!

> Fournimer's Text Box: my orange peeled.

> Palcath's Text Box: My banana split!

> Anders' Text Box: My mint … uh … my mint …

Anders could not think up a mint pun. Everyone was expecting one, and he wanted to impress this party in hopes of finally fitting in. He was about to give up when a frozen scenic lamp fell from the sky and landed at his feet. Written on the lamp in both Caps Lock and permanent marker was his joke.

> Anders' Text Box: My mint leafed!

The two doors started to lower into the floor with a shaky and dusty cut scene. Anders was unsure why it needed a film grain and sepia tone filter, but it was nice nonetheless.

> Game Explanation Text Box: Some monsters are completely immune to certain kinds of attacks. Always bring a balanced party.

> Roodg's Text Box: f

Fournimer's Text Box: U

Anders' Text Box: DG

Palcath's Text Box: K! … 'dg'? Don't you mean 'c,' lad?

Anders' Text Box: No, you were supposed to use 'e'.

Roodg's Text Box: LoL. fUDGE!

Suddenly a gigantic *Icicle Explosion* erupted from what used to be the red corner.

Roodg's Text Box: iT ATE MY SPELL! hAS BIG HAMMER! hELP. mELEE-ONLY IT SAYS!

Miss sounds were heard from what used to be the blue corner.

Fournimer's Text Box: mine is immune to everything but Healing Magic.

Loud wing beats erupted from what used to be the yellow corner.

Palcath's Text Box: I can't hit this flying monstrosity lads! Only ranged attacks can hurt it.

Anders had almost been too nervous to check behind him, but he knew he had to confront the monster. Judging by what the others had said, whatever was behind his door would be immune to everything but Attack Magic. Surprisingly, nothing gigantic or scary was behind him, just a single, very tiny beetle. It flipped upside down and was still the exact same tiny beetle. Anders used a *Laugh Animation*—finally, some luck! It was just a stupid beetle. He lifted up his *Leather Boot* and stepped on it, but it felt like stepping on a stone. When he lifted up his foot, the beetle was still there, unharmed. He was informed via Game Explanation Text Box that this monster was immune to everything but Attack Magic.

Anders' Text Box: I have the Attack Magic one, but it is no problem.

Palcath's Text Box: Meet in the centre, everylad, and bring your monster! We can trade off there.

Fournimer's Text Box: all right, but do we have Healing Magic? Dude what are you?

Anders' Text Box: Elf *Night Ranger (Ranged Style)*.

Fournimer's Text Box: we can't hurt mine!

Palcath's Text Box: Maybe not … but regroup, lads, and we can worry about it last.

Still naked, Anders did not want to go meet up with everyone just yet. He had gotten very good at ranged attacks and could probably stay behind a wall or something. The quest would be over, and he had new clothes just waiting to put on. Great hope swelled within him, if this worked, there might be some fantasy loving friends to go on adventures with.

He glanced down at his vicious boss. It would be easy just to pick it up, walk down the path, and throw it in front of Roodg to blast to bits. Anders bent down and picked up the little guy. It felt like a normal beetle, but he couldn't crush it in his hand either. It was so illogical. Walking confidently down the corridor to the centre area with his soon-to-be-defeated monster, he heard the sounds of battle and chaos all around him and smiled. Green was the safe corner to be in! He knew he liked that colour for a reason.

Not moving particularly quickly, he noticed that the combat sounds had all moved to the centre glade, the boys (and possibly one girl) were going to handle things in very short order, he suspected. The longer he took to get down there, the less time until the quest would be over, and the less chance of exposing his compromised clothing state to these fine gentlemen (and possibly one gentlewoman).

He walked lazily down the path at only one move unit per turn. Eventually he stepped on something and stumbled. He nearly twisted his ankle. It felt like a rock. He lifted up his foot and saw a little beetle, identical to the one in his hand. Spending his turn picking this one up as well, he noticed three more quickly scurry by. By the time his next turn had arrived, about five more had scurried past him down the path. Feeling uneasy now, he spent his next turn looking back up the corridor.

In the centre glade, Palcath was combating the large Hammer Spider from Roodg's corner and was holding his own against it. Fournimer had taken on Palcath's huge Bombing Bee, and wasn't having much trouble despite not being a great archer. Roodg had made a makeshift blockade out of frozen scenic lamps to trap Fournimer's Great ZombAnt and was trying to throw different random things at it out of desperation. So far, *Desert Bacon*, *Aqua Velour*, and *Ground Beet* had done nothing but bounce off the undead beast.

Palcath's Text Box: Try throwing a *Health Potion* at it, lass.

Roodg's Text Box: wHY?

Palcath's Text Box: Trust me, lass. I've played things like this before.

Roodg's Text Box: oH RIGHT. dUH! mE TOO!

Roodg threw a *Health Potion* at the ZombAnt, undamaging it, but as with all undead things, undamaging it caused damage. Roodg spent the next few rounds up close with the ZombAnt, slapping it in the face with various cures and remedies.

Roodg's Text Box: hEY LOOK! i'M MELEE!

Fournimer's Text Box: hey, great call Man!

Anders' Text Box: !!!

Palcath's Text Box: ?

Fournimer's Text Box: ?

Roodg's Text Box: ?

The three avatars abandoned what they had been doing and adjusted their camera angles to what used to be the green corner. Out came the fastest-running avatar they had ever seen. They all thought that Anders must've had a spell of *Serpent Speed* cast upon him to run that fast. Covered in at least a thousand tiny black beetles, their mystery companion came bolting from the corridor. From the top of his *#6 Hairstyle* to the soles of his *Leather Boots*, the insects writhed all over him, and he was screaming in *Blind Panic*. A wave of similar beetles followed close behind, attempting to latch themselves onto Anders. They were called Swarm Beetles and numbered in the thousands. How the rendering stayed smooth with all of the individual beetles onscreen at once was a mystery to everyone.

Roodg's Text Box: oH GROSS!

Palcath's Text Box: Ugh!

Fournimer's Text Box: oh Dude!

Anders' Text Box: !!!

Anders felt the Swarm Beetles scuttling all over him, but that was not why he was panicking. He normally liked bugs. He was certainly not afraid of them under normal circumstances. He was not panicking because the Swarm Beetles had attacked or bit him in any way. He was panicking because he felt several Swarm Beetles attempting to ram open his elfhole to get inside. The thought of thousands of anything all crawling around in his insides doing whatever they pleased was making him feel sick, whether they were insects or anything else.

His magical bum was not making clenching it closed easy in the slightest. *Stretch More* from the Hydra encounter was still active, and the Swarm Beetles were flipping themselves around in the slick juice they had managed to pry loose. Priming them for easy entry.

Palcath's Text Box: Use magic on them, Roodg!

Roodg's Text Box: oH, RIGHT!

Abandoning their respective monsters for the moment, everyone was spellbound by the horrible display, but not in the status effect sense. They were all secretly glad now that they had not ended up on the green path. Roodg was expertly throwing Attack Magic at the Swarm Beetles. If there was one thing Roodg could do right, it was magic. Precisely targeted Swarm Beetles would fall off in a crisp fizzle or ice shard, only to be replaced with more instantly.

> Roodg's Text Box: tOO MANY! iT'S NOT WORKING!

> Anders' Text Box: !!!

Several beetles had fallen off dead, but it only urged the survivors on. They had a reason to get inside now: Magical tingle protective butt goop! Anders was feeling them group together to start trying to ram themselves inside. He was loosening up a little despite his concentrated effort to keep the little swarm buggers out. Anders was horrified; now the slicker ones were joining the horrible beetle battering ram.

> Palcath's Text Box: Use your area attack on them, lass!

> Roodg's Text Box: nO WAY! i GOT IN so MUCH TROUBLE LAST TIME!

> Palcath's Text Box: I don't think he will mind a little damage this time, lass. I give you permission as long as Anders says it is all right.

> Anders' Text Box: !!!

> Roodg's Text Box: tHAT'S A YES IN MY BOOKS!

When the mushroom cloud from the *Nuclear Fire Grenade* finally cleared, a very relieved elf Night Ranger stood before the trio, surrounded by the charred husks of thousands of little swarm perverts. A very relieved and still very naked elf Night Ranger, to be precise.

> Roodg's Text Box: iS HE… NAKED? tHE sWARM bEETLES ATE HIS CLOTHES!!! nO WAY!

Anders increased to *Blush Shade #3* to everywhere. In his *Blind Panic* status effect, he had completely forgotten he was naked underneath his new *Swarming Pervert* clothing. Everyone else except Roodg blushed as well, Fournimer turning to *Blush Shade #4*.

> Anders' Text Box: Uh, They… uh….

> Roodg's Text Box: i… i… i BLEW UP YOUR CLOTHES? omfm! i AM AMAZING!

It was now the forgotten other bosses' turns (they had been very polite to wait until both the Swarm Beetle incident and plot advancement were over). They all abandoned their current targets and changed targets to Anders. On their first turns, they all glitched: the Hammer Spider's Hourglass flipped over, the Bombing Bee's buzzing sound effect became a distant important object twinkle sound effect, and the ZombAnt became the AntZomb. They all moved toward Anders, brandishing their various stingers in a lewd manner.

> Anders' Text Box: Oh, crumpets!

> Fournimer's Text Box: crumpets?

> Palcath's Text Box: What is wrong with those bosses? Hit them while they are distracted, lad and lass!

With one swing of his *Small Steel Hammer*, Palcath crushed the Hammer Spider with a *Sneak Attack*, turning it into a *Hammer Spider Hammer*. The Bombing Bee was shot by Fournimer with a *Sneak Attack* and it exploded into six *Jars of Delicious Honey* (that tasted like a hand mixer on setting 4). The now-AntZomb was hit directly in the face with a *Health Potion* by Roodg, who also scored a *Sneak Attack* and it melted into a *uoᴉʇod ɐuɐɯ*.

> Palcath's Text Box: Lass, did you just get a Sneak Attack with ... a *Health Potion?*

Thundering trumpets soared through the air, much louder than normal; everyone had completed the Main Story Quest: Crystal Returned. They had exceeded their original goals and now were Level 22.

Anders quickly opened his *Ultra-Pack* to find his *Mithral Vest (s)* and *Mithral Leggings (s)*. He saw them in physical form for the first time, and his eyes nearly fell out of his skull. He bolted for the dungeon's exit after using a *Stamina Potion* and almost all of his Stamina Bar out of embarrassment, leaving the party behind dumbfounded.

> Fournimer's Text Box: no wait, Anders Dude!

The sound of the entrance to the dungeon door opening and closing let them know that it was too late; he was gone.

> Roodg's Text Box: hE WAS NUDE!

> Palcath's Text Box: What the lad was that all about?

> Roodg's Text Box: i AM MAGIC! i BURNED OFF HIS CLOTHES! fIRE MAGIC IS AWESOME AGAIN!

> Palcath's Text Box: Not that, lass, I was talking about the monsters fritzing out again. How in the Flaming Pit did you get a Sneak Attack with an item?

Roodg's Text Box: i AM MAGIC! wEREN'T YOU LISTENING?

Fournimer's Text Box: Guy just burnt off that elf Dude's clothes and you are worried about the monsters acting funny?

Palcath's Text Box: Why did that lad just run away like that?

Fournimer's Text Box: um, Roodg just burnt off all his clothes Man, weren't you listening?

Roodg's Text Box: eVEN HIS *sTANDARD* *iSSUE* *uNDERGARMENTS!* aLL GONE!

Palcath scratched at his *#5 Facial Hair*, lost in thought.

◈ **Chapter 13** ◈

THE (S) GEAR

Anders climbed further up the Lova Mountains and found a dead-end path with no treasure to speak of. Pointless paths like this were much more private as it made it much less likely that any avatars would happen by. He opened his *Ultra-Pack* again and reached inside.

> Anders' Text Box: Well ... maybe they will look better if I put them on?

He examined the *Mithral Vest (s)* first. It was similar to the icon, but had significant differences. Shining on in all its glory, the icon of a metal vest had ultra fine scales inset with bright emeralds. Hanging around the neck of the vest icon was a cape of dark green stitched with big squares of lighter green, all surrounded by golden fringe.

Anders tried on the *Mithral Vest (s)*, and it was almost like the icon version he had seen in his *Ultra-Pack*. There it was in all its shining glory, the real thing. The metal had ultra fine scales that glinted in the Lova Mountains' sun just like the icon, but they covered only certain select areas. His forearms and a small strip on his underarms were covered, leading toward the main portion of the vest. It covered his neck and upper torso but only just barely, ending an entire length unit above his nipples. While it did have beautiful white piping along all the open spaces, his shoulders and entire abdomen were still completely bare excluding what was covered by his *Jewel Necklace* and *Snazzy Belt*.

Three emeralds dotted the garment in a triangle pattern near the collar on the left side, (not where the icon showed them at all). The dark green cape was there, but it could more accurately be described as a crop cape. It went down only about four length units further than the vest in the back and had two diamond shapes of lighter green fabric, outlined in golden trim. One such diamond hung at the very back of the cape, making it end in a triangular point, the other was hanging from right below his collar. It covered the area of the vest right above his nipples, and went down to his sternum, completing the look.

> Anders' Text Box: Biscuits, it looks like it does, not like the icon.

Next was the *Mithral Leggings (s)*. They followed the same overall theme as the *Mithral Vest (s)*, trim, fringe colours, and all. The scale portion covered everything below the knee and had two thin bands that went up the insides of his legs. The thin bands went around his crotch and ended at the small of his back in a triangle dotted with three tiny emeralds. Some light green fabric diamonds hung from a very low and tight-fitting, whisker-thin sash of rich green fabric. There were five in all, two very small ones on the sides, two only slightly larger in the back, and one in front. The front diamond only just barely covered his shame, and even a calm breeze or a *Run Animation* would show him off to the world if they were paying attention. The back diamonds were just a bit larger, but the bottoms of his ass cheeks were still very visible. These were clearly designed for someone with *Standard Issue Undergarments* or no sense of modesty.

> Anders' Text Box: These are not (s) as in special, they are (s) as in slutty. That's it, (s) gear. You made me run around naked for how long, waiting to put you on, and now you are slutty? You just made my list!

Anders' List:
1. Scenic Pillars
2. Glades
3. Status Effects
4. Constrict Bars
5. Traps
6. (s) Gear
7. Oh, yeah! Swarm Beetles

Seeing his new "epic" outfit with the screenshot camera, Anders felt almost more naked now than he had felt while being actually naked. His *Snazzy Belt* still hung by itself across his waist. It looked out of place, since the sash was hanging several length units lower. He took a new screenshot anyway, just from the piping line up. The outfit was pretty nice, if you didn't see anything below his nipples. While posting the picture on his Player Pager, he noticed something in the distance of the screenshot. There was a familiar clock tower in the background.

Checking back through his Player Pager bookmarks (stopping only to admire Fourni's picture for a few rounds), he found the familiar tower on Lissa's profile. It was the tower in the very last picture where she spoke of hiding out until things calmed down. He noticed that she was wearing a new outfit in this picture compared to the rest, but it was probably not rated (s). Originally she had been mostly covered up in a *Calming Jacket* and *Leggings*, but now she had on some gentle *Silver Robes* that were not even slightly revealing. This picture was probably taken just after she got to Level 20, and was dated only a hundred turns or so older than from when he had first seen it last night. It was only about half a cycle old now.

Hearing a dungeon door open in the distance, he decided quickly to follow the path up to the tower to see if Lissa was still there. If she was, he could talk to her about this whole sexy mess. He really didn't want his former party to see him looking even more naked now than he had been moments ago when he had actually been naked. Keeping the outfit on just for the massive defensive bonus (he told himself), he hurried up the path. He stopped only briefly to insert the green *Earth Crystal* into his bow. In truth, he had almost forgotten about it. Waiting until later to insert the crystal would have made it worse.

> Fournimer's Text Box: hey Dude? you out here?

Anders heard the Text Box in the distance but didn't reply. Instead, he opted for continuing up the path and leaving the area.

> Palcath's Text Box: See, I told you he would be gone, Fourni.

◈ Chapter 14 ◈
THE CHIEFS

Palcath used the *Pose to Think About It Animation,* but took special care to show off his new, almost complete set of *Heavy Full Plate* Armour while doing so. He was again missing only a helmet.

> Palcath's Text Box: Okay, that whole thing was weird. What do you make of it, lad and lass?

> Roodg's Text Box: i MADE HIM NAKED! i AM EPIC!

In his, maybe her, new complete set of *Navy Gear,* Roodg cast a fire magic spell on herself (or maybe it was himself) for the sixteenth time since leaving the Lova Mines. A strange determination to make it happen again had gripped the avatar, but nothing out of the ordinary happened.

> Fournimer's Text Box: you made him run, that is what you did Guy. we could have used a real archer! You know how bad I am at shooting the buttons that lower those bridges.

> Roodg's Text Box: yEP Fournimer, YOU SUCK AT THAT!

> Fournimer's Text Box: hey, you didn't use caps lock! a miracle!

> Roodg's Text Box: hEY i HAVE JAM!

Fournimer's Text Box: jam? what could that possibly even mean? just turn off Caps!

Roodg's Text Box: LoL, i LOVE THAT! cAPITAL LETTER ADVICE FROM YOU. sHIFT IS RIGHT THERE BTW!

Fournimer was sporting a brand new *Silver Vest* with purple trim. It clashed a bit with the rest of his outfit, which was all earth tones with green accents. The fact that it clashed was upsetting to the human, even though no one else noticed.

Palcath's Text Box: No, it is more than that. I am going to think about a few things. Give me a moment.

Palcath's Text Box: Lass!

Roodg's Text Box: iT'S MORE THAN SHIFT AND CAPS LOCK?

Palcath's Text Box: No, lass, not that silly argument; no one really cares. I mean more than making him run away!

Roodg's Text Box: oH YOU MEAN Anders! bURN uNDERPANTS BURN!

The *Toe-Tapping Animation* was executed by Fournimer, as Roodg continued to try to destroy the brand new *Navy Robes*. Fournimer spent his rounds secretly taking screenshots of the Magic Mage blasting himself … herself … whatever into the sides of various scenic objects. He really needed to ask Palcath what a gender neutral term was.

Palcath's Text Box: I knew it! There is something, lad. In the Chat Log, here, he called you Fourni, but I never called you that the entire time we were in the dungeon.

Fournimer's Text Box: yeah, only you call me that Man, but well it's sort of an obvious nickname. trust me, I'm all about nicknames.

Palcath's Text Box: Yeah, you're right, lad … oh, here! It's his Player Pager. Look at that first picture.

Fournimer's Text Box: hey a Green Slime, we searched for that damn Slime Cave dungeon for like a full cycle. Mr. Max said he didn't even know where they were!

Roodg's Text Box: iCY WINDS i COMMAND THEE, DESTROY MY PANTS!

> Palcath's Text Box: It is dated only a few hundred rounds in, and here the lad is with one, right at the start.

> Fournimer's Text Box: all right, that is interesting I guess, but why do you care so much Man?

> Palcath's Text Box: Honestly? I have played through this whole giant-evil-something-will-destroy-the-whole-world crap a hundred times before. The graphics here are very pretty and it is fun that you are here, Fourni, but it is all the same. Also, all these *Puzzle Block* quests are starting to piss me off. A quest about figuring out how a solitary elf lad can kill a Hydra boss, single-handed, in half the time it took the three of us to do it ... well, that is just is so much more interesting.

Palcath watched as his team thought about that for a round or two. They made the right choice when they both nodded, this was more interesting than finding out what had been happening to the NPC's horrible tasting crops.

> Fournimer's Text Box: great point Man. that is more interesting. let me open the WorldForums. wow! everyone has been giving Bro a hard time about not finding the Green Slimes for them yet.

> Palcath's Text Box: Fourni, who is Bro again, lad?

> Fournimer's Text Box: oh sorry, that Mr. Max guy is Bro.

> Roodg's Text Box: i THOUGHT i WAS Guy! sTOP USING NICKNAMES THEY ARE CONFUSING!

> Palcath's Text Box: Okay, I need to keep a list of your nicknames or something, lad.

> Fournimer's Text Box: I already made one, should I send it to you Man?

> Palcath's Text Box: Please do, Fourni, lad. I will merge it with my Important Avatar list. Anyway, so if Mr. Max Bro couldn't find the Green Slimes, how did this elf lad?

They were at a loss for what to do. When Palcath suggested that they do some research, Roodg fought such silly ideas by not doing any. Founimer started to idly browse the WorldForums for fun things to read. Palcath took his research more seriously than the others and was busy researching elves, but Fournimer's tactic paid off.

> Fournimer's Text Box: hey, here is another WorldForums post just

slamming Bro about The Titan boss, lots of avatars are pissed off about needing to reload. it's not even that old. check our logs, are the times close?

Palcath's Text Box: Um … wow, we missed the boss changing by only a few hundred turns, lad. The dungeon even changed names after; that is really strange. I knew something was off about that place!

Roodg's Text Box: nUDIE Anders HAD 2 TRUESTUFF WEAPONS.

Fournimer's and Palcath's Simultaneous Text Boxes: What?

Roodg's Text Box: yEAH DIDN'T U SEE THEM? BURN YOU DAMN ROBES BURN!

Fournimer's Text Box: Could he have gone there twice?

Palcath's Text Box: Maybe … hmm … take off your shirt, Fourni.

Roodg perked up.

Roodg's Text Box: yEAH DO THAT!!

Fournimer's Text Box: what? gross Man!

Palcath's Text Box: Relax, Mr. Jumpy Pants, I just want to see the Night Ranger's starting *Standard Issue Undergarments*.

Roodg's Text Box: mE 2!

Fournimer changed to *Blush Shade #1*.

Fournimer's Text Box: why?

Roodg's Text Box: cAUSE i'M GUNNA TRY BOLT ON THEM!

Palcath's Text Box: On these other screenshots, there is a picture by this entrance skull and another one in the maze. Wow, just look how far down the pictures go; his waist is completely bare. In this skull one, I can see past his bellybutton.

Fournimer viewed the picture, perhaps for a round too long, and he bookmarked the page for later. The stubble-dusted human got up and took off the *Silver Vest*, showing his *Standard Issue Undergarments*, a cloth wrapping that went up past his nipples.

Palcath's Text Box: Hmm … so the lad had to have been already naked. He wasn't just no equipment naked; he was like naked naked before even entering the dungeon.

Roodg's Text Box: sO… i'M NOT MAGIC?

Palcath's Text Box: Nope, lass, you are not.

Roodg's Text Box: aWW!

Roodg sat down on a rock, defeated.

Fournimer's Text Box: so the Dude was naked naked and still defeated the Hydra in half the time that it took the three of us? how did he do that?

Palcath's Text Box: See, lad, I told you this was more interesting than finding out how to stop the Plague of Shadow.

Fournimer's Text Box: what about when those three monsters went all crazy and went after just him?

Roodg's Text Box: yEAH, THIS ITEM IT DROPPED IS ALL FUCKED UP. 'uoɐod ɐuɐɯ'. hOW DID i EVEN TYPE THAT?

Roodg examined the uoɐod ɐuɐɯ closely. All attempts to flip it upside down and make it become a regular *Mana Potion* would not work, the item refused to cooperate.

Fournimer's Text Box: yeah and you two got *Sneak Attacks* again. you can't even get those. I just checked! didn't that happen already?

Palcath's Text Box: Lads! We all got *Sneak Attacks* like that after the Flamealith broke.

Roodg's Text Box: wE SAW HER BOOBS! bOOBS ARE RAD!

Palcath's Text Box: That is actually an interesting point, lass—nudity there as well. Not to mention all the other stuff that went weird. My Constrict Bar going down when Fourni missed, the other Constrict Bar I hit away.

Roodg's Text Box: wHY DID U MENTION IT THEN?

Fournimer's Text Box: so, right after we left there, the dungeon's name got changed up and the boss went crazy? do you think that Anders Dude was there right after us?

Palcath's eyes lit up. Fournimer had given him a great idea. The only idea that could logically fit given the data they had collected.

Palcath's Text Box: No, I think the lad was right there with us. Now he shows up here right when we do.

Fournimer's Text Box: so a naked elf Dude is following us around just to show us up? that doesn't make any sense.

Roodg's Text Box: i'M GUNNA SET nAKED eLF qUEST AS MY ACTIVE QUEST.

Palcath's Text Box: Not a lick, lad.

It may have logically made sense, but Palcath had no idea why anyone would be following them, even if someone was. There was a piece to this puzzle he was missing, and not knowing it was more infuriating than every *Puzzle Block Puzzle* combined.

Roodg's Text Box: hE HAS A NEW PICTURE NOW, WITH CLOTHES EVEN! jUST OVER THERE!

Palcath's Text Box: Well, at least that part makes sense, lass. He wanted to get to Level 20 to put on his level-restricted Armour like us.

Fournimer's Text Box: so, did the Dude use us just to get through that maze? is that why he followed us?

Palcath's Text Box: I don't think so, lad. Mr. Max's guide didn't say anything about needing four avatars. If he already knew that four were needed, he would either be past Level 20 or stuck in the maze waiting for us. Hmm ... he didn't offer to help until we got stuck in different areas of the maze with only three of us....

Fournimer's Text Box: so he is a shy stalker? wait ... why would a stalker say anything at all? why not just wait, or help secretly without saying anything?

Palcath's Text Box: Hmm ... good point, lad. He must either not be a very good stalker or have another plan altogether....

Roodg's Text Box: oR HE WAS HIDING BECAUSE HE WAS NAKED AND DIDN'T WANT ANYONE TO SEE HIS ELF BITS. bUT THEN BEETLES WERE TOTALLY GOING TO RUN UP HIS BUTT AND HE GOT REALLY SCARED SO HE CAME OUT OF HIDING EARLY BEFORE THE QUEST WAS OVER FORGETTING HE WAS ALL NUDE AND STUFF! tHEN WE SAW HIM BEING NUDE, SO HE RAN OFF CAUSE WE ALL SAW HIS JUNK AND HE WAS ALL SHY! LoL!

Palcath added a checkmark to the Roodg-is-not-smart column.

> Palcath's Text Box: Doubtful, lass. I wish we had more information about this.

The trio thought for a few moments, absentmindedly looking through various game materials. Roodg was disorganizing the contents of his or her *Backpack*, Palcath was researching his Battle Logs, and Fournimer was cruising the WorldForums. It was Fournimer's tactic that paid off, and he told everyone about it right after he closed the post about proper elf hunting tactics.

> Fournimer's Text Box: hey a new WorldForum topic was just posted called Codes! it is already the highest viewed one in history.

> Palcath's Text Box: Codes, lad?

> Fournimer's Text Box: yeah Codes, Dwarfman, there is a whole list here posted by someone named Breaker.

> Roodg's Text Box: Breaker? tHAT SOUNDS FAMILIAR.

> Palcath's Text Box: He isn't on my list, Roodg, so he isn't someone we have met. Put it on the screen, lad. I want to see it … hmm … start scrolling down.

> Roodg's Text Box: r U SURE? i THINK WE MET HIM…

> Fournimer's Text Box: look at them all Man and Guy!

The list scrolled down slowly, showing a great deal of cheat Codes. Most sounded worthless so far, but they had scrolled down only to G (which included Codes called Gecko Face and Gel Insoles). Maybe the better ones were still to come.

> Roodg's Text Box: omfm! nO WAY! tHAT WASN'T A CHOICE! i WANT THAT ONE so BAD!

Roodg: [>COMMAND> RE-ASSIGN START PT1> M/F/_ > SELECT _]

After that, Roodg flew up into the air and began to spin, and colourful lights erupted from every single body and robe part, slowly increasing in intensity until all that could be seen was an outline of a spinning, white-hot, Roodg-shaped light. With a powerful noise, Roodg exploded outward and revealed … Roodg, who was exactly the same as before all the spinning as if nothing had happened.

> Roodg's Text Box: omfm! iT WORKED! sO AWESOME!

> Palcath's Text Box: Huh … what worked? You are the exact same, lass.

Roodg felt himself/herself all over.

Roodg's Text Box: nO, i'M ALL CHANGED, CAN'T YOU TELL?

Fournimer's Text Box: ...

Palcath's Text Box: Okay ... keep scrolling down, lad.

Fournimer's Text Box: that one: *Maximum Battle Log* – learn everything that is kept from your view, including who does what damage in the current area, what monsters are planning behind your back, and even respawn rates of defeated creatures. plus much more! that is so a Dwarfman thing!

Palcath's Text Box: Sold, lad.

Palcath: [>COMMAND> Battle Alter MBL> Unlock N/F/FF > Select F]

Six-hundred-and-forty-eight bluebirds and a single starling flew right at Palcath's head in just under four rounds. They came from every direction and harmlessly exploded upon impact. Palcath's eyes lit up bright yellow, and glazed over into a permanent gold.

Roodg's Text Box: hOLY CRAP! bIRDS!

Palcath's Text Box: Wow, lass and lad ... I can ... I can ... read the air. Everything is all now so ... significantly full of stats.

Fournimer's Text Box: hey Man, go back and check the Battle Logs!

Palcath's Text Box: I already was ... hmm, that Anders lad didn't do a single point of damage to the Hydra. He failed the very first *Poison Spit* check and was put into *Dire* status for having no Stamina. The Hydra didn't do any damage to him either; it just kept using moves.

Fournimer's Text Box: that's weird. what happened Man?

Palcath's Text Box: I don't know, lad. I can't see the battle, just the Battle Log.... Hmm ... the monster had a secret agenda to 'Force its heads to work together'.

Roodg's Text Box: iT ONLY HAD 1 HEAD!

Roodg paced in front of the exact same scenic tree multiple times, unable to stay still. On the eighteenth pass by, a branch defied all game logic. It began to interact with a player character, snagging the back of Roodg's *Navy Robes*. There was a loud ripping noise followed by an explosion of numbers and black pixels. The loud screeching of a word being yelled erupted into the entire area.

Fournimer's Text Box: cheque?

> Palcath's Text Box: Chart?

> Roodg's Text Box: aHHH! mY *nAVY rOBES!* wHAT JUST HAPPENED?

Frantically feeling the back of the *Navy Blue Robes* and finding nothing wrong with them, Roodg began to calm down.

> Roodg's Text Box: wHA?

Fournimer and Palcath both confirmed that the *Navy Robes* were exactly the same as they had been before the horrible yelling noise.

> Fournimer's Text Box: that was weird Man!

Palcath didn't answer as his eyes were making strange movements again and were scrolling up. He was checking the Battle Log.

> Palcath's Text Box: Nope, nothing, lad. The Battle Log is empty, but I did find out something else … no, wait, there is more.

> Fournimer's Text Box: what Man?

Palcath got up and began to pace while processing the information. Pacing always seemed to help with that.

> Palcath's Text Box: One: that I was right, of course. Anders was at the battle with the Flamealith. The lad shot at her at least once, and jumped into the battle to attack my *Constrict Bar*. When she saw him, she Constricted him. I broke his *Constrict Bar*. That's odd.… When she had me in Constrict, her secret motive was to destroy my worst piece of equipment, my shield. When she had him, her secret motive was to store for later use.

> Fournimer's Text Box: so the Dude helped you Man? what is number two?

> Palcath's Text Box: Way back, like fifty turns after we first recruited Roodg, Anders was being *Bound Most* by the vine creature you cut in half, Fourni. It was going to do … cliché things to him. But you stopped it.

> Fournimer's Text Box: so we saved the elf Dude way back? how did you read all that so fast Man?

> Roodg's Text Box: ctrl F. dUH!

> Palcath's Text Box: Looks like it, lad. We saved his ass awhile back and

didn't know. Let me think about it some more while pacing around.

Roodg's Text Box: tHAT THING HAD SO MANY FLOWER DICKS! i SWEAR IT DID. cOCKS ROCK!

Fournimer wanted to use a Code as well, something fun sounding like *Auto-Locate, Vishnu Hands, Laser-Guided Bunny Missiles That Shoot Out of Your Eyes,* or *Lizard Lips.* Right near the end of the list, he found what he was looking for.

Fournimer: [COMMAND> Weapon Extra Effects > N/Y > Select Y]

Jumping in the air, Fournimer executed a *Double Jump* (which he couldn't actually do), then a *Triple Jump*, then a *Quadruple Jump*. The others lost sight of him well after losing count of the jumping. They were shocked to see him come back into the area by erupting from the ground as they had been staring up. Holding out his weapons, Fournimer used the *Grin Animation*. They were covered in neatness.

Palcath's Text Box: Whoa, lad, that is neat. What do they do?

Fournimer tried his main weapon. It made a florchinking sound effect and used all sorts of swoopy things; plus, it had a trail of sparkles. A shot of his secondary weapon caused an arrow to fly out, followed by a trail of multicoloured glitter.

Fournimer's Text Box: uh … they are the same I think…

Palcath's Text Box: Yeah lad, but now they are really neat!

Roodg's Text Box: gLITTER?! tHAT IS 2 COOL! i WANT IT!

Roodg: [>COMMAND> wEAPON eXTRA eFFECTS > n/y > SELECT y]

Roodg excitedly readied himself/herself to jump in the sky like Fourni had just done. Roodg stood there for quite some time.

Roodg's Text Box: ?

Roodg: [>COMMAND> wEAPON eXTRA eFFECTS > n/y > SELECT y]

Nothing.

Roodg: [>COMMAND> wEAPON eXTRA eFFECTS > n/y > SELECT y]

Still nothing.

Roodg's Text Box: nO FAIR!

Palcath's Text Box: That's odd … hmm….

Palcath: [COMMAND> Weapon Extra Effects > N/Y > Select Y]

Palcath's Text Box: I wonder….

Palcath: [>COMMAND> Battle Alter MBL> Unlock N/F/FF > Select N]

Nothing happened. Palcath's eyes stayed the same. Thinking, he began to pace again. As he paced past the same scenic rock formation, it stopped being so specifically scenic. This time, one rock rolled away from the others and landed on top of him. While it didn't weigh anything or hurt him in any way, it did smack him in the head. Palcath stopped moving. The rock remained leaning against his face. He moved to the side, but it didn't move. He tried to push it back to where it started and heard a loud ripping followed by the same ear-bleeding sound.

> Roodg's Text Box: cHIRP?

> Fournimer's Text Box: cleat?

> Palcath's Text Box: What the lad was that?

A quick once over on the dwarf proved that nothing was amiss and all his Armour was still intact.

> Roodg's Text Box: hUH?

> Palcath's Text Box: Nothing in the Battle Log again. Maybe it is just something from the Codes? I can't activate the other Code either, lass, and mine isn't turning off. Let's see if it happens to you, Fourni.

They all watched Fournimer intently. He was determined to not be attacked by scenery like the others had been. He stood fast in his position and didn't move a muscle. A few quiet rounds went by, but nothing happened.

> Fournimer's Text Box: I guess it is not from the Codes. I'm glad beca—

A cloud interrupted the Text Box by falling from the sky and landing on Fournimer.

> Palcath's Text Box: Ha!

The cloud turned dark gray and shot out random bolts of lightning and upside-down rain.

> Roodg's Text Box: nEAT.

A rainbow of light burst from the cloud and destroyed it. A loud tearing noise was followed by an explosion of numbers and black pixels and the screaming loud word.

> Roodg's Text Box: cRETE?

> Palcath's Text Box: No, it was definitely Chiefs. It is calling us Chiefs. Chiefs because we are so darn awesome at this detective thing, lass.

Fournimer rose from the ground. He was completely soaked, and his entire *#6 Hairstyle* was standing straight up due to the new lightning logic.

> Roodg's Text Box: omm! i CAN SEE UR NIPPLES!

A very blushing Fournimer checked. It was true; he couldn't see his *Standard Issue Undergarments* at all. He very quickly put his *Silver Vest* back on.

Roodg looked down Roodg's *Navy Robes*.

> Roodg's Text Box: i CAN SEE MY NIPPLES! wE R NAKED NAKED NOW! jUST LIKE Anders!

> Palcath's Text Box: Lemme just … yep. Me, too.

> Fournimer's Text Box: Man, Guy … something is coming … from down there.

Three boss-level monsters approached the party; it was as if they had come from nowhere. As they advanced, they all flipped with a familiar strange glitch that the avatars had seen before.

> Palcath's Text Box: Okay, get ready to fight. Fourni, I want you to attack from the side with your crazy neat weapons. We need to see if they actually do anything. I'll take the front to distract them. That way, I can tell you all what they are secretly planning. Roodg, you try to blast them. If that doesn't work, just … do whatever it is you just Coded on them … or just throw some scenery at them or something, lass. Okay now, if they are … oh, sweet Maker.

> Fournimer's Text Box: what in the…?

> Roodg's Text Box: i CALL THAT ONE!

Chapter 15

BATTLE IN THE B
(STRONGHOLD)

Anders opened his Micro-Mini Map and double-checked. This was definitely the only way through. An entire dungeon stood between him and the Tower of Mechanis. It wasn't a very long trip since the mountains blocking the way would house only a small dungeon. The terrible thought that a tall, multi-levelled, annoying dungeon with many floors could be stashed inside as well made him slightly shaky. Stronghold B didn't have a normal dungeon door, though. It had a set of double doors, which made Anders research it first.

According to the Insta-Wiki, the Stronghold was part of a group of dungeons that housed dangerous raid monsters. Mr. Max's guide had said that at least 100 avatars needed to be present in the same place for the monster to even spawn. It also said that Mr. Max himself was recruiting avatars to join his quest to finish them all (and to help complete his Insta-Wiki, obviously). The group had already destroyed the creature from Stronghold A, with Mr. Max leading the charge and dealing the killing blow solo in one round. The group was headed here next.

That would explain the forty or so avatars all hanging around here. Anders did his best to walk slowly, worried that, with any strong movement, the scant scraps of fabric would reveal a little too much. While he was relatively sure no one had seen anything, he did get many a wide-eyed stare. A few female avatars had even told him they were jealous of his outfit, and asked where he got it. Anders didn't recognize any of these higher leveled avatars except for the loud, boisterous fellow in the middle. Anders recognized him immediately as Mr. Max. He was flexing his huge muscles with the *Flex Animation* to anyone that saw him. Anders, who was absentmindedly checking out the large, bare, muscular arms revealed through the ill-fitting *Diamond Plate*, earned himself a beefy wink from Mr. Max. Anders quickly moved away and went to stand behind some low scenery. He was hoping to avoid showing off his outfit—and now interested bits—to any avatars.

When Mr. Max put forward his call to action, the other avatars listened, showing up in droves. Within just a few more rounds, there were more than sixty ready-to-go hopefuls that could probably handle themselves, and about eighty more that would probably not survive the encounter. Anders got some information by keeping his eye on the Text Boxes in the area. Apparently, a high level player named Breaker brought about sixty lower level avatars with him and charged them all handsomely for the escort.

Anders helped a little gnome named Gliint get off a roof that he apparently had accidently lagged onto while jumping. Gliint told Anders about Breaker's entry fee of 500 Gold Pieces for this battle. The gnome seemed trustworthy—perhaps a little too fond of using animations, but trustworthy. Anders felt a twinge of pity for the little guy. Gliint had been brought here only to serve as bait for the Stronghold B monster. The gnome had given nearly all of his spending gold to Breaker just for the privilege to die. Anders felt bad for the naive gnome and gave him the only piece of outdated gear he had, his *Leather Armlets*, and a bunch of other less important junk that would never be mentioned again in the future books of this series.

Mr. Max made the *Shh Animation* to settle the crowd. Soon, the random inane Text Box chatter filling the air petered out. Once the very last avatar had stopped jumping in place, Mr. Max did his trademark *Flex Animation*. A few others did the pose but were quietly reprimanded by their peers. It was Mr. Max's pose to use, and no one else should do it. Anders chose not to try the pose for other reasons, one of the main ones being that he was pretty sure if he did try it, his balls would fall out of his outfit.

> Mr. Max's Text Box: Hail, fellow adventurers!

> 139 Simultaneous Text Boxes: Hail!

> Gliint's Lag Text Box: Hail!

Anders didn't say anything. Gliint the Level 4 gnome was now getting singled out for being just a round too late. Anders decided to forgo the evil glances and not add his "hail" late either.

> Mr. Max's Text Box: Fellow adventurers and adventurettes, we stand here this cycle to attack and bring down the mighty monster of Stronghold B after a thrilling victory at Stronghold A! We know not what dwells within these walls, and while not all of you will survive this battle, you can all say that you were here, with Mr. Max the very first time that whatever is in there was defeated! So, grab your weapons and

> come with me. Together, we will see a mighty victory! TO VICTORY!

With that, Mr. Max *Flexed* his muscles, took out his gigantic sword, and raised it high in the air. Mr. Max was holding his giant, new two-handed sword (the aptly named *Four-Handed Sword* that had replaced his older *Three-Handed Sword*) firmly in just one gauntleted hand. The *Gauntlet* was important looking and covered in liquid metal spikes.

> 139 Simultaneous Text Boxes: TO VICTORY!

> Gliint's Lag Text Box: TO VICTORY!

Gliint used the *Sorry About That Animation* in response to the many leers he received.

> Gliint's Text Box: Sorry … there are a lot of people here, and my connection isn't great.

Mr. Max charged into the double door dungeon followed by the crowd of hollering avatars. Anders thought about joining in; Mr. Max's speech was pretty good, all things considered. He had a flash in his mind of a gigantic beast the size of a mountain picking him out from the crowd. With a mighty roar, it would charge at him (after doing a back flip without explanation) and try to rape him in front of 141 other avatars with its one-hundred-and-sixty move unit long pseudo-penis. The thought was not very appealing.

Anders decided to not risk it, even if he did sort of have pants on now. He would stay outside and wait until it was over. Once the battle was finished, all the other avatars would leave. The high leveled ones were far too strong for this area and would probably go to Stronghold C, and the lower leveled ones would be dead. That way Anders could just walk through Stronghold B to the tower. He wouldn't even have to encounter the pseudo-beast at all since he would be alone and Mr. Max said you needed 100 avatars to even get the beast to spawn.

More than three hundred turns went by while Anders hid behind a scenic frozen bush and absentmindedly chewed on his *Mountain Bacon* reserves. The double doors finally burst open and out poured Mr. Max and most of the higher leveled avatars; only about ten were missing. Each had gained a few levels, except Mr. Max—he gained only one and was now Level 97.

The only lower level avatar that Anders saw was Gliint, who was now Level 19.99. The little gnome Backstabber was bragging that his bad connection had made him miss getting hit by the AOE attack that killed all the rest of the lower levels. (Anders had considered being the Backstabber class because they were the fastest class and had an easy to aim crossbow, but it sounded too much like a judgement of moral character, and he didn't want to play a bad guy, even if it was just the name of the class.)

Mr. Max signaled for silence, and the ruckus that had been going on quickly stopped. He famously used the *Flex Animation*.

> Mr. Max's Text Box: Fellow adventurers! We fought well, and the Gigas lies dead. Onward we shall march! First to complete the Hero of the

> Cycle's quest in record time! Then to the Shores of Eternal Night and to Stronghold C for another great victory!

53 avatars performed the *Cheer Animation* at once.

Glünt performed the *Cheer Animation*.

Mr. Max used the *Flex Animation* one last time and led the charge back down the Lova Mountains path.

Anders thought for a round after the group ran. What was the Hero of the Cycle's Quest? Maybe it had a good reward or something, but why was it possessive? He also had no idea at all as to where the Shores of Eternal Night were. Deciding with good reason to not follow the random cheering avatars, he ducked into the empty Stronghold B.

The inside was one very large chamber, covered in ice. Peppy drum music was filling the room; it felt more annoying than mood-setting. The chamber was completely smooth and allowed natural light to pour in through the roof. The realistic ice was pretty, but the room was empty. There was nothing inside. The area must have reset already, Anders guessed, due to the lack of lower-leveled avatar corpses. A very distant set of double doors was at the other side of the chamber. It was almost too small to see from here, but he could just make out the clashing pigments of the standard double door colouring. Anders headed in the direction of the clashing.

When the Frost Gigas suddenly dropped from the ceiling, it not only knocked Anders flat on his butt but also scared him so badly that he squeaked out loud. The ground was still shaking, and Anders stayed sitting, unable to stand. His view was only that of a giant blue humanoid foot.

> Frost Gigas' Text Box: Beware, adventurers seeking battle, for I am the mighty Frost Gigas!

The Frost Gigas started to charge up something but stopped halfway through the animation. He looked around with a mighty crackling of his neck.

> Frost Gigas' Text Box: ...Beware, adventurers seeki—

> The Frost Gigas was frozen in place, waiting. Anders checked the Insta-Wiki before trying anything else.

> **Creature Name:** Frost Gigas
> **Class:** Gigas B
> **Level:** 98 (Requires 100 avatars to be present to spawn)
> **Special Attacks:** Gigas Burst, Gigas Stomp, Gigas Ice Shower, Gigas Barrage, Gigas Blast, Gigas B

> **Drops:** *Frost Gigas Boots* (only for avatar that gets last strike)
> **First Player Encounter Notes:** I can't believe I got to be the Hero of the Cycle and get the final hit! Mr. Max, you are my hero! – Gliint

Anders realized that Mr. Max was taking 53 high level characters to go finish Gliint's Level 20 quest just down the road. There wasn't a real Hero of the Cycle's quest to do.

The Frost Gigas didn't move. It just stared blankly.

> Frost Gigas' Text Box: …

> Anders' Text Box: …

> Frost Gigas' Text Box: …

> Anders' Text Box: …let me guess: you are a NPC, right?

The Frost Gigas suddenly snapped out of it.

> Frost Gigas' Text Box: Not exactly, little one, I am a Combo NPC/Monster. I need to be able to follow my script and to attack. They made me both.

The Frost Gigas got out of battle stance, which sent a wave of relief down Anders' body.

> Frost Gigas' Text Box: I only show up for 100 or more avatars, though. Where are you hiding the others?

> Anders' Text Box: It's only me. I waited until they all left.

> Frost Gigas' Text Box: Strange of me to show up! Why did that happen again?

The Frost Gigas bent down.

> Anders' Text Box: I agree. I just want to go over there and leave. Is that okay?

> Frost Gigas' Text Box: Allow me to carry you. It is only polite after I scared you half to death like that.

> Anders' Text Box: No, it's okay. I can walk. It is fine.

The Frost Gigas picked up Anders by the crop cape of his *Mithral Vest (s)* and held him up to see better.

The very facial profile of the Gigas was larger than Anders himself.

> **Frost Gigas' Text Box:** I insist. It really isn't any trouble at.... What ... what ... what are you wearing?

The Frost Gigas was staring at Anders intently. Anders had been afraid of this. If every monster changed when it saw him, this NPC/Monster would at the very least half-change. From the angle the Frost Gigas was holding him, Anders knew that the champion of Stronghold B had a full view of his exposed crotch and butt under the very skimpy *Mithral Leggings (s)* sash squares.

Anders' face turned slightly pink just as the Frost Gigas' turned slightly purple. Anders' heart sank, however, when the Gigas' face glitched and turned two-hundred-and-fifty-five other colours before settling on blue again.

> **Anders' Text Box:** Let me guess, Combo NPC/Pervert now, right?

The Frost Gigas revealed an ice-toothed grin directed at the tiny elf in his hand.

> **Frost Gigas' Text Box:** You got it, Elfboy!

> **Anders' Text Box:** That's it, Combo NPC/Monsters, you just made my list!

Anders' List:
1. Scenic Pillars
2. Glades
3. Status Effects
4. Constrict Bars
5. Traps
6. (s) Gear
7. Swarm Beetles
8. Combo NPC/Monsters

The Gigas moved the struggling Elfboy downward with one hand, while he undid the strap to his one-piece Gigas Armour with the other. It had a single shoulder strap and a kilt-like skirt. The beast removed the skimpy kilt and threw it across the domed room. It hit the floor with a massive thud. Anders noted that it now completely blocked the main entrance to the cave that he had came in from originally.

Anders was absolutely shocked to see that the Frost Gigas was wearing tight-fitting, dark blue, short-legged boxer brief underwear; a label on the front across the waistband bigger than Anders' head said Gigas™ in a fancy logo. The dark briefs on the pale blue skin of the muscular Frost Gigas were flattering, even sexy. Anders blushed and felt himself perk up (despite the real danger of the situation). Whatever was behind that tight, name-brand Gigas boxer brief was massive—and it was beginning to stir.

The Gigas pulled Anders toward him and rubbed him against the front of the underwear. Anders could feel the member beginning to enlarge. It pulsed and grew with the Gigas' heartbeat; with each beat, it got a little bit larger and a little bit harder. The Gigas' cock was pushing toward the outside of the giant thigh to the left, and Anders was getting rubbed all over it. Finally, the member stopped growing. It was noticeably past the Gigas' thigh and straining hard against the waistband, desperately wanting to escape. It was hard to guess at the size while it was still covered up and compressed tight by the straining fabric, but Anders guessed stupidly big.

The double doors of the dungeon creaked open. Anders wasn't sure if he was glad that the Gigas' outfit had landed there or not. On one hand, the avatar trying to open it probably couldn't see what was happening. On the other, they couldn't help him get away.

The Frost Gigas didn't hear the double doors since he was enjoying himself far too much. After a few more long, hard rubs against his hidden and straining member, he pulled Anders back for a better view of the big reveal. With a thumb into the waistband, the Gigas pulled down his boxer briefs in a swift motion. One side made it down to about his knee, while the other caught on his member and ended up about mid-thigh. The fumble was pretty sexy, though Anders thought it would have been slightly more provocative on someone more his size. The cock forcefully bounced free from its prison; the very sight of it made Anders' heart skip a beat.

It stood erect, almost perfectly straight out, basically staring Anders in the face. Thick, blue veins as big as Anders' wrist pulsed on the member, flowing from the base to the exposed light purple cock head. Had this Gigas been shrunk down to regular human size, he would have been more than proud. But here, as it stood, it was a cock easily twice as long as Anders was tall. Much thicker than Anders' #2 *Body Type (Average)* stood this behemoth. When the Gigas flexed slightly, the thing bounced. The monstrous cock reminded Anders a little of Mr. Max; it was about as thick as he was with all his muscles. The cock was pulsating noticeably, and a drop of precum as big as Anders' head dripped out over the tip.

Anders saw the two massive Gigas balls. They were a little bit larger than what would be normal for a creature his size. While they were nothing compared to The Titan's big Ts (which was almost a relief), they were achingly swollen and a much darker colour than the Gigas himself; they were definitely blue balls—or bluer balls, to be precise. Anders could hear the cum swirling around in them. The Gigas flexed again. The balls compressed upward while the big dick bounced. A little more precum was produced, the smell filling Anders' nostrils.

Frost Gigas' Text Box: Lick it.

Anders got ready to do what he was told. Licking it was far better than anything else that this monster might decide to try doing with him, at least in terms of survivability. Being guided while held in the Gigas' firm grip, the giant started by splashing Anders' face right into the precum drop. Anders was instantly covered with it, causing him to choke and splutter. Anders was not off to a great start. Despite his efforts, he couldn't manage to do anything but cough while the Gigas rubbed him against the giant throbbing cock.

> Frost Gigas' Text Box: I gave you a chance, Elfboy, and you ruined it.

Horror flashed through Anders' eyes as he was turned around and no longer faced the giant member.

> Frost Gigas' Text Box: It's been literally forever. My blue balls are getting ready to burst. I don't have time to waste with failed cocksuckers.

The Gigas aimed Anders' hole directly at the cock and started to push it toward him. Thicker by almost double than Anders was himself, it wouldn't ever fit in his hole, not even in his entire body. Right now it was just moving around on his entire lower body.

> Really Far Away Text Box #1: Oh my Maker, lad! I can't watch.

> Really Far Away Text Box #2: no, we have to stop it! help me move this giant skirt.

> Really Far Away Text Box #3: !

The Gigas grabbed Anders tightly and lined him up, ready for entry on the next round with some Gigas-themed action, most likely. At least three avatars were going to watch him get split in half by a giant boss cock. That made it almost better. He cursed at himself for not clearing away the debris in front of this computer's power switch. It was too late to look for it now.

On Anders' turn, he cast *Stretch More*. He tried casting the spell as many times as possible for the rest of the round, doubtful it would work, but he had to try.

With a death grip on Anders, the Gigas began to pull him back toward the waiting cock. The Gigas was met with expected and fierce resistance. Judging by how much Anders felt go in, it became apparent the extent of Anders' *Stretch More* ability was just about a little bigger than the Rockagin's member. The Gigas continued to try to push, and Anders felt like he was going to be ripped open at the seams.

> Anders' Text Box: Ugghh!! Stretch More! Please Stretch More! Urk!

The Gigas pushed harder, forcing himself in. He was enjoying the tightness and challenge.

> Anders' Text Box: Blerk!!! Stretch More! Please Stretch More! PLEASE! *STRETCH MORE! MORE!*

The Frost Gigas was getting impatient. When his turn began, he started to squeeze Anders hard, pulling him strongly toward his Gigas dick. Anders eyes were closed, but he heard a buzzing noise around his head. He felt a huge gush of fluid from his body. Obviously it was his blood from splitting in half. He let out a cry that rivaled the Frost Gigas' volume and font size.

> # Anders' Text Box: UUURRRGGGHHH!

> Really Far Away Text Box #1: Tell me when it's over, lad.

> Really Far Away Text Box #2: holy fuck!

> Really Far Away Text Box #3: cRUMPETS!

> Really Far Away Text Box #1: What? Holy Fuck!

Anders opened his eyes, confused that he could even open them at all. He wasn't dead. Quickly going over himself with his eyes and hands, he saw and felt no blood. He glanced up at the Frost Gigas' bewildered face first, then at everything else Gigas related. Thick but neatly trimmed blue pubic hair was scratching the bottom of his legs, and he felt something large and slightly chilled resting at the back of his bum. It smelled earthy, sweaty. The thing against his butt pushed up a bit, like when the Gigas had flexed before. It was the greatest pressure Anders had ever felt.

Reaching down below him with his foot, Anders' boots slid against the slick drops of fluid covering the object's base. A few rounds later, it sounded like buckets of fluid were splashing down onto the frozen floor. Anders realized what had happened. *Stretch More More* had been added to his list of spells. He reached down with his hand and gingerly felt for his opening. His body completely surrounded the cock, holding it tightly. It shouldn't have been possible; the cock was bigger than Anders' entire body. Anders' ass began to tingle when he realized that somehow now he had the entire Gigas' cock inside him. His legs were splayed unnaturally, and his hips were really out of proportion. He could feel the pressure, but had no idea how it wasn't exploding through him. It had entered him, and vanished.

> Really Far Away Text Box #1: I see … so the lad has an ass of holding. That is the only possible explanation for how that works.

> Really Far Away Text Box #2: an ass of what?

> Really Far Away Text Box #3: LoL! cRUMPETS!

Another quick tingle was all it took to bring the Gigas back to his senses.

> # Frost Gigas' Text Box: Holy fuck, who would have

thought that the Elfboy had a secret attack?

The Gigas took hold of Anders and moved him around. Even though the cock was twice as big as the elf, it somehow still fit. He was dumbfounded. The Gigas took Anders all the way off, just to be sure. With a big blue hand he pushed the Night Ranger down again, all the way to the base. The Gigas repeated the action again and, surprisingly, the avatar on him moaned loudly. On the next slow return, Anders screamed with what sounded like pleasure, and thousands of little pressure tingles hit the Gigas' cock. The tingles were an incredible feeling, so the Gigas began to pump the elf on his cock with increased speed to get more.

The huge thing constantly thrusting into Anders put so much pressure and pleasure on his insides that, although with each thrust he should have been cumming, he couldn't climax. The feeling was just too intense, and with every thrust, he let out a powerful scream.

He could feel the Gigas' huge cock pulsate with every thrust; through the big veins, he could feel the blood flowing. With each thrust, he was pulled down against the giant, pulsating balls, and he could still hear the cum churning within. It felt painfully full and tight. It needed release, and Anders realized that, soon, he'd need to be released almost as bad as the Gigas did. He couldn't keep this up for very long. *Stretch More More* was at the absolute limit.

> Anders' Text Box (of one word per thrust): ... take ... it ... out ... I ... want ... to ... feel ... you ... push ... it ... all ... in ... again.

The Gigas complied; it desperately wanted to get more of the wonderful tingles. He slid Anders all the way off and began to penetrate him anew. It took Anders twenty of the full-pressure entries to finally release himself. He gasped in relief and contracted and clenched his rump in pleasure.

The tightening of Anders' bum slowed the Gigas slightly. It was gripping hard against the Gigas' cock. The increased pressure of the elf and all of the orgasmic tingles were getting to him. The Gigas let out an intense scream. He clutched Anders tightly, keeping him secure on the base of the giant penis. Spurt after thick spurt pulsed into Anders. He just barely had enough time to *Absorb* before the next wave hit. The Gigas was shaking as he came. Each spurt made his balls quake violently. He slowed his pace, but the massive balls continued to drip out more in quiet gushes. Once it was finally over, the Gigas' balls had shrunk down to what would have been normal for a creature its size, and were no longer shades of painful dark blue.

It took twenty turns of inactivity and resting before the Gigas slowly slid out. With only a slightly softened cock, it took far more care now and gently placed Anders on the ground. Thick ropes of cum and juice covered Anders' legs, posterior, and *Mithral Leggings (s)* that hadn't even needed to come off for the encounter. Sheepishly, the Gigas pulled something out of the waistband of his underwear (after pulling them up) and placed it carefully into Anders' *Ultra-Pack*.

> Really Far Away Text Box #1: So that's how the lad does it. I thought so.

> Really Far Away Text Box #2: way to go Elfboy!

> Really Far Away Text Box #3: cRUMPETS!!!

The Gigas left Anders to go to the far side of the dome to his Gigas bed and fell asleep as soon as his Gigas head hit the Gigas pillow. He didn't even pick up his set of Gigas clothes still blocking the door to put them in the Gigas hamper. Anders stood there shaking and heard his Insta-Wiki ding. He was given the chance to write the additional comment about the Frost Gigas to be immortalized for all time.

> **Additional Comments:** Mrrf … mrn mff er nnneer mif nnnble mubmub ip ner smah niffim mibufinerm. – Anders

Anders collapsed to his knees and fell face first onto the cold floor. His entrance was still painfully stretched, with big globs of fluids pouring out all over his body. Passing out was an appropriate idea, so he did. He drifted off while listing to exciting trumpet music.

◈ **Chapter 16** ◈

THE TOWER OF
MECHANIS

Anders opened his eyes slowly, with great effort. He had no idea where he was. He felt groggy. It took some rounds for his eyes to adjust to the light before he could see anything.

He was inside a structure, not a very large one, maybe about the size of a Dungeon Entry Room. The muslin roof was held up by poles, and paintings of various types of terrain were hung around the four walls. The other side of the room, he noticed, was a mirror image of this one. He heard a brisk wind pick up outside, and saw dark yellow walls rustle in the breeze. A shaft of bright light entered the structure as the nearby door blew open. Anders screamed out a curse comprised of random baked goods and covered his eyes.

The longer he lay there, the more that came back. He noticed that he was nestled comfortably in a real bed. Around him were three other beds in a semicircle, making for a total of four nice beds. There was room for more beds, they looked like they would spring up from the floor as a party needed. There was room for least a few more beds. Each bed had a brown chest at the foot of it. Anders thought that brown was a bit of a boring colour for chests. Thinking about it, Anders remembered the one thing he'd really learned from the tutorial: real beds existed only in two places, Inns and *Portie Tents*. This was either a very lame Inn made of canvas, or a very nice *Portie Tent* (possibly a *Portie Tent Ultra* judging by how much art was inside).

His sheets felt stiff and new, so he was probably the first one to ever use the slot four sheets. He didn't much feel like standing yet, and there wasn't anyone else here, so he reviewed the other beds and their standard-sized personal areas more closely.

The first was toned with the red colour palate. The red was a little forceful and intense; seeing it gave Anders more of a headache. A little bit of lighter red would have done it some good, but pink was probably a different colour set completely. The personal area was more than a little bit haphazard, and the bed sheets had been set to *Very Messy*. There were various destroyed pieces of scenery that all had met with very messy ends, all just randomly thrown about. Anders decided not to linger on this personal space any longer.

The second had a much calmer demeanor with its blue palette selected. The bed was set to *Immaculate*, and not a single flaw could be seen. The personal area was very carefully decorated. None of the objects were expensive, but they all were interesting to look at. All had been carefully placed through what had been many turns of strenuous point and click.

The third area was set to yellow, though much of it was really gold The bed was set to *Almost Made Properly* and only had a few wrinkles on the comforter. Important Quest Items were in the personal space, and while they had been placed with care, they were not obsessively placed like the ones in the blue area. They were at different angles from each other, and some had fallen over, giving the impression of someone who cared that they were on display, but didn't really care if they were perfectly arranged.

Anders had forgotten that you could change colour palettes for personal areas in *Portie Tents*. He had only ever been in one once at the store in Coorparbeaan when he had no way of affording one. He went to the menu to change his to green, hoping the party that owned the tent wouldn't mind. He opened the menu but noticed that they had already been set to green. Someone else had changed the default settings for him. Also a few of his fanciest items had been removed and displayed very carefully in the personal space. His *Combi-Fusion Pot*, the *Allure Potion*, the remaining *Auto-Trap Release*, and his half-used *Repair-It* dotted his personal area. Judging by the care that went into the placement, Anders guessed that the blue-area-dwelling avatar had done it.

He stretched and accidently hit the *Combi-Fusion Pot* in the display area, moving it slightly to the left. It wasn't in perfect alignment anymore and was not facing the camera at a direct angle, but Anders was easy-going and it didn't convern him.

Testing the waters, he moved himself to the edge of the bed and put his toes on the floor. He wasn't hurting nearly as bad as he had been when just waking up. He tried to stand up and did a very good job of it. He felt pretty much at full Hit Points. He waited a round before moving ahead, but he eventually was able to step forward without falling over. He legs no longer felt like jelly, so he felt ready to leave this *Portie Tent*.

Taking a few steps away from his bed (and leaving it in the *Just Got Out Of It* setting), he felt absolutely fine and was able to walk normally. When another breeze hit the tent and sent a gust of air through the open door, he felt the crispness hit him pretty much everywhere. Taking a moment to check his equipment page, he realized that he was completely naked. Turning back to the green personal area, he looked around but couldn't see any of his things. He had a moment of brief panic, but when his eyes fell on the brown chest, he realized his items had probably just been stored. He opened it and found everything he owned inside.

Not wanting to greet the map naked, he slowly put on his equipment. Finding a new pair of boots in his bag, Anders viewed their stats.

Frost Gigas Boots
Rating: More More Epic
Level: 98
Defence: 500 (+498 more than current equipped)
Class Restriction: Only those who dealt the final blow to the Frost Gigas can wear these boots.
Special Qualities: Immune to being destroyed; Cannot be traded
Steadfast: Avatars wearing these boots can no longer be pushed, pulled, or lifted. They cannot suffer from any other effect that would impede movement unless they choose to allow it (except when swimming).
Cling: Avatars can climb special walls using *Steadfast* while wearing these boots.
Level Restriction: Level 20+
Colour Slider (Rd-Oe-Yw-Gn-Be-Pe-Pk-Bn-We-Gy-Bk)

Anders' eyes nearly changed colour to shocked. *Level 98 More More Epic Boots?*

They had more Defence than his entire outfit had combined, and he pulled them on. These were some awesome boots. Made of liquid metal, they fitted up to his knees and ended with cool spikes. There were accents that pulsed with colour; the default colour had been blue, but he quickly changed them over to green. They also were familiar for some reason, then he remembered where he had seen a *Blank Gigas Gauntlet* before, on Mr. Max. (He wasn't sure which Gigas it was, which is why he had to call it the Blank Gigas, but he did know that Mr. Max had gotten the final blow on the Stronghold A Gigas, so it was a *Whatever That Gigas Was Gauntlet*.)

He checked his new stats with the *Frost Gigas Boots*, he felt faint. He sat back down on the bed. He saw that he was now Level 34 and that his Magic Points total was 99,999,967/1,950. He had gotten something like 30,000,000 MP pumped into him by the Frost Gigas and was 12 levels higher now for the experience. That was not a The Titan amount of Magic Points, but it was still respectable.

Anders stood to try out *Steadfast* and could not move his feet at all while doing it; however, he could still move —the rest of his body. It was a fun little trick. He wanted to try out the *Cling* ability but, a *Portie Tent* wall was not classified as a "special wall".

Leaving his oldest friends, the *Leather Boots,* in the chest at the foot of the green bed, Anders gathered himself and got ready to leave the *Portie Tent* and head outside. The door to the tent was open, but Anders saw a note attached with bACK IN 10 MINS scrawled on it. Never being one to listen to notes with poor grammar, Anders stepped outside into the bright snow-dusted area.

The mountain air felt nice as it filled his lungs. There were a few evergreens dotting the area around the tent, they were the only living things around. Anders could see no monsters or avatars, not even when he strained his camera into the distance.

This campsite was set at the base of the tower he'd been originally heading for, nestled in a small area beside the stairs that seemed almost made for a *Portie Tent*.

> Anders' Text Box: Looking at it, this area was exactly made just for a *Portie Tent*.

In the far distance, he could see the set of double doors that would go to the Frost Gigas' bedroom.

The Tower of Mechanis had four huge gears sticking out of the sides at awkward angles. All manner of pistons, levers, and pipes were jutting out of the tower, but despite the fantasy setting, it didn't feel out of place. Anders theorized that this area might be high fantasy or possibly even steampunk.

Lissa might still be in there. Hopefully she was. Anders desperately wanted to talk to her. A very quick check of her Player Pager had not shown any new postings, so he set his fingers to the crossed setting.

After waiting for about twenty turns (Anders had no idea how many *mins* were left in total) for whoever it was that left the note, Anders decided that the longer he waited for them to show up, the less chance he had of finding Lissa. He needed to ask what she knew about this whole mess, so he had to get moving. He added a note to the note that said, "Me, too."

Climbing up the stairs to the Tower of Mechanis proved immediately difficult. He couldn't move his feet after they hit the stairs. After a few rounds of *Clinging* to the stairs, he figured out the ability and could walk relatively well by using *Steadfast* one boot at a time, but it took a little practice. The entire structure was made of the same metallic material. This tower might actually prove to be fun.

It was like walking through heavy snow, snow that was on a wall. Anders had guessed right. He entered the standard dungeon door into the tower, and began to climb vertically with his boots. Standing on walls and ceilings while hitting the strange little clockwork monsters that lived here was really fun. He took a screenshot of himself standing on the ceiling with his bow drawn—it was so awesome—and he added the comment of "I am so awesome."

Up high on the walls and shooting down arrows from above with deadly *Earth Crystal* attacks, Anders made a discovery. The longer he charged the attack, the more MP it used and the more damage it did. He had a lot to spare, so he went Heat Pig wild, and killed everything in one hit. He could tell he was getting closer to the top and had only touched the actual floor here with the very first step inside.

The novelty eventually began to wear off as the trudging up walls continued (but not enough for him to climb down from the walls), so Anders headed for the clock face room of the tower. It was a large half-oval-shaped room with a high back wall. There were two different closed doors on the back wall, one on either side of a gigantic clock face. Various mechanical scenic objects surrounded the clock, from gears to pipes to pistons.

Anders approached one of the doors carefully. It was along a narrow platform beside the clock face. Anders cautiously attempted to open the door inwardly, but it was blocked from the other side. He could see through the crack that a scenic crate had been pushed up toward the door. After a few rounds of knocking with nothing happening, he shifted his camer to the other door.

This door was harder to get to, and that might make a better hiding spot for Lissa. He soon discovered that he couldn't just walk to the other door by climbing on the walls, since his boots wouldn't stick to the clock face. He had to re-evaluate. Between where he was standing and the other door was a series of moving blocks. They twisted, turned, and slid in and out across the open space. This was a *Jumping Puzzle*. He watched the pattern for a few rounds, and he noticed two things: the blocks were made of the magnetic material, and the puzzle really wasn't that hard.

Since the blocks were magnetic, he could simply skip the *Jumping Puzzle* altogether by putting both legs on specific starting blocks. While this would make him flip upside down at one point, he'd still be safe because he could use *Cling* and *Steadfast*. His options were that he could either skip the easy puzzle completely by being lazy, or jump three times.

Going with the lazy method, he put one *Frost Gigas Boot* on left Starting Block 4 and one *Frost Gigas Boot* on right Starting Block 1. He started his journey across the large clock room and was having fun. The floating blocks pulled in different directions at times and were making him feel like he was walking on spinning random clouds in big *Jumping Puzzle* boots.

> Game Explanation Text Box: Timing your jumps correctly is essential to success.

> Anders' Text Box: Now what?

It had felt like the difficulty of this puzzle was off. Anders noticed a series of obstacles suddenly pop out of the wall. Various mechanical pistons jutted out into the puzzle with extreme force, so he went to *Double Jump* away.

Anders realized immediately that he didn't *Double Jump* away because he had forgotten to disengage *Steadfast*. His *Frost Gigas Boots* held *Steadfast* to the two *Jumping Puzzle Blocks*, which were spreading his legs apart painfully. On their turn, the blocks rotated, flipping Anders upside down; if he released his *Cling* now, he would plummet down the tower. It was a good 600 Move Units down. A series of fast-moving drills, pistons, and turn cranks were now lined up to directly assault his delicate places with blinding *Serpent Speed,* and all he could do was slowly drift toward them. If he wasn't on the bottom of these darn *Jumping Puzzle Blocks*, he would have been fine.

> Anders' Text Box: This is a clock GLADE! How could I be so stupid! That's it, *Jumping Puzzle Blo* ... Urk!

Chapter 17
KNOCKING

Knock Knock Lissa was not going to answer that. She had already fallen for it once before and was still finding motor oil. She looked over her secure prison, impressed with herself. This was a large, open-domed area with two doors. One was held secure with scenic crates and an array of makeshift traps made from scenery and rope. The other door was her special way out, just in case. Monsters could not jump. There would be no way that they could make it over there. No one would bother doing the very difficult *Jumping Block Puzzle* outside to get to the other door. But, if anyone managed to enter the door, the first thing *Knock* they'd see would be a flashing lever. The lever was an elevator release that took the avatar back to the bottom of the tower and gave them a Red Chest. They would think they found the end of this tower dungeon and leave (they were right—this was the end). She felt safe; nobody could resist a flashing lever.

> Lissa's Text Box: #Secure.

Knock She had a great view of half the map from here. The prison was walled by glass. Everything she could see (until the polygons broke up in the distance) was beautiful. The back of a giant clock face *Knock* completed her prison, giving her the exact time of the cycle (even if what she saw was the backside of the model and the time was reversed).

She was getting very sick of this Ainsley's Arrow background music song, though.

Even if she *Knock* really liked them, the chorus of "Tower Tower Burning Brighter" just would not get out of her head.

Her supplies were stacked behind a crate in the corner and were *Knock* slowly running out. She could manage at least another seven cycles in here before being forced to leave her prison. She *Knock* used the *Sigh Animation*. This prison was beautiful and secure, but it was still a prison, even if it was of her *Knock* own making. Hopefully she would figure out *Knock* something soon and could leave.

Using the *Sitting Animation* to rest on a crate, she opened up the *Knock* WorldForums and took a gander. The Codes had been taken down almost *Knock* as soon as they had been posted. Too many avatars that tried them had complained about their save files becoming corrupted. *Knock* Damn it! There still wasn't any additional info. She had *Knock* hoped that there would be a way that someone had discovered how to fix an *Knock* avatar if its data was corrupted, but it was as she *Knock* feared. She tried to look up the feed of the game's IT team, but it hadn't updated in a while. All she saw were her own frustrated hashtags piling up.

There was only one generic administrator post, suggesting that if a character suffers from any major glitches, the only fix was to *Knock* restart. So far, that was what the majority of the avatars had chosen to do. Many with the problem *Knock* that tried to resist death simply vanished, likely dead. Dead dead. They weren't able to reload their corrupted file. Just like Vendimm, *Knock* Zal Finn, and the others.

The other WorldForums posts were generally the standard fare, but *Knock* she scrolled down the list anyway, hoping someone else had *Knock* posted something relevant. There were a few topics by angry avatars *Knock* who had to restart, but their *Knock* details were sketchy at best. It made sense. Who'd want to admit the *Knock* truth and say that their *Knock* avatar was just fucked to death by a *Knock* horny Manticore?

Her own WorldForum topic demanding the developers' *Knock* assistance was still ignored. It was already buried all the *Knock* way backonpage seven. She was tired of bumping the *Knock* thing and was just going to let it *Knock* die unanswered. She had also tried a thread to get them to respond about the TorTech-Headsets, *Knock* hoping to figure out what was making the game so realistic, but nobody had *Knock* commented at all. It had been buried too. There were only a few *Knock* other interesting WorldForums topics.

One was about *Knock* a new avatar named Brenna Jay *Knock* who was posting in character. *Knock* Lissa had checked the page because the title "Breaking through" had been misleading, but it had nothing to do with *Knock* broken avatars. It still had a lot of posts, and was popular. *Knock* Brenna Jay's commitment to stay in *Knock* character was impressive. Lissa gave her WorldForums post a *Knock* Thumbs-Up! despite her distaste for role-play. Brenna Jay had done a good job of subtle role-play, so it didn't bother Lissa to *Knock* read it. If she'd encountered that kind of overacting in actual game play, she would probably *Knock* have flown off the handle. Role-playing was *Knock* tiresome. It took twice as long to say anything and nothing was entirely clear. Save it for the forums, dorks.

Another post was an announcement by *Knock* Ivy, the Administrator Head of WorldForums. The race *Knock* was pretty close, and *Knock* the Insta-Wiki contest was almost *Knock* over. Two avatars had reached above 90% *Knock* now, and the winner could be anyone!

Knock Lissa guessed that the winner would *Knock* be one of the two *Knock* avatars that were *Knock* already above 90% *Knock*, and not *Knock* *anyone* as the announcement claimed. *Knock* Her Insta-Wiki was *Knock* only at 22.56%. This WorldForums post was *Knock* old, though. The first avatar *Knock* had made it to *Knock* 90% over two cycles ago *Knock* at least.

Opening her Player *Knock* Pager, she decided to *Knock* update her status for *Knock* the first time in *Knock* a while. She took a *Knock* screenshot of the view from *Knock* her prison and started *Knock* to type in a *Knock* caption. She tried to *Knock* keep it upbeat, for at *Knock* her very core she was *Knock* still an opt*Knock*imist (She told *Knock* herself).

> The beautiful view *Knock* from the top of *Knock* Mechanis Tower *Knock* is breathtaking. *Knock* I knock <backspace backspace backspace backspace backspace> know that *Knock* more of the map *Knock* remains hidden, *Knock* but this dungeon will *Knock* always knock <backspace backspace backspace backspace backspace backspace backspace backspace> ys hold a *Knock* special place *Knock* in my *Knock* knock! < backspace backspace backspace backspace backspace backspace> *Knock* knock! <Post>

> Lissa's Text Box: #Annoyed.

> <Edit *Knock* Post> < backspace *Knock* backspace *Knock Knock* backspace *Knock Knock Knock* backspace *Knock Knock Knock Knock* backspace *Knock Knock Knock Knock Knock* backspace *Knock Knock Knock Knock Knock Knock* H *Knock-Knock-Knock* E *Knock-Knock-Knock-Knock* A *Knock-Knock-Knock-Knock-Knock* R *KNOCK-KNOCK-KNOCK-KNOCK-KNOCK* T *KNOCK-KNOCK-KNOCK-KNOCK-KNOCK-KNOCK* !> *KNOC-KNOC-KNO-KNO-KNO-KN-KN-KN-KN-KN-KN-KN-KN-KN-KN-KN-KN-KN* <P *KN* o *KN* s *KN* t *KN*>

A very *Knock* frustrated avatar *Knock* ran to *Knock* the crates *Knock* in front *Knock* of the *Knock* door and *KNOCK KNOCK* destroyed them *KNOCKKNOCK* with her *KNOCKKNOCK* *Holy Mace*. *KNOCKKNOCK* She knocked *KNOCKKNOCK* on the door.

> Lissa's Text Box: Damn you!

KNOCKKNOCK She opened *KNOCKKNOCKKNOCK* the door.

> Lissa's Text Box: WHAT ALKNOCKY?!

Knock

> Lissa's Text Box: Fuck! I mean WHAT ALREADY?!

Knock

> Lissa's Text Box: #Speechless.

Knock

> Lissa's Text Box: Oh, that is #SoFuckedUp.

A *Body Type 2 (Average)* Night Ranger elf with *Hairstyle #6* and very little Armour was glued sideways onto two *Puzzle Blocks* by his overly fancy boots. Lord Pistonis, the boss of the tower, was holding the *Jumping Puzzle Blocks* firmly in his mechanical hands. His long piston was moving at full speed into the elf; the animation was almost too fast to watch. With each thrust, a knocking sound was made as the piston returned to its start position.

Butt boy was making a moaning sound that sounded like a *Gatling Gun*. The knocking sound effect wasn't even getting a chance to complete before the next knock started. The air smelled like burnt elf skin. Lissa saw that Lord Pistonis' piston was heating up to dangerous levels. It was white hot, and there was smoke starting to come out of her mystery guest's hindquarters.

Thinking quickly, Lissa cast *Fire Resistance +50* on the avatar named Anders, trying her best to aim the spell directly at his smoking ass. The area glowed a faint blue for a round, and the smoke stopped coming out of both his ass and ears. She was amazed at how captain ridiculous had been able to take so much abuse.

> Anders' Text Box: T-T-Th-Th-h-h-ha-ha-a-a-an-an-n-n-nk-nk-k-k- - -y-y-yo-yo-o-o-ou-ou-u-u-!-!-!

Lord Pistonis continued his ass assault. His main piston was no longer visible to the naked eye, for the speed was just too great. After a few more high speed rounds of assault, Lord Pistonis grabbed his ball bearings, arched his gears, and buzzed out in intense speedgasm. The speed of his piston began to slow at about the same rate it had sped up. The *Puzzle Blocks* began to drift away from Lord Pistonis, and only his first few speedspurts of hot motor oil ended up inside the intrepid adventuer. Quick, tiny spurts of the thick oil continued to pump over the dtill slightly smoking elf, who was apparently stuck on the drifting away *Jumping Puzzle Blocks*.

By the time Lord Pistonis had reached his starting piston speed and finished speedcumming, the robo-humper had fallen off the *Jumping Puzzle Blocks* all the way back at the start of the puzzle. He was so completely covered in thick, hot oil that only his eyes were visible. White eyes in a sea of black comically saw Lissa and blinked, still standing in the doorway. She guessed that he changed his *Blush Shade* somewhere under all that oil.

On Lissa's next turn, she closed the door and ported in from the door across the room, near where Lord Pistonis had fallen asleep. With a quick smack of her *Holy Mace*, she scored a *Sneak Attack* and broke the boss' head in two equal parts, effectively killing him (but only until he respawned).

> Lissa's Text Box: Two timing jerk-off!

Lissa was given a chance to edit her original Additional Comment to Lord Pistonis' Insta-Wiki page, so she did.

> **Creature Name:** Lord Pistonis
> **Class:** Mechanical Piston
> **Level:** 22
> **Special Attacks:** Piston Push, Piston Spring, Gear Crush, Knock, Knock Knock
> **Drops:** Motor Oil
> **First Player Encounter Notes:** Fellow adventurers! Only attempt to battle this monster if you can handle his ultra-fast piston attacks! – Mr. Max
> **Additional Comments:** This guy is a two-timing jerk. #SoFuckedUp. – Lissa

Lissa used an *Absorbing Cloth* that she'd found in Anders' *Backpack* to help wipe down the greased Anders. Soon he was almost completely motor oil-free (though she suspected his ass would never creak again). The *Absorbing Cloth* was now used up and she tossed it aside. She was glad to have found it, otherwise she'd have to touch that disgusting looking *Initiate's Jacket*.

She had already darted down the first few flights of stairs by the time the elf had realized he should follow her. back down to the start

Chapter 18

PARTY MAXED

O utside the Tower of Mechanis near the *Portie Tent* Placement Area a trio of adventurers were Animating. Palcath used an *Arms Crossed Animation*, Fournimer used a *Tsk Tsk Animation*, and Roodg used a *No Big Deal Animation*.

Fournimer's Text Box: what is wrong with you Guy?

Palcath's Text Box: We leave you alone for, like, ten turns, lass, and you let him just get up and leave?

Roodg's Text Box: i NEEDED A SANDWICH! i LEFT A note!

Roodg held up the note.

Palcath's Text Box: We really needed to talk to that lad. Now he is missing.

Roodg's Text Box: hE LEFT A NOTE ON MY NOTE! hE JUST WENT TO GET A SANDWICH 2!

Roodg held up the note again.

Fournimer's Text Box: what are we going to do now?

Roodg's Text Box: wAIT 10 MINS!

Fournimer's Text Box: yes, but starting from what time?

Palcath's Text Box: Does that even matter, lad? We needed to talk to Anders about how he got his ass of holding!

Roodg's Text Box: dID YOU WANT ONE 2?

Palcath's Text Box: Flaming Pit, no, lass.

Fournimer's Text Box: what exactly is an ass of holding anyway?

Fournimer watched as Palcath got into his explanation pose. This was the pose that Palcath used when explanations were needed, which was great to Fournimer as he was curious as to what an ass of holding could possibly be.

Palcath's Text Box: It is simple, Fourni. An ass of holding would work like any number of other similar objects. It can hold much more than would normally be physically possible, just like the magic satchel that the goddess Athena gave to Perseus!

Roodg's Text Box: nEAT!

The explanation didn't help Fournimer understand.

Fournimer's Text Box: the what that who gave to who?

Palcath's Text Box: Right, never mind that example, lad. Okay, it is like a Bag of Holding … wait … oh, I know. It is like that cartoon bunny you like with the purse, or that trash can on the reality show with that music lad who went into rehab.

Roodg's Text Box: Better Homes & Orphans? i LOVE THAT SHOW!

That was the explanation that helped Fournimer to understand. When in doubt, go with the bunny.

Fournimer's Text Box: oh, I get it now. just like how Ni Hao Bunny© can fit her entire car into her little tiny purse!

Palcath's Text Box: Exactly, lad! Except with Anders, his tiny purse is his butt. I just want to know how the lad came upon that power. I want to know if it was the same way we got ours. Also, I want to know if he knows anything else.

Roodg's Text Box: Anders' BUTT IS NOT TINY. hE TOTALLY HAS A BUBBLE BUTT. i BET IT GOT BIGGER THAN NORMAL FOR HIS SIZE WHEN HE GOT A BUTT OF HOLDING!

> Palcath's Text Box: I noticed that it was bigger as well, lad ... strictly out of curiosity, of course. How about you, Fourni? Did you notice that the stylistic appearance of Anders' butt was different than standard male elf avatar models? Is it fuller? Rounder perhaps?

Fournimer changed to *Blush Shade #1* and looked for an excuse to change the subject. He found it.

> Fournimer's Text Box: I ... uh, well ... um ... oh, the door is opening!

Palcath made use of the *Sly Smile Animation* as they heard the sound of a dungeon door opening.

> Roodg's Text Box: sEE THERE IS Anders! i TOLD YOU SHE WOULD BE BACK. nO, WAIT.

A human female Mendicator wearing a very typical Mendicator outfit, but not a very typical Mendicator attitude, was strolling down the steps of Mechanis Tower. She had a *#12 Hairstyle*, which was just at her shoulders, and it was a brilliant shade of purple with two highlights of black framing her face. Her *Walk Animation* tossed it back and forth in a way that caused other avatars to watch her instead of where they were going, even possibly leading them to walk right off of a cliff (if one was available). She had *Body Type #3 (Curvy)*, which was also known as having it "goin' on".

> Palcath's Text Box: ...who?

The next round, the dungeon door opened up and their quarry Anders walked out. His legs were more than a little shaky, and he wasn't walking at full speed.

> Lissa's Text Box: You didn't tell me you had a party down here, Loverboy. Why would you be so stupid and go into Mechanis Tower all by yourself? You haven't told me anything about yourself.... Actually, you haven't even said anything yet. #SpeakUp!

> Palcath's Continuing Text Box: ...purple?

Had Palcath been walking at the moment, he would have walked right off a cliff (if one was available).

> Fournimer's Text Box: there you are Dude, we were looking everywhere for you!

> Roodg's Text Box: sEE. iT'S ONLY BEEN LIKE 8 MINS!

> Fournimer's Text Box: you shouldn't be up yet Dude, you still must be sore from the Frost Gigas.

Anders turned *Blush Shade #3*. He now knew who owned the *Portie Tent* and who had watched him "defeat" the Frost Gigas.

> Anders' Text Box: I ... um ... yeah. Sore from him.

> Palcath's Continuing Text Box: ...but...

> Lissa's Text Box: Yeah, Loverboy here has just been knocking around his joints to keep them loose. He is fine now.

Anders exchanged his *Blush Shade #3* for *Blush Shade #5*, skipping *#4* entirely. Lissa just gave Anders a *Secret Smirk Animation*.

> Fournimer's Text Box: you shouldn't be up yet Dude, go and lie down.

> Palcath's Text Box: ...that's...

> Roodg's Text Box: oH COME ON, IT'S BEEN LIKE 4 CYCLES ALREADY! eNOUGH REST i'M BORED!

> Anders' Text Box: FOUR CYCLES? I was passed out for four cycles?

Anders' own Battle Log confirmed it. The *Frost Gigas Boots* were added to his inventory well over four cycles ago.

> Anders' Text Box: But how?

> Palcath's Continuing Text Box: ...not...

> Fournimer's Text Box: you are just lucky to be living Dude. how anyone could have taken that much Gigas and still be standing is beyond me. ass of holding or not.

> Lissa's Text Box: Ass of holding, huh? Why wouldn't you just walk by the Frost Gigas when he froze up? I did. You seriously took the entire Frost Gigas as well, Loverboy? How big was it? I am working something out.

Anders exchanged his *Blush Shade #5* for *Blush Shade #6*, which was the highest level of *Blush Shades* available.

> Anders' Text Box: It's a long story.

> Lissa's Text Box: Perfect! Let's talk later. I am sick of this mountain area. #Snorefest. Let's get out of here!

> Roodg's Text Box: i LIKE HER!

> Fournimer's Text Box: wait Guy and ... uh ... Chick ... we need to talk to Anders Dude before we go. right Man?

Lissa's Text Box: Chick?

Fournimer's Text Box: right Man?

Palcath's Continuing Text Box: ...

Fournimer's Text Box: Dwarfman?

Lissa's Text Box: Chick?!

Palcath's Continuing Text Box: ...default!

Fournimer's Text Box: huh?

Palcath's Continuing Text Box: ...

Fournimer's Text Box: are you *Spellbound* or something Man?

Lissa's Text Box: CHICK!!!

Palcath's Continuing Text Box: ...

Fournimer's Text Box: Palcath!

Lissa's Text Box: You are not going to call me CHICK! #GirlPower!

Palcath looked up, using a *Snapping to Your Senses Animation.*

Palcath's Text Box: Oh, good. You are lucky, Roodg lass. There is Anders!

Roodg's Text Box: wHAT?

Palcath's Text Box: Now we can talk to the lad, but first I don't think we have been properly introduced, lass. Hello, fair maiden. I am Palcath Ironburrow, son of Gloni and Defender of the Dwarven Clans. I have traveled here from far beyond the Crystal Vale to help defeat the Plague of Shadow and save the land from destruction.

Roodg's Text Box: nO. wE STOPPED THAT sHADOW THING TO DO THE nAKED eLF qUEST REMEMBER?

Lissa appeared to reel at the advanced role-play coming from Palcath. He was one of those role-play over-actors. Her posture switched from aggressive, to slightly more aggressive. Time to mess with the dork.

Lissa's Text Box: Okay then, a role-playing fan, huh? Let's RP. I am

Lady Lissandra Collinswood from the order of her Majesty's ... Third Mendicator Battalion. I have traveled far ... to seek a remedy for this vile 'Plague of Shadow' myself. Is it a disease...? I dunno, but I do not wish to see my homeland ... destroyed and my people suffer, or something. Happy now? Can we move on, Knightboy?

Roodg's Text Box: wHY DOES YOUR NAME SOUND FAMILIAR AND MUSICAL?

Lissa's Text Box: It doesn't!

Roodg used the *Suspicious About That Animation,* but decided to drop it for now.

Roodg's Text Box: k

Palcath's Text Box: Oh, nice one, lass! Expertly role-played! Call me Knightboy whenever you wish.

Lissa's Text Box: Oh, sweet Maker.

Fournimer's Text Box: oh so he can call you lass and fair maiden, you can call him Knightboy, but I can't call you Chick?

Lissa's Text Box: You got it, genius, five smart star points to you!

Fournimer's Text Box: okay fine. Lissa.

Lissa's Text Box: Nope. You can't call me that either.

Fournimer's Text Box: huh? why not? what am I supposed to call you?

Lissa's Text Box: Call me Fair Maiden. I liked that one.

Fournimer used the *Stubborn Pose Animation.*

Fournimer's Text Box: but, fair maiden ... that's longer than Lissa! how does that even make it a nickname?

Lissa counted with an *Indignant Pose Animation.*

Lissa's Text Box: Nope, just because you can't be bothered to use capital letters doesn't mean you get off easy. You will now call me Fair Maiden (both capitals). Also, to point out your flawed logic, Lissa and Chick are both five letters long! Lissa is even easier to type than Chick, so how exactly did that save you any time?

Fournimer's Text Box: stop ruining my character trait!

Lissa's Text Box: It was ruined before I got here. Nicknames are annoying, and you need to stop it!

Roodg's Text Box: tHAT'S WHAT I TRIED TO TELL HIM.

Fournimer used the *More Stubborn Pose Animation*.

Fournimer's Text Box: but you have already made up two nicknames of your own!

Lissa counted with a *More Indignant Pose Animation*.

Lissa's Text Box: Mine are #Charming. Yours are #Stupid.

Roodg's Text Box: u PEOPLE R WEIRD.

Palcath's Text Box: Enough foolishness! Roodg lass, we need to talk to Anders.

Roodg's Text Box: hUH? i WASN'T BEING FOOLISH AT ALL.

Palcath's Text Box: Really? Wow, I guess you were not being foolish, lass. I stand corrected. How strange, you were the one making sense.

Roodg's Text Box: i KNOW! tHAT IS STRANGE.

This was going nowhere; Anders needed to move things along.

Anders' Text Box: What did you need to talk to me about?

Mr. Max's Approaching Text Box: ♪♫ Da na na na nah! Dah na na na na nah nanananah!♪♫

Anders' Text Box: ?

Roodg's Text Box: ?

Lissa's Text Box: ?

Fournimer's Text Box: ?

Palcath's Text Box: ?

Mr. Max's Text Box: I said … ♪♫ Da na na na nah! Dah na na na na nah nanananah!♪♫

Mr. Max's song was catchy, which was impressive to Anders as it was just a series of Da na na nahs.

Anders' Text Box: Huh?

Roodg's Text Box: hOW DID YOU MAKE THE MUSIC NOTES?

Lissa's Text Box: We heard you.

Fournimer's Text Box: yeah we can totally read Bro.

Palcath's Text Box: But the question is … why did you say it, lad?

Mr. Max's Text Box: For my dramatic role-playing entrance, of course, fellow adventurers! ♪♫ Da na na na nah! Dah na na na na nah nanananah! ♪♫

Mr. Max jumped into the area in a single bound. Taking care to make sure everyone was indeed looking at him, he did his patented *Flex Animation*.

Mr. Max's Text Box: I will force you to talk!

Anders' Text Box: Force who?

Roodg's Text Box: wHAT???

Lissa's Text Box: Pardon me, but I was getting introduced here. This was my big character introduction, not yours.

Fournimer's Text Box: what Bro?

Palcath's Text Box: Lad, you must be mistaken. I already have talked to you. I must say, though, I am a big fan of your work and would welcome the opportunity to compare notes and even damage formulas.

Mr. Max's Text Box: Not you, you!

Mr. Max used the *Point Animation*, but because of where he was standing and the direction he was standing in it didn't actually point at anyone.

Anders' Text Box: ?

Roodg's Text Box: ?

Lissa's Text Box: ?

Fournimer's Text Box: ?

Palcath's Text Box: ?

Mr. Max's Text Box: Urgh! Role-playing is so hard! A little girl gnome

> told me about role-playing, and I wanted to try it, so … I am!

> Lissa's Text Box: Is that what you are trying to do? I changed my mind. The overacting is way better than whatever that fuck that was.

Mr. Max took a round to position himself properly. Executing the *Point Animation*, he thrust his finger out and pointed it almost directly at Anders.

> Mr. Max's Text Box: I will force you to talk!

> Anders' Text Box: Me? What did I do?

> Mr. Max's Text Box: Now, defend yourself, you buxom elf maiden knave!

Starting with an *Upward Uppercut Swordslash*, Mr. Max unleashed his giant *Four-Handed Sword*. It bounced off Anders with a "tink" noise. Several more wordy sounding moves followed, which all bounced off Anders with similar "tinking" noises.

> Fournimer's Text Box: wow, chill Bro.

> Mr. Max's Text Box: Quiet, madam! I'm role-playing for the first time ever! It's going to be really dramatic. Just watch!

> Fournimer's Text Box: madam?

Anders could only stand there in complete shock. Mr. Max, the most famous and beefiest avatar around, was attacking him with everything the beefman had. A single attack would have struck him down, but he was well protected under the "No Player VS Player" rules.

Returning Swordarang bounced off Anders' face with another "tink", followed by a *Sword-a-pult*.

> Lissa's Text Box: Stop interrupting my introduction with your dorky role-playing!

> Mr. Max's Text Box: I am role-playing! I am glad you noticed. This is all just for the extra drama! I know you are slow, sir, but try to keep up!

> Lissa's Text Box: Slow? Sir? Okay … I am going to call you meathead from now on, you big sack of meat. No capital letter either.

> Fournimer's Text Box: another nickname? come on!

Double-Handed Force Slash was followed by *Rage of the Sword Gods*. They hit Anders with "trink" noises.

> Roodg's Text Box: pvp ONLY WORKS WITH AREA SPELLS,

> ATTACKS DON'T WORK. i TRIED IT A BUNCH.

> Mr. Max's Text Box: I know it doesn't! That is the entire point. This is for role-playing, sillynilly!

> Roodg's Text Box: wHAT IS A SILLYNILLY?

The Sword of Fate was followed by *Six Chances of Glory*, which was followed by *Hurt of the Triad*. Each move was making "trilink" noises, and Anders could feel himself begin to fall over. He activated *Steadfast* and covered his face.

> Anders' Text Box: Stop! I give up.

> Mr. Max's Text Box: You can tell me what I want to know after I finish 'beating the information' out of you, fellow adventurette! Hahaha!

> Anders' Text Box: But I already gave up. What do you want? Please! Stop!

Great Blades of Fire, Blade 4, Hack n' Attack, The Blade of Shout, and a few others were striking Anders and making "trilinkle" noises. He could feel the force of these attacks. If he wasn't held to the ground with *Steadfast,* he would have fallen over. The wind caused by the sword attacks was rushing into his space. He could feel the sword's animations breeze by his face.

> Palcath's Text Box: Um … lad, role-playing is a subtle art. Perhaps we can compare notes on it as well.

> Mr. Max's Text Box: I know that! I have over 70 ranks in Role-Playing, and I don't even have a *Danger Dice* on me right now! Here comes the big yet very subtle finish! Take some screenshots. It will be your Player Pager main picture for the rest of time, little gnome girl who says 'lad'!

> Palcath's Text Box: Gnome? What kind of gnome says 'lad'? Gnome say 'pip pip' … you said so yourself.

Mr. Max used the Level 98 unlocked two-handed sword attack, the *Flurry of a Thousand Strikes.* It would drain his Stamina Bar rapidly, but he could unleash as many attacks as he wanted until it was gone. Roodg followed Mr. Max's advice to the gnome girl Palcath and took many screenshots.

Mr. Max barraged Anders with a flurry of 78 strikes per round. He was slashing at the poor elf like he was never going to stop. With Mr. Max's gigantic Level 98 Stamina Bar, he almost didn't have to. Flurry of 78 attacks after flurry of 78 attacks hit Anders. With each set, Anders felt himself losing a bit more balance. He closed his eyes, but the sword attacks kept coming. The torrent of attacks was all too much for Anders, and he fell backward a little, still holding *Steadfast.* Mr. Max did not stop his barrage; he had plenty more where that came from. He leaned into the attacks with all his force.

> Mr. Max's Text Box: HOW DID...

78 Sword slashes "tra-linked".

Anders cowered.

> Mr. Max's Text Box: ...YOU...

156 sword slashes "tra-linkered".

Anders was knocked downward.

> Mr. Max's Text Box: ...FIND...

312 sword slashes "tra-la-linkered".

Anders fell to the ground; *Steadfast* was failing.

> Mr. Max's Text Box: THEM?!

A *Single Final Attack Combo End Sword Slash* swished.

Anders was hit into the air and flew backward. *Steadfast* was completely broken, despite what it had promised. Anders landed hard against the stairs to Mechanis Tower, and he felt something warm on his cheek. Bringing his hand up, he felt it; it was painful. On his fingers there was a trickle of blood.

Mr. Max caught his breath and Stamina Bar, then panned up. He was taken aback when he saw the blood. His expression went from intense pretend anger to complete bewilderment and regret.

> Mr. Max's Text Box: What? I ... I ... how could I ... do that ... to ... to a fellow adventurette...? I was only role-playing! For drama!

Mr. Max fell to his knees overcome with shock. "Falling to your knees overcome with shock" was not a standard animation, however. When he did that, everyone heard a rip followed by a screeching, ear-piercing sound, and a blast of numbers and black pixels overcame him.

> Mr. Max's Text Box: Cheer?

> Roodg's Text Box: cHEAP

> Palcath's Text Box: Character Sheet?

> Fournimer's Text Box: chick?

> Anders' Text Box: Ouch.

Lissa stepped forward and performed a *Raising One's Hand for Silence Animation*.

> Lissa's Text Box: It said Cheat.

Everyone Else's Text Box Together: OH CHEAT!

Mr. Max's Text Box: I'm sorry, fellow adventurette. I was just so close....

Anders didn't know what to say in return, so he said nothing.

Mr. Max's Text Box: I've been at 99.7% complete for cycles, and I am almost done. I just wanted to win so badly.

Roodg's Text Box: hUH? wIN WHAT?

Palcath's Text Box: The Insta-Wiki contest, no doubt. Mr. Max has been the fan favourite from the start, but I've heard others are getting near 90% now as well.

Mr. Max's Text Box: Breaker is at 96.58%, and he has been laughing at me in the WorldForums for cycles now for getting stuck and being so close.

Palcath's Text Box: Let me guess ... it is the Green Slimes still, right?

Mr. Max's Text Box: Yes, whoever you are, Green Slimes and whatever is with them. I'm only missing those two, a recipe from one item, the *Three Vials of Green Goo Quest*, and the Plague of Shadow, but I can't challenge it until the rest are done.

Palcath's Text Box: Whoever I am? Well ... I can guess that you, Mr. Lad, saw the screenshot of Anders with the Green Slime on his Player Pager! That's sort of why we followed him, too.

Mr. Max's Text Box: Yes, after searching through thousands and thousands of Player Pagers, I found a picture of someone looking at a Green Slime.

Lissa's Text Box: Thousands and thousands? There are only like 10,000 avatars in total, and his name starts with 'A', meathead.

Roodg's Text Box: mAYBE HE STARTED BACKWARDS WITH z?

Mr. Max's Text Box: I camped the page but kept on losing it. This master of stealth was very sneaky with it. Must have kept changing names or something. Finally something was posted from Mechanis Tower so I ran here as fast as I could. I don't know what came over me. I just got so angry at everything. I just wanted to try out some role-

> playing. I didn't know I could actually hurt someone.

The beefy avatar walked over to Anders and held out his hand.

> Mr. Max's Text Box: I am sorry, fellow adventurette. Please accept my sincerest apology.

Anders thought it over. Mr. Bad Role-Player did look genuinely sorry; he really shouldn't have been able to hurt him. The game logic had broken, and it had hurt Anders, not Mr. Max himself. The role-playing was almost passable. It was obvious Mr. Max had not done a lot of it, but he did try to increase the drama, although in a very stupid and beef-headed way. It also didn't hurt that Mr. Max was famous and had really big muscles. Anders took the outstretched hand and Mr. Max helped him up, but his 60+ extra levels of strength showed and the *Jerking Up Animation* hurt a bit.

> Anders' Text Box: It is okay, I guess, Max.

Mr. Max *Flexed* and then *Winked* at Anders, and Anders would have blushed back, but he was already at the maximum level.

> Lissa's Text Box: Sorry to break up the hippy love fest you have going, #Puke, but you should probably get ready, Mr. Meat.

> Mr. Max's Text Box: For what, fellow adventurer?

Lissa used the *Point Animation*. A large worm had risen from the ground and was looming over Mr. Max.

> Lissa's Text Box: For that, meathead.

Mr. Max was unconcerned and showed it with an *Unconcerned Animation*.

> Mr. Max's Text Box: For a Land-Sucker boss? Really, whatever you are, it is not difficult, just a Level 18 boss! They're fairly common in these parts, but there shouldn't be one right here. My kill count on these things is at like 200 already, so no big deal. It just flipped around, great wasted action. What is it going to do next, dance? Eep!

> Lissa's Text Box: Whatever I am?

It was hard to watch, but impossible not to. Everyone but Lissa did try to help at some point, but Mr. Max's pride was far too great to allow himself to be defeated by a Level 18 boss. He turned away all offers for backup.

The great worm-like thing spent its turns pulling down the *Diamond Pants* and flipping Mr. Max onto his stomach, exposing his toned ass. Mr. Max countered the move by flipping the worm over instead. Mr. Max growled and Text Boxed that wasn't the way things worked around here and began scolding the thing with his massively larger levels.

To everyone's surprise (besides Mr. Max's), the Land-Sucker relented and became submissive. Mr. Max got ready to strike a final blow with his sword, but the Land-Sucker had instead latched onto Max's impressive *Body Type #8* cock and had began to service it happily with its *Land-Suck* move.

In a valiant attempt to remove the creature, Mr. Max grabbed and tried to pull, but this only enticed the thing to try harder. Rounds of *Land Sucking*, *Land Sucking More*, *Land Sucking More More*, some failed removal checks, and many refusals of help later, Mr. Max was beginning to get flustered.

> Mr. Max's Text Box: Why will you not come off? I can't attack you if we are Grappling!

> Lissa's Text Box: It likes you far too much, I think. Can we get back to leaving, now?

> Roodg's Text Box: nO i WANT 2 SEE WHAT HAPPENS! yEAH! gIVE IT TO IT!

> Palcath's Text Box: Pip pip! You still sure you don't want help, lad?

> Fournimer's Text Box: Bro…

> Anders' Text Box: Shoot it! That is the only way it will ever let go!

> Mr. Max's Text Box: I don't have a bow! Or even a secondary weapon!

> Anders' Text Box: No … uh….

Anders did a *Thrusting Animation* to demonstrate. Mr. Max gave him an incredulous look.

> Anders' Text Box: Trust me, shoot it, or it will never stop.

> Mr. Max's Text Box: Uh, okay. Thank you for the advice … uh, someone!

> Anders' Text Box: Someone? You just said you were stalking me!

Grabbing the giant worm by the scruff of its wormy neck, Mr. Max began to thrust into it. Sounding like a happy little vacuum (which existed here despite no electricity), the Land-Sucker did what it was made to do: suck. The Sucker got so excited that it gobbled up Mr. Max's balls as well.

In a manner that could only be used by someone as well versed in fighting monsters as Mr. Max, the beefy avatar used his new secondary attacking weapon with extreme skill. He finally knew why Warriors did not get a secondary starting weapon like every other class. He had this wonderful one all along.

Using all sorts of advanced new moves on the Land Cock-Sucker, Mr. Max's showed off his aptitude with the battle mechanics. With a final blow, he shot his first load into the happy mouth.

> Mr. Max's Text Box: Take that, you fiend!

Sated, the Land Cock-Sucker let go of the member and slinked away. Mr. Max did his victory dance, which meant he did the *Flex Animation*.

> Mr. Max's Text Box: Another victory for me, fellow adventurers! Why are you all looking at me like that?

Everyone had been staring at the well-muscled avatar (which to him was not that unusual), but they didn't stop and they all had their eyes and mouths open (which was).

> Mr. Max's Text Box: What? Is there something on my face?

Anders tried to blush, but couldn't.
Fournimer tried to blush, and could.
Lissa covered her mouth.
Palcath covered his eyes.
Roodg shamelessly leered on.

> Roodg's Text Box: wOW. lOOK AT THAT THING! Mr. Max GOT ALL MAXED!

Mr. Max was confused for a round, maybe even a round and a half. He finally saw what everyone else did. His previously impressive, big-as-they-come, Body Size #8 cock had been used to attack the Land-Sucker with such great skill that it was now completely maxed-out (stat wise). Soft as it was, it hung to just below his beefy knees and was about as fat around as his big forearm; his foreskin still covered the entire thing but was not happy about it. His balls had increased to match, massive and swelling with Max juice.

Suddenly very impressed with himself, Mr. Max used the *Flex Animation*. Mr. Maxum (that was his new nickname for it) responded by rapidly getting hard. It turned upward, only gaining a few length units as his cockhead began to peek out from under his foreskin.

> Mr. Max's Text Box: Hey, I have spells now. I've never had spells before.

Mr. Max cast *Increase Max More*, and his giant cock grew a few length units longer and a little bit thicker. It was a stacking spell, and each new casting increased the member. It became as thick as one of his beefy legs and about half as long as he was tall when it reached full castings. Straining now, his foreskin came down, revealing a massive, meaty cockhead. His balls increased in size to stay in proportion, eventually hitting his knees. The increased weight almost toppled him over, but he grabbed it with his *Earth Gigas Gauntlet* to prevent himself from falling.

> Mr. Max's Text Box: Good thing I delivered the final blow on the Earth

> Gigas and have this *Earth Gigas Gauntlet* that lets me hold oversized weapons, or I'd be on my ass!

Mr. Max cast *Increase Max More More*, and his pride grew to a size that was very nearly the same size as himself in one quick instant. His foreskin was strained now with the stretching cause by his giant member. Mr. Max's balls grew even bigger, now hanging down past his knees.

> Mr. Max's Text Box: I also have a locked ability? That is crazy! I should be high enough level to get everything … oh, and a passive ability called *Fill*, which restores MP but gives double to anything with *Absorb* … whatever that means.

Anders passed out again.

◈ Chapter 19 ◈
COMBI-FUSION RECIPE -> PLOT + FLOUR = THICKER PLOT

nders awoke from his comedic passing out quickly, or he least assumed it was quickly. Everyone was still "admiring" Mr. Max and his new impressive tool. Just looking at it nearly made Anders pass out again.

> Lissa's Text Box: See, I told you not to interfere!

> Fournimer's Text Box: no you didn't!

Lissa used the Shrug Animation with very little enthusiasm.

> Lissa's Text Box: Well, I meant to! But now look at the big meathead!

> Roodg's Text Box: k

> Palcath's Text Box: How could we not, lass? He is filling almost the entire area.

Palcath was trying not to look at Mr. Max for personal reasons. Anders was also trying not to look but for different personal reasons.

> Lissa's Text Box: No, I mean look at his new tools to defend himself with!

> Roodg's Text Box: i ONLY SEE 1 TOOL.

Lissa's Text Box: I mean the fact that he has something sexual now that he could use to combat monsters. #Insightful.

Fournimer's Text Box: I'm confused now … Fair. Maiden. what do you mean?

Palcath's Text Box: Okay, lads, lasses, maybes, and Mr. Lads. We should all just sit down for a round and go over what is happening here … for the slower kids in the class. Let's all go inside and talk.

Lissa's Text Box: Fine. But I am still mad that he stole my thunder.

Palcath pointed at the *Portie Tent* and everyone walked inside eventually.

Mr. Max had to take a few turns to calm down and let the spell wear off. He also had to try to jam his oversized Mr. Maxum into the *Diamond Pants*. Eventually it made it inside, but the codpiece was in obvious discomfort.

Anders joined the rest when he woke up.

Lissa immediately claimed a newly-created bed. Within half an instant, the color scheme was switched to purple, and a bunch of her prison cell memorabilia was thrown into the personal space. She jumped up on the bed as if it had always been hers. Palcath was a little bit upset, but didn't say anything. Seeing what Lissa had done when he finally could fit through the door, Mr. Max changed the newest bed that sprang up to orange. He simply sat on the floor in front of the bed. He didn't bother putting anything in the personal space. Anders ran in and immediately tripped on the scenic carpet and fell on his face, thanks to his new big boots. That gave everyone a nice view of his (s) equipment before he sheepishly went and sat down on the green bed.

Palcath's Text Box: Okay … so … then….

Lissa's Text Box: Yeah, so then. From what I can tell, the first boss that targets you specifically after you hear the 'cheat' message gives you special powers that might help you survive future encounters with the other … horrible monsters.

Anders' Text Box: Perverts.

Lissa's Text Box: Right, perverts. I can't be sure, though. I need to know more. Loverboy gave me the idea at the top of the tower. Originally, I thought I was the only one that was fully broken with an ability.

No one was brave enough to ask what Lissa's powers were—or how Loverboy had given her the idea.

Lissa's Text Box: Okay, so I need to know what happened to everyone so I can be sure.

Nobody spoke.

> Lissa's Text Box: Fine. I'll start, so all you Nancy boys … and uh … Roodg don't feel self-conscious. I got this game early due to a shipping error, but I didn't know that. I made myself, watched the cinematic opening, and started to play. I smacked the first Start Rat and became the very first avatar with an Insta-Wiki. Bingo! I got a special Promo Code that let me change my hair colour to a non-standard one.

> Palcath's Text Box: That doesn't sound much like cheating, lass.

> Lissa's Text Box: It wasn't. I ran out of typing characters. Text Boxes can only be so long.

Palcath used the *Nod Animation,* and allowed her to continue.

> Lissa's Text Box: Anyway, eventually more people joined the game, and soon a group of five other adventurers saw my cool hair and invited me to join their group. I was low level and naive at the time and didn't know how easy it was to get into a party because I was a healing class. When they threatened to leave me alone in the wilds, I stupidly gave them my Promo Code, and they switched their own hair colours as well.

> Lissa's Text Box: The screaming sound called out at them instantly, and their *Standard Issue Undergarments* were gone. Soon a big gang of Elderly Transformed Rōnin Tortals came along with other intentions, but my group was stronger, and they just killed the Tortals by working together. Along the road, they got picked off by monster perverts, but since they never gained their abilities, they didn't have a way to defend against the sex attacks and died.

Everyone but Lissa used the *Gasp in Surprise Animation.* Fournimer was so surprised he used the Animation twice.

> Fournimer's Text Box: wait. died died? real people died?! the TorTech-Headsets are killing people?!

> Lissa's Text Box: No, the players didn't actually die die. That would be stupid and impossible. They probably walked funny for a few days though. From what I read on the WorldForums, their saves were corrupted, and they couldn't reload. #GameOver. They blamed me and my shoddy hair Code for the fact that they had to restart, and they stopped talking to me.

Palcath's Text Box: So, you mean they died? If we die ... our avatars are dead dead? No regen? Respawn? Revive? Renew? Restore?

Lissa's Text Box: No. None of those. #PlotPoint. That is why I was hiding out and trying to find a solution. I got my hair Code fair and square!

Mr. Max's Text Box: What? Dead dead? No! After all this work, that can't be true. I do not believe you, whoever you are! I will not let it happen!

Fournimer's Text Box: why didn't you die? if you don't mind me asking.

This was going to take several long Text Boxes to explain, and Lissa knew it. She stood up and used a *Clear Your Throat Animation* before continuing.

Lissa's Text Box: Monsters don't target the healing classes until we are last standing or we hit them. It's one of our abilities. The perverts were never going after me because I wasn't broken yet. I didn't know that until much later. I started to ask in the WorldForums about what was going on and learned my hair Code was blacklisted, after I got reported for Code abuse by my old party.

Lissa's Text Box: I got a visit from Administrator Ivy, and she told me I couldn't use the Code again. She said I was going to be on a time out for Code abuse. Right after my time out was over, I walked by a BitBat and it ripped off my panties and flew off with them! I knew I was broken now, and I needed a place to hide. This was going to be my only chance for keeping purple hair. I saw the tower and came here, and I skipped that idiot Frost Gigas when he froze up. He never targeted me.

Lissa's Text Box: I went to the top room of Mechanis Tower and blocked myself in with scenery, but like an idiot, I answered the door when Lord Two-Timer knocked. He found me and targeted me since I was alone.

Lissa's Text Box: So, the very first boss I fought and was targeted by gave me my awesome powers. Once I saw Loverboy here take on Lord Jerkoff and use his own 'ability,' I knew I wasn't the only one.

Palcath's Text Box: So ... you have powers, lass?

Lissa used a *Dramatic Pose Animation* before Text Boxing, to better accentuate her point.

> Lissa's Text Box: Yes. They are #Awesome.

> Mr. Max's Text Box: Who is Loverboy? She has some kind of 'ability' as well?

> Anders' Text Box: What?

> Roodg's Text Box: dAMN RIGHT HE DOES! sO CRAZY!

Palcath had a big Text Box to get out, so to better make his point he also stood up and used a *Clear Your Throat Animation*.

> Palcath's Text Box: Interesting theory, lass. I can confirm that story. Fourni, Roodg, and I used some Codes when trying to track down Anders, and then, uh … yeah, we um … got separated and didn't really win our encounters. Now we are different as well, in more ways than Codes. The Codes we used gave Fourni really neat weapons. I have these *Battle Log Eyes*, and Roodg is … different apparently.

> Mr. Max's Text Box: Different how? Who are all these avatars you are talking about little gnome girl?

> Palcath's Text Box: What, lad?

> Fournimer's Text Box: I still can't believe I ruined my avatar for glitter.

> Roodg's Text Box: i DUNNO WHAT U R TALKING ABOUT, i LIKE SO WON MY ENCOUNTER!

> Anders' Text Box: You three were tracking me down?

> Palcath's Text Box: Well, you were stalking us, lad! You started it!

Anders joined the growing trend and used a *Clear Your Throat Animation*. He used the Animation for different reasons than the others had, wishing that there was a *Nervous Clear Your Throat Animation* instead.

> Anders' Text Box: I wasn't stalking you. I was hiding because all my clothes and *Backpack* dissolved at Level 4 and I didn't want anyone to see my elf bits. But then beetles were totally going to run up my butt. I got really scared. I came out of hiding early before the quest was over, totally forgetting that I was all nude. Then you guys saw me being all nude, and I ran off because you all saw my junk and … I was shy.

> Roodg's Text Box: … iSN'T THAT LIKE WORD FOR WORD WHAT i SAID HAD HAPPENED?

Anders' Text Box: Besides, I was only stalking Fourni!

Fournimer's Text Box: huh?

Mr. Max's Text Box: Who is this Fourni? Wait … your *Backpack* dissolved? But you are wearing an *Ultra-Pack*, which is the Level 2 *Backpack*.

Anders' Text Box: I made this one with my *Combi-Fusion Pot*.

Fournimer's Text Box: seriously go back for a round there. stalking?

Mr. Max's Text Box: May I see it?

Anders' Text Box: Sure, there is my *Combi-Fusion Pot* on display. See, it's golden and better than other ones since it's free to use!

Mr. Max's Text Box: No gold Combi-Fusions would be nice, but I want to see the *Ultra-Pack*, fellow adventurette.

Shrugging, Anders handed over the *Ultra-Pack*. Mr. Max examined it for only a round.

Mr. Max's Text Box: Holy Maker. Since you don't have a base *Backpack* anymore, your max Carry Capacity is ???? Therefore, your new Carry Capacity with this is 100% more of ????

Anders' Text Box: So?

Mr. Max's Text Box: So?! You have 22,475 Carry Units in here! I have the *Ultra-Mega-Pack-Super Mark 2*, and my Carry Capacity is only at 1,000 Carry Units! Where are you keeping all this stuff?

Lissa's Text Box: I can think of a place…

Roodg's Text Box: Anders, DO YOU WANT TO BORROW MY aQUA vERA BECAUSE YOU JUST got BURNED!

Lissa and Roodg slyly used a *High Five Dual Animation*.

Mr. Max's Text Box: Who is this Lissa fellow now? What does borrowing items accomplish? Who is High Five?

Lissa's Text Box: You legitimately don't know any of our names, genders, or classes, do you?

Anders' Text Box: I never went back to Corckerblantah. I thought my

> *Ultra-Pack* would tell me when it was full or something!

> Palcath's Text Box: Okay, back up a turn here. Your clothes and *Backpack* dissolved, lad? Why?

It was Fournimer's turn to use a *Clear Your Throat Animation*. He wanted to get some answers to important questions.

> Fournimer's Text Box: no, back up two turns. you were stalking me?

He was ignored.

> Anders' Text Box: I accidently didn't buy a melee weapon and couldn't fight up close. I was standing on a miscoloured pixel above a scenic pillar and was sniping off Green Slimes that didn't have ranged attacks. When the boss came into the starting room and hit me off the pixel, all my *Vials of Green Goo* shattered, and the acid ate my stuff. Then the Pink Slime, taught me uh … ***Blush Shade is already at maximum*** not to do that anymore.

> Mr. Max's Text Box: But how did you find the Slimes, buxom archer? I searched everywhere.

> Anders' Text Box: That first NPC said to go right, so I went left instead.

> Palcath's Text Box: So, where are they, lad? No one in the whole map besides you knows where they are!

> Anders' Text Box: Behind a scenic bush. I put it there because I didn't know what was going on and didn't want someone else to get slimed. It really should not have fooled anyone, but I found out later that scenic bushes are magic veils of mystery. Crackers, I guess I messed up!

It was Roodg's turn to use an Animation. Everyone was expecting a *Clear Your Throat Animation,* but Roodg instead used a Crackers Are Amazing Animation.

> Roodg's Text Box: cRACKERS? i LIKE CRACKERS!

> Mr. Max's Text Box: What? I spent cycles looking for them to complete my Insta-Wiki and win the contest, stalked you, forgot who you were, found you again, stalked you, role-played, and completely broke my character so I can die and be permanently corrupted because of a bush! I'll never win the contest now!

> Palcath's Text Box: Kill you, lad? You are ridiculously over-leveled. I heard you killed the Earth Gigas in one round while the 99 other

avatars were waiting for you to say charge. Heck, a giant worm thing just came to rape you, and you out-beefed it in a single round and got it to suck you off instead. I seriously doubt anything here can kill you.

Mr. Max's Text Box: That isn't the point, little girl!

Anders' Text Box: What's the big deal? So, you don't get a new haircut or a shirt in the mail that doesn't fit or something?

Mr. Max's Text Box: Don't you fellow adventurers even know what the contest was for?!

Anders' Text Box: I never talked to anyone in Crickledorpbin besides the first NPC, whoever he was. Some Wizard guy. Oh, and the shopkeeper that scammed me. I have no idea.

Palcath's Text Box: I knew I wasn't going to win, lad. I never bothered to check.

Lissa's Text Box: I already won a contest. I thought I couldn't win another, so I didn't think to read it.

Fournimer's Text Box: Dwarfman was into the story parts. I let him handle that stuff.

Roodg's Text Box: tHERE WAS A CONTEST?

Mr. Max was completely in shock. It was if his big beefy heart had been taken out and stomped upon.

Mr. Max's Text Box: You and a party of your choice get first dibs at the expansion. They take your avatars and port them over there so you have a whole new map to yourselves for like two hundred cycles! It was going to be awesome, an entire new map just for me to explore....

Palcath's Text Box: !

Anders' Text Box: So, what, a whole different map full of giant perverted rapey monsters to get all perverted and rapey with? Who in the Flaming Pit wants that?

Palcath used a *Jumping To Your Feet With An Amazing Revelation Animation* (after first sitting down so that he could actually do it).

Palcath's Text Box: We do, lad!

Anders' Text Box: Pardon?

Palcath's Text Box: Didn't you hear the lad? They take your avatars and port them over. To do that they would have to make a hard copy backup from the server!

Lissa's Text Box: So, we would get backed up and imported with new save files, right?

Palcath's Text Box: Very possibly, lass.

Lissa used a *Falling To Your Knees With An Amazing Revelation Animation* (mostly to show up Palcath who had forgotten about that varation).

Lissa's Text Box: That's the solution to our problem! #SaveThePrincess!

Fournimer's Text Box: so all we need to do is get Mr. Max to win the Insta-Wiki Contest and we maybe can stop from becoming dead dead?

Roodg's Text Box: tHERE WAS A CONTEST?

Lissa's Text Box: What are we waiting for? Let's go move that bush and kill some slimes, let Mr. Beef kill the Plague of Shadow while we cheer him on from the sidelines, and we can all keep our custom hair colours!

Mr. Max's Text Box: What's the point? Breaker is already getting a party ready to go challenge the Plague of Shadow, and he has 96.58%.

Palcath's Text Box: Breaker? The lad with the Codes?

Anders' Text Box: The guy that charged Gliint and all the other low levels to die at the Frost Gigas?

Roodg used a *An Amazing Revelation Animation* (mostly to show both Palcath and Lissa that you could just use a standard version of an Animation and still be just as dramatic.

Roodg's Text Box: i KNEW WE MET Breaker BEFORE! hE IS Buddy! tHE EMO WITH THE SILENT SIDEKICK & THE TWO LESS IMPORTANT OTHER SIDEKICKS.

Palcath's Text Box: Damn. If I knew that was who Breaker was, I never would have let us use the Codes, lass.

Lissa's Text Box: Okay, Max, time to think about this. What percent do you have?

Mr. Max's Text Box: 99.97%. Before I finished everything in the last area I had 96.58% though.

Lissa's Text Box: And Breaker has what percent right now?

Mr. Max's Text Box: 96.58%, but he is getting ready to go to the last area to get to 99.97% right now!

Lissa's Text Box: ...

Palcath's Text Box: ...

Fournimer's Text Box: ...

Anders' Text Box: ...

Roodg's Text Box: ...

Mr. Max's Text Box: ...

Mr. Max's Text Box: ! Breaker hasn't killed a Green Slime either!

Five avatars executed the *Slow Clap Animation*.

Mr. Max's Text Box: But Breaker probably already has paid to get a full party with the Six Gigas' Equipment. You need all six and a full Insta-Wiki to challenge the Plague of Shadow. I posted that info in my guide like the loveable fool I am. I only delivered the killing blow to the Earth Gigas. We only have one piece of the Gigas Equipment! We will never make it in time!

Mr. Max used a *Clear Your Throat Animation*, Lissa used a *Scowl Animation* back, she couldn't believe that Max was not only oblivious to vital plot points, but that he hadn't noticed that the party had stopped using the *Clear Your Throat Animation jokes* and were onto *An Amazing Revelation Animation jokes*.

Lissa's Text Box: Seriously? Okay, look, meathead. First of all, Loverboy over there has on the *Ass-Pounding Boots*, so we have two pieces. Second, Breaker's party doesn't know where the Green Slimes are, so they will waste a bunch of time finding out they are missing something and have to come back. Even if they make it back, the slimes are hidden and impossible to find. You already know where all the Strongholds are, and you are so over-leveled that you can kill the Gigases all by yourself!

Anders' Text Box: *Ass-Pounding Boots?*

Mr. Max's Text Box: But you need 100 avatars for one to show up.

Lissa's Text Box: Trust me, you don't.

Mr. Max's Text Box: ♪♫Da na na na nah! Dah na na na na nah nanananah!♪♫ All right, fellow adventurers, a quest has been decided. A quest to save ourselves! There is no time like the present. Let me mark their locations on your Micro-Mini Maps! Now, onward to the closest Gigas! The Frost Gigas! Right through that door there! Follow me to Stronghold B!

Palcath's Text Box: Anders already has that one…

Mr. Max's Text Box: Well, where is this Anders? Maybe we can get her to help us!

Lissa's Text Box: Come on! You said you camped his page. All of our names are even written in the Text Boxes, for crying out loud!

Roodg's Text Box: i KNOW WHY IT TOOK HIM SO LONG TO FIND Anders' pLAYER pAGER NOW.

Mr. Max's Text Box: Onward to The Straight of Endless and to the next closest Gigas just past the Shores of Eternal Night!

Mr. Max executed his patented *Flex Animation*. Everyone else left the *Portie Tent* except Roodg and Mr. Max.

Roodg's Text Box: ¶ cRACKERS! ↓ cRACKERS! ▲ cRACKERS! ☐ cRACKERS! ♥ oHH! hEART!

The robed whatever it was walked right past Mr. Max, not noticing the stunned expression on his Mr. Face or how painfully full his Codpiece was after the *Flex Animation* ended.

Chapter 20
HE'S ALWAYS RIGHT

Palcath froze. This couldn't be happening. This just couldn't be happening. It was just too horrible to comprehend. He would need to make a stand here, he would need to stop this madness before it was too late.

Palcath's Text Box: No, I am not getting on that.

Fournimer's Text Box: why not Man? you are acting all crazy.

Lissa's Text Box: It doesn't say anywhere in the manual that dwarves are scared of water. Why in the map are you role-playing it?

Palcath's Text Box: I am not scared of water. I'm scared of boats!

Anders' Text Box: Scared of … boats?

Fournimer's Text Box: that's just crazy Man! we need to get on to find Stronghold C, come on already!

Lissa's Text Box: If you don't stop this overacting, I am going to role-play that I get seasick and stand beside you the entire time fake vomiting. #MoveItOrLoseIt.

Palcath's Text Box: I'm not role-playing. I haven't said lad or lass once in this entire Chapter!

Mr. Max's Text Box: Come, fellow adventurers, the ship sets sail once we get on. It has a tight schedule to keep that depends completely on us getting on and nothing else!

Palcath's Text Box: No, we just joined up. I am not getting on a boat. It is way too soon for this.

Anders' Text Box: Too soon for what?

Palcath's Text Box: Hasn't anyone else ever played a fantasy game before? Boats are bad news! Every time! We shouldn't do this!

Fournimer's Text Box: will someone please just help me move the Dwarfman?

Roodg's Text Box: k

Palcath needed to be brought onto the S.S. Party Splitterup kicking and screaming.

Chapter 21

A LIKELY PAIR

It started with quadruple vision, but after a few turns (both of time and of his stomach) it slowly fell to triple, then just to double. Things slowly became more solid on round 6, and Palcath stood up, thankful that the world was only a little shaky. He had been right, of course, getting onto a boat was a bad plan. He remembered an attack on the S.S. Party Splitterup by a Kraken that was very smitten with Anders. It had split Anders down the middle and, sometime later, the ship as well.

> Palcath's Text Box: I knew it. I was right. I always am. Boats are always dangerous! They're practically designed to split up parties, newly formed or not. Now I need to find out … am I all alone here, or did we get split up into pairs or groups? Lads?

Surveying the area, Palcath saw someone covered in sand. He wasn't sure who it was, but he dug up some of the sand, saw beautiful purple hair shining in the sunset, and thanked the Maker.

> Palcath's Text Box: No lads here. This is a lass!

> Lissa's Text Box: Urgh. Who is that? Did you see what that Leviathan did to Loverboy after the Kraken was done? Totally #SoFuckedUp.

> Palcath's Text Box: Fair Maiden, I am relieved to see that you are okay after your horrible ordeal. Allow me to assist you.

Lissa's Text Box: Oh, Maker, are you forcing me to do that dorky stuff now? Fine. Thank you, brave "Sir Knight". I am now greatly in your debt since sand has always been my one true weakness. How shall we continue, noble Sirdy Sir Sir? #TotesSerious.

Palcath, either unable to understand sarcasm or too smitten to notice Lissa was making fun of him, applied the role-playing on thick. He was sure she liked it.

Palcath's Text Box: 'Tis almost night upon us, Fair Maiden lass. We should rest for the eve and continue on next cycle's morning at the crack of the rooster's caw.

Lissa's Text Box: Wow, really? Still on with that? Okay, well, I would very much enjoy that, 'tee hee,' for the rest is well needed. Perchance we shall even write of this predicament in our journals, Sir Knight, Lord of the Halls of Lad.

Palcath's Text Box: An excellent suggestion, Fair Maiden Lissandra Collinswood. It may very well be in our best interests to check out our situation as well.

Lissa's Text Box: You remembered my full name? #ShockingTurnOfEvents. I mean, whatever, you do realize that I'm making fun of you, right? Should I do the *Campfire Making Animation* thusly, humble Sir Knight?

Palcath's Text Box: Of course I would remember your name. 'Tis as gentle as you yourself. You are trying to make fun of me, lass, but I know that only a true role-player would make fun of another one by doing it. Also, that *Campfire Making Animation* offer is generous of you. However, I must insist that I do that, if nothing else to prove that chivalry is not dead.

Lissa's Text Box: Okay, fine. I am obviously really into role-playing. Crap! I never even got to use the *Portie Tent*. Oh, how I am going to be laying on the role-playing thick now due to disappointment, for I am most distressed that I shall not ever rest my bosoms upon the delicate purple sheets, as I very much wanted to try one.

Palcath's Text Box: Then it is a good thing I was the one with it in my inventory, Fair Maiden.

With a flash of *Tent Animation*, a perfectly nice *Portie Tent* complete with various campfires and wonderful outside camping furniture was erected upon the shore. Palcath smiled with pride (and the use of a *Smile Animation*).

> Lissa's Text Box: Looks like I got randomly stranded with the right nut from the mix. Time to go rest my bosoms!

The pair entered the safety of the *Portie Tent*. After a few moments of very important Player Pager updates, they began to do some research. Lissa noted that research was the way to get Palcath to calm down his role-playing, at least by a little.

> Lissa's Text Box: No one else has posted anything yet on their Player Pagers or the WorldForums. That is #SoFuckedUp of them.

> Palcath's Text Box: That isn't surprising, lass. The only one who kept their stuff up-to-date was Mr. Max, but he stopped updating awhile ago. Well, him and Roodg, but I simply cannot hope to understand the lass' brain or Player Pager.

> Lissa's Text Box: So, that was a she?

> Palcath's Text Box: I have no idea, really. I thought so, but Fourni though they were a guy.

> Lissa's Text Box: All right. I will need to take a closer look next time. Regardless, I posted that we should meet back up in Centreofmapia. It is right in the centre of the map, after all.

> Palcath's Text Box: It's so far away I can't even see it on my Micro-Mini Map. I can't even find it unless I zoom out, but everything just turns to dots when I do.

> Lissa's Text Box: You can zoom out? What in the Flaming Pit? Oh hey, right there, never saw that button command. Wow, we are very far east. The land does connect the entire way, though. We don't have to get on any boats to get back, 'fraidy dwarf!

Lissa used the *Smirk Animation*.

> Palcath's Text Box: I don't really mind boats that much anymore, lass. That is funny…. There are only 5 Xs on here. Mr. Max must have forgotten Stronghold F.

> Lissa's Text Box: Does that really surprise you? The meathead probably forgot to mark the one we were sitting at.

> Palcath's Text Box: Nope, I see that one. That's odd; he forgot Stronghold E. Stronghold D is pretty much right on the road we would

> need to take to get back to Caffaquenitablib.

> Lissa's Text Box: It is, but we are not super over-leveled overachievers full of meat. We probably shouldn't even go outside! This is marked as a High Level Area, and it becomes a More High Level Area after the Stronghold.

> Palcath's Text Box: Well, let's just test the waters next cycle, lass. We should try to get to the Stronghold at the very least so we can wait for Mr. Max to come get us there.

> Lissa's Text Box: Agreed. If we are not there when meathead shows up, he will forget that we are supposed to be helping him. Now I'm actually going to rest these bosoms. #Goodnight.

Palcath listened to her turn around in her new bed for some time but couldn't just let the falling asleep music take him. When he finally got close to drifting off, loud aggressive snoring from the purple bed area snapped him out of sleep. He couldn't help but use the *Chuckle Animation* at the "delicate flower".

~ ~ ~

After a hearty meal of *Mountain Bacon* and *Desert Bacon*, Palcath pretended to wash their dishes (that only showed up during meals; they never truly needed washing) while Lissa tapped her foot, annoyed with the needless role-play. A quick pull on the *Portie Tent*'s string and it was safely put away.

They cautiously ventured into the Bogness Swamp. It was humid here, and the background music of pipe organs was telling them it was dangerous. Without warning, a *King Gribblet's Spear* flew through the air directly at Lissa's forehead. She screamed and covered her face. She hadn't seen a regular Gribblet yet, let alone this advanced version. It shouldn't even be allowed to attack her first. Why else would she have risked going outside to die die? The dwarf falling over dead was supposed to be her warning to run. This would be the end of her purple-haired glory; she just knew it.

The *King Gribblet's Spear* hit with a thunk, but Lissa didn't feel any pain. Opening her eyes, she saw standing in front of her a dwarf in Defensive Stance, *Trueblock Shield* at the ready. On the ground was a *King Gribblet's Spear* blinking out of existence.

> Lissa's Text Box: You … you saved me.

> Palcath's Text Box: I'm a Defender, lass. It is kind of what we do. Honestly, I never used the ability before now. Fourni could hold his own, and Roodg always deserved to get hit. I almost couldn't find the hotkey in time.

The King Gribblet and his Gribbletlings were upon them now, but Palcath deflected most of the attacks. He was extra careful to prevent Lissa from taking any damage, even at the expense of losing a little more health himself. He was a dwarf and had a Constitution bonus, after all.

A few rounds passed with Lissa and Palcath smacking the monsters with their respective weapons. The progress was slow going, but they were making some headway. The King Gribblet became frustrated with them and started to cast a high level Attack Magic called *Gale of Gribblets*.

> Palcath's Text Box: Crap. I can't defend us against magic, lass. Brace yourself!

The spell went off in a flurry of Gribbletness. Palcath had braced for the worst but was surprised when Lissa raised her bracelet and a small energy shield pulsed into existence. The spell was deflected and ripped a random Gribbletling to shreds.

> Palcath's Text Box: You … you saved me!

> Lissa's Text Box: I'm a Mendicator, lad. It is kind of what we do.

> Palcath's Text Box: I stand impressed, Fair Maiden. You have spunk and a love for the defensive arts that I have yet to see in another.

> Lissa's Text Box: Trust me. No spunk is on my person.

The King Gribblet, however, was not one for plot advancement, and executed his *Stunning Spear*, which Palcath missed defending against because he had started role-playing. He fell to the ground at about one-quarter Hit Points and would miss his next turn. A random Gribbletling made an attack directed at Lissa, but Palcath chose to take the attack instead, leaving him in *Critical* status.

> Palcath's Text Box: Urk!

Lissa went next and cast *QuikHeal* and *Stun-Gone*. Palcath was now at Full Hit Points, and *Stun* was removed. He could take his turn normally and used it to bury his *Hammer Spider Hammer* into the King Gribblet's crown. This sent the *King's Crown* into his *King's Brain* and finished him off. The remaining Gribbletlings ran. The duo heard some trumpet music; they'd finished the battle and gained a level.

> Lissa's Text Box: You dumb role-playing fool! I can take a few hits, you know. You almost got #Deleted.

> Palcath's Text Box: No, I will not allow it, lass! I swear that I will prevent you from taking damage.

Lissa needed to pretend role-play to pretend that she wasn't blushing.

> Lissa's Text Box: Well, fine, I give you permission to let me get hit if

> you are in dire trouble. But only then. Otherwise, you will take all my damage and like it!

> Palcath's Text Box: I am not sure I agree with you taking any damage at all, but otherwise yes. I will take it all and like it. But, more importantly … you can do healing and status effect removal both in one round? Where have you been all my play time?

> Lissa's Text Box: This is going to sound a bit too obvious, but I have been locked in a tower.

The King Gribblet had been standing in front of a Blue Chest; Palcath opened it up and read what was inside.

> Palcath's Text Box: Nice, it's equipment! An *Uplifting Blouse (s)*? It says that you can wear it, but not until Level 36.

> Lissa's Text Box: Ohhh! (s) must mean Swank! That's still a bit away, but that one monster gave me like a level and a half.

> Palcath's Text Box: Yes, I as well. Let's keep going, lass.

As they continued on, they learned that, through the lost arts of working together and the Defend command, they could kill pretty much any common monster in this area. It wasn't even making them break a sweat. Palcath would get healed after taking even a little damage or succumbing to a status effect. The status effects were thankfully rare as he was a dwarf and made most of his saves. A surprise attack on Lissa was quickly averted when Palcath easily broke the Constrict Bar from the Constricting Cat in just a single hit. They were the perfect pair for battle. This was missed by most players who never saw the natural synergy because they were both such unpopular classes and would have never used Defend, thinking it a waste of time.

Reaching the Lava Flats much sooner than expected, they were pleasantly surprised to already be at level 34. A few lucky chests on the way had earned them some nice consumables as well as some gear they couldn't equip yet. They had found only one thing that they couldn't use at Level 36: a pair of knives called a *Severator* for Backstabbers which was sold to a passing Shop-Kitten for a tidy profit.

Stronghold D was just down the road, but a door to a volcano caught their eye.

> Palcath's Text Box: Care for a quick diversion inside, lass? We are making excellent time, and any Red Chests inside will only add to our Level 36 upgrades.

> Lissa's Text Box: I have to agree. Any bosses inside will be a good warm-up for the Gigas' ass we are totally going to kick next! We are rocking this area like we have our cocks out.

Palcath's Text Box: I agree! I was going to suggest we try to kill the Gigas as well, lass. We have been nigh unstoppable.

Lissa's Text Box: I sure hope that there is an *Adamantium Hat* or *Helm* or *Something (s)* inside to go with the *Adamantium Breastplate (s), Leg Guards (s), Boots (s),* and *Gantlots (s)* I already found. If so, I will have a complete set of your stuff that I can keep for myself and not use! I would look better in it than you anyway.

Palcath's Text Box: Yes, I bet you would, lass. I hope there is an *Uplifting Hood (s)* or *Circlet (s)* or *Whatever (s)* for me inside to complete your outfit. I probably look better in this skirt anyway. I can totally rock the right skirt.

Lissa used the *Laugh Animation.* She hadn't expected that retort in the least.

Lissa's Text Box: Why the game doesn't just give the stuff to the right avatar, I will never know.

Palcath's Text Box: Hey, let's make a pact, lass. If there isn't a full set, we don't swap them, or put them on, or even look at them until we both have a full set to trade. We can show them off together!

Lissa's Text Box: I agree with that, lad. It is far more exciting that way. I simply can't wait to see your skirt. I have the perfect purse to go with it.

Palcath's Text Box: Aww, you just called me 'lad'!

Lissa's Text Box: Still making fun of you.

Palcath's Text Box: Sure you are.

The Fire Pits of the Dead Mountain proved to be not as exciting as they sounded. The mountain wasn't even dead. It was clearly an active, live volcano. Lissa cast *Fire Resistance +50* as needed, and by the time they found the boss chamber, they were sitting at Level 35. Two nice plump Red Chests were at the back of the volcano glade just waiting to get plucked.

Lissa's Text Box: Let's kick some ass!

Palcath's Text Box: Damn right, you ass-kicking lass!

A warning from the Game Explanation Text Box about using *Aqua Vera* if you got seriously *Burned,* (which would have helped Anders to understand a joke in Chapter 19) a Fire Volcanis burst into the area. It spent its first turn chewing its nails with interest and moving toward Lissa while unbuttoning its reptilian trousers. Lissa defended while

Palcath scored a *Sneak Attack* on the creature. This caused the Volcanis to change its target and whip out its scaly penis while heading toward Palcath. Palcath defended, and Lissa scored a *Sneak Attack*.

The Fire Volcanis gave up on the whole rape idea after losing about 80% of its Hit Points to *Sneak Attacks* from avatars that couldn't even do *Sneak Attacks*, and it tried to scurry off.

Lissa enchanted Palcath's *Hammer Spider Hammer* with an *Ice Edge* (even though it was a hammer), and the increased elemental damage caused the Fire Volcanis to explode into ice crystals. Trumpets indicated that Level 36 was upon them.

> Palcath's Text Box: Lass! You can enchant as well?

> Lissa's Text Box: Well, not that well, it is only a #OneHitWonder. I'm sure it would be much more useful if it stayed on for a bit. But, yeah, I am pretty awesome.

> Palcath's Text Box: I'll say!

> Lissa's Text Box: I guess we are pretty awesome. That perv didn't even get in an attack.

Opening the juicy Red Chests proved anticlimactic. They did not contain the missing Armour pieces, but what they did contain was new primary and secondary weapons for Level 36.

> Lissa's Text Box: Okay, let's use the weapons, but I am keeping your Armour until I have the full set.

> Palcath's Text Box: I agree, lass. The Lava Flats is a pretty big area yet.

Trying on their new weapons was exciting. It had been awhile since either had new things, and both were using *Truestuff* or Level 20 boss drops.

Palcath had a brand new *Overkill Hammer* that had three separate hammer heads. It certainly was more than a bit of overkill. He was most proud of his new shield, though. The *Golden Shield* gleamed in the sun (even though they were inside). While the shield itself was brown, all the trim was golden. A big yellow citrine was gleaming in the center. This bad boy allowed him to *Shield Smash* while defending.

> Lissa's Text Box: Okay, even I will admit that shield is a whole bunch of levels of yellow badassness.

Lissa now had a brand new *Overkill Mace* which had four large spikes on the ends, while everyone knew that three would have been plenty. Her new bracelet was called a *Silverlet*. It covered up almost her entire arm in its silver lattice and was inlayed with a single amethyst. When she tried defending, a purple disc projected from the gem.

> Palcath's Text Box: Nice, it is even purple for you, lass!

> Lissa's Text Box: The Overkill Weapons are a little bit of overkill in their designs, though. Very well named, in fact.

> Palcath's Text Box: Yes, lass, way too much overkill in these things. Who could possibly like this much extra useless crap on a weapon?

They used a *Smile Animation* at each other. Laughing out loud, they both answered at the same time.

> Lissa and Palcath's Simultaneous Text Boxes: Roodg.

Before going to leave, they checked up on their Player Pagers. They updated the fact that they were doing awesome, and that their next target was the Gigas in Stronghold D.

> Palcath's Text Box: What? None of the other lads have posted about what has happened to them yet!

> Lissa's Text Box: #SoFuckedUp. I am glad I got forcibly stuck with the dwarf!

> Palcath's Text Box: I am very glad I got paired with you as well. You are whole entire levels of human-lass awesomeness!

> Lissa's Text Box: Huh? I'm not a human.

> Palcath's Text Box: What? Yes, you are, lass! What are you talking about?

> Lissa's Text Box: I am clearly a half-elf. Lissa is short for Lissandra, remember? That is so elf like. Don't you see my half-pointy ears?

> Palcath's Text Box: Um … oh yeah, I guess they are a little pointy.

> Lissa's Text Box: I only picked *Elf Ears #1*. They are pretty pointy close up, though.

Palcath reluctantly changed his *Relaxed Pose* to a *Standoffish Stance*.

> Palcath's Text Box: So, lass … does that mean I am supposed to half-hate you now?

> Lissa's Text Box: What, Mr. Role-Player? If you thought I was a human, your opinion of me should have increased by half since I am only half-human.

> Palcath's Text Box: What are you talking about, lass? Dwarves hate

elves. I should half-hate you now.

Lissa's Text Box: No, dwarves hate humans in Gentalia, after they waged a Great War with each other. The elves and dwarves banded together and have refused to forgive the humans, even though it was hundreds of years ago. Didn't you read the flavour text? How can you call yourself Mr. Role-Player and not know that?

Palcath's Text Box: I thought in the Great War, the humans had battled against orcs or something. Honestly, I didn't read that part. I just assumed that dwarves and elves hated each other because they always do.

Lissa's Text Box: No, I think the developers tried to be original this time. I mean, did you see the Trolls?

Palcath's Text Box: They were pretty normal to me, lass. Ugly as sin. I almost puked when I saw one.

Lissa's Text Box: Really? You must not have seen a girl one. The girl ones were not normal!

Palcath's Text Box: I've never seen one of the female models. So wait, if humans and elves are supposed to hate each other … why is half-elf a starting race?

Lissa's Text Box: Duh, because half-elf chicks like me are #HotAsFuck!

Palcath's Text Box: No arguments here!

Lissa's Text Box: Well, all that flavour text and role-play crap doesn't really matter. Let's just find some hats before killing that Gigas so we can look good while kicking ass. At this rate, we will be able to kill all the Gigases … Gigai … whatevers … while waiting for the others to post that they even frickin' woke up.

Getting ready for the *High Five Dual Animation*, Lissa was left hanging for several turns before Palcath even noticed and quickly completed the action.

Lissa's Text Box: You were reading the stupid flavour text, huh?

Palcath used a *Sheepish Smile Animation* and admitted that he had been doing exactly that.

Chapter 22

AN UNLIKELY PAIR

I t took Anders a few moments to clear the thoughts out of his head—and the sand out of everywhere else. He wrung out the *Initiate's Jacket* and put it back into his *Ultra-Pack*. The last thing he remembered had been the Killer White Shark topping off his Magic Point reserves.

He was on a beach, and it was night. He was certain of that much. He opened up his menu but noticed that the Game Time registered early evening. It shouldn't be this dark yet. This was probably the Shores of Eternal Night that Mr. Max had mentioned. He knew Stronghold C was close by. Callisthenics was close as well, but he was to the west of either. Checking his Player Pager, he noticed that Palcath and Lissa had been stranded far to the east. Palcath, who understood everything, predicted that everyone had been split up into teams of two. Lissa had ordered everyone to meet back in the starting city.

It would be best to do the *Campfire Making Animation* now and rest until daybreak, even if at the Shores of Eternal Night it would just be another permanent night break. As Anders was stacking the wood, as he had done many times before, his mind began to wander.

Groups of two? He wondered who else was here, if anyone. There were a couple of great options, and Anders couldn't decide which one he liked better.

On one side, there was the perfect-faced human avatar with the chin stubble. Anders could see him there, weapons all glittery and ready to defend him from any more clichés that showed up. His perfect ass filled up those *Hard Leather Pants* so nicely that Anders had forgiven him entirely for snatching them from him in the first place. He even had a nickname for Anders: Dude. Anders was the only one that Fourni had given a nickname (as far as he could recall), so he felt pretty special.

On the other side, there was the very nicely-bodied human avatar with the recently grown mega-penis. Not only was he famous, but he was so over-leveled that nothing would be able to even get close to Anders. Plus, he was so beefy that Anders could probably just ride on his shoulders the entire time and take a nap. Anders also owed him an apology, and was sure he could handle an apology with *Increase Max More* with no problem at all. Even if Max had no idea who he was, it would still be nice.

Letting his thoughts continue to wander, Anders finished the *Campfire Making Animation* and suddenly felt all warm inside. What if it was both of them? That would be awesome. He could cuddle in the middle. That would be both the perfect team—and the perfect sandwich!

Anders saw something out of the corner of his eye. Written in the sand, he could see a note; it was visible now that the fire was going.

> Anders' Text Box: bACK IN 10 MINS.

That note could only have been written by one avatar.

> Anders' Text Box: Oh fudge me!

> Roodg's Text Box: i'M SURPRISED U WOULD HAVE ANY ENERGY 2 FUDGE RIGHT NOW! aFTER WHAT THOSE mERMEN mERAUDERS DID 2 U BACK ON THE BOAT. i WAS JUST GETTING THE PERFECT SANDWICH BUT i AM BACK!

Anders hadn't even thought about this pairing. He frantically looked around and felt his little elf heart sink when he didn't see signs of anyone else. Fourni and Max were probably together. There went the sandwich dream.

> Roodg's Text Box: i READ Palcath & Lissa's pLAYER pAGERS. sO i UPDATED MY pLAYER pAGER & SAID WHERE WE WERE. nOW THEY KNOW 2.

Anders was a little surprised. He was forced to use the *Confused Blink Animation*.

> Anders' Text Box: Really?

> Roodg's Text Box: yEAH. nEXT CYCLE WE WILL PASS sTRONGHOLD c ON THE WAY 2 MEET THEM. Mr. Max's POINT ON THE MAP SAYS SO. iF THE gIGAS IS DUMB WE CAN TOTALLY KILL IT! iF IT LOOKS HORNY SAME DIFF. cLITORIST IS JUST ANOTHER CYCLE AWAY AFTER THAT.

> Anders' Text Box: How can you tell that? I can't see any of that.

> Roodg's Text Box: dUH. zOOM OUT AND LOOK AT THE MAP.

> Anders' Text Box: Well, that is not such a bad id—

> Roodg's Interruption Text Box: sHHH. sLEEPING NOW. zzz!

Falling asleep didn't come easy for Anders. Had he just gotten told by Roodg what was what?

~ ~ ~

Anders was not looking forward to the next cycle of travel but was quickly surprised by his new companion. Roodg was an excellent ranged attacker, and with both of them blasting away at foes, no monsters could get near them. Using magic was second nature to the avatar, and both hapless monsters and scenery fell to the spells. With the amount of innocent scenery Roodg destroyed through imaginative spell usage, it was easy for Anders to see why his, or her, last name had been set to Scenerybane. After Anders used an *Earth Shot* from his *Trueshot Bow+*, Roodg stared at him with a curious expression. At least Anders guessed that it was a curious expression; he couldn't see any face at all under all that *Navy Cowl*.

> Roodg's Text Box: u CAN USE THE CRYSTALS 2 Anders? i DIDN'T KNOW! tHEY GO IN MY RING. hERE TAKE Palcath's AIR ONE. i already had one but didn't tell him.

Taking the *Wind Crystal*, Anders was once again surprised by the Magic Mage. He could barely muster up the Text Box to say thank you. Now when he pulled back his *Trueshot Bow+*, he could fire either arrows with little leaves that followed them or ones with lightning sparks. Fourni would be jealous of all the neat effects.

The morning cycle was passing quickly, even though it was night here. The duo handled their challenges swimmingly, except for in the section where they had to swim (they didn't know the controls very well for that). There were only about two-hundred rounds left before second night when they came to a fork in the road: one way led to a sunset, while the other revealed nothing but darkness.

> Roodg's Text Box: k, THAT DARK WAY LEADS THRU THE cHAMBER OF oTAU, AND GOES 2 sTRONGHOLD c.

> Anders' Text Box: How did you know that, Roodg? Is it on the map?

> Roodg's Text Box: nO. iT IS ON THE SIGNPOST RIGHT THERE.

Anders still managed to keep his composure, despite feeling silly.

> Roodg's Text Box: iT SAYS THAT THE cHAMBER OF oTAU IS AN aNTI-mAGIC zONE. tHERE IS AN OPTIONAL VERY

HARD BOSS, BUT THE NORMAL MONSTERS R NOT THAT BAD. wE NEED 2 GO THRU THE cHAMBER 2 CHECK OUT THE gIGAS.

Anders' Text Box: It says all of that on the signpost?

Roodg's Text Box: LoL. nO. iN Mr. Max's GUIDE, SILLY BOOTS. tHERE R NO SPOILERS THOUGH.

Anders' Text Box: I admire that guy for keeping spoilers under wraps, but honestly I just wish that he spoiled a few things at this point. I want to know what the Gigas is before we even bother to go there.

Roodg's Text Box: wHERE IS THE FUN IN THAT? k, I'M GUNNA BE HORRIBLE INSIDE AN aNTI-mAGIC zONE. i DON'T KNOW WHAT IT DOES, BUT IT WILL BE ALL SORTS OF HORRIBLE FOR ME. i ALREADY KNOW.

Anders' Text Box: If all the monsters are lower level inside, I can just shoot them. The boss is tough, but we can avoid it anyway, right? Should we try?

Roodg's Text Box: yES! wE BOTH STILL HAVE OLD EQUIPMENT! i HAVE A NEW cASTER'S rING FOR LEVEL 36, AND i'M LEVEL 35 NOW SO SHOOT EVERYTHING! i HOPE THERE IS RED CHESTS INSIDE.

Anders' Text Box: I'm Level 35 as well. There is new stuff for 36? I skipped a few levels. I was kind of disappointed with this Mithral stuff. I waited so long to see it, and it is not really what I had imagined. Yeah, let's go in there, and you can watch me kick butt!

Roodg's Text Box: bUT i LIKE YOUR OUTFIT. iT IS HOT. i LOVE HOW IT SHOWS OFF YOUR BUBBLE BUTT OF HOLDING!

Anders changed to *Blush Shade #1*. He was glad it was constant nighttime here so Roodg probably didn't see that. He walked up the path to the Chamber of Otau. The place probably had huge black walls, possibly hundreds of feet in the air, but it was very hard to see anything due to not having special night vision of any kind. The duo opened the regulation dungeon door and stepped inside.

The very first step inside of the dungeon felt immediately claustrophobic. Everything special became ordinary. Anders noticed that his boots were no longer *Steadfast*, his *Truestrike Sword+* wasn't wavy anymore, and his *Trueshot Bow+* wasn't full of fabulous effects. At least this dungeon was a lot brighter than outside, and seeing was no longer a challenge.

> Roodg's Text Box: oH HEY! u HAVE A SCAR!

> Anders' Text Box: I do? Where? I didn't think scars were in this.

> Roodg's Text Box: tRUE, SCARS R NOT IN THIS GAME, BUT NEITHER IS GIANT gIGAS COCK SO ... iT IS ON YOUR FACE. tHE SCAR NOT THE COCK LoL.

Anders touched his hand to his face and felt a mark on his cheek.

> Anders' Text Box: It's the attack from Mr. Max.

> Roodg's Text Box: cRAP.

> Anders' Text Box: Why? Is it bad?'

> Roodg's Text Box: nOPE. iT IS BADASS. bUT MY SPELLS ARE ALL LOCKED. i CAN ONLY HIT THINGS WITH POTIONS OR MY REALLY BAD RING BITCHSLAPS NOW. i HOPE THEY ARE ALREADY DEAD.

Only one of the types of monsters here were already dead, lively little fellows called Specters. They had magical attacks, which was not very sporting of them. Anders left them to the item-slapping crazy Roodg and shot the other four types as he saw them. They were not exceedingly high level, and the progress to Level 36 was slow going. Midway through the dungeon, the pathway split into two. Anders could see that one path was long and windy and the other short. They both ended at the same point. Neither contained monsters, but the short path contained an uncomplicated *Vine Swinging Puzzle*.

> Roodg's Text Box: uM. bIG LONG WINDING PATH RIGHT?

> Anders' Text Box: Why? There are no monsters in either, and that one is much shorter.

> Roodg's Text Box: tHERE MIGHT BE HIDDEN STUFF?

> Anders' Text Box: We can see everything, though. I don't think there is anything else.

> Roodg's Text Box: pLEASE?

Confused, Anders agreed, and they choose the longer, windy path. When they came to a ledge, Anders needed to jump, but Roodg didn't. Being so lanky, the Magic Mage could just reach up and grab the ledge.

> Roodg's Text Box: tHANKS FOR GOING THIS WAY Anders. i AM ALL LANKY AND IT MAKES ME SUCK AT vINE sWINGING pUZZLES! LoL. i CAN'T GRAB THEM AT ALL AND ALWAYS FALL!

Anders was taken off guard when the Magic Mage gave him a *Big Friendly Hug Dual Animation.*

They slowly made it to the end of the dungeon by taking the longer paths each time. Roodg was thankful that Anders had taken the Vine Swinging weakness into consideration. While they had explored every side path of the entire Chamber of Otau, they found no equipment. Luckily, they did find some useful *Combi-Fusion* materials. That would have been great if Anders' hadn't left his *Combi-Fusion Pot* on display in Palcath's stupid *Portie Tent.*

They finally reached the end of the dungeon and again found two split paths. This time neither path went to *Vine Swinging Puzzles.* One was clearly marked as leading to the door outside. The other somehow seemed deadlier, as if it led to the very hard boss.

> Roodg's Text Box: tHIS PLACE WAS LAME. eVERYTHING DIED IN 1 HIT.

> Anders' Text Box: It wasn't even worth wasting my infinite arrows to kill these things.

> Roodg's Text Box: cOME ON. wE SHOULD GO SNOOP AND SEE WHAT THE BOSS IS.

> Anders' Text Box: I haven't had a lot of luck with bosses. Maybe we shouldn't.

> Roodg's Text Box: nOT WHAT i HEARD.

> Anders' Text Box: I suppose we can just turn back if it is dangerous.

> Roodg's Text Box: k

> The side path turned just once and headed straight for a very rare chamber glade. There was a large stone table in the centre of the room, but there weren't any stone chairs. The most striking feature of the room was a stairway at the end leading to a higher section. Nestled in the higher section were seven chests. Two were probably unimportant because they were blue, but four were red and full of temptation. The final, resting in the middle, was a shining beacon of gold possibilities.

> Roodg's Text Box: omm! tHERE ARE 7 CHESTS THERE! tHE

> MOST i'VE SEEN TOGETHER IS 2! hMMM. sTRANGE Mr. Max ONLY LISTS 6 HERE, NO GOLD ONE.

> Anders' Text Box: I have seen three once, with one gold one. It is where I got this (s) equipment.

> Roodg's Text Box: tHE (S) STANDS FOR sAWESOME RIGHT?

> Anders' Text Box: Clearly it does. I would be lying if I said I wasn't very tempted to make a run for those chests, though. I wonder what is inside them.

> Roodg's Text Box: nO SPOILERS HERE. wHERE IS THE BOSS?

> Anders' Text Box: Waiting to jump down on us if we enter the room. I just wish we knew what it was so we could try to get some info.

> Roodg's Text Box: i GOT AN IDEA.

Roodg turned and ran back down the path they had come from before Anders could even ask what the idea was. Roodg must have had *Serpent Speed* constantly active, judging from how fast the avatar executed strange whims. Returning a few rounds later carrying a stunned Regular Gribblet, the mage stopped before the entrance to the chamber glade and threw the little monster inside. The plan was to draw out the hiding boss with a random creature. After a few rounds of confusion, they realized that the plan failed. The Gribblet started to prowl as if nothing had happened, so Anders put it out of its misery.

> Anders' Text Box: Cookies! That was a good plan.

> Roodg's Text Box: LoL. cOOKIES! i HAVE ANOTHER PLAN. u COVER ME.

Moving slowly at just a single move unit a turn, Roodg crossed the glade. Taking great care to avoid anything that was important by walking around it, the mage crept by the table and slowly ascended up the stairs by crawling on all fours. All the while, Anders followed the movement with a bow, ready to strike anything that showed up. After a few endless rounds, Roodg was at the top platform near the chests. It was the slowest Roodg had ever moved. Assuming the ready-to-sprint position, the mage used the *Wince Animation* and swiftly *White Wolf Kicked* a chest. Nothing happened except for Roodg stubbing a toe.

> Roodg's Text Box: ???

> Anders' Text Box: Try opening one. I'll keep covering you.

Roodg opened a Red Chest while ready to run.

> Roodg's Text Box: oH! *bLACK cASTER bOOTS (S)*! bLACK IS BADASS!

Roodg opened another Red Chest a little less nervously this time.

> Roodg's Text Box: *bLACK cASTER pANTS (S)*!!!

Roodg opened the other two Red Chests, excited now.

> Roodg's Text Box: *bLACK cASTER gLOVES (S)*! *bLACK cASTER cOWL (S)*! aLMOST A WHOLE SET!

The Red Chests remained closed from Anders' point of view as they still had things inside them for him.

> Anders' Text Box: Why didn't anything happen? Try the blue and gold ones.

The first of the blue boxes contained an *Absorbing Cloth*, which Roodg read the description to learn was used to remove the *Soaked* status, so Lissa wasn't that far off when she used one to mop up the oil covering Anders after the fun with Lord Pistonis. It would have been nice quite a few turns ago after crossing the Othur River and getting actually *Soaked*, but it was too late for that now. The second contained an *Overkill Casting Staff* to Roodg's delight.

Still wary of the Golden Chest, Roodg opened it and jumped back, but nothing happened.

> Roodg's Text Box: iT IS A *pORTABLE aNVIL*. iT SAYS THAT U CAN USE IT TO ADD STATS TO CERTAIN EQUIPMENT. iT DOESN'T WEIGH ANYTHING! i'M GUNNA TAKE IT.

Roodg very carefully took the *Portable Anvil*, then panned the camera around.

> Anders' Text Box: Still nothing? This place is broken, I think.

> Roodg's Text Box: lAME! cOME GET RED CHESTS.

Walking into the glade confidently, Anders passed the stone table and headed for the stairway.

> Game Explanation Text Box: Even when travelling with a full party, you can still be outnumbered. Always be careful.

> Anders' Text Box: What?

> Roodg's Text Box: oH COOKIES!

This boss encounter was activated only by having a party in the glade. The encounter began. It was not like a normal boss battle, however, because from the sky dropped seven of the things. They were big, hairy beasts, each with the head of a bull and the body of a man. They were only about two heads taller than Anders. Each Minotaur had on a pair of fairly skimpy bikini briefs: two were in blue, four in red, and the largest of the bunch, the Minotaur Leader, was in gold.

> Anders' Text Box: That's it! I am fed up with you, stupid Game Explanation Text Box. You are never helpful. You just made my list!

Anders' List:
1. Scenic Pillars
2. Glades
3. Status Effects
4. Constrict Bars
5. Traps
6. (s) Gear
7. Swarm Beetles
8. Combo NPC/Monsters
9. Jumping Puzzle Blocks
10. The Game Explanation Text Box

The six normal Minotaurs dropped in at the bottom of the area, near the table, and blocked Anders from leaving. The Leader dropped in at the top of the stairs, blocking in Roodg and hiding the Magic Mage from Anders' vision.

The Insta-Wiki was instantly opened by Anders, but not by Roodg.

> **Creature Name:** Minotaur Leader/Regular Minotaurs
> **Class:** Man Beasts
> **Level:** 50/35
> **Special Attacks:** Gore, Spin, Assault, Charge, Grapple, Snatch
> **Drops:** Minotaur Musk
> **First Player Encounter Notes:** Fellow adventurers, bring all your friends. This is two battles in one. The Leader and Regular Minotaurs do not battle side by side. Use this to your advantage. – Mr. Max
> **Additional Comments:** That was no problem with all the *Musk*, kay. – Kray

On their first turn, the Minotaurs hopped back a few move units without animation of any kind and advanced toward them menacingly.

> Anders' Text Box: They outnumber us!

> Roodg's Text Box: lET ME CHECK SOMETHING ... k. yEP i CAN

HANDLE THIS BIG GOLD ONE, u TAKE ON THE LITTLE ONES. sO EXCITING!

While he could complain, Anders remembered that, without magic, Roodg did not have any way of really attacking them, so taking on the other six was probably fair. He wasn't so sure about facing six bosses at once, though. Jumping onto the stone table to get a better shot, Anders unleashed a *Flurry of Arrows* and said, "Biscuits," when he missed with every single shot.

The Regular Minotaurs used their turns to surround the table and begin to touch themselves through their skimpy underwear. Judging by the sizes of the emerging bulges, none of them was particularly well-endowed, at least not compared to what Anders was used to. While they would probably be larger than an average human, they were certainly not hiding the disproportionate slabs of meat of the previous bosses he'd encountered. It was a bit of a relief.

After shooting twice at a Minotaur in blue skivvies, Anders was shocked to see the man-beast use *Snatch* to pluck his arrows out of the air. He would have to try his melee weapon.

The Minotaurs took their turn by dramatically pulling out their "secondary weapons". Anders judged the now-exposed Minotaur cocks. The smallest belonged to one of the red-bikinied man-beasts and was about seven length units long and not that terribly thick. The largest, surprisingly, belonged to one of the blues, and while it was an impressive twelve length units of thick meat, it was the smallest impressive thing Anders had seen thus far.

On Anders' turn, he thought about this. The Minotaurs would be a nightmare to battle with his limited melee skills and inability to use his *Critical Strike* from the *Truestrike Sword+*. His alternate way of battle would involve taking half a dozen Minotaurs and getting sexy with them. They were probably small enough to take without even using *Stretch More*. When Anders heard Roodg moaning from the platform above, it cemented the idea in his head. It was time to get sexy, and on his own terms.

He was pretty sure he could defeat the Minotaur orgy and enjoy the Flaming Pit out of it at the same time. There was nothing in the rules against that (that he knew about, at least). He did not cast any *Stretch Mores* or *Stretch More Mores*. Instead, he used his turn to lift up the cloth accent squares on his *Mithral Leggings*. This gave the Minotaurs a good view of his elf bits. For good measure, he ran his finger suggestively down his butt crack.

The Regular Minotaurs got excited at the eagerness of the Elfboy; on their turn, they stroked their proud meat in anticipation. The scent of their *Minotaur Musk* was filling the area, a strong odor that made Anders' own cock twinge with excitement. On his turn, Anders leaned over and grabbed one of the Minotaur cocks, and deftly licked up the drops of the *Minotaur Musk* that covered the member; it had a thick, full flavour.

It was the next round. The first Minotaur buried his musky cock in Anders' face.

The next two used their turns to gently flip Anders over onto his back. The fourth used *Spin* to rotate the stone table, giving Anders a full view of a different beastly cock, which Anders responded to by greedily taking it into his mouth. The fifth reached over and started to tease his nipples, and the sixth lowered its bull head down and started to lick Anders' balls. The strange tongue did an incredible job. weird but incredible.

For several pleasant rounds, the table was spun from Minotaur to Minotaur. New cocks ended up in Anders' waiting mouth, and new things happened to his body. They fell into a pattern. Each Minotaur did something different, while the one across the table was sucked off by the greedy little elf. The ones not involved in the exchange would either be slowly jacking off or gently slapping their cocks against Anders. Minotaur 1 enjoyed teasing and twisting nipples, sometimes even licking them. Minotaur 2 was the expert ball licker and oftentimes swallower. Minotaur 3 would massage Anders all over while teasing with his hot breath. Minotaur 4 loved kissing anything he could reach, including the other Minotaurs. Minotaur 5 was very skilled at cock sucking and would have been Anders' favourite, if not for Minotaur 6.

Minotaur 6 would lick Anders' hole with his hot, flickering tongue. Every round that the elf was sucking off Minotaur 3 (the largest of the bunch), the expert tongue would work his hole and make him moan. The other Minotaurs enjoyed the elf moaning so much that eventually each of them abandoned their original talent. Each turn, Anders' hole was tongued and licked. Minotaur 6 was still by far the best at it, getting more moans per round than the rest.

It was this skilled Minotaur that was the first to make a new move. On one of its turns, it instead licked its man-beast finger and started to feel at Anders' elf hole, causing the most moaning by far. The other Minotaurs stopped spinning (but not cock-jerking and slapping) and started to watch intently. The first finger slid into Anders, and he winced. It felt much larger than he expected, and he was shocked. Nevertheless, when the finger wiggled inside him, it hit some nice places and Anders felt himself loosen a little.

Another finger was added, and Anders gasped. He was surprised how uncomfortably large it felt at first, but slowly he relaxed, and it started to become enjoyable. A third finger was trying to enter, but the elf butt was being stubborn; it wouldn't let another in.

Anders didn't understand what was going on until he heard some angry cursing at cookies from above him. He had forgotten about the platform and Roodg a long time ago. Roodg managed to get part of a Text Box out, something about all magic sex abilities being sealed as well, but it was hard to hear through the moans of the Minotaur Leader.

Anders realized what was going on. Minotaur 6's fingers were not gigantic at all. They were just normal-sized fingers. Anti-Magic-Zone Anders just didn't have access to the magical passive ability of *Stretch* right now. That was the problem. He was just feeling how things should have felt normally.

Anders let out a gasp as the Minotaur removed the fingers from inside him. These cocks were suddenly a lot more impressive. Thankfully, Minotaur 6 happened to be the smallest of the bunch, and was not exceedingly thick. Anders, however, had not really been preparing for this, and the sudden pressure of the Minotaur trying to enter caused him to tense up. Thankfully, the Minotaurs had already been swayed with his acceptance of this situation earlier and did not become aggressive.

> Minotaur 6's Text Box: I guess we need to be gentle with the Elfboy for now, guys.

> Minotaur 3's Text Box: That is a good idea, Steve. We are not really in a hurry here. Go slow and try again.

Minotaur Steve simply stopped trying to enter and began his licking again; the thick, hot tongue began to work its way inside Anders. After a few rounds of the hot licking, both the Minotaur and Anders felt a loosening deep inside. Anders was even more thankful for the tonguing he'd received because, without the passive ability provided by the *Pink Goop*, this might get pretty painful. Minotaur Steve positioned Anders again, but this time Anders was prepared and pushed himself onto the man-beast's member. It fit but was still a little tight. Minotaur Steve took his time, going slowly to try to work his way deeper inside.

Some rounds later, one perfect thrust caused the Elfboy to moan loudly. The Minotaur was fully inside, and Anders was fully ready. The other Minotaurs cheered and soon were treated to hand and blowjobs from the moaning elf (when he could breathe). After a few rounds, Minotaur Steve pulled out. Anders gasped.

The table was spun. A slightly bigger Minotaur was attempting entry this time. Anders was warmed up enough that this change in size didn't intimidate him. The new Minotaur pushed in tentatively. Once the Minotaur was sure Anders was all right, he began humping rapidly and moaning loudly.

The table continued to spin, but only the three smallest could get inside Anders right now. An attempt from the fourth (about nine length units long) did not work. Signalling Minotaur 4 to keep trying, Minotaur 3 spun the table around and stuffed its giant cock into Anders' face. It aimed the tip of its musky cock at Anders' nose and sprayed a few drops. Anders was breathing so heavily at this point that he breathed in a big whiff. It was exotic and felt like a great warm hug. By the time the musk cleared away, all nine length units were stuffed inside, and Anders hadn't even noticed.

Anders moaned. He wanted to tingle so badly. His tush was being stubborn and refused to tingle, which made Anders upset. What it did do was start to quiver and tighten on the Minotaur's member. After a few hard thrusts, the nine length units slid out and began to cover Anders' body in the thick *Minotaur Musk*. The other Minotaurs and Roodg cheered.

> Roodg's Text Box: wOOO! gO Anders!

The mage had evidently finished the upper encounter and was now watching. That made Anders get a little bit shy, but the table was turned and his butt was getting licked again by Minotaur Steve. The feeling was so intense, Anders forgot to blush. After another fantastic round of licking up some of the *Musk*, Steve positioned himself and re-entered the moaning elf. Taking turns with Minotaurs 5 and 2, Minotaur Steve thrust harder each time he got a chance. The table was spinning at an alarming rate. Anders imagined it would have caught fire by now if it were wooden—or real. With one more turn, 5 and 2 came hard. They shot their musky man-beast seed all over Anders' waiting body in thick, fragrant ropes.

Minotaur Steve came a few hard thrusts later, spilling out a particularly big load into Anders. More thick, musky ropes shot out of Steve, mostly hitting Anders' butt and legs after Steve slid out of the entrance just a bit too late to show off completely.

Now it was only the biggest ones who were left. Number 1 was a good ten length units and was thicker than the rest that had tried. He aimed his man-beast pole at the waiting elf ass, guiding the tip in. Anders wanted it, too, and with a good press took it in with some very painful pleasure. Again, careful not to hurt Anders, Minotaur 1 took things slowly, taking his time to build up the speed. Anders used his turns to think about other things, concentrating on licking the giant number 3 cock to get it as wet as possible. With each thrust, Minotaur 1's thick cock began to fill Anders. He couldn't help it, his bum twitched and convulsed on the beast, and the number 1 cock shot a full two squirts inside before pulling out.

Cum *Musk* still dripping out of his hole, not absorbed, the table turned one last time. The huge twelve length unit member was locked right on Anders' *Musk*-dripping elfhole. No matter how relaxed, how stretched he'd gotten with the previous Minotaurs, there was no way this one was going to fit. The other five Minotaurs moved toward Anders' face. With one squeeze each of their spent nut sacks, a super thick *Musk* droplet dribbled out, sending wonderful twitches down Anders' body. It was intoxicating. He came to as the giant cock pushed into him and began to thrust. Anders was stretched to new limits.

> Roodg's Text Box: yEAH! u R ROCKING THAT PORTABLE HOLE!

The thickness inside him was reaching new areas and was pressing hard on his place. It felt almost as big as the Frost Gigas had, but was warmer. The Minotaur pulled out. Anders assumed it was ready to cum, but instead it flipped him over. Bending Anders over the table, it entered with a thick push that caused him to shake.

Anders desperately wanted his ass-pounding boots to be working so he could become *Steadfast*. He needed a different plan, so he shifted to a standing position. The big Minotaur took the bait and lifted Anders into the air and began to fuck the elfhole hard. Five other pairs of furry arms helped pull Anders up and down onto the man-beast, but soon the arms shifted him downward. Anders was confused as to why, but saw the reasons in short order. The others were hard again, not content to just shoot once and be defeated. Anders happily helped, reaching eagerly to take one in each hand to pump them. Not to leave the others unattended, he alternated Steve, number 4, and number 2 in his mouth, sucking wildly and slurping greedily.

Roodg's Text Box: nO FUCKING WAY! gO Anders! u RULE!

Anders was spurred on by the mage's cheering. With renewed enthusiasm, he started to work the Minotaur dicks with unbridled vigor. The giant inside him was throbbing, and he was pushing back on it and gripping. His hands were working the members, and he had three cocks in his mouth as best as he could.

The pressure in his hole was pushing the limit, and he gripped down hard with the next powerful thrust. All twelve wonderful length units inside him began to pulse. Thick bursts of cum exploded through him, lathering his insides. Many bursts filled him, but with the magic lock still in effect, they were not absorbed into Magic Points. Number 3 finally pulled out, and globs of the *Musk* were getting ready to drip out of Anders' stretched hole. Before any of it could, he was turned in the air and entered by another thick member. Anders couldn't even tell one from another anymore; he just moved back and forth on the man-beast's beast and tried to feel everything that he could.

The new cock in his mouth began pulsing and was taken out at the last round. Anders tasted the first spurt of cum, but the rest shot over his face. Before he could even catch his breath, it was replaced by another that started to pound wildly.

The cock at Anders' backdoor began to release, and every drop entered the waiting elf. A new cock replaced the previous and instantly began to *Musk*fuck him. He felt something strange and unexpected. Another cock was pressed up against the first. Anders glanced down as best as he could and saw that the two smallest of the Minotaurs had both entered him at the same time.

Roodg's Text Box: hOLY FUCKING COOKIES! gO Steve!

The feeling was the most intense yet. Anders moaned wildly as the cock in his mouth released, shooting thick, musky cum down his waiting throat. With only two Minotaurs left, Anders began to work at milking them for all they were worth. He pushed and squeezed on the cocks with his ass, and he reached down and started to rub both sets of fragrant nuts.

This was all too much for the remaining Minotaurs, and they began to squirm under the pressure. Two pulsing cocks began to cum inside him at the same time, and Anders was going to take them for everything they had. Getting multi-blasted was incredible for Anders. He was sad when the Minotaurs exited his tired hole, meaning it was all over.

A few rounds of feeling full ended when Anders' insides began to quiver. Thick drops of the *Minotaur Musk* began to ooze out. Then it began to pour. As more and more flowed out, the sensation became more and more intense, and with the last wave of anal dripping, Anders started to shoot his own eager elfseed in dribbles until his nuts ached. This earned him a round of applause from everyone, and a *Handshake Dual Animation* from all the Minotaurs, the most vigorous coming from Steve.

Anders was completely covered from head to toe in thick, goopy Minotaur stuff. Strands were dripping from his stretched hole and were pouring out onto the floor.

Roodg walked over to Anders and handed him something with the *Hand Something to Someone Else Dual Animation*.

> Roodg's Text Box: u NEED THIS MORE THAN ME i THINK.

Anders opened his hand and saw the *Absorbing Cloth*. He couldn't help but *Chuckle Animation*.

◈ **Chapter 23** ◈

THE OTHER PAIR

Fournimer stared across the campfire (which he had animated all by himself) at the big bag of beef. That over-leveled meathead had fallen asleep before the fire was even fully animated. He just expected Fournimer to do it all by himself while he got all nice and rested (Fournimer guessed). He used the *Scoff Animation* at the big wall of muscles and knew that he would have to be the one that kept the fire stoked all night to keep the nighttime-only monsters at bay.

While reading through the others' Player Pages, he paused at each for a round and thought.

Palcath's was even more flowery and full of role-play than normal. There were so many "thee"s and "thou"s that the entire thing was a little hard to follow. That dwarfman certainly was pleased to finally have found a member of the Healing Class to adventure with. All of his latest screenshots had him grinning from ear to dwarfy ear. Only ever having seen Palcath use the *Frown*, *Upset*, *Worry*, and *Thinking Animations*, it was a bit strange. It made Fournimer happy for Man. It had been awhile since Man had done anything but play games and be grumpy.

Lissa's face was stuck as well; however, she was stuck on *Scowl*. Fair Maiden … no, wait … Chick (it was his thoughts, and he could call her whatever the Flaming Pit he wanted to) had mentioned that she and her "Knight" were going to head back to Copirpletgoth. She also wrote that they might stop off at Stronghold D along the way to check out the Gigas.

Her Knight?

More difficult-to-follow role-playing speak, no doubt. Fournimer really found it hard to follow anything more complicated than Palcath's patented "lad" style of role-playing. In the last update picture, Fournimer thought he saw Lissa cracking a half-smile, but it was probably a trick of the light.

Roodg's page was as hard to follow as ever. That Guy certainly kept it up-to-date, but it was so haphazard it was like trying to read a ham sandwich. A new screenshot of just water with the caption, "LoL. wET!" A short paragraph that involved walking somewhere without vines. Mention of a horned Gigas trip. Another screenshot of Anders sleeping on his side with a nice view of the back of his *Mithral Leggings (s)* and a caption of "LoL ELF BITS!" Fournimer just couldn't follow it. He saved the picture and moved on.

Anders' page was next. Fournimer hoped that Dude was still okay. Those Whaler Killers had done a number on him with their spears. It hadn't been updated at all, which wasn't surprising. The only avatar Fournimer knew that updated less was himself. It still had some nice pictures, though. Fournimer looked closer at the main profile picture compared to the others. Anders' ass was smaller back then. It was just like Roodg and Palcath had said. Anders did indeed now have a perky bubble butt of holding. Anders was also always smiling, despite all the horrible things that had happened to him. Fournimer made a mental note to update his own Player Pager (eventually) and to smile more (which he did now).

With a *Heartfelt Sigh Animation*, the avatar closed the Player Pager and looked back at his new partner. This muscle-bound overachiever Bro had just gotten magical penis powers that completely complimented Anders' magic butt of holding. Fournimer's stupid power didn't match either of them, not even remotely. Well, how nice for both of them!

Mr. Max turned over in his sleep. Apparently, the magical penis had read Fournimer's thoughts and was standing up, hard and proud. The codpiece had moved aside, finally disgusted with its new job. Thankfully, the *Diamond Pants* were unbreakable. However, with the massive appendage pressing against them, they may as well have been a 50% diamond/50% spandex blend. The tent Mr. Max was pitching could shelter an entire family of gnomes, and the thing wasn't even magically *More* enhanced yet.

Fournimer had a staring contest with it for a few rounds, but Mr. Max rolled over again, and the giant thing flopped right into the campfire.

> Fournimer's Text Box: oh biscuits!

As fast as he could, Fournimer shut off the campfire and used a half-full *Waterskin* to douse the fired-up crotch. Mr. Max didn't notice the ordeal; despite the burn marks on his pants, he just kept sleeping. A new campfire was set up by Fournimer, not far enough away to allow monsters to find Mr. Max in the night, but still far enough away that his balls would be frozen by morning. Satisfied with himself, Fournimer started to drift off to sleep, but just before the music took him away, he felt himself use the *Giggle*

Animation.

> Fournimer's Text Box: did I just say 'oh biscuits!'?

~ ~ ~

> Mr. Max's Text Box: Okay, fellow adventurer! Time to get up!

Opening his eyes groggily, Fournimer was not impressed with the vigorous shaking from Mr. Max. It wasn't morning yet. It felt as if he had been asleep for only a few hundred rounds at best.

> Fournimer's Text Box: no it isn't! what is wrong with you Bro? it is still the middle of the night!

> Mr. Max's Text Box: Of course it is! We are in the Big Badlands area, the second hardest area in the game! The nighttime monsters here are only about half as strong as the daytime ones. With your obvious lack of levels, you would be torn to avatar bits with just a few hits. You don't want to be like that elf lady on the boat with that trio of Mega Shrimp! We can't have your parts all over the place. I am not cleaning that up.

> Fournimer's Very Sarcastic Text Box: well thanks. that means a lot.

> Mr. Max's Text Box: No problem, partner! Boy, it was a cold one last night. I nearly froze my balls off.

Holding back a *Laugh Animation*, Fournimer got out from under his blue blanket and stood up. That was strange; he didn't remember having a blanket, blue or otherwise. Confused, he rolled it up and placed it in his pack.

> Mr. Max's Text Box: Okay, let's see what we can do about that horrible outfit of yours.

Fournimer was getting ready to send a very aggressive Text Box when a giant ball of glowing light popped up by Mr. Max. It shifted colours and emitted a constant humming noise.

> Fournimer's Text Box: what is that thing Bro?

> Mr. Max's Text Box: It is a *My Spiritual Storage Device from the Crags of Hulm*. What level are you anyway?

> Fournimer's Text Box: Level 24.

Fournimer was a bit embarrassed by his low level. He had let his levels fall way behind while watching over Anders in the *Portie Tent*. Palcath and Roodg had done a lot of killing and were already in their 30s now.

> Mr. Max's Text Box: Silver ... you already have the vest. Your sword is better... this, though.

Mr. Max used the *Hand Something to Someone Else Dual Animation*, and Fournimer reached out. Fournimer immediately followed with a *Jawdrop Animation*. He had just been handed an entire set of *Silver Mail Armour* (except the vest), a brand new *Flockshot Bow*, a *Super Snazzy Belt*, and an assortment of potions.

> Mr. Max's Text Box: Okay, tell me when you get to Level 28.

Fournimer was in complete shock. He has just been handed thousands of Gold Pieces' worth of really nice equipment.

> Fournimer's Text Box: uh ... thank you. a lot.

> Mr. Max's Text Box: No problem, fellow adventurer! I needed to collect everything for the Insta-Wiki. There is no point in having it just sit around collecting dust when someone can use it. Stay close to me and probably just stick to using the *Flockshot* for now, okay?

Staying close to Mr. Max was difficult. The big avatar ran around constantly and took all sorts of hidden paths to treasures. This was coupled with the fact that Mr. Max was now using his new "secondary weapon" with lethal force. After a forceful cock-slap to a Chronos Lizard, Mr. Max used the *Flex Animation* and accidently killed a Whipping Crane when his penis sprang back to life. The poor little non-boss monsters didn't have the abilities or the skills to do anything about a sexy power, which the beefy avatar was exploiting at every cock-blocking turn.

Shooting the very aggressive high-level monsters with the glittery precision of the *Flockshot* didn't do much damage, at least compared to a Mr. Max hack (or thrust) which cleaved most of them apart in one hit. After just fourteen monsters, Fournimer had made it to Level 28.

> Fournimer's Text Box: ding! I just made Level 28 Bro!

> Mr. Max's Text Box: Wow, already? I thought it would be 15 monsters. Good show.

Opening the *My Spiritual Storage Device from the Crags of Halm* again, Mr. Max pulled out a *Zweihänder Blade* and a *Super Duper Snazzy Belt*.

> Mr. Max's Text Box: Only this for now, I am afraid. Tell me when you get to Level 31, okay?

> Fournimer's Text Box: thank you Bro, I will. here.

Fournimer attempted to use the *Hand Something to Someone Else Dual Animation*, but Mr. Max declined.

> Mr. Max's Text Box: Don't worry about it! I have like twenty of the things anyway. Let's hurry and level you up as much as we can before morning.

> Fournimer's Text Box: wow thanks Bro! but why are you being so nice to me?

> Mr. Max's Text Box: You desperately need things that I have a bunch of in storage. I don't want you to get ripped up into bits! That would make me look bad.

He was now uncertain if the avatar was genuinely being nice or not. Fournimer really did appreciate what he was doing, regardless of the spirit it was in. After a few more monsters were impaled (some even with swords), Fournimer reached Level 31 and was given a complete set of *Leatheriron Armour* and an *Ultrashot Bow*. Mr. Max reviewed his inventory stash again.

> Mr. Max's Text Box: Well, the next is 36. Overkill Weapons and … for you … Hard Leaf Equipment. Crap, I gave away my only *Hard Leaf Jacket* to that Backstabber gnome, whatever his name was, the Hero of the Cycle or something like that. Well, here is an almost full set. Change as soon as you can. It is almost morning!

After a few normal encounters and some high-level bosses which Mr. Max made some quick thrusting work of, Fournimer was Level 36. While Mr. Max pulled both of his weapons out of the dead Flork Demon's skull, Fournimer changed his equipment.

The new *Hard Leaf* stuff was great. It was made of triple-laminated bright green plant life that breathed with the winds. The bright red *Leatheriron Armour Vest* clashed horribly, though, and seeing the combination made Fournimer's brain hurt.

> Mr. Max's Text Box: Wow, that is some hardcore awful clashing. I regret giving up that *Hard Leaf Vest* now, sorry. Check the Red Chest. Maybe it will spawn out a low drop and give you a *Hard Leaf Vest* out of sympathy.

Fournimer used the *Chuckle Animation*. He was an eyesore right now. It was not something he would normally stand for. Reaching into the chest, he pulled out a *Fancy Scarf (s)*.

> Fournimer's Text Box: it is a *Fancy Scarf (s)*.

> Mr. Max's Text Box: I remember my *Fancy Scarf*. It was great fun to

have it flowing all dramatically in the wind like that. They are such low-level accessories, though. That chest just screwed you. The belt family has much better stats.

Fournimer's Text Box: really Bro? I can't even find it in here. wait here it is. it says I need to be Level 50 to even put it on and it is under the Body Slot not Accessory.

Mr. Max's Text Box: That is strange. Maybe it is bugged. Can I see it?

Handing over the *Fancy Scarf (s)*, Fournimer waited patiently.

Mr. Max's Text Box: Strange, it is the same model, but it is in the wrong spot. It has much better stats than the other one as well. My *Diamond Plate* is much better, but this does have much better stats than the Night Ranger standard Level 50 *Emerald Chain Jacket* does. It is definitely bugged. We should contact an Admin.

Fournimer's Text Box: that's okay Bro. if it is better, I really don't think I will complain.

Mr. Max used the *Shrug Animation* and handed it back along with some *Emerald Chain Armour*, a nice pair of *Boots*, some *Gauntlets*, and a *Circlet*. A rooster cawed, to let everyone know it was officially morning.

Mr. Max's Text Box: Yeah, you keep it. I don't even have any Emerald equipment left except these. You might as well hang on to them. It is morning now, and Level 50 will come quickly. After that, it slows down. So much slow down … just wait until your 90s. I've been Level 98 like forever already.

Level 50? Fournimer was in shock. He was only Level 24 about a quarter cycle ago; this was serious progression. He hadn't even had time to try out all of his new Night Ranger abilities.

Fournimer's Text Box: thanks so much for the help Bro. where are we going anyway?

Mr. Max used the *Confused Blink Animation*.

Mr. Max's Text Box: To Stronghold F, of course! To kill the most badass Gigas around! I don't know where after that; probably D is the next closest.

Fournimer's Text Box: Dwarfman and Chick are right by there. we can meet up with them!

Mr. Max's Text Box: Uh, yeah, sure, sounds great.

Mr. Max's Internal Text Box: Who the heck are they?

Mr. Max's Text Box: Okay, it is far more dangerous during the day, but you are a little more prepared now. You probably will not be ripped to shreds as quickly. Hopefully you get to Level 50 soon because that outfit of yours is hurting my eyes! ;)

Mr. Max used the *Laugh Animation*, and was quickly followed by Fournimer.

Fournimer's Text Box: mine too, Bro!

This area really was much harder during the day. Even Mr. Max had to hack or penetrate a couple of times for each monster to go down. Fournimer did hold his own with his new equipment and abilities, but he knew if Mr. Max hadn't been there, he would have been cut into Fourni ribbons long ago. By the time they made it to Stronghold F, Fournimer was an impressive Level 49.22.

Fournimer's Text Box: what is with all the avatar names up there? there are like over a hundred. way too many nicknames to think up.

Mr. Max's Text Box: There are 226 avatars up there! That is the most I have ever seen out of the starting area. It has to be a raiding party intent on killing the Stronghold F Gigas. There, amongst that smaller group of higher-level-sounding names.

Fournimer's Text Box: who Bro? The emo haired one? yeah, that is Buddy.

Mr. Max's Text Box: No, that is Breaker. There is no one named Buddy here.

An idea clicked suddenly for Fournimer. Buddy was Breaker. The rude emo guy that had tried to get them to pay to go to the raid was the same guy that had released the Codes. Yes, Roodg and Palcath had already said that, but Fourni hadn't been paying attention.

The duo approached the clearing but stayed back and out of sight.

Mr. Max's Text Box: Ha! Only 9 of those avatars up there are high level; the rest are under 20.

Fournimer's Text Box: so Buddy brought a bunch of chumps as bait? that is pretty harsh.

The large group above entered after Breaker did some sort of overly complicated *Animation*. Breaker did not follow right away, instead waiting quite a few rounds to make sure all of his bait had served its purpose. Breaker was a Backstabber. His class did not surprise Fournimer in the slightest, given the fact that he had brought so many low-level avatars as bait. Breaker was wearing the same *Frost Gigas Boots* as Anders had. He also had on a similar style *Breastplate* and *Helmet*. All were set to black accents.

> Fournimer's Text Box: Bro, should we go up and help, maybe we can steal the kill?

> Mr. Max's Text Box: No, I don't want Breaker to know we are here. We should just watch for now. Damn, and he has almost the full set.

> Fournimer's Text Box: he has like what, three pieces Bro?

> Mr. Max's Text Box: If he has the helmet, he has four I bet. The other one wouldn't be visible from here. Damn, he just needs the *Light Gigas Pants* and *Earth Gigas Gauntlet* probably.

After quite a few rounds, the group came out. They had lost one high-level character, but a good half of the low levels. Breaker was yelling and pointing at one of the low levels. He was livid. The low level was wearing some stylish and puffy *Light Gigas Pants* and doing the *Pleading Animation*.

With a *Stretching of His Arms and Dramatic Hand Flourish Animation* Breaker pointed at one of the other high-level avatars. This high level was the same class as Mr. Max, given the big sword, but his sword was a *Katana* (Mr. Max told Fournimer that the *Katana* was very outdated equipment for that level). Fournimer recognized him; it was Jive Turkey! Well, it was warrier; that was his real name. He still had the look of being transported here from one of those old-timey silent black-and-white games Fournimer's grandfather used to play. Fournimer looked around, but he didn't see that four-armed avatar or the one without eyes. Roodg had been right. At least two of those avatars had shown up again. Fourni would need to remember to tell Palcath about that.

The avatar signaled that he understood Breaker by simply using the *Nod Animation*.

With a single sword slash of his *Katana*, the jive avatar slashed at the low-level troll in the nice pants, who was neatly cut in half. The *Katana* was held aloft with a single *Earth Gauntleted* hand.

With a *Stretching of His Arms and Dramatic Hand Flourish Animation* Breaker signalled again, and everyone went back inside. The lower levels had clearly not been having a good time for some time now.

> Fournimer's Text Box: dear Maker! did that just happen? PVP isn't allowed!

> Mr. Max's Text Box: Well no, not unless your avatar is broken for it.

warrier is Breaker's number one stooge. I've seen them together before. That means Breaker has all the pieces but this one under his command.

The duo ran up to the lower-level troll named Brenna Jay, who still remained in two pieces on the ground. Black pixels were flowing out of the avatar instead of blood. Fournimer was surprised. An avatar named Brenna Jay definitely didn't sound like a burly male troll Defender, but here was proof that even trolls had surprises.

Mr. Max's Text Box: That is odd. She should have retried by now.

Fournimer pressed his hand against Brenna Jay's neck.

Fournimer's Text Box: Bro, this is a male. but I think this avatar is Dead. as in Dead Dead.

Mr. Max's Text Box: That is clearly a girl. I think we should become scarce for now and wait until this Stronghold is clear. That will give us enough time to get you to Level 50 and out of that horrible outfit ... Fournimer!

Fournimer's Text Box: how can you think that is a girl? just look at him, all bumpy and warty. male trolls sure are ugly. but yes, let's get away from here for now Bro!

They hurried back toward the killing fields and away from the horrible scene.

Fournimer's Text Box: hey wait.

Mr. Max's Text Box: What?

Fournimer's Text Box: you used my name!

Mr. Max's Text Box: That is your name, isn't it? Crap. I didn't get it wrong, did I?

The big can of beef was using the *Anxious Animation*.

Fournimer's Text Box: nope, you got it right Max. I was just surprised you used it.

Mr. Max's Text Box: Good, I have a hard time remembering names, you see. There are always so many avatars around, and they all think that they deserve to know me. I meet so many that I just stopped paying attention. Plus, I have a lot of other things on my plate right now with all this Insta-Wiki Contest stuff and the Maximum Level Contest. Honestly, I just can't remember them all. I can only remember the really important ones' names.

Fournimer turned to *Blush Shade #4*, skipping the first three shades entirely. He had just been called important by the most famous avatar around. He placed a gentle hand on the big beefy *Diamond Breastplate*.

> Fournimer's Text Box: well thank you Max for remembering.

Mr. Max *Wink Animationed* at Fourni and did his famous *Flex Animation*. Fournimer used the *Smile Animation* and turned away to walk back to the very high level area. The big idiot wasn't nearly as bad as he had originally thought.

> Mr. Max's Text Box: No problem ... uh, err ... you just go ahead, Fournimer. I'll catch up in a round or so.... Get down, you!

◈ Chapter 24 ◈

A QUICK BREAK

Finally properly pants-equipped and after adventuring through the night, Breaker watched as warrior dealt the final blow on the Protector of the Summoning Pillar. warrior really was a faithful little lackey and was by far the longest lived in the long list of lackeys. To his credit, warrior had been the one who had been broken for PVP, so it made sense that he had not cut himself in half yet. It was a dirty job, and Breaker was glad that he had made warrior test out the PVP Code so that he could keep his own hands clean.

The latest victim of warrior's PVP chop had been that insolent pant-stealing son-of-a-bitch Brenna Jay, but more important were his two first kills that had cemented his servitude—warrior's long-time friends and companions. The three had been a group long before Breaker had met them, but now two were dead dead, and all Breaker had to do was *Point Animation* at them. Grandiger, the one with the Vishnu Arms Code, and Hellsfight with the Tremmorsense Code were no more. They sacrificed themselves for Breaker's cause and had "donated" their *Gigas Gear* to his outfit.

Breaker had also tested Codes on those two, and others, by claiming this was a holy mission from the Maker. What kind of idiot would believe that garbage?

warrier's Text Box: …

warrier used the *Nod Animation*.

Breaker's question was answered. That kind of idiot would believe that garbage. He couldn't believe that warrier had been so determined to serve this fake mission from the Maker that he would chop his old friends into perfect eighths. The silent avatar had never talked after getting broken and meeting his first boss monster. Breaker had no idea why, but he also really didn't care. warrier hadn't talked much before either. Breaker was willing to tolerate warrier for now, seeing as how other avatars he sliced apart couldn't fight back. He admired the slaughtering, but the slaughter was annoying.

Come on, man, you only need to enter your name once. Use a frickin' capital letter and spell it right. Furthermore, he was still using very outdated equipment in an ill-fated attempt to resemble a gray samurai.

> Breaker's Text Box: I agree. We should summon the Plague of Shadow, now that we have a full set of Gigas Gear.

> The Plague of Shadow's Text Box: You have come with a full set of Gigas Gear, but you have not completed the remainder of the Insta-Wiki. Breaker and warrier, your challenge has been denied.

> Breaker's Text Box: What the fuck?

> warrier's Text Box: …

warrier used the *Shrug Animation*.

> Breaker's Text Box: Dah! I have the same stupid percent remaining as that foolhardy Mr. Max. What am I missing…? I have finished everything, except … that stupid Green Slime crap! That is missing from the whole game! How will I complete my plan to get into the expansion first now?

> warrier's Text Box: …

warrier used the *Eyebrow Raise Animation*.

> Breaker's Text Box: To finish our holy quest from the Maker to rid the land of all evil! You already knew that, warrier. I told you that already, right? That my holy quest was in the expansion.

warrier just looked at Breaker with his gray eyes. He didn't say anything (as usual).

Now that he needed to complete this stupid Insta-Wiki as well, Breaker was not pleased. He had to find some idiot to use an Auto-Locate Code to try to locate them. He could use it himself, but he wasn't stupid enough to break himself forever. Breaker heard someone coming and hid behind the summoning pillar.

> Zal Finn II's Text Box: Wow! Sweet Gliint, you were right. This place is rad.

> Caëlahenâilenẇhei's Text Box: I am sorry for doubting that you had been here before, Gliint. Clearly, you have; otherwise, we would have

gotten lost numerous times. I must remember to write down the way before I forget what it was.

Gliint used the *Cheer Animation.*

Gliint's Text Box: Of course I know the way! Mr. Max taught me a song when we first came here.

Breaker used the *Smirk Animation.*
Oh, look—some idiots!

◈ Chapter 25 ◈

DOUBLED IN THE D (STRONGHOLD)

It was a quarter-cycle after dark, and the duo had finally given up. Lissa's *Uplifting Circlet (s)* had been found within just a few rounds, but after searching every chest in the area, they could not find an *Adamantium* head slot piece for Palcath. They had made it all the way to Level 41 while exploring. However, it was just too late now to continue and they had a big next cycle.

After setting up the *Portie Tent* for Lissa, Palcath stayed outside for a few rounds to update his Player Pager, and to check on the others. Roodg was with Anders—Palcath had not seen that one coming—but that was really as much as he could get out of any of them. It wasn't surprising that Fourni hadn't updated, but it was that Mr. Max hadn't. Lissa impatiently came outside and motioned for the dwarf to hurry his butt up.

> Lissa's Text Box: Okay, I know we made a pact and all, but I think if I am going to take on that Gigas next cycle, I will need to see you in the skirt. I want my last memory to be hilarious.

> Palcath's Text Box: Maybe I will lend you the skirt, but just for now. You were great to try to help me find my last piece, lass. But, to be honest, the Helmets are always my least favourite part of the outfits, and I would rather not even wear one.

> Lissa's Text Box: I was only helping to get more experience points, but you are welcome.

> Palcath's Text Box: Okay, lass. Let's trade these fancy (s) outfits and try them on.

> Lissa's Text Box: Great! I couldn't really wait any longer. I want the skirt. These old clothes are so drab.

The two avatars first handed each other the Armour set that they had found in chests, due to strange game logic, and moved to opposite sides of the *Portie Tent*. They got changed in private, even though changing Armour didn't show anything, since the models just swapped out. Perhaps it was just to make the reveal more exciting. Plus, Palcath insisted that it was for modesty.

> Lissa's Text Box: #OhMy!

> Palcath's Text Box: Wow.

The two met in the middle of the *Portie Tent*.

> Lissa's Text Box: The (s) doesn't stand for swank at all! It stands for slu—

> Palcath's Interruption Text Box: Sexy! Look at you in that outfit! Not a healing standard outfit at all! You are hot, lass!

The *Uplifting* outfit was not what Lissa had expected. The *Uplifting Circlet (s)* was pretty standard *Circlet* affair, with a bright pink gem in the centre, but that was where the similarities ended. The rest of it was making her blush about the same colour as the gem, which was *Blush Shade #3*.

The *Uplifting Blouse (s)* was very uplifting, but it should have been called an *Uplifting Corset (xxx)*. It was jet black and in three sections, two split in the sides and one in the back. Bright pink laces up either section ended at the top in lace bows, but her skin was visible underneath. It was definitely uplifting her, and her new cleavage was much more than she had thought she possessed.

See-through light pink fabric made up the *Uplifting Sleeves (s)*. They were long and covered Lissa's hands completely, but they stopped covering at the shoulders, probably to give the blouse full access to that area. Only a thin strip joined the sleeves together in the back where they were tied with a black bow.

Lissa was a good four height units taller in the *Uplifting Boots (s)*, which went up well past her knees. They were shiny black leather and tied up with pink laces on the sides. Her *Uplifting Skirt (s)* was not standard issue length. It was multiple shades of purple and just barely covered up the essentials, while the see-through purple trim and bows really did nothing to help. Palcath was very glad right now that he was a dwarf and closer to the ground for a slightly lower camera angle.

Lissa composed herself. She was badass and strict in the outfit. She shrugged off being embarrassed and decided instead to own the look, even if it was pinker than she would have liked.

> Lissa's Text Box: Well, it wouldn't have been my first choice. Not nearly enough of my perfect skin is showing.

> Palcath's Text Box: You didn't suit that standard stuff anyway, lass. I think this works better for you. Some of it is even purple—not a lot of it, that is a pretty short skirt, and … uh … what was I walking about? Talking! I mean talking.

> Lissa's Text Box: I think you did suit the standard stuff better, but it isn't horrible. I would maybe even consider saying the (s) stands for svelte, if given a big enough bribe.

Palcath had been so smitten with Lissa's outfit that he had completely forgotten to check out his own. He gave himself a once over and was pretty impressed.

The *Adamantium Armour (s)* was almost what he had expected. Plates of Adamantium covered vital areas and were outlined in nice black chainmail trim. Places such as his shield arm, feet, neck, one pectoral, and his dwarfy bits were covered in a nifty Armour spiral that started at his feet and went upward. But, besides these small plates and their interesting trim, the outfit had forgotten to put any material on.

> Palcath's Text Box: It isn't horrible … but how is this supposed to defend me better than what I was wearing before? There is hardly any Armour even here!

> Lissa's Text Box: I suspect that the laws of Chainmail Bikinis are in full effect. It is refreshing that a man is showing off way more than I am—and, honestly, I am showing a lot. #GirlsBeatBoys!

It was Palcath's turn to change to a *Blush Shade*, but unlike Lissa, he didn't hide it well.

> Palcath's Text Box: Well, uh *cough* Dwarves do get a Constitution bonus after all, lass.

> Lissa's Text Box: It's getting late. We should probably recover Health and Mana. Tomorrow is a big cycle for the fine forces of sexy justice! Also, I guess you will be there.

> Palcath's Text Box: Until next cycle, lass!

Nestled in his bed, Palcath stared at the ceiling of the *Portie Tent* for a few rounds before closing his eyes. They promptly opened again when a map-shattering snore escaped from his "delicate lass" companion. He used a *Smile Animation* and closed his eyes again.

~ ~ ~

After a few rounds experimenting with the *Combi-Fusion Pot* that Anders had foolishly left behind in the *Portie Tent*, Lissa decided it was time to advance the story. Palcath closed the *Portie Tent* with the pull cord and stuffed it into his newly *Combi-Fused Ultra-Mega-Pack*, and they were off. After only a few turns, they were standing by the double doors.

> Palcath's Text Box: I wish that Mr. Max lad wasn't so nice about spoilers. I want to know what is in there before we try, lass.

> Lissa's Text Box: I would have liked for the big meathead to have told us while he had the chance, instead of standing in front of all those reflective surfaces flexing. I am still mad at him for stealing my big introduction.

> Palcath's Text Box: Well, should we try, Fair Maiden? Stay close to me, and I'll protect you.

> Lissa's Text Box: Let's give it our best, Sir Knight. Stay close to me, and I'll protect you.

The double doors of D opened, and the pair went inside.

> Lissa's Text Box: Wow. This place #SoFuckedUp.

> Palcath's Text Box: I agree, lass. It is so fucked up.

They were on top of a mountain; half of the mountain was a smouldering volcano, with oozing lava, black smoke, and ash. Heat was radiating from that half of the room, and the sky was dark and full of blood-red clouds. The other side had rain pouring down everywhere from thick storm clouds above. Lightning flashed and thunder boomed nearly constantly. The air on that side was charged and caused their hair to stand on end. While the two areas never merged properly, it was evident that the mountain was the same model underneath all the drastically different effects.

> Lissa's Text Box: I will admit it. I'm confused.

The duo took one step up the mountain. Immediately reacting, the different skies parted, and two Gigases descended dramatically to the ground with a *Descend Dramatically to the Ground Animation.*

> The Fire and Wind Gigases' Simultaneous Text Boxes: We are the twin Gigases of Fire and Wind, here to challenge you avatars for supremacy over the....

The Gigas twins looked down at the Defender and the Mendicator and stopped mid-sentence with an expression of confusion stamped on their faces. That wasn't a standard animation in the slightest.

> Palcath's Text Box: Oh, crap.

> Lissa's Text Box: What?

> Palcath's Text Box: I just noticed. This Armour has a Crystal Slot to increase elemental resistance, and I loaned my banana *Wind Crystal* to Roodg.

> Lissa's Text Box: Crap!

> Palcath's Text Box: What?

> Lissa's Text Box: I have a Crystal Slot as well, but I have only an *Ice Crystal* that tastes like oranges.

> Palcath's Text Box: Well, that isn't going to help us either, lass. Oh, well.

> Lissa's Text Box: It is a shame, really. Well, now that we know what is here, should we leave and come back with the right buffs?

> Palcath's Text Box: Why haven't they finished their sentence yet, lass? Are they on pain medication or something?

> Lissa's Text Box: Don't worry about it, #AllGood. Let's go. I think I remember a recipe in Loverboy's *Combi-Fusion Pot* for some Wind Resistance items.

Palcath reviewed the Battle Logs and thought for a few rounds.

> Palcath's Text Box: This whole thing is odd. I'm going to find out why, lass!

> Lissa's Text Box: No, don't talk to th—

> Palcath's Interruption Text Box: Okay, Gigass ... Gigases ... Gigasi ... whatever. First of all, why would the Wind and Fire Gigases be twins? It should be Fire and Ice, or Wind and Earth! Not one from either group. Besides, you are hardly twins; you look nothing alike! You are not even on the right damn sides of the area! It should be Fire with volcano, Wind with lightning. What is wrong with you?

> Lissa's Text Box: Idiot! Couldn't just leave well enough alone, huh?

Now they are going to unfreeze and attack us!

Palcath's Text Box: Well, just look at them, lass! They are so mixed up. I couldn't just stand by idly.

Lissa's Text Box: Yes, you could have!

The Fire and Wind Gigases' Simultaneous Text Boxes: ...Mountain? Wait, what? Uh ... well, we are fraternal twins, we think.

The Fire Gigas' Text Box: Right, Sis? At least ... I think we are. We don't look anything alike.

The Fire Gigas was twice as tall as a human. He was very muscular and had glowing orange tattoos covering his body. The custom fire tattoos were genuinely hot to the touch. He had large, curled goat horns and rugged black hair that matched his pointy goatee. Only a miniscule singed black loincloth covered his red skin. An aura of fire surrounded him as he floated in the air. The Fire Gigas was both menacing and confused.

The Wind Gigas' Text Box: You're right. I always wondered that, Brother. I always assumed we were at the very least related.

The Wind Gigas was only slightly shorter than her supposed twin brother. She had seafoam-green skin and was wearing gold ornaments covering only her essentials. Her bright yellow hair was tied up in two braids that extended past her feet. An aura of electricity surrounded her as she floated in place. The Wind Gigas was both powerful and confused.

The Fire Gigas' Text Box: We really should ask one of the Administrators after we fight these 100 avatars, probable-sister, and find out for certain if we are related.

The Wind Gigas' Text Box: True, I like that plan, possible-brother. But, there aren't 100 of them, there are only 2. We shouldn't even have spawned right now anyway.

The Fire Gigas' Text Box: That is odd indeed. What shall we do?

The Wind Gigas' Text Box: I don't know. Two avatars hardly seem like a challenge.

Lissa used a *Shh Animation* directed at Palcath.

Lissa's Whisper Text Box: Quiet, dwarf. I can still save this. I have a plan.

Lissa's Text Box: The reason that you spawned was that we were sent here by the Administrators to answer those exact questions you are talking about right now! You just need to shut up and listen.

The Fire Gigas' Text Box: Oh, that is perfect! Please tell us.

The Wind Gigas' Text Box: Yes, please do!

Lissa's Text Box: You are twins and related. #HolidayMiracle! They switched the models out last moment to give you these better ones because the original models were not cool enough. Now look at you both; how cool are you?

Palcath's Text Box: It is the start of the summer. How could it be a holiday miracle? I mean … yes! And they switched elements at the very last moment as well even though it doesn—

Lissa's Interruption Text Box: Quiet, dwarf! You've done enough already.

The Fire Gigas' Text Box: Really? Well, that makes sense. We both have pretty badass models.

The Wind Gigas' Text Box: I know, right? I am so badass! All sparky and junk.

The Fire Gigas' Text Box: You know what? We should thank these two for helping us solve the problem that they themselves created.

The Wind Gigas' Text Box: Perfect idea! Let's thank these two properly for helping us. What should we do?

The Fire Gigas' Text Box: Let's give them the Gigas drops. We have hundreds of the things anyway in the cellar. I want more room to do my paintings.

The Wind Gigas' Text Box: Excellent idea! Let's do that. I want more space to do my pottery!

The twins floated closer to the duo. They were ready to hand over something to the pair and had gotten their *Hand Something to Someone Else Dual Animations* primed.

Lissa's Text Box: Sweet! #NailedIt!

About three move units away from the grounded pair, the floating pair halted. They were looking over the pair more closely now, especially at all the skin and near-glimpses of naughty bits. Their auras flickered for a round, and both twins grinned.

> Fire Gigas' Text Box: Yes, let's 'thank' these two 'properly.'

> Palcath's Text Box: Lass, I don't like the quotation marks he made around the words 'thank' and 'properly.'

The Fire Gigas erupted into burning flame, and with an intense blast of heat, his loincloth was burnt into a cinder. Underneath was his Gigas penis. It wasn't the size of it that was alarming; it was a modest appendage, given the size of the creature. The alarming fact was that the entire thing was on fire.

> Palcath's Text Box: Crap! Where is Anders when you need him?

The Wind Gigas' golden straps retracted in a swift motion and revealed her special attacks. Her nipples were sparkling tesla coils, and her ladyness was sucking in air at an alarming rate. A loud whistling could be heard emanating from within.

> Lissa's Text Box: Crap! Where is meathead when you need him?

After a few harsh rounds of defending, both Lissa and Palcath had been hurt pretty badly. Palcath decided that there was nothing fun about getting smacked in the face by a burning penis, while Lissa decided that getting zapped with electric nipples was not on her list of favourite things to do.

> Palcath and Lissa's Simultaneous Text Boxes: Okay FSaiirr MKaniidgehnt, we need to split up. I will take out the FWiirned Gigas. I know I can handle it better than you.

> Palcath and Lissa's Simultaneous Text Boxes: Pardon?

> Palcath and Lissa's Simultaneous Text Boxes: Stop talking when I'm talking dlwaasrsf. It makes the words all fmuecskseedd up.

> The Wind Gigas' Text Box: Splitting up isn't as kinky, Brother.

> The Fire Gigas' Text Box: True, Sis, but just in case we are related, let's take their advice again. I don't really think I am comfortable with incest.

> The Wind Gigas' Text Box: All right, I'll take this one. He will be fun until it breaks off.

> The Fire Gigas' Text Box: I'll take this one. She will burn up eventually, but I'll still have fun.

The Fire Gigas grabbed Lissa and took her into the stormy side of the mountain while the Wind Gigas dragged Palcath deeper into the burning side. Palcath complained bitterly that they went to the obviously wrong sides for their elements. Still, both avatars went willingly since they both had plans.

> Palcath's Text Box: Sorry about this, lass. I wish you didn't have to watch.

Palcath moved aside a small section of his *Adamantium Crotch Guard* and revealed himself. His penis was even harder than the mythical metal that had been hiding it. It was almost unnatural with an industrial metallic sheen. He activated *Vibrato Penis* and it began to vibrate on its own accord—it even had its own sound effect.

> Lissa's Text Box: An ace up your sleeve, huh? Well, you are not the only one with a sleeve, you know!

Lissa uplifted her *Uplifting Skirt* and revealed herself. Her privates were made of pure purple-coloured rubber, and an unnatural strange sheen covered her womanhood. She activated *Auto-Fuck Pussy* and it began to vibrate on its own accord, equipped with its own different sound effect.

The Twins were shocked and could only watch stunned as the plot developed around them.

> Palcath's Text Box: That is different, lass. What the heck does it do?

> Lissa's Text Box: It lets me beat my Gigas way the Flaming Pit faster than you can beat yours, lad!

> Palcath's Text Box: I don't know, lass. Mine has changeable speeds.

Turning his penis slightly, Palcath changed the speed of his erection from low, to medium, then to high. The buzzing increased rapidly with each, as did the sound effect.

> Lissa's Text Box: Big deal! Who doesn't have speed settings?

Lissa pressed her clitoral button and also turned her speed from low, to medium, then to high.

> Palcath's Text Box: That is nothing, lass. I can do this!

After activating *Pound*, Palcath's unit began to thrust by itself, like it was attached to a hidden piston. He was originally embarrassed by the situation, but trying to one-up Lissa was making his dwarf blood hot.

> Lissa's Text Box: That all you got, dwarf?

A new move called *Convulse* was activated by Lissa, and now her opening was convulsing by itself in a rhythmic fashion.

> Palcath's Text Box: I have different settings for both motions, lass. I also have an Ultra Speed setting!

> Lissa's Text Box: Naturally I can do that as well. Those were all pretty

much givens, though. Got anything else?

Palcath's Text Box: Well, mine is metal and conducts elements!

Lissa's Text Box: Mine is rubber and repels elements, big deal.

Palcath's Text Box: I guess we are pretty much an even match, lass.

Lissa's Text Box: Not even close. I do have one more thing that I know you don't have.

Palcath's Text Box: What, you do? No fair, lass, that was all of mine! What is it?

Lissa's Text Box: #Smirk. I know how to properly use mine.

Lissa gave the dwarf a *Grin Animation*.

Palcath's Text Box: Is that some sort of challenge, lass?

Lissa's Text Box: You are damn right it is, dwarf.

Palcath gave the half-elf a *Smirk Animation*.

Palcath's Text Box: All right, I know how to use this thing. Trust me.

Lissa's Text Box: Fine! Let's make it interesting. The first to finish off their twin gets all the Gold Pieces they drop.

Palcath's Text Box: What, all of it? Seriously, lass?

Lissa's Text Box: Scared or something?

Palcath's Text Box: Uh … no! Not even a little! In fact, that isn't enough, lass. The first to finish gets all of the random drop items we find until we get back to Coaloegrander!

Lissa's Text Box: That all? That isn't going big enough at all. The winner gets all of that other stuff and gets to be called the leader of the group!

Palcath's Text Box: But I am already the leader!

Lissa's Text Box: Of a group of three. There are five of us now (six, if you count meathead)! So, the rules have changed.

Palcath's Text Box: Fine, you are on!

Lissa's Text Box: No using *Ultra Speed* either! There is no skill in that!

> Palcath's Text Box: That goes without saying, lass.

> The Fire and Wind Gigases' Simultaneous Text Boxes: Actually, we changed our minds. You both are really freaking us out. Please, just take the drop items.

Both Palcath and Lissa ignored the comment and jumped into the air. They each tackled their floating twin with dangerous force. They wasted no time going to work on their respective twin. They each brought forth an intensity that the twins found extremely alarming (and on the high speed setting, no less). Palcath was immune to the sucking of the Wind Gigas' tunnel as he had promised, and was making very quick work of her. Lissa was immune to the flames of the Fire Gigas' member and was making him buck like a wild beast.

Buzzing from Palcath and whirring from Lissa filled the area and completely drowned out the annoying bagpipe music in the background. As their respective genitals worked into a blur, the heat and electricity in the air increased. Neither avatar took any notice as they pounded away. Their resistance to the extra damage stopped them from getting hurt, but it did not rid them of the magic energy building from the bosses that was now surrounding their bodies. Sparks were forming between Palcath and the Wind Gigas. Lissa and the Fire Gigas were now glowing a hot blue. Both avatars were preparing for their big finish, and neither wanted to lose. The entire combat area was now magically charged, and spouts of fire and electricity were arcing through the space. A thin line of energy eventually linked the conduction and reflected off the avatar's genitals, and a new frackling noise filled the air.

> Lissa and Palcath's Simultaneous Text Boxes: Behold my finishing move!

> The Fire and Wind Gigases' Simultaneous Text Boxes: No, wait! Don't!

The avatars ignored them, lifting up from their Gigases at the same instant and getting ready to do their signature finishing move—but neither expected what happened next.

The breaking of the Gigas link caused the conducted and reflected elemental damage that had been piling up from the two pairs of linked crotches to release all at once. When the two seperate links collided a huge eruption of both fire and electricity burst through and combined into one large *Firelectrical* attack. The explosion was exacerbated by the ambient flame and voltage of the mountain room. When the effect storm finally broke, the mountain was a smoldering crater and both avatars were flat on their asses. The Twin Gigases were nowhere to be seen. Only a burnt goatee and half a sparking braid remained, but their drop items were smoking in the wreckage. They had probably been defeated.

A stunned Palcath, hair standing all on end, picked up his drop. A speechless, only slightly charred Lissa picked up hers.

> Palcath's Text Box: Ouch. What in the Flaming Pit just happened, lass?

> Lissa's Text Box: I'll tell you what happened ... we tied.

They had become Level 45 after the encounter and were both given a chance to write Additional Comments in the Insta-Wiki. Once they could finally stand, they took the opportunity to do just that.

> **Creature Name:** Wind Gigas
> **Class:** Gigas D
> **Level:** 98 (Requires 100 avatars to be present to spawn)
> **Special Attacks:** Gigas Shock, Gigas Storm, Gigas Electrode, Gigas Lightning, Gigas Blast, Gigas D
> **Drops:** *Wind Gigas Helm* (only for avatar that gets last strike)
> **First Player Encounter Notes:** Typical! A busty female monster designed for all the little adolescent males to ogle! Stop objectifying women! – Hippolyta
> **Additional Comments:** Just hit her with your hammer as fast as you can. She is a pushover. – Palcath

> **Creature Name:** Fire Gigas
> **Class:** Gigas E
> **Level:** 98 (Requires 100 avatars to be present to spawn)
> **Special Attacks:** Gigas Burn, Gigas Incinerate, Gigas Flame, Gigas Fire, Gigas Blast, Gigas E
> **Drops:** *Fire Gigas Choker* (only for avatar that gets last strike)
> **First Player Encounter Notes:** He has beaucoup d'attack. Sure to be the prepared for all that can be happening. – Jorthan The Male Troll Warrior
> **Additional Comments:** Have fire resistance active, and he will never see you coming. – Lissa

The dwarf got ready to try on his prize, but now that his blood had cooled somewhat, there was something in the back of his mind troubling him. He needed to ask.

> Palcath's Text Box: Lass, we just sort of had ... unprotected sex back there. Shouldn't you be worried?

> Lissa's Text Box: About what? Catching a computer virus or something? We are in a game, remember?

> Palcath's Text Box: No, not that, lass. I know that. I was wondering more about ... well ... you maybe.

Lissa's Text Box: Oh. You mean like getting pregnant? No, that isn't going to happen. I totally turned off my pregnancy settings in the Options Page.

Palcath's Text Box: You can do that, lass? You're right. There it is. Why do I have that? I can't get pregnant.

Lissa gave Palcath an *Incredulous Look Animation*, which caused Palcath to *Shiver Animation*.

Palcath's Text Box: You're right, lass. Better safe than sorry!

Palcath put that terrible thought out of his mind and tried on his brand new *Wind Gigas Helmet*. Liquid metal ran up one side of his face and ended in large spikes, which he quickly changed to yellow. A small visor with white writing and symbols covered his left eye. Only the dwarf was close enough to read it.

Palcath's Text Box: Finally, lass, a badass helmet I like the model of. It also gives me … an *Expanded Battle Log*?! Are you fucking kidding me?

Lissa's Text Box: The Flaming Pit? I can't find mine. Oh, it's an accessory. There are only five Armour equipment slots after all. I guess someone had to #GetBoned.

Lissa tried on the *Fire Gigas Choker*. It had a liquid metal strap and a jewel which she instantly changed to purple. It had a little bit of fancy metalwork in the front that fell on her cleavage with a (now) purple gem right in the centre.

Lissa's Text Box: Mine increases all my stats by 50! Plus, it gives me an ability called *Burnfire* which can increase my resistances once a cycle.

Palcath's Text Box: Nobody won our other contest, but you are the clear winner of style. Yours is stunning and has a more useful ability.

Lissa's Text Box: We tied! Don't be jealous of the necklace! We can get you one if you want. Let's just go outside and come back to respawn them. I will cast *Fire Resistance +50* on you. All you would have to do is take a red hot, flaming Fire Gigas' cock up your dwarf chute, and then—Bam! Just like that, you have one!

Palcath changed to *Blush Shade #5*.

Palcath's Text Box: It looks better on you.

Lissa's Text Box: Well, what now, Sir Lad? We probably have four pieces of Gigas Gear now, unless Loverboy or meatbasket got himself split in half or drained respectively.

Palcath's Text Box: We should continue with our plan, lass. We can be back in Cundersplunter by the end of the cycle or sooner.

Lissa's Text Box: Agreed. Let's update our Player Pagers so they know to meet up with us in Chillerrillerdon.

The rest of the trip back to whatever that starting city was called went by uneventfully, and they pitched the *Portie Tent* next to a calm river off the main path to wait for the rest of their party. Lissa decided that, since they had tied, they had to split everything. Palcath decided that he was okay with being the joint leader, but only if it was with Lissa. Lissa retired into the *Portie Tent* while Palcath sat outside, pretended to smoke a pipe as he reflected on the past few cycles.

When he entered the *Portie Tent* a few rounds later, Palcath instantly noticed that the Purple Sleeping Area had been switched with the Blue Sleeping Area. There was all the same stuff in the Blue Area, but it had just been thrown haphazardly about. Remembering how many rounds it had taken Fourni to place those specific items there, Palcath knew that the obsessive-compulsive human would be upset. Palcath, however, was not upset in the least—now the Purple Sleeping Area was right beside his. Lissa was sitting on her newly liberated bed, uncharacteristically grinning happily claiming that the joint leaders needed to have the best spots in the *Portie Tent*. Palcath just used the *Smile Animation* and said nothing.

◈ Chapter 26 ◈
CRAMMED IN THE C
(STRONGHOLD)

Nine vials of *Minotaur Musk*. That was how much Anders collected off himself. Reviewing the Battle Log, he knew there should have been eleven, but he simply couldn't find any more (no matter how hard he checked). The *Musk's* description said it had a physical effect that could relax anything, but the Insta-Wiki also said it was a *Combi-Fusion* item only. Anders knew that wasn't the case under these broken rules. As for the *Absorbing Cloth*, it had given up and became an *Absorbed Cloth* long ago. His *Initiate's Jacket* was also extremely worse for wear.

> Roodg's Text Box: wELL GO OPEN YOUR CHESTS!

Anders treaded carefully to avoid waking any of the sleeping Minotaurs and made his way up the stone stairs. Inside were a *Hard Leaf Vest (s)*, *Hard Leaf Pants (s)*, and *Hard Leaf Gloves (s)*. He was really happy to discover in the last chest a *Hard Leaf Helmet (s)*, as he still didn't have a helmet yet. Getting *Hard Leaf Boots (s)* would have sucked.

> Anders' Text Box: Come on, we shouldn't linger here too long. I don't want them to wake up.

> Roodg's Text Box: wHY NOT? wE GOT DOUBLE XP FOR MOST OF THEM! lEVEL 42 NOW! jOY!

> Anders' Text Box: I want to get out of this Anti-Magic Zone before we try this stuff on. Plus, it is getting pretty late, and we need to get

> some rest.

> Roodg's Text Box: k

Leaving the Chamber of Otau and the Anti-Magic Zone behind, the unlikely pair came into a clearing and before a set of double doors. It was monster-free and a likely place to set up camp. Anders had just finished the *Campfire Making Animation* as Roodg finished updating his, or her, Player Pager. When Anders was pretty sure Roodg wasn't watching—it was hard under that Cowl to really know where he, or she, was looking— he sheepishly stuck a finger in himself and was strangely relieved to feel all goopy again.

> Roodg's Text Box: i CAN'T WAIT ANYMORE! i NEED TO SEE IT!

Anders watched as Roodg began to rummage through their disorganized *Backpack*. Anders thought that it probably wouldn't have hurt the Magic Mage to do the organize menu option inside it. Nothing was in alphabetical order at all.

> Roodg's Text Box: tHESE *bLACK cASTER gLOVES (S)* ARE WICKED! sO MANY NEAT THINGS ON THEM! i ♥ THE TRIM, iT IS ALL RED!

Anders watched as the new *Black Caster Gloves (s)* popped onto Roodg's hands. They looked completely identical to the previous pair from what he could see of them, which wasn't a lot because of the avatar's *Navy Robes*. The only thing Anders could see were the fingertips anyway, and they were black now.

This repeated with the *Black Caster Boots (s)*, which Anders could see change slightly, losing the points at the very ends. Since the robes covered up most of them anyway, he couldn't really tell the difference, but Roodg claimed they were aBSOLUTELY WICKED.

The *Black Caster Pants (s)* were even less dramatic. Anders couldn't have seen those even if he flipped Roodg upside down and shook. Roodg again claimed these were uNIQUE and nEAT as well as sEXY!

Finally, with the *Black Casting Cowl (s)*, there was a visible change. It did resemble the *Navy Cowl*, but it was black and had some interesting red patterns and silver doodads on the trim. Half of this *Cowl* had been pushed to the side, you could see a silhouette of half of the Avatar's face, and now a thick tuft of long white hair from an unknown *# Hairstyle* stuck out. A single piercing *#36 Eye* could be seen shining at Anders from under the *Cowl*. Anders hadn't thought anyone would ever pick *#36 Eyes*. He had never seen them on an avatar before. They were the last on the list and were genuinely freaky. The iris was so thin that their colour was impossible to tell, and the pupil was small, beady and piercing. The eye was mostly white space, and it made Anders nervous to look back at it. Roodg used the *Grin Animation*, and Anders saw a flash of pearly whites.

> Roodg's Text Box: hOLY CRAP! i CAN SEE MY FACE AND HAIR!

> i HAVEN'T SEEN THOSE SINCE LEVEL 2! tHE (S) DOES STAND FOR sAWESOME!

Anders thought "face" was a bit of an overstatement; he still couldn't see the skin colour of the mage, or even guess at the race or gender. The *Cowl* and what he could see of the gloves and boots did have a nice model, though, and Roodg was very proud of them.

> Anders' Text Box: They do look pretty Sawesome to me!

Roodg put on the new *Caster's Ring*, which Anders couldn't see. That didn't stop Roodg from informing him of how nEAT it was. Roodg equipped the *Overkill Staff*. With all the needless spiky baubles and flashing things all over it, it certainly lived up to its name.

> Roodg's Text Box: sO COOL! tHE MODEL IS SO NICE. lOOK AT HOW MUCH EXTRA USELESS CRAP IT HAS!

Trust the Magic Mage to like something called the *Overkill* anything.

> Roodg's Text Box: tRY ON YOURS NOW! i WANNA SEE IT!

Anders knew that the (s) would probably still stand for slutty, but he remained optimistic as he started to put the equipment on. It was sort of unfair that the magic user's (s) equipment covered so much, but Anders double backed on his thought. That might not be true. He couldn't see any of them besides the cowl, so for all he knew, the pants could be ass-less chaps.

The *Hard Leaf Gloves (s)* really were more like bracers than gloves. Thick, hardy leaves covered the lower portions of his arms, with one big leaf resting in the middle. A few extra stray green leaves also covered his upper arms. All in all, they really were not that bad.

As soon as Anders put on the *Hard Leaf Gloves (s)*, his *Trueshot Bow+* and *Truestrike Sword+* started to glow. He didn't even have time to react before they flew up and exploded in a very loud pop. Before Anders could even swear with a random kind of baked good, a brand new bow and sword were in their place. Given their ridiculous embellishments, they had to be *Overkill* weapons—they had even more useless bits of junk than Roodg's new *Overkill Casting Staff*. When he checked them, he saw they were indeed *Overkill+es*. They hadn't increased in awesomeness, though. They were exactly the same, but seeing as how they had been levelling up with him, he couldn't really complain.

> Roodg's Text Box: aUTO uPDATING wEAPONS? nO FAIR! hOW DID YOU GET THAT?

Anders turned his weapons around in his hands, confused. He honestly had no idea how he got that, and it *was* a little bit unfair (not that he was going to report it as a bug).

He noticed something on the weapons that he had not seen before. Instead of nothing, which was normal, his weapons had monogrammed "T"s in the jeweled embellishments. He had two weapons that were two "T"s. These were far more special gifts from The Titan than Anders had originally known. They were weapons to last a whole play-time. Anders thought that these weapons were now "T"otally … uh … grea"T"!

> Anders' Text Box: I got them from The Titan. They are for Anderses only. I didn't know that they would upgrade, though!

> Roodg's Text Box: i KNEW YOU HAD BOTH FOR A REASON. i SHOULD HAVE SPANKED THAT tITAN WHILE i HAD THE CHANCE! bUT ON THE BUTT.

Anders tried on the *Hard Leaf Helmet (s)*. The word "helmet" was a definite overstatement. A single large leaf was now plastered on his forehead, pointing upward. It did provide a significant bonus to his stats, even if it was a little bit odd sitting there all alone.

Now it was the time of truth. Anders pulled on the *Hard Leaf Vest (s)*. Thick, hardy leaves covered up a portion of his upper body, but not much. It was like someone had started to make this vest, got bored halfway, and just stopped. It was full near the neck and shoulders, but quickly stopped after that. Two bigger leaves stood out, coming down from his neck and just covering his nipples. A few stray leaves dotted the rest of his torso, giving the impression that he had rolled in some foliage awhile ago. This did cover up more than the *Mithral Vest (s)* though; at least his nipples were hidden now. Anders took that as a win.

The final test was the *Hard Leaf Pants (s)*, and Anders nervously put them on. These were made by the same lazy tailor as the vest. Many leaves started near his waist, but quickly tapered out. The outside of his legs were now covered almost to the boots, but the insides of his legs were still pretty much bare. A larger leaf covered up his privates pretty well, and little leaves completely covered his butt. Anders checked over his butt closer and noticed it did look bigger and perkier than he remembered it being from character creation. He had thought it was just a trick of the ass-hugging *Mithral Pants (s)*, but everyone was right. He did have a perky bubble butt of holding. While a sharp gust of wind would probably expose everything, these leaves at least covered him up more than the *Mithral* had.

The leaves felt a lot like leather, and were not a bit unpleasant rubbing against his skin. Anders decided that these were nicer, even if they weren't covered in neat accents and gems like his old Armour was. Anders enjoyed the nice extra bonus which was that these were really green, and green was wonderful.

> Roodg's Text Box: u LOOK LIKE A SEXY DANGEROUS PIXIE! aLL READY TO KICK ASS. lOOK HOW CUTE YOUR ELFBUTT OF HOLDING IS IN THOSE!

Anders thanked the Magic Mage because he was pretty sure that was a compliment, and the duo settled down to sleep for the nighttime portion of the cycle.

> Anders' Text Box: I wish I could make more *Health Potions*, but I left my stupid *Combi-Fusion Pot* in the *Portie Tent*.

> Roodg's Text Box: u CAN MAKE THOSE? i'M ALL OUT OF POTIONS EXCEPT THE BROKEN UPSIDE-DOWN SOUNDING ONE, AND i AM NOT TRYING IT.

> Anders' Text Box: Well, what does the *Portable Anvil* do?

> Roodg's Text Box: i FORGOT ALL ABOUT THAT!

The *Portable Anvil* menu was as sleek as the *Combi-Fusion* one, except a bit frayed around the edges. From the instructions on the menu, you could drop in a piece of Armour with a combination of monster drop items and upgrade the Armour. They both tested everything they had on, but only Roodg's *Navy Robes* were upgradable (along with some of their old outdated gear they didn't care about).

> Roodg's Text Box: i DON'T HAVE ANY mOLTEN bLUE lIZARD sKINS 2 TRY THIS OUT WITH.

> Anders' Text Box: Hey, I do! I want to see what happens!

Roodg switched back into the old *Crimson Robes* for a moment. After a few rounds and a few *Molten Blue Lizards Skins*, the *Portable Anvil* dinged. Out came the newly forged *Navy Robes (s)*. Roodg quickly switched back into them. They were much more form-fitting and trimmed delicately in a light sky blue. Now with the bottom hem only coming down to the avatars' thigh, the *Black Caster Pants (s)* and *Shoes (s)* were visible. They certainly were as interesting and bobbled as the *Black Castor Cowl (s)* had been. The new *Navy Robes (s)* also was a bit lower cut and had barely any sleeves to speak of, showing off the arm-length *Black Caster Gloves (s)* and even some cleavage.

Wait, Anders thought, *is that cleavage?*

Anders was surprised that, even in this new, nearly skin-tight set of robes, the avatar's skin was still completely covered up by other Armour pieces, giving no indication of what colour it really was. The form-fitting robes also confused Anders because even in their skin-tight glory and lower-cut top, he still had absolutely no idea what gender this avatar was. Having the skin-tight outfit actually made Roodg more confusing, which was very confusing, to the poor confused Anders.

> Roodg's Text Box: i TOLD U THEY WERE ALL sAWESOME!

> Anders' Text Box: Muffins! Look at you now ... all ... being you and stuff.

> Roodg's Text Box: LoL! mUFFINS!

> Anders' Text Box: So, this *Portable Anvil* turns perfectly normal equipment into (s) equipment? How is that useful?

> Roodg's Text Box: cAUSE (S) EQUIPMENT IS MORE sAWESOME!

> Anders' Text Box: Good point.

> Roodg's Text Box: i'M sAWESOME NOW 2! tIME TO DIE gIGAS!

With only that split turn of warning, the Magic Mage entered the double doors and was gone. Anders had no choice but to follow.

The first thing that Anders noticed was that this place was dark. Very dark. Anders guessed that a *Dark More More* spell had been cast in here, and he bumped right into Roodg, who had stopped walking at some point.

> Roodg's Text Box: sO DARK!

> Anders' Text Box: You do know that we forgot to rest and recover!

> Roodg's Text Box: oH YEAH! …zzz

> Anders' Text Box: Really? Right here?

> Roodg's Text Box: sHHHH! sLEEPING!

~ ~ ~

Once they woke up, they proceeded into the hall. A very faint purple light started to glow in the distance, dozens of move units away. The pair really had no other option but to stumble forward as it lured them on. Once they were a single round's walk from it, the light shone with an amazing intensity, and they were forced to close their eyes—or their only visible #36 freaky eye as applicable.

When they opened them, an airborne Gigas flew before them. She was a member of the She-Demon subclass. Anders knew instantly that she was a Succubus, even though he had never met one before. She followed the acceptable limit of normal female monster Armour, and was therefore wearing barely anything at all. Only a few small strips of black leather were covering up the very busty She-Demon's milk white skin. Her breasts were (Anders changed to *Blush Shade #6* while describing them in his head) really big and really bouncy. Flowing atop her head was long, purple hair that was intricately styled. It was important to her and was very well maintained, accented with two small, cute horns.

> The Dark Gigas' Text Box: Cower before me, avatars, for it is I, the Gigas of Darkness, here to challenge you to mortal…

The Gigas began to just hover there midair and drool in the general direction of the avatar pair.

> Roodg's Text Box: mORTAL WHAT?

> Anders' Text Box: No, don't talk to her!

It was too late, however, and the Dark Gigas snapped out of it and continued the speech.

> The Dark Gigas' Text Box: Mortal battle? … Where is everyone else? I am supposed to *Dark Blast* all the little ones first!

> Anders' Text Box: It is just us two. We are here to, um…?

> Roodg's Text Box: 2 CHECK YOUR SEXY gIGAS DROP! yEAH. tHE aDMINS SENT US BECAUSE THERE HAVE BEEN COMPLAINTS ABOUT HOW GOOD AND SEXY IT IS. dROP 1 SO WE CAN LOOK AT IT! iT IS TOO AWESOME THEY SAID.

> The Dark Gigas' Text Box: Understandable, really, my drop is pretty much the best of the bunch. It was the other Gigases that complained, wasn't it? You can tell me, little pet!

The Dark Gigas simply took out her drop and placed it on the ground.

> Anders' Text Box: Nice one, Roodg, now whatever you do, stay back. Do not go clos—

> Roodg's Interruption Text Box: sWEET! iT'S AN ARMOUR!

Roodg ran up without listening and picked up the *Dark Gigas Armour*.

The Dark Gigas got a closer look at the avatar, and her wings skipped exactly 1.2 beats. She used the *Smirk Animation*, twirling her She-Demon tail in a long finger-nailed hand.

> The Dark Gigas' Text Box: Oh, I see how this is. The Administrators sent you to really test me. Really, really, really, really, really test me. All of me in my glorious splendor!

Anders didn't like reading of all of those "really"s. With only a single touch of her barely-there Armour, the entire thing fell off, and the Succubus was completely naked. Her oversized breasts bouncing loose would have excited many a spectator, had 100 avatars been here. She began to rub her netherworldregions with two manicure-tipped claws. Her netherworldregions were really odd in appearance to Anders. He admitted that he really hadn't seen many of those in his day, but this one just looked different. What he guessed was her button was very swollen as she teased herself, and with a final flick of her claw, Anders found out why.

An impressive demon penis with attached balls sprang up suddenly from the She-Demon's crotch. Her clitoris was in reality also a full, throbbing penis. This Succubus was an Incubus (Anders had not met one of those before, either). Anders considered it more carefully. No, this demon still had her lady parts as well, so this was a Sincubus (Anders made that last word up).

> The Dark Gigas' Text Box: Now, let's get you … boys? Boy and girl? Whatever, I am the last one who would ever judge that kind of thing. Let's get you ready!

A very fast slash of The Dark Gigas' tail in a move called *Gigas Sunder* ran through her opponents. Anders cried out in alarm but didn't get hit. This move ignored break-proof Armour. Roodg, however, still had some breakable Armour, the *Navy Robe (s)*. Roodg hung in the air for a turn as dark strands of ribbons sprung forth from the tail again, slicing the avatar all over. The next round, the *Navy Robe (s)* shattered into a million little navy pieces, and Anders shielded his eyes from the polygon fragments.

> Anders' Text Box: Roodg, are you okay?

> Roodg's Text Box: i GOT THIS 1! so PERFECT! u STAY BACK & SAVE YOUR CUTE MAGIC ELF BUTT OF HOLDING FOR LATER!

> The Dark Gigas' Text Box: How did you get those?

Anders shook the pixels off his eyes and opened them. What Anders saw would have made him fall to the floor, if not for his *Steadfast* ability. Roodg's actual skin was a dark charcoal colour, nearly identical to the *Black Casting Equipment*. Anders had been seeing it all along but had just thought it was more cloth. That meant that Roodg was a night elf. Anders hadn't picked that race because he thought night elf Night Ranger sounded exceptionally silly.

Anders' secret thought earlier had been accurate; those *Black Caster Pants (s)* were indeed ass-less chaps. More important than ass-less chaps, though, Roodg's torso was completely naked now, and Anders still had no idea what gender he was seeing. Roodg was actually not as skinny as possible for an avatar as Anders had thought all this time. In fact Roodg was actually *Body Style #4 (Average)*. Night elves were just had exceptionally skinny models even by idealistic video game standards. A *Body Sytle #1 (Slim)* night elf would probably snap in half during a camera pan. The now meatier, but still impossibly slim, Roodg had neither an absolute male nor female shape. On Roodg's chest were very flat, but still very there, breasts. From the avatar's crotch sprang up a fully erect and modest penis, and two testicles hung down close to the avatar's body. Under that male display, there was a fully functional vagina.

Anders finally understood that this had been what Roodg had meant when they'd said the Code made them "Sawesome," but no one had known what in the Flaming Pit they were talking about. Anders had no idea which sex Roodg had started out as originally, but at this point the avatar was clearly a both.

For this battle, there was simply no avatar better. Anders stayed back to protect his magical elf butt of holding as instructed.

> Anders' Text Box: Go get him/her, tiger/tigress!

The multi-sexed avatar used the *Smile Animation* at Anders (Anders saw the flash of white teeth) and turned to her ... his ... its ... prey. As instructed, Roodg tiger-pounced at the Dark Gigas and deftly tacked him ... her ... it to the ground with an audible thud.

Anders had a strange problem. He had no idea what personal pronouns to use to describe either side of this encounter. "It" would probably work, but it just didn't seem proper to call someone an "it". The Dark Gigas could probably be an "it" as there was only Code involved and no feelings to be stepped on, but Roodg was a real avatar. Maybe "they" and "their" would work, but those still were a little impersonal. Anders thought about taking a round to look up the proper genderless personal pronouns, but he realised that he would miss watching this once-in-a-lifetime opportunity of a battle. Even with the lady bits involved, it was going to be something to see. Pronouns could wait; he would just make do as best as he could with proper names or nicknames for now, even if his thoughts got a bit clunky.

The Sincubus had quickly gained interest in the similarly gendered avatar. While both had barely started to do anything yet, they were already making enough noise to drown out the upbeat (but still sinister sounding) lute music. Roodg was on top of the Sincubus, and they were both kissing each other with a definite sense of urgency. *Black Caster Gloved (s)* hands, clawed She/He-Demon hands, and something Anders didn't expect were feeling the other all over sensually. Anders was surprised that the Sincubus' tail was prehensile (and more than a bit lewd)—and it was also feeling Roodg all over.

During the round in which Roodg was buried face first and deep within the Dark Gigas' ample-sized love pillows, the tail grabbed Roodg tightly. The tail was wrapped around the Magic Mage who was lifted up in the air. Anders got ready to step in to help, but seeing that the tail was only propping Roodg into a better position, he backed down.

Now that Roodg was straddling the Sincubus' stomach with a penis placed exactly between the ample breasts, it left little doubt as to what was going to happen next. The Sincubus squeezed its breasts together tightly, and Roodg began to thrust into them back and forth. While taking the head of Roodg's penis into a vampire-style fanged mouth, the Sincubus' tail began to work over the avatar. The tail was an expert at its job. First the tail was only rubbing Roodg's nipples, but it turned its attention to feeling and slightly prodding both of the avatar's openings.

Not wanting to disappoint, Roodg used an action to turn around. Now they were fully engaged in a 69 position, and they were switching each round between which sex to enjoy the taste of. The part that was not getting licked would have hands feeling it all over or inside. Anders could only watch, and get strangely aroused, as the rounds progressed and the pace picked up. By the time both the avatar and Gigas had been given a heavy gloss of spit, Roodg changed positions again.

Now the couple were kissing and thrusting together. The fanged teeth of the Sincubus were dangerously sexy and really smiling. Although the face of the avatar wasn't exactly visible, Anders saw a flash of teeth that showed that Roodg was smiling. After some needful dry humping, Roodg spread apart the Sincubus' legs and started to get lined up. That is when both noticed a problem. They both had male parts nestled above female parts. They would have to flip around or do a different position to make this work, which was unfortunate, as they both had obviously enjoyed kissing.

> The Dark Gigas' Text Box: :(

> Roodg's Text Box: ;)

Roodg used the *Smirk Animation*, activated *Switch* twice, and stood back as if to perform a show. The first round had Roodg's penis and balls collapse inward and become a new vagina. The second round had Roodg's initial vagina expand outward and become a brand new penis and balls.

> The Dark Gigas' Text Box: ♥

Now that both sets lined up, a very enthusiastic avatar and Gigas were being penetrated and penetrating at the same time. Anders wasn't sure which was louder: the moaning of the couple, or the juicy sounds that were coming from the pair of interlinked crotches.

The tail of the Dark Gigas was now feeling Roodg all over, but the avatar did not think that was enough. With a forceful yank, Roodg quickly moved the exploring appendage toward the other opening. The Sincubus let out a yelp when the tail was yanked, but didn't waste any time in pressing it up against Roodg's backdoor. This earned a very thankful moan from the avatar.

The pace of the dual thrusting was quickly increasing, and both were at the edge. It was the Sincubus who double-orgasmed first, and it was even more powerful than Anders would have guessed. The Dark Gigas' breathing slowly began to calm down, and with a double "shlunk", she broke the pairing. A *Giddy Smile Animation* was plastered across her fanged teeth. Standing up and fixing the long, purple hairstyle, the Dark Gigas began to settle down.

> The Dark Gigas' Text Box: Thank you! That was the best defeat that I have ever experi—

> Roodg's Interruption Text Box: wHO SAID WE WERE DONE!?

> The Dark Gigas' Text Box: ?

Roodg activated *Switch* again and this time had two identical pussies on display. Roodg pounced on the startled Gigas again. Neither the Sincubus nor Anders saw that coming, and both gasped in surprise.

Roodg's face was now bobbing up and down furiously on the softening Sincubus penis. With only a cowl and the glint of an eye visible, the act was something different to witness. The Sincubus was flat on the floor again and in shock. Roodg seemed to know what would work—despite just ejaculating hard, the demon cock was quickly coming back to life. It took a few rounds, but eventually Roodg was satisfied by the stiffness of the member.

Jumping up yet again, the avatar switched positions with unnatural *Serpent Speed*. Roodg inserted the demon dick into the front vagina and began to ride it, double cowgirl style. The Sincubus was moaning again, but the noise was now deeper by at least an octave. With a vicious yank that earned a *Wince Animation* from the Dark Gigas, Roodg grabbed the prehensile tail and forcibly shoved it into the back vagina.

Roodg was quickly moving up and down on the demon, while the tail was happily doing its new job. The increased sexual energy was wearing out the Sincubus slightly, but Roodg was more than eager to pick up the slack. With unparalleled enthusiasm, the night elf was riding the demon cock while the tail shoved in constantly deeper.

With a full body shudder and a very low moan, the Sincubus was cumming again, even harder than the last time. Anders saw some of the juices leaking out when Roodg got up off the Sincubus. Standing up and visibly shaking, the Sincubus didn't even bother trying to fix the obviously once-important hair.

> The Dark Gigas' Text Box: That *pant pant* ... was seriously *pant* ... intense. You have ... *pant pant* definitely earned ... *pant pant* my ... *pant* *Dark Gigas Arm*—

> Roodg's Interruption Text Box: i NEVER SAID WE WERE DONE YET!

> The Dark Gigas' Text Box: ?

Activating *Switch* twice, Roodg was now showing off two proud night elf penises, each with its own set of balls. The Dark Gigas was dumbfounded as the avatar sprung toward the exhausted boss. Anders was not surprised. He pretty much saw this one coming.

Within just a few rounds, Roodg had the Sincubus on all fours. Pressing a cock against each of the available openings, Roodg entered the Dark Gigas. The lower penis had much less resistance and entered first, but the Sincubus was out of resisting energy, and it didn't take much for the tighter of the two openings to relax.

Very shocked and very deep moans were now coming from the Dark Gigas. Despite the already spent state of the demon dick, once Roodg's hand was working it firmly, life began to return again. The avatar was thrusting with a needful lust and, with another forceful yank, had the demon's tail again grabbed and pressed firmly against the night elf's backdoor. With a swift move, Roodg forced the tail inside and after a good slap it began to trust in and out.

Roodg was doing a few different actions on alternating turns—spanking the Sincubus' curvy backside, yanking on the very spent (but very hard) Sincubus' demon dick, feeling up the oversized Sincubus' breasts (paying extra attention to the nipples), and finally pulling on the Sincubus' long, important-to-her hair, just to mess it up.

On a round of important-hair pulling, the Sincubus began to buck and moan. Roodg instinctually grabbed the Sincubus' dick with one hand and feverishly pulled on it. While pulling back hard on the demon's hair, the avatar pushed inside both holes as deeply as possible. Roodg let out a genderless scream while releasing a double shot of spunk into the Dark Gigas. The Dark Gigas was sex-crazed and let out what could only be described as a bellow. Spurts of demon seed shot out the Sincubus' cock, all while a huge rush of female juice gushed out of the demon pussy. Roodg finished shooting and exited the Gigas.

Roodg sprang up, as if not even remotely exhausted.

After quite a few rounds of stumbling, the Sincubus finally managed to almost stand up.

> The Dark Gigas' Text Box: Muurfle mumble mmmum. Mmmurf mumm, mumble.

> Roodg's Text Box: & DON'T U FORGET IT!

With that, the Dark Gigas passed out into a pool of sexual juices.

Now that the show was over, Anders could think again. The first thing Anders thought about was how he felt a large wet spot in his *Hard Leaf Pants (s)*. Watching Roodg's encounter had gotten him far more aroused than he wanted to admit. He tried to shift himself so that his erection wouldn't be as visible.

An Insta-Wiki additional comment had been unlocked for Roodg, and the Magic Mage filled it out as could be expected.

> **Creature Name:** Dark Gigas
> **Class:** Gigas C
> **Level:** 98 (requires 100 avatars to be present to spawn)
> **Special Attacks:** Gigas Shade, Gigas Double, Gigas Sunder, Gigas Blackout, Gigas Blast, Gigas C
> **Drops:** *Dark Gigas Armour* (only for avatar that gets last strike)
> **First Player Encounter Notes:** Well ... I um, she really was rather not ... dressed ... actually, what I mean to say, well, uh ... she, um ... wasn't really

> wearing … much clothing. Gosh. – Trev Terra
> **Additional Comments:** zE IS A PUSHOVER WITH THE RIGHT TOOLS, BE SURE TO BRING THEM BOTH WHEN YOU FIGHT HIR! – Roodg

> Roodg's Text Box: i'M sAWESOME!

Anders had to admit that the Magic Mage had done a stand-up job with the encounter. He heartily returned Roodg's *High Five Dual Animation* that was currently hanging.

> Anders' Text Box: Only you could possibly have out-sexed a sex demon.

> Roodg's Text Box: mY SEX POWER IS SO sAWESOME SINCE i HAVE BOTH ALREADY! i CAN sWITCH BOTH!

> Anders' Text Box: 101 uses, that is for sure.

> Roodg's Text Box: sWEET! lEVEL 46!

Anders, who didn't remembered hearing trumpets, checked his level, which was still Level 42. He hadn't participated in this encounter, besides just watching, and therefore didn't get any of the experience for defeating the Gigas three times. That was kind of a letdown. He returned the other *High Five Dual Animation* and just didn't say anything.

> Roodg's Text Box: tHINGS!

That meant that Roodg was putting on the *Dark Gigas Armour* (and changing the default accent colour to red, no doubt). The Armour was strange, however, not at all like Anders was expecting it to be. It was mostly made of two different sets of liquid metal straps that were the lower layer of two different outfits. A few plates of solid metal made up spiky shoulder guards and a neckpiece. A swath of liquid metal emerged and thought hard about Roodg's body. It did not stay constant. It was confused as to what it was working with. After trying to settle on a shape, it gave up and made a hybrid shape that suited Roodg perfectly. Just as it was impossible to tell if the Magic Mage was a man or a woman, this Armour was a mix of both.

> Anders' Text Box: I think you confused it. It probably has set styles based on gender.

> Roodg's Text Box: wELL i SHOWED IT THEN!

> Anders' Text Box: So … what do I call you now, exactly?

> Roodg's Text Box: dUH! Roodg.

The avatar had been able to type in lowercase when required, Anders noted, for names at least.

> Anders' Text Box: Fair enough. Let's get back to Crahraggendes. The others might be waiting for us.

Anders didn't move after saying that. He just kept his *Dramatic Adventure Pose Animation* active.

> Roodg's Text Box: u HAVE NO IDEA WHICH WAY 2 GO DO U?

> Anders' Text Box: Not even a little!

> Roodg's Text Box: fOLLOW ME.

◆ **Chapter 27** ◆

EFFED IN THE F
(STRONGHOLD)

Mr. Max's Text Box: It is exactly how I remember my *Fancy Scarf* looking. Why are you complaining? I think it looks fetching.

Fournimer's Text Box: because it is only a scarf! where is the rest of it? there is no shirt at all! my nipples are right in the open. the (s) must stand for slu—

Mr. Max's Interruption Text Box: Studly! I don't think there is a rest of it. I think that is all of it.

The *Fancy Scarf (s)* was exactly like a regular *Fancy Scarf*, wrapping around the neck and dramatically flowing in the wind, even when there was no wind to speak of. That was, however, all it was. There was nothing else to this chest Armour slot piece, and Fournimer stood there completely bare-chested.

Mr. Max's Text Box: At least it is blue?

Fournimer's Text Box: it had a colour slider, I switched it to blue!

Mr. Max's Text Box: Well, yes, it would be better if you switched it to orange. Orange would be good on anyone! Hmm, you have bigger muscles than I thought. Give us a Flex!

Fournimer's face was slightly shielded by the *Fancy Scarf (s)* so Mr. Max didn't see the changing to *Blush Shade #2*—or, at least, Fourni hoped he didn't.

> Fournimer's Text Box: really?

> Mr. Max's Text Box: Yeah, most avatars go really skinny, and it is nice to see someone who picked the more muscular side for once. It was just hard to see those muscles under all the Night Ranger stuff. The stealth classes all have 'skinny boy' only gear! What is that *Body Type 6 (Average)*?

> Fournimer's Text Box: no, *Body Type 5 (Toned)*.

> Mr. Max's Text Box: Nice. Well?

> Fournimer's Text Box: well what Bro?

> Mr. Max's Text Box: Give us a Flex!

Fourni suddenly didn't mind so much about the scarf Armour; it had great stats and made him very manly, all things considered. It suited Fourni. At the very least, it heightened the sense of drama for no good reason. The *Emerald Gloves* and *Boots* were also pretty nice, and thankfully had colour sliders to change them from green to blue gems. The *Emerald Helmet* was completely hidden under his *#6 Hairstyle*, but he had still changed it to blue just in case of sudden wind gusts.

Executing the *Flex Animation* was something Fournimer had never done, but it wasn't that hard to figure out as Mr. Max had done it pretty much constantly.

> Mr. Max's Text Box: Good show, Fournimer!

That earned a *Butt Pat Like At Sporting Events Dual Animation* from Mr. Max, which Fournimer accepted.

> Mr. Max's Text Box: Let's rest for the night. It is safe here. Tomorrow we will be all refreshed go take on that Gigas!

Falling to the ground, Mr. Max was out cold with an impressive speed. His blanket only made it to his belt due to his beefiness. Fourni was glad Mr. Max was a quick sleeper. That meant Mr. Max didn't see Fourni attempting to hide the quickly hardening member pressing against the *Hard Leaf Pants* as a result of the butt pat.

Fournimer happily made a fire, this time far enough away to prevent Mr. Max from either burning or freezing. It turned out to be a good idea because Mr. Max was already dangerously flopping around his sleeping erection. Using the *Chuckle Animation* and covering up with the mystery blanket, Fourni drifted off to sleep.

~ ~ ~

When he woke, Fournimer saw that he had slept through the entire night and then some. It was at least 100 rounds in the morning. He had forgotten to wake up and stoke the fire in the night. He couldn't even see the X mark where the fire had been left to die. It was strange that he wasn't at all cold, though. Noticing the woodpile was at his head, he looked down. There was the fire's death X; he was sleeping right on top of where the fire had been.

His blanket was also the wrong colour. This one was not blue, but orange, and he didn't remember having this big, beefy arm wrapped around him before keeping him warm either. Or something that huge pressing against his back like that.

Fournimer got up with a start. At some point in the night, either he had crawled under Mr. Max's arm or Mr. Max's arm had crawled over him. It might even have been both, given the fact that they were currently in the middle of the fire pit.

> Mr. Max's Text Box: *Gurgle* Just 5 more rounds. I don't wanna go to Warrior School today. *Snort*

> Fournimer's Text Box: time to wake up Max. time to go kill the Gigas!

Mr. Max awakened with a single jump in the air, landing on his feet like a big, beefy cat.

> Mr. Max's Text Box: Definitely! Let's be off, Bro.

Fournimer observed Mr. Max carefully, but the meaty man wasn't showing any signs of knowing what had happened. Fournimer also noted that Max had used the assigned Bro nickname.

> Fournimer's Text Box: I meant to ask earlier Bro. what is the Light Gigas? how do we fight it?

> Mr. Max's Text Box: Well … it's all light and stuff and … it has like this light … maybe some laser beams?

Sending a *Quizzical Look Animation* over to Mr. Max was all it took to break the famous avatar down.

> Mr. Max's Text Box: Okay, I admit it. It was really late that cycle, and we had just finished killing all the other 5 Gigases. I charged in with 147 other avatars and hit a big ball of glowing light once. After that, I kinda fell asleep. When I woke up, the thing was already dead. All I have is the Insta-Wiki entry, but it just shows me a picture of the light ball and says a bunch of Gigasy named moves.

> Fournimer's Text Box: you feel asleep?

> Mr. Max's Text Box: Okay, fine, I went to make a sandwich first; then I

> fell asleep after eating it. Please don't spread that around, Fourni!

There was another of the nicknames on his list, but that was Palcath's name for Fournimer. Fourni was being called nicknames by someone who almost didn't even know his real one.

> Fournimer's Text Box: I promise Max Bro, I will not.

They opened the double doors to Stronghold F and stepped inside. It was painfully bright and covered in stark white tiles. It was like a massive, ornate bathroom. Just like most bathrooms, harpsichord music could be heard playing in the distance. After venturing a few move units inside, a ball of glowing light dropped down from the clouds in the open ceiling.

> Mr. Max's Whisper Text Box: That is the ball of light I was telling you about.

It took every ounce of strength Fournimer had not to just type in the "duh" that the comment deserved. Thankfully, he was a melee style Night Ranger and had more strength than most other classes.

> Fournimer's Text Box: come on Bro, let's get closer.

After just a few move units, the glowing sphere started to whirl around in a quick, complicated animation cycle.

> Game Explanation Text Box: This Gigas is immune to all but physical attacks.

> Mr. Max's Text Box: Ha ha! Perfect! Charge!

Almost before the Text Box was off-screen, Mr. Max was excitedly chopping at the little ball of light. Fournimer quickly joined him to add slightly more damage to the fray (as well as copious amounts of glitter). Every round or so, the light ball pulsed and did its own damage to the duo, but it was certainly not hard to recover from. Mr. Max had so many Hit Points that he didn't even need to use a *Health Potion*, while Fournimer used only eight. The ball was dwindling fast, and Fournimer was curious as to why this took Breaker's full party so long to complete. Mr. Max was curious as to what kinds of sandwich meat he had left in the fridge.

With a final slash of beef and glitter, the ball's life bar was destroyed and the Light Gigas faded into a small blip of nothing. There were no trumpets playing to congratulate them, but Fournimer hadn't expected them. Mr. Max was right. After Level 50, Experience Points were slow going.

> Mr. Max's Text Box: We rocked it partner Bro!

> Fournimer's Text Box: we sure did partner Bro!

> Game Explanation Text Box: This Gigas is immune to all but ranged attacks.

> Mr. Max's and Fournimer's Simultaneous Text Boxes: Huh?

Without any warning (except from the Text Box that had just warned them), the little blip of nothing that was left of the Light Gigas flashed and expanded. Now a ball of light with six fantastical fabric sections was in its place. The fabric floated and moved as if it were in an underwater area. While Fournimer was staring, the drifting cloth slashed out and did a large number of Hit Point damage to Mr. Max.

> Mr. Max's Text Box: Crap, that will rip you to bits if it hits!

Fournimer didn't even have time to react. Mr. Max ducked under his legs and lifted up, pulling Fournimer up on his beefy shoulders. Mr. Max grabbed on tight and started to run around the arena frantically. Rays of light emitted from the pulsing cloth ball, directed at the pair. Thankfully, the full-out sprinting manoeuvres of Mr. Max made them too difficult for the Gigas to track.

> Fournimer's Text Box: this can't be a legal action, Bro!

> Mr. Max's Text Box: Well, I don't want you ripped to bits. I don't have any ranged attacks. So, once every 14 rounds, use a *Stamina Potion+* on me. For the rest of the rounds, just shoot at it!

Already not the best of shots, Fournimer was now attempting to aim at a pulsing ball of light that shot out eye-blinding lasers while riding on a giant charging man-bull. To make matters worse, his arrows suffered due to the extra glitter and were moving with a bunch of lag. He did what he could with what he had, but was missing more often than hitting.

Mr. Max knew this wasn't going to work. They had only a limited number of resources at their disposal. He had to switch tactics. He choked down a *Stamina Potion+* while in full gallop. Mr. Max began a brand new way of running around like an idiot. Now he was strafe-running around like an idiot. It helped with Fournimer's aim, but it also was more difficult to avoid the cloth lasers. Now and then, a few hit and did reasonable damage.

Adding *Health Potions+* to the mix of *Stamina Potions+* that he was force-feeding his new mount, Fournimer was taking far less time shooting and far more time helping out Mr. Max.

> Fournimer's Text Box: this isn't working, I don't have time to shoot and help you.

> Mr. Max's Text Box: *Ultra Mega Pack Super Mark 2.* Under *glug* Items. F *glug glug* Under F.

Searching in Mr. Max's impressively stocked *Ultra-Mega-Pack-Super Mark 2*, Fournimer found that a lot of things started with "F", but he couldn't imagine what Mr. Max was thinking of. After two full dumbfounded rounds, Fournimer thought he had found it. He pulled it out and shoved it right down his companion's throat. This *Funnel* (which for some reason was used to *Combi-Fuse* with a *Glass Box* to make a *Lantern*) was exactly the rule-breaking logic they needed. Now with Mr. Max's ability to chug back the potions with little effort on Fournimer's part, the entire battle was going more smoothly. The only problem was how painfully full of potions Mr. Max was. He was now turning shades of yellow and red, the respective colours of the potions he was drinking.

After 468 rounds, 357 glitter arrows, 16 *Health Potion+s* for Mr. Max, 2 *Health Potion+s* for Fournimer, 18 *Stamina Potion+s* between them, and an accidental vial of something that sort of looked like a *Health Potion+* but was really just red *Furniture Polish+,* the blasted ball of light finally blipped out. Each celebrated the victory in different ways. Fournimer was doing the *Cheer Animation* in triumph while Mr. Max was burping out multi-coloured bubbles in triumph.

> Fournimer's Text Box: we did it Bro! I am out of all potions completely, but we did it!

> Mr. Max's Text Box: Nice *Funnel* *white bubble* idea. I was *rainbow bubble* talking about a *Full Health Potion,* but I see now that I am *green bubble* out of them. *blue bubble* I gave you all my *yellow bubble* spares and forgot. I'll need to *red bubble* open *My Spiritual Storage* *purple bubble* *Device from the Crags of Halm* and *orange bubble* get more out.

> Mr. Max's Text Box: It is not letting me *47 bubbles of various colours* open it for some reason.

> Game Explanation Text Box: This Gigas is immune to all but magical attacks.

> Fournimer's Text Box: well crap.

The pinpoint of light erupted into a flash of multi-coloured luminous balls, all pastel shades within the same palette. It was an amazing model with amazing light effects. The Light Gigas began to form out of these balls of light and started to solidify into a humanoid shape. Laser cloth was wrapping around, forming the clothing of the creature. It was now almost completely covered in cloth strips and ribbons. It had a masculine shape, but only its eyes could be seen, peering out from behind the cloth. A single white-feathered wing erupted from the back of the Light Gigas, and it began to hover in place. It was very possibly the angel of bandages.

> The Light Gigas' Text Box: Behold, I am the master of the Gigases. I

> am the Light Gigas, and I will….

The Light Gigas saw only two avatars.

> Fournimer's Text Box: okay, I know we are going to probably die now Mr. Max, because we don't have magic attacks … but that was pretty dang nifty to watch.

> Mr. Max's Text Box: I know. That was some sort of fancy, Fourni.

> Fournimer's Text Box: why did it just stop moving like that?

Fournimer again had not been paying attention to vital plot points and had missed the memo on not talking to a frozen Gigas. He was busy looking through his unimpressive notes but was quickly interrupted by Mr. Max, who had a tendency to miss every vital plot point and instinctively just spoke up.

> Mr. Max's Text Box: I am not sure. Hey! Light Gigas, why did you stop moving like that?

> The Light Gigas' Text Box: …challenge you to…. Wait! Mr. Max? The Mr. Max! No way! I can't believe it's you. You are so famous! This is not happening. This is not happening!

> Mr. Max's Text Box: Always nice to meet a fan! Hey, can you do us a solid, Light Gigas? Can we just have your drop? We kind of need it for a quest.

> The Light Gigas' Text Box: OMFM! Yes! Can I please have your autograph?

> Mr. Max's Text Box: Sure thing! Always happy to help a fan. Do you want it on your tits or your ass?

Mr. Max got out the *Handy Permanent Marker* (well, permanent until it was washed off) he had in his pocket for just such emergencies and stepped closer to the Gigas. Seeing Mr. Max closer, the Light Gigas blinked funny, and one of its pale blue eyes turned pale purple.

> Fournimer's Text Box: crap Bro, you broke it!

> The Light Gigas' Text Box: On second thought, famous or not, you two don't have any magical attacks. I would very much like to be the one who breaks the most famous avatar in the game.

The Light Gigas pulled a single thread on its mass of bandages, causing most of the cloth strips to fall off in a dramatic twirl. Only a select few cloth bandages remained to frame the important bits, but otherwise the Gigas had revealed his naked body. A statuesque male humanoid with copper-coloured skin was standing in the light he himself created. He had an impressive physique and chiseled jaw that smiled as a very impressive tool sprang up from its crotch. The pristine cock was aimed squarely at Mr. Max.

Fournimer was a lot nervous. Mr. Max stepped forward without skipping a beat.

> Mr. Max's Text Box: Oh, no, you don't. I am Mr. Max, damn you. That is not how it works around here. I don't give a crap if you are an Epic, More Epic, or More More Epic Monster. The fact is that you are still a monster. I don't take any crap from monsters. Besides, you have it wrong chump. I do have a magical attack.

With one swift motion, Mr. Max had pulled down his pants to reveal his giant flaccid member. With a hearty *Flex Animation*, it sprang up to full mast.

> Mr. Max's Text Box: I am not going to say this twice. You are going to service this giant magical cock, and you are going to damn well like it. Now, do it without any Maker damn bitching. Got it?

The Light Gigas was flustered now. He opened his mouth a few times in an attempt to say something, but nothing came out. After a few tries, all he could manage to get out was a stutter-filled Text Box.

> The Light Gigas' Text Box: Yes … uh … y-yes, s-sir?

> Mr. Max's Text Box: Damn right, yes sir. Now float your ass over here and get to work.

Watching the Light Gigas float over to start work on Mr. Max was a bit surreal for Fournimer. He couldn't believe that the muscular avatar's gamble had worked. Furthermore, he couldn't believe a few other things that followed: That Mr. Max had basically broken the Gigas' will in such a short time. That this was going to happen right now. That Mr. Max had managed to sound so aggressive when he had spoke. And finally, that he himself was so very turned on by the entire thing.

The Light Gigas began to work over Mr. Max's Mr. Maxum with his golden tongue. There was no way that he was going to be able to handle much of it in his mouth. The Gigas tried anyway, and attempted to choke back the first little bit of it. Mr. Max reached down and began to play with the Gigas' opening. Apparently Mr. Max didn't really leave much room for foreplay.

Worried, the Gigas continued to lick the member. Mr. Max continued aggressively and shoved a beefy finger inside the boss. The Light Gigas continued to be uncomfortable as Mr. Max began to finger-fuck it quickly. It was even sweating it was so nervous.

> Mr. Max's Text Box: You are just lucky that you agreed right away.

> Otherwise, I was going to make this sucker grow before I stuck it in you.

With a very aggressive turnaround, Mr. Max pushed the tip of his giant-sized member into the barely relaxed opening. With an initially unsuccessful push, a very stern warning, and a big glob of spit, Mr. Max was inside. Fournimer was surprised how quickly the Light Gigas adapted to the giant intrusion. Within just a few turns, the Light Gigas was doing all the pumping work and apparently was enjoying himself immensely. Moans of pure delight and harpsichord music filled the air.

> Mr. Max's Text Box: I knew you wanted it. Now get moving. I don't have all cycle.

> The Light Gigas' Text Box: Yes, sir!

Mr. Max finally grabbed the NPC Monster by the hips and started to thrust into it. He was going to beat this magic damage problem the only way he could. He noticed that Fournimer was blushing and frozen to the spot, but also that Fournimer was sprouting some very obvious wood under the *Hard Leaf Pants*. Mr. Max used the *Wink Animation* at him, which only made Fournimer blush harder.

> Mr. Max's Text Box: Okay, Gigas. Let me lay down the law for you. I am part of a team now, and we are both going to win this.

Hoisting the Gigas up, but still not taking it off his cock, Mr. Max manoeuvred the Gigas over toward Fournimer. The Night Ranger didn't know what to do. He was still mesmerized by the chain of events that had led up to this.

> Mr. Max's Text Box: Service my Bro.

> The Light Gigas' Text Box: Yes, sir!

Before Fournimer had a chance to take his turn, the Light Gigas had the *Hard Leaf Pants* down and little Fourni down his happy throat. All Fourni could do on his next turn was skip it while letting out a gasp. On the following turn, he grabbed the creature by the still-bandaged up hair and began to thrust into it. The light particle tongue felt amazing against his skin as it worked up his shaft and teased his balls.

The Light Gigas was on all fours, rocking back and forth to better please his new masters. With a few good spanks from Mr. Max, the Gigas began to work and moan even harder as it shifted around on both cocks. It certainly was enjoying getting spit roasted.

Fournimer watched Mr. Max's face as the Warrior pumped the creature with his giant meat. It was an intense thing to see, and it was increasing his own lust as he continued to thrust into the Gigas' mouth.

It was now nearly impossible to hear the harpsichord music over the Gigas' loud moans. The poor thing, it was evident that it wasn't going to last much longer. Mr.

Max pulled out from the Gigas with a giant wet, slurping noise. This surprised both Fournimer and the poor Gigas, who had been on the brink. Mr. Max manhandled the Gigas and turned it around, giving Fournimer access to the now gaping hole. Fournimer took the bait. He entered the creature and began to pump as Mr. Max watched and started jacking off on the sidelines. The Gigas tried to reach for Mr. Maxum, but Max pushed him away.

> Mr. Max's Text Box: Finish him off, Fourni!

After a final pump of his meat, Mr. Max shot his improved-sized load in thick spurts all over the fucking couple. When the final rope hit him, Fournimer lost it. With a loud scream, he buried himself deep into the Gigas and released. The pressure pushed the Gigas over the edge as well, and it began to cum out balls of goopy light.

Mr. Max was the first to recover due to his larger Stamina Bar. So, as if in spite, he used his turn to pull out the *Handy Permanent Marker*. He wrote something on the Light Gigas' ass, which he signed with a spank. The Light Gigas left toward its Gigas bed and was admiring the pen mark the way only a fanboy could. Fournimer guessed that the creature's ass cheek wasn't going to get washed for a long time. Fournimer read the writing and used an *Eye Twitch Animation*.

> Fournimer's Reading Text Box: your pussy was just owned by Mr. Max and his Bro Fourni.

> Fournimer's Text Box: uh Bro … about that writing….

> Mr. Max's Text Box: You did do a lot of the work, Bro. It seemed fair.

> Fournimer's Text Box: well, yes, but … uh … Bro, the thing is that wasn't a—

A brand new pair of *Light Gigas Pants* interrupted the Text Box by rising up from the ground at Fourni's feet. The scarfed one completely forgot about whatever it was he was thinking. This new thing had a liquid metal oversized belt and silky blue fabric after the colour slider was adjusted from being orange. Not only did they complete Fourni's outfit, but they also had an ability called *Improve*. *Improve* increased the effectiveness of his abilities, which sounded great, even if Fournimer had no idea what that meant.

Mr. Max wasn't kidding about the Experience Halt at Level 50. The entire Gigas battle had gained Fournimer only 0.3 of a level.

> Mr. Max's Text Box: Sweet! Level 98.32! That is up an entire 0.01!

It had gained Mr. Max even less.

Fournimer was given the chance to add a comment to the Insta-Wiki. This would be his very first, and he was excited.

Creature Name: Light Gigas
Class: Gigas F
Level: 98 (requires 100 avatars to be present to spawn)
Special Attacks: Gigas Unshade, Gigas Cloth Laser, Gigas Ball, Gigas Lightout, Gigas Blast, Gigas F.
Drops: Light Gigas Pants (only for avatar that gets last strike)
First Player Encounter Notes: Was Mr. Max sleeping for that entire encounter? I know, he totally was. Hey, how are we both talking at the same time? I don't know. Look, we were totally in sync and got the final hit on the boss at the same time! Really? Yes! That is so cool! Go us! – In'ferni and De'vini
Additional Comments: bring your best Bro to come help, and together you will be unstoppable! – Fournimer

Fournimer's Text Box: wait, you pulled me into that and pulled you out of that just so I could get the finishing hit Bro?

Mr. Max's Text Box: Well, your pants were very under-leveled. It felt like the right thing to do.

Mr. Max accented that Text Box with a *Wink Animation*.

Fournimer's Text Box: well thank you Max.

Mr. Max's Text Box: You didn't even need to use your special magic powers!

Fournimer changed to *Blush Shade #5*.

Fournimer's Text Box: no, I guess not.

Mr. Max's Text Box: You do have special powers right? Like how I have my giant Mr. Maxum? What exactly is your pow—

Fournimer's Interruption Text Box: we should get going Bro!

Mr. Max's Text Box: Fine, Fourni, be all secretive with it!

Chapter 28
REPEATING ONESELF

Palcath was merrily sitting in front of his *Portie Tent* on one of the supplied outside chairs. A rooster had just crowed a few rounds ago, and it was a brand new cycle. Role-playing that he had been smoking on a pipe, he saw someone familiar come over the nearby ridge and use the *Wave Animation*. *Wave Animationing* back, the dwarf pretended to put the pipe away but stayed sitting. There was a very obvious question that Palcath needed to ask, and his curiosity quickly got the better of his political correctness.

> Palcath's Text Box: What the Flaming Pit happened to you, Roodg? I'm more confused than ever. What are you?

> Roodg's Text Box: dUH! i'M Roodg!

Roodg sat down in one of the supplied outside chairs, legs opened wide, which only spread more confusion.

> Palcath's Text Box: Well, that answers that then, Roodg.

Lissa came out from inside the *Portie Tent*, smiling and carrying a platter full of delicious *Mountain Bacon* with a selection of various other heavy foods that she was trying to get rid of to lighten up her *Ultra-Mega-Pack*.

> Lissa's Text Box: Palcath, do you want something to eat?

Lissa placed the platter so that the heavier, ill-tasting appliance foods were closer to Palcath than the much tastier *Bacon*. Palcath reached over the foul food and grabbed the correct food choice.

> Palcath's Text Box: Just some *Mountain Bacon*, please. Those *Sweet Peaches* taste like a stackable washer/dryer combo.

> Roodg's Text Box: u GUYS FOUND sAWESOME STUFF 2?

Lissa used the *Smile Animation,* and sat down in a chair that had been changed from brown to purple. Chair colour was how Palcath had asserted his authority over the group some time ago since he was the only one who could change it.

> Roodg's Text Box: hEY! hOW COME SHE GETS A COLOUR CHAIR! cHANGE MINE TO RED Palcath!

> Lissa's Text Box: Nope. There are two leaders now. That is just how it is. Only we get to change the chair colours.

> Roodg's Text Box: wE HAD A LEADER BEFORE?

> Lissa's Text Box: I'm glad you are fine at least, Roodg.

> Roodg's Text Box: wHOA! WHEN DID HUMAN GET SO NICE?

> Palcath's Text Box: Last night.

> Lissa's Text Box: I'm not a human. I am a half-elf.

Roodg relaxed a little bit more in the default-coloured chair. Lissa noticed for the first time this conversation Roodg's obvious increased amount of gender-confusion. She used an *Eyebrows Furrowed and Face Twitch Animation.*

> Lissa's Text Box: Wow. What in the map? What are you exactly, Roodg? #SoFuckedUp?

> Roodg's Text Box: dUH! i'M Roodg!

> Lissa's Text Box: Well, that answers that then.

> Lissa's Text Box: Roodg, do you want something to eat?

Lissa tipped the platter so that the *Bacon* was further away than the other food items.

> Roodg's Text Box: sWEET! *bACON*. nO *vHEAT cAKES*, THEY TASTE LIKE A MINI DEEP FREEZE.

Anders came over the embankment and was now wearing what Palcath could only guess was a sexy Pixie outfit. He sat down in a supplied brown chair but kept his legs closed for obvious reasons.

> Palcath's Text Box: What are you wearing? You look like some kind of dangerous sexy Pixie.

Trying to turn the conversation away from his dangerous sexy Pixie outfit, Anders refused to answer the question and followed up with a deflection question.

> Anders' Text Box: Hey, you two found some new (s) gear as well?

Anders watched as both Lissa and the dwarf used the *Smile Animation*.

> Lissa's Text Box: Don't change the subject, Loverboy. What kind of dangerous sexy Pixie outfit is that, anyway?

> Anders' Text Box: Whoa, when did the human start to smile? I didn't think she knew how.

> Palcath's Text Box: Last night.

> Lissa's Text Box: Hey, I'm a half-elf. Wow. You have a scar, Loverboy. Did you know?

> Roodg's Text Box: iT IS BADASS!

> Lissa's Text Box: Loverboy, do you want something to eat?

> Anders' Text Box: Just some *Mountain Bacon* please. None of that *Groundermellon*, though. It tastes like a discounted microwave oven.

> Lissa's Text Box: Okay, avatars need to start eating things besides my *Bacon*! This other crap might spoil or fill up my inventory or something!

> Anders' Text Box: Why do you get a purple chair, Lissa? Palcath, can you change mine to green please? I like green.

> Lissa's Text Box: Nope, he can't! Only joint leaders get fancy chairs. That is just how it is.

> Anders' Text Box: We have leaders?

> Fournimer's Text Box: hey Mr. Max over here! I found them!

Fournimer came into the circle, wearing nothing on his chest but a fancy scarf that flowed dramatically in the wind. The human sat down and looked around, first stopping at Roodg.

> Fournimer's Text Box: whoa Gu … Guy? what happened to you? what do I call you now?

Roodg's Text Box: dUH! Roodg!

Fournimer's Text Box: well that answers that then.

Roodg's Text Box: u FOUND sAWESOME STUFF 2?

Determined to change the subject, Fournimer looked around desperately, settling on the human female who was smiling.

Fournimer's Text Box: whoa when did the human Fair Maiden get all smiletime?

Palcath's Text Box: Last night.

Lissa's Text Box: Half-elf! Don't change the subject, Scarfy. What kind of sexy scarf outfit is that, anyway?

Fournimer's Text Box: me? what about Anders? he looks like a dangerous sexy Pixie! my *Hard Leaf* stuff was nothing like that!

Roodg's Text Box: wANT IT 2 LOOK LIKE THAT? i CAN DO THAT NOW.

Fournimer's Text Box: hey, Elfdude. you have a scar, did you know?

Roodg's Text Box: iT IS BADASS!

Lissa's Text Box: Scarfy, do you want something to eat? Preferably not more of my *Bacon*!

Fournimer's Text Box: you have *Bacon*? I'll take one of those. *Strawbarrels* taste like a premium four-cycle dishwasher.

Lissa's Text Box: Stop taking my *Bacon*!

Fournimer's Text Box: hey! why do you have a purple chair! Man, I have been asking you to change mine to blue since forever!

Lissa's Text Box: Coloured chairs are for joint leaders only, sorry, Scarfy.

Fournimer's Text Box: you told me that I was the joint leader Man!

Palcath's Text Box: I ... um ... hey. Is that Mr. Lad I see?

Mr. Max's Text Box: Fellow adventurers and adventurettes! Fourni and

> I have returned, valiant as ever!

Mr. Max came in and sat in another brown chair.

> Anders' Text Box: Wait, Fourni? How do you know someone's name?

> Mr. Max's Text Box: Because that is his name ... and I know everyone's name ... uh ... what was that one again ... Dood?

> Fournimer's Text Box: Dude? that's my nickname for him!

> Mr. Max's Text Box: Nickname for who? I don't remember anyone named Dude.

Mr. Max scanned the vaguely familiar avatar faces, and his eyes settled first on someone he had never seen before—a dangerous sexy Pixie that was scowling for no real reason. Aiming his camera at the others in an attempt to get away from the evil eye, Mr. Max saw the whatever-that-was in the *Dark Gigas Armour* and just had to ask.

> Mr. Max's Text Box: Hey there! Which one is this? Guy, right? No ... what do I call you, Magic Mage?

> Roodg's Text Box: dUH! Roodg!

> Mr. Max's Text Box: Well, that settles that then.

> Fournimer's Text Box: Guy? that's my nickname for ... uh.

> Mr. Max's Text Box: Hey, Dwarfman and human Fair Maiden got themselves some studly gear as well! Oh, and she is less ... wait, I don't remember what she looked like before, but it is different. Right?

> Palcath's Text Box: Yes, it happened last night.

> Lissa's Text Box: Half-elf!

> Fournimer's Text Box: Man? Fair Maiden? those are my nicknames for them!

Mr. Max looked over again at the unfamiliar scowling elf, and he felt a very sharp tinge of guilt when he noticed that scar. He suddenly remembered that his sword had deeply cut an avatar's cheek; might it have been this one? But that was all he remembered about this nameless elf.

> Mr. Max's Text Box: I'm sorry if I attacked you while role-playing. That was you, right? I can't believe you have a scar. Was that you?

> Anders' Text Box: That is okay, Max. The scar is badass.

Fournimer's Text Box: Max is my nickname for him!

Anders' Text Box: No, it isn't! You don't give nicknames to avatars! You only gave me a nickname because I thought I was special!

Mr. Max's Text Box: I knew it was you, someone! You can't select scars in character creation! Monsters better watch out, though, because you are all ready to be a badass ... dangerous sexy Pixie or something! Looking good, lady! By the way, that's not what *Hard Leaf Equipment* is supposed to look like!

Roodg's Text Box: iT CAN LOOK LIKE THAT NOW!

Lissa's Text Box: Meathead, do you want something to eat? I'm all out of food, though, so you will have to eat your own damn *Bacon*.

Lissa put away her food, (despite having lots of extra) to avoid giving any to Mr. Max.

Mr. Max's Text Box: I don't like *Bacon*. I have lots and lots of food! Mmmm! I don't know why everyone says this stuff tastes likes appliances. They taste delicious. Appliances are tasty. Do you want some ... err....

Lissa's Text Box: My name is Lissa! Just read the Text Box. But ... yes, sure thing, hand over whatever you got!

Mr. Max's Text Box: That is right. You are Fair Maiden ... I think. Here are a few spares I have on me right now.

Mr. Max handed Lissa 1,146 different kinds of appliance-tasting food. Lissa took them all happily (to sell later).

Fournimer's Text Box: wait why did you call her Fair Maiden? that's my forced nickname for her!

Palcath's Text Box: You did that one already, Fourni.

Mr. Max's and Anders' Simultaneous Text Box: Fourni? That's my nickname for him!

Palcath's Text Box: um...

Lissa's Text Box: Don't change the topic, meathead. How did you learn our nicknames and not our real names? Our names are in the Text Boxes you are reading right now, by the way!

Mr. Max's Text Box: I thought those were your names! That is what Fourni was calling you. I tried really hard to remember.

Fournimer's Text Box: it's true, I made Bro take a test. but not with the nicknames because that is my thing.

Anders' Text Box: Bro? Why are you calling him Bro?

Fournimer's Text Box: because that is the nickname I gave him!

Anders' Text Box: But you only gave me a nickname!

Lissa's Text Box: Seriously, Loverboy? Weren't you listening? He almost always uses nicknames. Right, Scarfy?

Fournimer's Text Box: it is my character trait, yes Fair Maiden. that and not using capital letters except for names and nicknames. can't I just call you Lissa now?

Lissa's Text Box: No, you can't, Scarfy. But don't change the subject! What is with the sexy scarf and no matching sexy gloves and boots?

Roodg's Text Box: i CAN CHANGE THEM 2 MATCH. i CAN DO THAT NOW!

Fournimer's Text Box: you can change them? How can you do that … uh…? I don't know what to call you anymore.

Roodg's Text Box: dUH! Roodg!

Mr. Max's Text Box: Speaking of changing, why is this chair not orange?

Lissa's Text Box: Only leaders are allowed to have non-brown chairs!

Mr. Max's Text Box: Why do you two have coloured chairs? The only coloured chair here should be orange! I am surely the leader of this outfit!

Lissa's Text Box: #NewRule! Anyone but you is the leader!

Roodg's Text Box: cAN i BE LEADER? i HAVE GREAT LEADER POTENTIAL! wELL NOT REALLY … bUT CHANGE MY CHAIR 2 RED PLEASE?

Fournimer's Text Box: I was already told that I was a leader! I want a blue chair!

Anders' Text Box: This brown chair really is pretty complimentary with my green Armour. I don't think it needs to change…. I really don't want to be the leader, anyway.

Mr. Max's Text Box: Why isn't this chair orange yet? I am obviously the leader here!

Lissa's Text Box: Enough with the reasons! I won joint leader fair and square!

Palcath's Yelling Text Box: STOP IT!

Everyone Else's Simultaneous Text Box: Stop what?

Palcath's Text Box: We are stuck in a loop or something. We need to go over what has happened to everyone and stop interrupting. Lissandra and I defeated the Twin Gigases of Fire and Wind and got their Gigas drops.

Anders' Text Box: Lissandra?

Mr. Max's Text Box: Sorry, I was getting a sandwich. What are we doing now?

Lissa's Text Box: Urgh! Palcath and I killed the Twin Gigases of Fire and Wind and got their Gigas drops!

Roodg's Text Box: dID U BEAT THEM UP WITH KISSES LIKE ME? i SO USED KISSES.

Mr. Max's Text Box: Oh, good! I couldn't see the *Fire Gigas Choker*, but there it is on the Fair Maiden's boobs! Wait … boobs? You're a chick?

Lissa's Text Box: Chick?! Boobs! CHICK! My boobs! How dare you! My boobs are—

Palcath's Internal Interruption Text Box: Perfection!

Roodg's Text Box: bOOBS ARE RAD!

Mr. Max's Text Box: That means we have all the Gigas drops now! Let's go to the Floating Castle and challenge the Plague of Shadow!

Roodg's Text Box: fLOATING cASTLE? nEAT! gO!!!

Fournimer's Text Box: you still need to kill the Green Slimes first, Max.

Anders' Text Box: Max? That's my nickname for him!

Mr. Max's Text Box: Oh, yeah, I forgot about them.

Palcath's Text Box: We were supposed to stop interrupting, remember?

Anders' Text Box: Flapjacks, I forgot!

Fournimer's Text Box: flapjacks?

Roodg's Text Box: LoL! fLAPJACKS!

Palcath's Text Box: With Roodg's Armour and Fourni's pants, we definitely have all the Gigas Gear now!

Mr. Max's Text Box: We do? Let's go to the Floating Castle and challenge the Plague of Shadow! Hurry, fellow adventurers!

Palcath's Text Box: Dear Maker. Want to help me out here, lass?

Palcath's Text Box: ... lass?

Lissa's Text Box: Sorry, I was getting a sandwich. What are we doing now?

Palcath used the *Sigh Animation.*

Mr. Max's Text Box: Why are we still here? We need to go to the Floating Castle and take on the Plague of Shadow!

Lissa's Text Box: Seriously, meathead? Don't you remember that you need to kill the Slimes first?

Mr. Max's Text Box: Oh, yeah, I forgot about them.

Anders' Text Box: How? It has only been like a round since Fourni told you that.

Fournimer's Text Box: did someone say my name? sorry I was getting a sandwich, what are we doing now?

Roodg's Text Box: wE R ALL GETTING SANDWICHES! brb!

Mr. Max's Text Box: That's a good idea. I'm going to get one as well.

Lissa's Text Box: You already did go get one! Or did you forget that?

Mr. Max's Text Box: No, I remembered that. I am not forgetful. I am just still hungry is all, adventurette.

Lissa's Text Box: No, Lissa!

Palcath's Text Box: Or Lissandra Collinswood, if you want to be formal.

Mr. Max's Text Box: Lissandra Collinswood? Why does that name sound so very famil—

Lissa's Interruption Text Box: No, it does not! #DropIt.

Mr. Max's Text Box: I was thinking it did. But, okay, if you say so.

Fournimer's Text Box: really? I can use Lissandra?

Lissa's Text Box: No, Fair Maiden!

Mr. Max's Text Box: Sorry, Fair Maiden!

Lissa's Text Box: No, Lissa!

Fournimer's Text Box: Lissa!

Lissa used the *Furious Animation*.

Mr. Max's Text Box: Who are you? I forget.

Anders' Text Box: As compelling as this is, I am going to go get a sandwich before we go and kill the Slimes.

Mr. Max's Text Box: Oh, yeah, I forgot about them.

Lissa's Text Box: How you are winning the Insta-Wiki Contest, I will never know.

Roodg's Text Box: bECAUSE WE ALL AGREED 2 HELP HIM REMEMBER?

Mr. Max's Text Box: You are forgetful as well, Fair Adventurette. I clearly remember that. I don't feel so bad now.

Lissa's Text Box: No, I knew that already! It was rhetorical. Thanks a lot, Roodg, for that. You can wipe that *Smirk Animation* off your now-visible eye, you ... uh, what are you, exactly?

Roodg's Text Box: i'M Roodg, REMEMBER???

Mr. Max's Text Box: I thought your name was Guy, but I don't see how that works. Maybe it does. Uh, I hate to ask, but what are you?

Roodg's Text Box: !!! dUH Roodg!!!

Anders' Text Box: I can verify that. 100% Roodg right there!

Fournimer's Text Box: yeah but 100% of what?

Anders' Text Box: Of Roodg, weren't you listening, Fourni?

Mr. Max's Text Box: Fourni? That's my nickname for him!

Palcath's Text Box: Fuck this shit. I am going to go get a sandwich.

$\Diamond$ **Chapter 29** $\Diamond$

AN OLD FRIEND

It took several rounds of sorting out (and even more sandwiches) before everyone was finally up to speed on everything that had happened to everyone else. The only thing that was still confusing to some was the gender of the Magic Mage. Well, and Mr. Max was still confused by everyone's actual name.

> Mr. Max's Text Box: Okay you three, Fair Maiden, Sandwich Dwarf, and Duh Guy.

> Palcath's Text Box: That is hardly fair, lad. I only had one sandwich. I remember you getting five by the end of it, Mr. Max!

> Mr. Max's Text Box: Really? Strange, I don't. Anyway, you, fellow adventurers, are under leveled and poorly equipped.

> Roodg's Text Box: hEY! i AM 46 AND MAGICALLY AMAZING!

> Mr. Max's Text Box: That you are ... Duh Roodg.

> Roodg's Text Box: hOLY FLAPJACKS! hE SORT OF KNOWS MY NAME! i REALLY AM AMAZING!

> Fournimer's Text Box: I guess you are important now, too, Roodg.

Roodg's Text Box: nEAT!

Lissa's Text Box: We are 45! Plus, we just got this stuff ourselves, #BigMeatyJerk.

Palcath's Text Box: Yeah, lad, I remember that this gear had big, interesting descriptions and everything. It had important plot relevance and even took up several paragraphs.

Mr. Max's Text Box: I didn't mean to offend you, fellow adventurers. It is just a fact. There is a huge stat boost at Level 50. The Floating Castle in the Sky is the hardest area in the game. Even the normal monsters are like bosses. I didn't want you to get ripped apart before we even got to the Plague of Shadow.

Mr. Max pulled out some sort of discus-shaped device and handed it to Palcath.

Mr. Max's Text Box: We can handle the Slimes here. I have a great plan. All I need is Fourni and the other one.

Fournimer changed to *Blush Shade #2*, as did Anders.

Fournimer's Text Box: you need me?

Anders' Text Box: And me?

Mr. Max's Text Box: Fourni is already Level 50 and has all the epic stuff I gave him. Unfortunately, I already gave away all the best stuff for your classes. Use this *Zoomer Rezoner* and go back to where I left the other half. Pick up the glowing *Returner* on the ground. Just follow this map of the area, collect your Epic Level 50 gear, and get to Level 50.

Palcath's Text Box: But we just got back together, lad. Now we are splitting up again?

Mr. Max's Text Box: Not for long, though. You are a pretty balanced team, class wise, and it shouldn't take you much time if you don't do something foolish like defend the entire time. No more than 200 rounds at the most. When you're done, press the *Returner* and you will warp back to us. By then, we will be ready. I only need Fourni and someone else for my plan, anyway.

Lissa's Text Box: This plan is … genius and thoughtful! How in the Flaming Pit did you, of all people, come up with it?

Mr. Max's Text Box: Sometime during the third sandwich, it came to

> me. That is what it takes to be a leader. Besides, the plans I have for Fourni and that other one are far more elaborate and clever.

> Lissa's Text Box: You are not the leader!

> Palcath's Text Box: Tell us about it later, lad. I want to get this Epic Gear! I read that you can change the colours like on the Gigas Gear!

> Lissa's Text Box: What? You can change the colours? Let's go already!

> Roodg's Text Box: wOOOOO! cOLOURS!

The trio was off to level up and follow the very specific map to the very specific chests.

> Mr. Max's Text Box: Okay, the first part of stage two of my plan involves the one who isn't Fourni.

> Anders' Text Box: I probably should have gone with them. I'm only Level 42!

> Mr. Max's Text Box: Wow, really? That sucks! Well, it is too late now. Your part of the plan is … to show me where the Slime Cave is!

> Anders' Text Box: Really? That's it? It is only like a 20-round run from here. I could have shown you the entrance and then after gone to level up as well!

> Mr. Max's Text Box: That is a good idea. You should have spoken up before they left.

> Anders' Text Box: Whatever, Max. Just follow me, I guess.

> Mr. Max's Text Box: In that super sexy dangerous Pixie outfit of yours? Any time!

Anders turned to *Blush Shade #4* while Fourni turned to *Envy Shade #4*.

The trio reached the entrance to the Slime Cave in only a few rounds. Anders had no idea how everyone had missed the door. It was just behind a scenic bush; it wasn't even a very big bush. It was a scenic twig, if it was anything. However, the laws of scenic bushes being able to hide everything were in complete effect.

> Anders' Text Box: Here it is.

> Mr. Max's Text Box: Where? I don't see anything.

> Fournimer's Text Box: yeah Dude, I don't see anything!

Anders pulled the scenic bush away with a very unenthusiastic motion. The other two avatars acted as if he had just pulled the sun down and squeezed it to make fresh blue orange juice.

Fournimer's Text Box: wow! just like magic Dude!

Mr. Max's Text Box: Impressive, no wonder I never found it.

Anders' Text Box: The main road leads right to a bush near a sign that read 'Slime Cave'. Didn't either of you find that suspicious?

Mr. Max's Text Box: No matter. Now, onward to the next part of the plan! Fourni, it is your turn to shine!

Fournimer was very excited at this idea.

Fournimer's Text Box: okay, perfect! what do you want me to do?

Mr. Max's Text Box: Hold this *Returner* while I go inside.

Fournimer's Text Box: seriously Bro? that's it.

Mr. Max's Text Box: No, of course not! There is something far more important that you need to do.

Fournimer was too scared to ask, so Anders stepped in for the human.

Anders' Text Box: What else does he need to do?

Mr. Max's Text Box: Wait outside and cover the door back up with the bush until I get outside! I don't want anyone else to find this until we win the contest.

Anders' Text Box: You realize I could have just done that, right? Since you already brought me here with you, anyway. Or, hotcakes, you could have just moved the scenic bush back and stepped around it. You didn't need either of us here at all!

Mr. Max's Text Box: Hmm, I guess you're right.

Anders' Text Box: Scones! I feel sort of bad about all of this now.

Fournimer's Text Box: why? it's just Mr. Max forgetting how to use bushes.

Anders' Text Box: Not that. I mean that I would be dead dead now if I never had met the Pink Slime and got my powers. I sort of owe it a

> thank you. Fourni, Max, can you guys do me a favour?

> Fournimer's Text Box: yeah, sure thing, Elf Dude.

> Mr. Max's Text Box: I don't have any more epic gear to give you. I'm sorry.

> Anders' Text Box: Huh? That isn't what I was going to ask.

> Mr. Max's Text Box: Sorry. I thought that was it; I get that question a lot! That is the reason why I am out of the stuff.

> Anders' Text Box: No, that wasn't it. Max, can I come inside with you? I know this Pink Slime is the same one I met because it hasn't been killed by anyone else yet. I just want to thank it before you Insta-Wiki it.

> Mr. Max's Text Box: Wait, you're that buxom elf that I was searching for earlier! Okay, I agree, but only if you show me where the Slimes are.

> Anders' Text Box: Okay, Max, it is a deal. Fourni, can you stand guard outside for me and make sure no one finds the bush while we are inside?

> Fournimer's Text Box: sure! I can totally do that for you, Elfboy.

Anders used the *Confused Blink Animation*. Elfboy. He had almost forgotten about the name the pervert monsters had called him, but hearing it from Fourni, he suddenly liked the sound of it.

> Anders' Text Box: Thanks, Fourni. You're the greatest! I'll owe you one.

Anders touched the human on the lightly stubble-dusted chin, leaned over, and gave him a *Kiss on the Cheek Animation*. That made Fournimer use the *Too Stunned to Say Anything or Move Because a Cute Gay Elf Just Kissed Him on the Cheek and Completely Took Him Off Guard Animation*. Fournimer was not exactly sure why that was one of the *Standard Animations*, it was way too situational, but he turned the global count on it to 1 and was glad it was there to use. He was also glad that his *Light Gigas Pants* were not form fitting. Max and Elfboy quickly entered the dungeon, and Fourni waited outside, trying to be as non-epic and inconspicuous as possible while holding a bush for no real reason in this very low-level area.

As soon as they walked in, it was there, staring at Anders: his old nemesis, the Scenic Pillar, had a wry expression on its marble finish. Anders ignored the temptation to crawl back onto its subtle arch to reach his miscoloured pixel and instead focused on the task at hand.

> Anders' Text Box: Careful, the Green Slimes are acidic.

> Mr. Max's Text Box: So what? They are like Level 2 or something, and my stuff is Epic.

With just a few chops of his mighty sword, Mr. Max both raised the kill count of Green Slimes to 86 and completely dissolved his *Four-Handed Sword*. They each now had a good store of *Vials of Green Goo*, though Anders refused to put any in his *Ultra-Pack*. Mr. Max finished off his *Combi-Fusion* Insta-Wiki by mixing the *Vial of Green Goo* (which made sense) with a *Suntan Lotion* (which didn't) to make a low-level item called an *Acid Burn*.

> Contest Announcement Text Box: The Combi-Fusion Insta-Wiki Contest is over. Congratulations to all who tried.

> Mr. Max's Text Box: Nice! My prize was a bunch of experience! I am so much closer to max level now. An entire 0.01%!

> Anders' Text Box: That's all?

> Mr. Max's Text Box: What are you talking about? That is so much experience for Level 98—you have no idea! Crap, my *Four-Handed Sword* broke. That shouldn't have happened. My stuff is unbreakable. I sold all my *Repair-Its* for gold, and I think I gave away all my other swords. I don't even remember if I have one in storage.

> Anders' Text Box: The logic is broken here still. We need to be more careful. I have a *Repair-It*, but I just realized now that it is still on display in the *Portie Tent*. Toast! I forgot to go pick my stuff up! Just *White Wolf Kick* the Pink Slime or something to get the Insta-Wiki, and we can fix you later.

> Mr. Max's Text Box: *White Wolf Kick*? I forgot about that. Thank you … elf?

> Anders' Text Box: Elf is by far the closest you have come… and it is no problem, Mr. Beefcake! Let's search for the Slime Cave glade. I never went past this room and am sort of curious as to what this place is really like.

Anders shot all the Green Slimes that approached, all three of them. They turned the very first corner that revealed the boss glade, only 2 move units down the hallway.

> Anders' Text Box: Well, that was genuinely disappointing.

In the middle of the glade rested the undefined pile that was the Pink Slime. Inside the Slime's mass was a chest. It was probably red, but it was a bit strange, as if the Pink Slime had been sitting on it and trying to dissolve the chest for cycles now. It probably had been waiting there because no avatars were in the area, and Anders didn't kill the thing so it hadn't disappeared to respawn later. If there were some low-level pants in the chest that was just around the corner from where he first lost his, Anders decided he was perfectly justified in freaking out. The Pink Slime changed its view over to Anders and Mr. Max. It didn't glitch out or anything; it just looked.

> Anders' Text Box: Hello, um, Pink Slime. I came to say thank you. Even though you probably didn't mean to, you have saved my avatar countless times, and … uh, I will never forget it.

The Pink Slime quivered, like it was excited, like it understood Anders. It cast *Morph*, *Morph More*, and *Morph More More* and became the half-humanoid Anders had met so long ago. The Slime did something Anders didn't expect; it cast *Morph More More More*. Now it had almost full legs and a defined body structure, although still no real face to speak of. It moved off the chest it had been sitting on and gestured toward it.

> Mr. Max's Text Box: That chest is pink. There are no Pink Chests!

> Anders' Text Box: Well, there is one now. What should we do?

> Mr. Max's Text Box: Open it? It is clearly for you.

> Anders' Text Box: I think it might have been waiting for me this whole time … to come get this. Maybe it is thanking me for protecting it?

The Pink Slime nodded vigorously at that statement, and pointed at the Pink Chest again, very proud. Anders walked over and tried to open the chest, but it was very slick with a familiar goopy pink sheen. It even tingled his finger when he touched it. After a few rounds of slippery prying, he finally managed to open the pink semi-gelatinous chest.

Inside was a full set of gear rated More More Epic and allowed only for Anderses of Level 50 or more. The stats were impressive, nearly as good as his *Gigas Boots*. Anders couldn't really tell what they actually were modelled like; their icons were confusing, drippy blobs. They had a colour slider that was currently set to pink and a passive ability, but Anders couldn't equip them to find out what it did. They were called the *Slime Helmet (s)*, *Slime Gloves (s)*, *Slime Armour (s)*, *Slime Pants (s)*, and *Slime Boots (s)*.

Anders didn't know what to say. From what he could tell, the creature had spent every cycle of game time breaking logic rules to morph this chest into something special just for him. Maybe even morphed more. Tears welled up in his eyes.

> Anders' Text Box: Thank you so much, Pink Slime!

The Pink Slime sort of nodded, but that might have just been the jelly structure jiggling. Anders felt guilty.

> Anders' Text Box: I can't go through with this now! Look what it made me for protecting it. We can't just smack it down.

> Mr. Max's Text Box: I need its entry and drop item, though, or I can't win the Insta-Wiki Contest!

Anders used the *Smile Animation* at the celebrity avatar.

> Anders' Text Box: I think I have a plan for that.

Walking up to the Pink Slime in its *Morphed More More More* form, Anders put his arms around the creature's neck and kissed it on where its lips should have been. The creature quivered excitedly. Anders was already feeling the amazing tingles where the creature's gooey skin touched his. It was a very familiar and pleasant experience. He traced the creature's jellied muscles with his elf fingers and finally rested them where the creature's penis should be.

> Mr. Max's Text Box: Uh … what are you doing?

> Anders' Text Box: Defeating the monster. Don't worry, he looks scary on the book cover, but he is actually very nice.

The Pink Slime started to cast *Enlarge*, and with each casting, its penis grew a little more. Anders used his turns to lick and suck on the slick and growing member. Mr. Max used his turns to get more aroused by the scene in front of him. Once the jellied cock reached its final length of about 20 length units, it began to take shape and the balls began to grow. Anders did not let up; he licked everything. His tongue and lips were almost going numb from all the tingle stimulation.

Once the Pink Slime was enlarged as much as it could get, Anders turned around, spread his legs open, and activated *Steadfast* from his *Frost Gigas Ass-Pounding Boots*. The creature aimed the semi-solid cock at his opening and inserted a thin tendril again. Anders knew what was going to happen, and he moaned at the feeling of his slicked-up hole getting reslicked. After a few rounds, the creature's special reserve was drained into Anders, and Mr. Max was rubbing the front of his wet *Diamond Pants*.

The Pink Slime grabbed Anders around the waist with its arms and with a quick motion entered familiar territory. Anders gasped and pushed back toward the creature, forcing even more of it inside. Every tingle was a jolt of pleasure.

> Anders' Text Box: Do *Rolling Waves* again, please! It is still my favourite.

The Pink Slime complied happily to the avatar riding its member voluntarily. The pace began to pick up, pumping faster and faster. The moaning and bucking became more rapid and intense. Mr. Max was rubbing himself nearly raw through his unbreakable *Diamond Pants*. It was surprising that Anders could focus enough to remember anything important, but he Text Boxed it as soon as he did.

> Anders' Text Box: You need to help defeat it, or you will not get any credit!

Mr. Max was determined to get the wiki for this right now. Whoever that buxom elf lady was she needed help. She was certainly doing her best to help out by having sex with that sexy lesbian slime. Mr. Maxum was very turned on now, so that was a bonus. He dropped his pants and moved over toward the creature's jellied frame. He started to rub his big cock up and down the creature's morphed up nethers, and wonderful tingles overcame him. He wanted more and eagerly pressed his cock against what should be its opening.

The Pink Slime was just as happy to accommodate Mr. Max. It made a hole and accepted the epic penis without any problems. Mr. Max was so big, though, that he could see his penis reach the root of the Pink Slime's big clitoris. The tingles shot through Mr. Max, and the big avatar groaned. After a few pumps, he noticed that Mr. Maxum enjoyed the tingles of the lesbian slime vagina so much that it began to grow, as if Mr. Max was using *Increase Max More* every round. Anders felt and Mr. Max watched as the cock grew inside the creature and was slowly growing up the jellied clitoris, thickening it. In reality, it was a gay slime, a gay elf, a jellied cock, and a slime butt; however, Mr. Max was not the best at noticing vital plot points.

> Anders' Text Box: What are you doing?

> Mr. Max's Text Box: Nothing!! Mr. Maxum is doing it by itself!

With every thrust, Mr. Maxum grew just a little more. He had expanded the very bottom of the creature's member by about twice in girth. Anders noticed that it would no longer go in with the added size. He cast *Stretch More*, and it slid through to the hilt. Anders tingled like crazy as he realized that he was sort of getting plowed by the muscled avatar now. Mr. Max responded as if he felt Anders' tingles through the creature's skin because he moaned and pressed in deeper. Within just a few rounds, Mr. Max had completely filled up the jelly cock-sleeve, and was still expanding.

The creature's jelly was getting thinner each round, but it didn't mind; it just continued to fuck Anders by moving its and the human's cocks inside. Anders remembered how big Mr. Max had gotten even before the additional spell, so he cast *Stretch More More* as a precaution. Watching the big cock fuck him while surrounded by a different cock was such a bizarre turn on. He craved and savored every thrust.

Mr. Max thought that the Pink Slime was about at its stretch limit, but couldn't stop his erection from growing. It still had some time before it would stop at the second stage—or at least when he hoped it would. The creature fortunately did not break, and with each growing pulse more and more of its body was forced to become part of the cock-sleeve.

Once Mr. Max finally reached the second level, the creature had gone from being the size of a horse to that of about a normal human. The rest of its volume was stretched around Mr. Maxum.

Anders was moaning loudly.

> Anders' Text Box: Oh yeah, Mr. Max, give it to me!

Mr. Maxum bounced, and decided to take it further (without Mr. Max's consent). It began to grow toward the next stage. The lesbian slime tingles and the hot elf pussy were almost too much for it to handle.

Anders knew what was going on (mostly) and could feel the change. He remembered how big Mr. Maxum could get, and it would be even bigger with a creature cock-sleeve. He used his turn to access his *Ultra-Pack* and use a *Minotaur Musk*. By the time the musk cleared, Mr. Max was at full size and completely and comfortably in Anders. The only thing that could be seen of the Pink Slime now was its giant balls hanging in front of Mr. Max's. The rest of the thing was being used just to sheath the big, beefy cock.

Anders was relieved at how much the musk had helped him relax. This combo cock was at least as thick as the Frost Gigas, but this time he was only feeling the feels-so-good kind of pain. Anders began to work himself back and forth and felt two distinct sets of thrusting, the very obvious Mr. Max thrusts and the subtle Pink Slime thrusts from around the giant cock.

> Anders' Text Box: Yeah, Max! Go harder! Please?

> Mr. Max's Text Box: Fuck yeah! Let's get fucking. Take my big dick in your hot pussy!

Anders was not a really a fan of calling a guy's butt a boy pussy, but if that was what Max wanted to call it, he could let it slide this time.

Mr. Max started to thrust with more enthusiasm. Deep inside, the creature continued to use *Rolling Waves*. Multiple moans escaped from Anders who could feel a set of balls behind him begin to quiver, but he wasn't sure which they were. Soon, he felt the familiar *Pink Goo* shoot deep inside him and coat his insides once more. Anders grabbed his ankles to get a better view. The watermelon-sized slime balls had started to diminish. The creature was still writhing all up and down the giant shaft, and both avatars could feel it. The tingles were becoming too much.

> Mr. Max's Text Box: Oh, scones!

Anders watched as Mr. Max's giant balls began to throb. He could see them physically contracting. He couldn't feel anything from Mr. Max being added to the slime that was coating his insides. Anders tried to focus to see what was going on. He had half-expected Mr. Max to just break through the Slime when he came, but instead each shot was just replenishing the creature's balls. Anders realized that the Pink Slime must have *Stretch* and *Absorb* as well. As Mr. Max came, more and more slime goop was generated in the pink balls, and more and more of it would fill Anders.

A final tight thrust from Mr. Max, and Anders was gone, shooting his own load in barely there tingly drops that felt amazing. However, even after the elf and human were finished, the Pink Slime was still going strong. Mr. Maxum had finally decreased in size, and the creature now was no longer completely wrapped around the massive cock. It began forming a humanoid body once again. As soon as it had an anatomy, it continued to fuck and release its own goo. It took until Mr. Max was completely soft and Anders was completely full of goo for the creature's balls to wane. Anders felt his body slowly absorb the goo, but this time it went into his inventory, not into his MP reserves.

His *Ultra-Pack* listed the quantity of *Pink Goo*; he couldn't see it anywhere inside the pack, but it was listed there. The once maximum capacity of x99 *Pink Goo* had broken and increased to x188 … then x277, x366, x455, x544, x633, x722, x811, x900. It went all wonky for a round and tried to go to x1000, but finally settled on x999 with an extra that came out of Anders (glass vial and all) after the number change. When Anders could move again, he gave the extra to Mr. Max to help complete the Insta-Wiki.

> Contest Announcement Text Box: The Item Gathering Insta-Wiki Contest is over. Congratulations to all who tried.

> Mr. Max's Text Box: Nice! Even more experience! Another entire 0.01%!

The duo cleaned up with the unfortunate *Initiate's Jacket* and waved goodbye to the Pink Slime as it curled up onto its Pink Slime bed to get some much-needed rest.

> Mr. Max's Text Box: That is all the items, Combi-Fusions, and regular monsters! Now just one quick quest to finish for NPC Valisha and we can challenge the Plague of Shadow, you … lovable, sexy, dangerous Pixie, you!

> Anders' Text Box: Well! What are we waiting for, Max? Let's do this!

They opened the door to leave the dungeon and stepped outside.

> Palcath's Text Box: What's wrong with you, Mr. Max? Why did you do that, lad?

Mr. Max changed to *Blush Shade #6*.

> Mr. Max's Text Box: Do what?

> Lissa's Text Box: What took you guys so long in there? We've been out here forever.

Anders changed to *Blush Shade #6*.

Fournimer's Text Box: we were going to come inside looking for you but I lost the door.

⬥ Chapter 30 ⬥
BREAKING UP

Breaker was starting to get annoyed with all of his new minions. They had been told to do research, but had not yet produced any results. Breaker was expecting that his luck would soon change and waited for someone to speak up.

> Gliint's Text Box: Hey! *Wave* I found something.

> Breaker's Text Box: What?

Breaker scowled at the gnome after there was no reply for several rounds. He couldn't help but appreciate the irony. This Backstabber gnome had specialized in the Speed Style of the Backstabber class, the fastest of all classes. With the Speed Code he had used to make himself drastically faster and the bonus to speed he had gotten from being a gnome, he was the quickest avatar in the entire fantasy world. Unfortunately, he constantly froze up due to his poor internet connection. The Code had done nothing for the lag; it actually had made it worse. This completely aggravated the gnome. Breaker used the *Smile Animation* because the entire situation made him warm and fuzzy inside. Random server jumps during his combat actions often created scenarios where a monster would explode, and Gliint would be stuck hanging in the air, until a round later when he was able to finally complete the movements in ridiculously super speed. The fact that Breaker found this hilarious was the only reason he hadn't unleashed his best minion, the still very silent and poorly named warrior, on the lagger yet.

At least the gnome was a fellow Backstabber, even if he was the inferior Speed

Style as opposed to Breaker's Stealth Style. The strange decision the gnome had to pick brown as an accent colour would probably work for certain outfits, but it really didn't work for the gnome's current outfit. Gliint's *Daggers* and *Crossbow* were so inferior to his own that it was almost laughable. Oh, why not. Breaker decided that they were laughable and used the *Chuckle Animation*.

Well, at least his *#3 Hairstyle*, dark brown and a mohawk, was entertaining because Breaker had been calling it a gnomehawk, but that only went so far to redeem the little lagger.

> Breaker's Text Box: Well?

> warrier's Text Box: …

warrier used the *Shrug Animation* while looking in the general direction of the gnome.

> Breaker's Text Box: No, not yet.

> Caëlahenãilenŵhei's Text Box: I believe that the seeds of my research may have blossomed as well, for it has become apparent that I have ascertained something relevant to our plight.

> Breaker's Text Box: What C-Elf?

Might as well get to the point quickly with the impossible-to-pronounce light elf Rocket Sorcerer. Her name was the second hardest word to remember that started with the letter "C" that Breaker could think of. She was going to take forever to reply as well, but for completely different reasons than the gnome. She never spoke like a normal person, constantly using flowery language to sound smarter than she actually was. This took forever to type, due to either her low WPM or her constant thesaurus use. To top it off, she couldn't type without looking at her keyboard, which meant that her eyes were almost constantly closed thanks to her TorTech-Headset tracking them.

Breaker had always thought that the Rocket Sorcerer class was just a joke about stupid avatars until he had met her. In truth, it was simply the least popular class in the game. Well, technically, she was a Rocket Sorceress. She had used one of his Codes to change her class name, not knowing that it was from him—or that it would ruin her character, of course. Breaking your character over a grammar issue was probably the absolute worst reason Breaker had ever heard, which delighted him. Her accents were set to white, which always worked with the darker colours of the magical type Armour, but she was going to be in for a surprise when she got the Level 50 *Sapphire Cloth* and found out it was all white. It would have no contrast at all with her fair skin. She was wearing the *Circlet* style of head gear and not a *Cowl*. Too bad, the *Cowl* might have made her too hard to hear.

The *Magical Whip* she was using to cast her spells was much more like a riding crop than a whip. Her secondary backup melee weapon was a *Bigger Book*. Who fights with a book anyway?! That was stupid. Did you just slap things with it, or read it to bore monsters to death? Breaker assumed hers was the bore-monsters-to-death method of combat.

She was so very typically light elf that it almost made Breaker sick. She was *Body Type #2* and *Thin*, giving her absolutely no "jiggle". She would have been mistaken for a boy in a dress if not for her long *#24 Hairstyle* set to platinum blond and pale blue *#12 eyes*. The crowning elf achievement was her ears that were set to style *#28*, the biggest size. They stuck outward and were so oversized that they looked like they belonged to a completely different game altogether.

Breaker performed a *Toe-Tapping Animation*.

> Contest Announcement Text Box: The Combi-Fusion Insta-Wiki Contest is over. Congratulations to all who tried.

> Breaker's Text Box: What?! But how?

> warrier's Text Box: ...

warrier used the *Shrug Animation*.

> Gliint's Lag Text Box: Mr. Max's *Swoon* Player Pager is updated! His Insta-Wiki percentage is increasing!

> Breaker's Text Box: Thanks. I noticed.

> Gliint's Text Box: Sorry, *Apologize* bad connection.

> Zal Finn II's Text Box: That is so not sweet. I'm on it. Mr. Max hasn't updated his Player Pager for cycles now. Damn, I have no idea where he is.

Zal Finn II was as plain and generic as they came. Breaker was positive that she hadn't even changed anything during character creation. Everything was the default human female starting settings, which made her look identical to all of the generic NPCs. Her brown hair, brown eyes, and even ear type were uninspired and were all set to the default of *Style #10*. She was even the default starting class, a Warrior (Skill Style). Even before Mr. Max made that class popular, there were already far too many of them around. Her Armour was even brown and boring. While the accents were set to pink, it really couldn't save her genericness. However, she did her research well and was able to type very quickly. Breaker was amazed that she got lost in crowds without even having the *Stealth* ability—or a crowd to hide in, for that matter. She was way better at it than him, and he was actually built for that. Breaker remembered how her old helmet had completely covered her face, which had strangely made her easier to find.

At least she had the default body type for females (*Type #3* and *Normal*) giving her at least the default level of "jiggle". Breaker decided that even default jiggle was way in the Flaming Pit better than no jiggle at all.

> Zal Finn II's Text Box: Let me try my *Auto-Locate Eyes.*

Glowing pink text glimmered inside her eyes. Breaker thought it was pretty awesome of him to include that effect in the Code. She could scan the world for any monster, avatar, or NPC and discover their location. It was a fruitless endeavor, however, as the annoying Green Slimes and the other missing monster were hidden from view somehow. What a complete waste of breaking a character! Breaker was glad he hadn't wasted his avatar on something so stupid.

> Zal Finn II's Text Box: Strange, Mr. Max isn't showing up. He must be logged out.

> Breaker's Text Box: That just isn't possible. He just won the Insta-Wiki Combi-Fusion Contest! Try again!

> Caëlahenäilenẇhei's Text Box: So, I have checked into the annals of the avatars of this world and have found something most interesting and entirely relevant. My distant kinsman evidently has combated some vile creatures that our compatriots have yet to encounter. This Anders fellow has contended with the elusive Green Slimes, though none of our congregation has successfully unearthed their whereabouts. In addition, he appears to be a damaged character, based on these pictures. I am most pleased that his name started with A; otherwise, this venture would have taken much lo—

> Caëlahenäilenẇhei's Text Box: nger.

> Breaker's Text Box: Zal Finn?

> Zal Finn II's Text Box: I was already on it. Strange, he isn't showing up as logged in either. Let's see, a search of Anders' Player Pager leads me to someone named Roodg. Sweet Maker, this Player Pager is hard to read. They were stranded together and apparently killed a Gigas. He … uh … she is broken as well. Roodg's Player Pager mentions avatars named Fournimer and Palcath. Fournimer's is nearly blank. Palcath's is pretty full; just let me read all this.

> Breaker's Text Box: Hmm … we need to think abou—

> Zal Finn II's Interruption Text Box: Cra-zazy. This dwarf records everything. His party of Roodg and Fournimer started a quest to track down an elf that had killed a Green Slime, must be Anders. Things progressed, and he met up with others to start a new quest. What the

> chunk, no way! Impossible!

> Breaker's Text Box: No way what?

> Zal Finn II's Text Box: There is a picture of Palcath here with Lissa!

> Breaker's Text Box: So what? Who is that?

> Yallundy's Text Box: Lissa, the girl with the Hair Change Code. Zal Finn II talks about her all the time.

Breaker stared down the normally soft-spoken Soother. While Yallundy had every reason to be intimidating, she couldn't possibly pull off the *Intimidate Animation*. Standing at just under max height, her gray skin shimmered as if it had been mixed with silver. Her long pure white *#40 Hairstyle* and *#40 Style Eyes (Violet)* were not allowed by any race but troll. Unlike the male trolls, which Breaker had never even considered picking due to their extreme ugliness, the female ones were devastatingly beautiful. Even with the somewhat increased frame of the trolls, some girls just knew how to work their big curves, and Yallundy did so, although Breaker suspected it was accidental. This particular troll, however, couldn't intimidate a mouse (which existed in this world but all dressed in nice clothing).

The troll could cast spells thanks to her *Magic Wand*, but her secondary weapon was a musical instrument (currently a *Blue Lute*). You couldn't even attack with either of those weapons! No wonder hardly any avatars were from the Soother healing type.

The troll had broken her character due to her indecisiveness. She simply could not pick a favourite colour to set her accents to. So she had used the Colour Shift Code, which made her accents cycle through her two favourite colours, green and blue. This made her mostly have a teal accent appearance. Breaker couldn't believe she would destroy her character over something so trivial as colours, even if she didn't really know that would happen.

> Breaker's Text Box: Oh. Yes, of course. Lissa! How could I possibly forget someone as important and poorly named as Lissa? You know what? I really don't like her name.

> Zal Finn II's Text Box: Lissa's Player Pager has a picture of her standing next to Mr. Max on a boat during a storm! Lissa knows Mr. Max … sweet! She and Palcath were stuck together and have Gigas equipment now. So does Roodg, maybe … sort of anyway, and Fournimer. So does Anders!

> Gliint's Lag Text Box: Wow, really!? *Shock* Lissa? No way!

> Breaker's Text Box: So, Mr. Max knows about the Gigas equipment

and found a party with a full set. How did the jerk get his Insta-Wiki up?

Gliint's Text Box: Of course he does! *Reminisce* We found that Gigas thing out together!

Breaker's Text Box: You knew that all along and didn't tell me?!

Gliint's Text Box: I did tell you when we first met! *Face Palm* I was there when you tried and couldn't summon the Plague of Shadow yourself!

warrier's Text Box: ...

warrier used the *Hard Thinking Animation*. He really didn't like how Breaker had re-enacted out the scene of not being able to summon the Plague of Shadow to win sympathy over this group of adventures. He could have just asked for their help instead of tricking them into it. He was on a legitimate holy mission from the Maker after all.

Breaker's Text Box: No, about Mr. Max already knowing that!

Gliint did not reply; he lagged out.

warrier's Text Box: ...

warrier used the *Shrug Animation*. Breaker almost gave the go ahead to kill Gliint, but warrier had only shrugged, not shrug shrugged.

Zal Finn II's Text Box: The other four are all together just standing around. They aren't even that far away.

Breaker's Text Box: They are just peons. They don't matter.

Contest Announcement Text Box: The Item Gathering Insta-Wiki Contest is over. Congratulations to all who tried.

Breaker's Text Box: Crap! I need to find Mr. Max, and I need to find him now.

Yallundy's Text Box: NPC Valisha.

Breaker's Text Box: Who? What? Speak up!

Yallundy was nervous and flustered. Breaker was too forward and aggressive for her; it stressed her out.

Yallundy's Text Box: It ... just ... but....

Breaker aggressively used the *Toe-Tapping Animation* while being annoyed.

> Breaker's Text Box: Out with it already, ogre!

> Caëlahenãilenẇhei's Text Box: She is a troll.

> Breaker's Text Box: Whatever, C-word.

> Gliint's Lag Text Box: *Shrug* You never asked me that!

> Zal Finn II's Text Box: Calm down, Breaker. She just means that Mr. Max needs to complete the quest portion next. Amirite? He will most likely need to go convo with NPC Valisha to complete the Vials of Green Goo quest.

> Breaker's Text Box: That's right! Perfect. warrier, you are with me. You guys stay here. We will be back soon to pick you up.

> warrier's Text Box: …

warrier used the *Nod Animation.*

> Zal Finn II's Text Box: Sweet! No, not sweet. We should come with you.

> Gliint's Lag Text Box: *Arms crossed* Yallundy is a troll!

> Breaker's Text Box: No, you five just stay here. We will be faster alone. Buff us, troll.

With an array of Yallundy's best buffs and a burst of *Serpent Speed* from Breaker's set of abilities, the duo was nearly ready. But first Breaker had something important to do. With a *Stretching of His Arms and Dramatic Hand Flourish Animation* Breaker went off toward Clamincramil (or whatever the damn city was called). With the increased movement speed, they were out of Text Box range in only a few rounds.

> Zal Finn II's Text Box: There are five of us left here?

> Caëlahenãilenẇhei's Text Box: Yes, just because Kray hasn't Text Boxed anything recently doesn't mean he isn't part of the active party. It is actually a personal record for him being quiet. You should not complain about this turn of events. I certainly am not.

> Zal Finn II's Text Box: I know that, Caela, but I was saying it for the benefit … never mind.

> Kray's Text Box: Sorry, I was getting a sandwich. Kay, what's going on?

Kray was a male standard elf Night Ranger of nearly the slightest build (he still regretted picking average and not thin—oh, how it haunted him) and shortest height that made him resemble having the frame of a twelve-year-old girl. It wasn't a requirement, but almost all of the male elf avatars looked much like girls. For someone that picked a pretty boy elf with a flippy red *#4 Hairstyle* and cared so much about his appearance, it seemed odd that he didn't give a Start Rat's ass about accent colours and left everything on the defaults. None of his equipment matched; it was all from different sets. It was all just the stuff with the best bonuses—he didn't have a theme going in the slightest. From a distance, his outfit and hair actually hurt to look at; it clashed that badly.

He had all the distinctive attributes of a "twink" in both ways. He was definitely the gay slang version of twink—a little, skinny, gay pretty boy who only cared about his looks. He was also definitely the game slang version of a twink—a lower-level gamer with max-level stuff, chosen only to give him the best stats. He was the very rare double twink.

> Caëlahenãilenŵhei's Text Box: I would advise that you read the Battle Log and familiarize yourself with what has been revealed in our current situation. Once you've returned to the present, please be sure and speak up again, 'kay?

> Kray's Text Box: Kay, fine. I don't really think that I should have to read, of all things. I will just skim this.

> Gliint's Lag Text Box: Yeah *Nods*, Kay is in the party.

> Kray's Text Box: My name is Kray, not Kay, kay?

> Yallundy's Text Box: I have been thinking lately, and well—

> Zal Finn II's Interruption Text Box: So have I, Yallundy. I think I am going to do a little research.

> Caëlahenãilenŵhei's Text Box: I have already conducted an extensive investigation whilst searching through the various Player Pagers and WorldForums annals seeking out information regarding the missing Green Slimes. With careful scrutiny, I have come to the conclusion that just a small number of players have broken characters as we do. The most common way for breaking is from entering a Code. However, the initial Code list was taken down almost immediately after it was posted on the WorldForums, after some complaints were sent to the Developers and avatars got deleted perm—

> Caëlahenãilenŵhei's Text Box: anently.

> Gliint's Lag Text Box: Kay, *Formal Bow* sorry about that, Kray.

Zal Finn II's Text Box: Unsweet! Permanent deletion of avatars? How?

Caëlahenâilenẘhei's Text Box: Save File corruption was the cause. Once the corrupted avatar dies, it cannot reload a save.

Zal Finn II's Text Box: Breaker never told us that when he shared these Codes with us! He told me they were different from the Hair Code colour bug that messed up Zal Finn I!

Kray's Text Box: Kay, well, maybe he didn't know? He probably didn't know. He is tall. Tall guys do not lie.

Caëlahenâilenẘhei's Text Box: I am fairly certain that the height of an avatar has nothing to do with honesty. By your own inane logic, you are not trustworthy in the slightest as you are quite short in stature. Breaker not knowing about the Codes is possible, but doubtful. We four have only been broken for a few cycles. Kray, you were already broken when we met you, but you didn't use a Code, correct? The Codes were taken down cycles and cycles ago.

Kray's Text Box: It took me a long time of rubbing against them, kay. But I got those Minotaurs good after they finally broke me.

Kray used the *Reveal Personal Plot Point Animation*. No one else really took notice.

Zal Finn II's Text Box: Well, I guess Breaker could have written the codes down when they first were posted and kept a copy, right? It isn't that hard to cut and paste. He hasn't used one yet so I guess he just didn't know it broke avatars. It isn't like he made the damn things and knows them all by heart. He wouldn't just willingly lie to us and give us a way to break our avatars permanently for a good laugh if he knew that it would corrupt our save files.

Caëlahenâilenẘhei's Text Box: I suppose you are right as that is an unlikely scenario. I still think I will do more research on the matter.

Gliint's Lag Text Box: Hey, *Angry eyes* I'm not tall, and I'm super honest. Honestly!

Contest Announcement Text Box: The Quest Completion Insta-Wiki Contest is over. Congratulations to all who tried.

Zal Finn II's Text Box: I'm on it!

The eyes of the plain avatar began to glow as she was searching the world intently.

Gliint's Lag Text Box: Permanent deletion? *Sigh* No way! My stupid Code didn't even work. *Increased Speed*, my cute little gnome ass. It did nothing to end the horrible lag. I don't want to lose my awesome boots!

Zal Finn II's Text Box: warrior is not even halfway to … Cavranderwinwill yet. Strange, I can't even see Breaker. Mr. Max is standing next to NPC Valisha. He must have completed the quest. I still cannot see the Green Slimes, though. I have no idea how he found them. Mr. Max is with all those others—Anders, Fournimer, Palcath, Roodg, and even sweet Lissa.

Kray used the *Examine Your Nails Animation* with very little enthusiasm.

Kray's Text Box: Kay, we should hurry up and get over there!

Zal Finn II's Text Box: No, Breaker said to wait here for him to get back, so we should wait.

Caëlahenãilenŵhei's Text Box: My opinion is that would be a poor decision for the three following reasons. Account one: It is unlikely that Breaker will actually be returning, not after what just happened. The action he is most likely to take is that of continuing his relentless seeking out of Mr. Max; of this, I am certain. So, despite what he said, he is not coming back here. Account two: We can never get back to … the starting city in time, so going back there is unadvisable. Account three: Remaining here will not be beneficial at all, effectively accomplishing absolute—

Caëlahenãilenŵhei's Text Box: ly nothing.

Zal Finn II's Text Box: What do we do, Caela?

Caëlahenãilenŵhei's Text Box: Simple, Gliint has *Advanced Serpent Speed*, which is faster than Breaker's regulation *Serpent Speed*. We are also far closer to the Moving Stairway of Clouds than any of them. Most importantly, the rules clearly state that if we are not in the Floating Castle area and the Insta-Wiki Contest is completed, we will not be counted as being in the active party of those who killed the Plague of Shadow. We can likely save ourselves by getting ported over to the expansion due to save file transferring.

Kray's Text Box: Kay, I like that plan. Let's do this already. I heard in the expansion there are better hair-dryers. Mine is almost fried.

> Zal Finn II's Text Box: Sweet! Agreed! Gliint, cast *Advanced Serpent Speed* and let's go.

> Caëlahenäilenẇhei's Text Box: Gliint?

> Zal Finn II's Text Box: Craptacular. He's frozen up again. Yallundy, grab him. He can cast the spell when he catches up.

With a decision made, the party advanced. Yallundy performed the *Sigh Animation* and picked up the little frozen gnome.

> Yallundy's Text Box: Okay, but … that isn't what I was thinking about it.

~ ~ ~

> Contest Announcement Text Box: The Quest Completion Insta-Wiki Contest is over. Congratulations to all who tried.

Breaker stopped in mid-run cycle and nearly fell over.

> Breaker's Text Box: What? That son of a bitch! How?

> warrier's Text Box: …

warrier used the *Shrug Animation*.

> Breaker's Text Box: You're right. Of course he would finish that quest part next. What do I do? I have to win this. The Maker declared it to be so.

> warrier's Text Box: …

warrier used the *Shrug Animation*.

> Breaker's Text Box: I should have brought that dumb generic broken idiot to help spy on him. I have a better idea. Get me a new one, warrier. One that is really stupid.

> warrier's Text Box: …

warrier used the *Nod Animation*, but was having second thoughts about the entire thing.

It wouldn't be very hard, being this close to the starting area that was crawling with newbies. warrier knew what Breaker wanted him to do. He found an entire party in the middle of a boss battle. He first chopped the Bombilworm they were fighting in half. He reluctantly collected the four avatars in his slender gray arms to deliver to Breaker.

Nestled in his grasp was a party of four small characters, not the gnomes but that other small stature starting race that felt like it should be breaking some copyright laws. This was going to be pretty easy for Breaker. These fools were greener than a Green Horner.

> Breaker's Text Box: Sorry to grab you out of your battle, friends, but I need your help.

> Mary's Text Box: Whoa, they are like Level 66!

> Piping's Text Box: How could we possibly help you?

> Breaker's Text Box: Simple, I have reached the maximum amount of Gold Pieces. I need someone to take some off my hands. I also have some equipment to give away as my *Ultra-Mega-Pack-Super Mark 2* is full.

> Frillo's Text Box: Free things are great!

> Samantha's Text Box: I don't know. What is the catch?

> Breaker's Text Box: No catch at all. Right, warrier?

> warrier's Text Box: …

warrier used the *Nod Animation*.

> Breaker's Text Box: Here, take these, little ones.

Breaker performed the *Hand Something to Someone Else Dual Animation*, and the four little avatars eagerly took some items. Breaker had recently refined a technique to add Codes to equipment. It was a simple process that involved hacking the equipment itself—and it was perfect for taking advantage of low-level idiots like these.

> Mary's Text Box: 10,000 GP free as well! Wow! Oh my Maker Breaker! This is a *Loko's Helmet!* It is so awesome!

> Breaker's Text Box: It has a special ability as well. It will allow you to find people or monsters!

> Mary's Text Box: We can finally find those Green Slime things or even Mnt. Volcano! Oh … it says they are all hidden.

> Piping's Text Box: Hey, I have thi—

> Breaker's Interruption Text Box: We are doing this one at a time to avoid confusion. Let's finish with Mary first. Mary, do me a favour. Can you locate Mr. Max for me?

Mary's Text Box: I've heard of him. He is famous! Sure, no prob. Yup, there he is. He is by NPC Valisha with some others. Oh, wait, now he is running out of town.

Breaker's Text Box: Thanks, now move to the back of the line. Piping, you are up.

Piping's Text Box: These *Mad Daggers* are neat. What do they even do?

Breaker's Text Box: They let you cut a path directly to a few places. The starting city's fountain is the only one you have heard of, but now you can go there whenever you wish.

Piping's Text Box: That is so cool. Now we can go right back to … uh … I think it is called Colkeen.

Breaker's Text Box: Do me a favour. Can you open a path right now? Then move to the back.

Piping's Text Box: Sure thing!

Frillo's Text Box: This *The Glum Ring* is awesome! It has cryptic poetry on it and even lets me use *Stealth Mode*, and I'm a Warrior!

Breaker's Text Box: Crap! I didn't mean to give you *The Glum Ring*. I wanted to give you this pair of *Fritzing Gloves*. Samantha, I wanted these *Fritzing Gloves'* ability next. You haven't equipped yours yet, so put this on instead.

Samantha's Text Box: I don't think I want to do that.

Breaker's Text Box: Whatever. I don't have time for this shit. Deal with this one, warrier.

warrier's Text Box: …

warrier used the *Nod Animation*.

warrier took out his *Katana* and, with a single swipe, cut the low-level Samantha in half. He had to do what Breaker said; Breaker was on a mission from the Maker, after all. A fountain of black pixels spurted from the severed corpse. The rush of a nonexistent fire ripped through the three remaining little avatars, shooting out an array of black pixels and a shrill yell of "Cheat" that Breaker loved to hear.

Mary, Frillo, and Piping's Simultaneous Text Boxes: What the warg?

> Breaker's Text Box: Good luck with that new Bombilworm, by the way. I hear they are pretty nasty.

Breaker and warrier walked away while hearing some uncomfortably lewd noises from behind them. warrier very nearly used the *Sad Cry Animation*; he felt horrible for them. Bombilworms never left survivors.

> Breaker's Text Box: Now what?

> warrier's Text Box: …

warrier used the *Shrug Animation*.

> Breaker's Text Box: You are right. We don't really have enough time to get someone to put these *Fritzing Gloves* on. That dumb popular beef-headed idiot is probably halfway to the Stairway by now.

> warrier's Text Box: …

warrier used the *Nod Animation*. Why did Breaker care so much about Mr. Max? Why would Mr. Max be so important for a holy mission from the Maker? He was just a man.

> Breaker's Text Box: You're right. It is ready, cycles of cycles of work. Fuck it. If I am going in, I am going all in. I am not just getting one Code like some useless chump.

> warrier's Text Box: …

warrier used the *Scowl Animation*.

> Breaker's Text Box: Oh, shut up. You love PVP mode.

> warrier's Text Box: …

warrier used the *Sigh Animation*.

Breaker retrieved his *Breaker's Belt of Awesomeness* from his inventory (he named it himself). Every Code he thought that could possibly be useful (or at least was interesting) was enchanted on this unimpressive looking belt. It took the deaths of numberous idiot avatars and millions of hard-earned Gold Pieces from low-level morons to perfect the Coding. When it was done, it was a thing of incalculable power. It also contained the Code that he had never released to the public. The one he had saved for himself: Administrative Mode.

He had received a written warning and a two-cycle suspension about releasing the Codes. The suspension was actually very valuable to him. By watching the other avatars jump blindly into his Codes, he discovered that only one Code could be applied before the avatar was broken. But, as he found out later, applying more than one at the same time worked out fine.

The other thing he learned by releasing the Codes was that using your own avatar name for things was a bad idea. After his suspension, he set up a system of routing himself through a series of dummy accounts. That way, anything he did was untraceable. No Admins were ever coming to chastise him again; that was guaranteed.

Breaker equipped his *Breaker's Belt of Awesomeness*. When the buckle snapped shut, a ripple of sound and power emanated from his body. The wave of power rushed outward from him, spreading all through the map. A few of the closest low-level avatars exploded from the wave's impact.

warrier was knocked off his feet and had to cover his ears. The map-shattering "Cheat!" that was shouted nearly made his brain explode. Once warrier could finally open his eyes, Breaker was nowhere to be seen and the cut path to the fountain was gone.

> warrier's Text Box: ...

warrier used the *Fold Your Arms Animation*. That jerk on a holy mission from the Maker had just abandoned him on the side of the road.

◊ Chapter 31 ◊

TO THE CASTLE IN THE SKY

Mr. Max's Text Box: I am sorry, okay? Everyone would have found out once I completed the Quest for NPC Valisha, anyway.

Lissa's Text Box: While that is true, meathead, they found out hundreds of rounds sooner than they needed to!

Fournimer's Text Box: calm down, Fair Maiden, it isn't like someone has been secretly plotting against Bro or anything.

Mr. Max's Text Box: Well, Breaker is the only other one close to winning. He might be secretly plotting against me.

Lissa's Text Box: All the more reason to not alert him two hundred rounds earlier!

Palcath's Text Box: It doesn't matter anymore, lads, lass, and Roodg. We are already way out of range of ... uh, Cogcorcoggins, anyway. I completely forgot to write down the name again when we went inside.

Anders' Text Box: Yeah, and we hid the entrance to the Slime Dungeon behind the scenic bush. Breaker and everyone else will never be able to find it. Cheesecake, that doesn't sound really sporting of us now that I say it out loud.

Lissa's Text Box: #CheeseCakeIsFair! I agree to drop it for now. We should just hurry up and get to, um … where are we going?

Roodg's Text Box: dUH! tHE cASTLE IN THE sKY!

Lissa's Text Box: I know that, but it is in the sky, right? How do we even get there?

Mr. Max's Text Box: We use the Moving Stairway to the Clouds, of course! That is where we have been running to since you made me skip NPC Valisha's entire dialog. I wanted to read it so bad!

Lissa's Text Box: We are running?

Fournimer's Text Box: correction, we have been running. Palcath has been carrying you. you have been yelling.

Lissa's Text Box: What, really? Well, when will we get there?

Mr. Max's Text Box: We are there. Get on the Moving Cloud Stairway, and let's go.

Lissa's Text Box: I'm just going to shut up for a while.

Roodg's Text Box: pLEASE.

The Moving Stairway to the Clouds was nearly everything it promised to be. It was moving, and it was going toward the clouds. What it was not was a stairway. It was a platform, if anything. This made Anders upset for a reason he really couldn't place. He still sat down on one of the platform's provided chairs. He was futher disappointed because the cloud seating should have been comfortable, but it really wasn't.

Mr. Max's Text Box: See that half-dwarf already knows what to do. We need to sit down for this thing to start, fellow teammates!

Roodg's Text Box: oH! fELLOW TEAMMATES!

The platform (that was masquerading as a stairway) only started to move upward once everyone was correctly seated. It started with a lurch, a rumbling gust of wind and energy, and the faint sound of thousands of dead voices whispering the word "cheat". Anders wasn't sure if anyone else had noticed the dead whisper voices and was going to mention it since they had freaked him out,. but then the platform began to rise. It was above the treetop level, and the full map of Gentalia was revealing itself before them. Soon Anders was so caught up with the scenery from this vantage point that he forgot to mention the "cheat".

This background music was "Stairway Stairway Lifting Light" by Ainsley's Arrow. Even if it was a great song, Lissa hated it; she was no longer a fan of Ainsley's Arrow after hearing them constantly in the Tower of Mechanis. She hated them, but nowhere near as much as the most famous band that had supplied songs for this game—Caution Step. Oh, how she hated them.

> Palcath's Text Box: How long does this stairway ride take anyway, lad? We are not exactly moving up quickly.

> Mr. Max's Text Box: 257 rounds.

> Lissa's Text Box: What? That is like forever! Are we just supposed to sit here and waste that many rounds? Mega #SoFuckedUp!

> Fournimer's Text Box: you were going to shut up, remember?

Fortunately for Fournimer, Lissa had not used the Code to get *Laser-Guided Bunny Missiles That Shoot out of Your Eyes*, or he would have been burned to a fine bunny-roasted crisp.

> Palcath's Text Box: What are we supposed to do for that long, lad? Why did those programmer lads make this take that long?

> Mr. Max's Text Box: The programmer lady, I think you mean. The head programmer was totally a lady. I'd remember something like that. Well, normally an adventuring party would spend this time talking about the epic quest up to this point and planning their strategy for the battles to come.

> Anders' Text Box: We probably shouldn't waste time talking about the epic quest. I only completed two parts from an eight-part quest, and I have no idea what any of it meant.

> Mr. Max's Text Box: Why not? It was epic! So many threads and sub-quests!

> Anders' Text Box: Well, forgetting that … what is our plan?

> Mr. Max's Text Box: Just sing the song I wrote! '♪♫ We skip the epic quest parts and … we go left, we insert the *Jewel of Krackatosh* (a-tosh!), go left, then up the stairs and around the corkscrew (clock-wise)! Go right, and down the ladder. Then it is right, flip the three levers there,

but you need three people for the three switches (threeee)! After it is left, through the portcullis (but not at all below it). Go right and touch the Pillar of the Plague of Shadow to summon the final battle … we will fight! Da nah! ♪♫♪' Then use jazz hands!

Roodg's Text Box: tHAT SONG WAS sAWESOME!

Roodg used the *Cheer Animation*. Lissa did not.

Lissa's Text Box: No, it wasn't. That was a horrible song! But why isn't it leaving my head? Why was it so catchy? Why do I want to give you money to buy it now? What did you do to me, you devious bard! Make that horrible song leave my head!

Mr. Max's Text Box: Besides the song, we will be avoiding all but the necessary mid-boss battles and seven monsters on the first path to get whoever was Level 42 to Level 50. Until then, she should stay back. As a ranged style Night Ranger, she should be doing that anyway.

Fournimer's Text Box: whoa Bro, that was pretty specific.

Palcath's Text Box: I like it, lad. Well planned out. It is settled. That is our plan.

Palcath used the *Cheer Animation*. Lissa did not.

Mr. Max's Text Box: Trust in your leader.

Lissa's Text Box: What? You are not the leader! Besides, that plan only took three rounds to settle! ♪♫ but you need three people for the three switches ♪♫ We still have 235 rounds left until the top. I, for one, will not just sit here and wait quietly.

Roodg's Text Box: oBVIOUSLY.

Palcath's Text Box: Well, I suppose we do have some exposition to get through. We could always do that, lads, lass, and Roodg.

Lissa's Text Box: I have a question then. What is the Plague of Shadow? ♪♫ The Plague of Shadow to summon the final battle … we will fight! Da nah! ♪♫

Lissa used the *Jazz Hands Animation* and changed to *Blush Shade #6*, the highest possible shade.

Lissa's Text Box: Damn you and your stupid song, Max!

Mr. Max's Text Box: Besides the name of the kick-ass official Caution Step song for this game, the Plague of Shadow is also the main antagonist. The story thus far indicates that it destroys entire fields of crops in mere rounds and will slowly starve the NPC population to death.

Anders' Text Box: Who cares? All their silly crops taste like appliances.

Mr. Max's Text Box: Mmmm … appliances.

Lissa's Text Box: Yeah, okay. But what IS it exactly? This Plague of Shadow?

Mr. Max's Text Box: It is THE Plague of Shadow!!!

The rest of the party did the *Looking Expectantly Animation*.

Mr. Max's Text Box: Okay, I have no idea. I couldn't summon it, but it is probably big and likes food.

Lissa's Text Box: I guess we should hide our meat and potatoes.

Roodg's Text Box: hEAR THAT Anders? bETTER STAY BACK WHILE IN THAT SEXY PIXEY OUTFIT!

Lissa's Text Box: Nice.

Anders' Text Box: Hey!

Mr. Max's Text Box: Good point, Duh Roodg. That elf doesn't have Level 50 equipment yet, unlike everyone else. She should stay back.

Roodg's Text Box: yEAH! wE GOT ARMOURS & STUFF! mINE IS ALL WHITE & sAWESOME!

Roodg spent a round using the *Getting Up* and *Twirling to Show Off Animations*. After the platform stopped its ascent, everyone threw things at the avatar until Roodg took a seat once again. The new *Sapphire Cloth (s)* had layers of transparent fabric, and accents that had been changed to red. Layered on the jet black skin of the night elf avatar, the outfit had a far more beautiful model than it would on any other standard avatar. Even the avatar's one visible crazy *#36 Style Eye* was more intense. The outfit was completed by a shamanistic *Sapphire Casting Staff*. The glowing ball of energy in the centre, which Anders assumed was blue by default, had been changed to red. A *Bigass Bitchslap Ring* was on Roodg's hand. It wasn't the highest level ring, but it had made Roodg laugh more than the *Sapphire Ring*.

Lissa's Text Box: Mine is #SexyHot, even if the sleeves and boots cover up more than everything else combined.

Lissa was secretly grateful that, despite how short her new *Garnet Skirt (s)* was, it did not reveal anything (unless she performed the *Stretch Animation*). The *Garnet Sleeves (s)* were very large at the wrist but tapered into a thin band near her shoulders. Her tall boots ended only length units below her short skirt, and her new circlet was almost identical but had much better stats. Her *Garnet Blouse (s)* was boosting her cleavage even more than her *Uplifting Blouse (s)* had, but she was loving it. It had all been turned to purple accents before she even dignified the orange colour by trying it on. She really disliked orange; it was a very scene-stealing colour. Her new *Garnet Healing Mace* was far too menacing to have the word "Healing" in the title, and her *Garnetlet* would project a magic shield in the shape of a gem—a now-purple gem.

Palcath's Text Box: Well, I like it, Lissa lass.

Lissa *Animationed* something but hid it with her obnoxious sleeves.

Palcath's Text Box: I am just glad that I found out my *Wind Gigas Helmet* ability and my Code stack, lads. Now I can calculate hit odds, average damage, see elemental weaknesses, and find out hidden rules. Very exciting.

Palcath was proud of his new *Diamond Shield* and *Diamond Hammer*, and he kept them out even when not in battle. The silver of it matched his new *Diamond Plate*, which now had some yellow gold accents. The colour scheme for this outfit was kind of pale and not very exciting, but Palcath had chosen yellow as his colour, and Anders was impressed that Palcath had stuck with it. The dwarf's Armour was just like Mr. Max's except for the fact that all the cloth material under the Armour was missing, perhaps to provide clothing for underprivileged mice.

Mr. Max's Text Box: I don't get it, Dwarfman. How come your *Diamond Plate* is so different from mine?

Palcath's Text Box: Well, mine is *Diamond Plate (s)*.

Roodg's Text Box: hEY! i CAN DO THAT NOW!

Palcath's Text Box: Do what?

Lissa's Text Box: Yeah, you keep saying that. What can you do?

Roodg's Text Box: i FOUND THE *pORTABLE aNVIL* @ THE mINOTAURS.

Anders' Text Box: Oh, yeah, you did. It lets you turn normal equipment

> into (s) equipment.

> Mr. Max's Text Box: I didn't find that, and I have 100% Item Completion, Duh Roodg.

> Roodg's Text Box: iT LETS YOU ADD STUFF 2 ARMOUR & TURN IT sAWESOME!

> Lissa's Text Box: So, this *Portable Anvil* turns perfectly normal equipment into (s) equipment? How is that useful?

> Anders' Text Box: I literally said the exact same thing.

> Roodg's Text Box: cAUSE (S) EQUIPMENT IS MORE sAWESOME!

> Anders' Text Box: Then Roodg literally said that exact same thing.

> Fournimer's Text Box: can I see Guy?

> Roodg's Text Box: k

After messing with the *Portable Anvil* for a few rounds, Fournimer used the *Perk Up Animation.*

> Fournimer's Text Box: whoa! if I change these *Emerald Boots*, *Gloves*, and *Helmet* to their (s) versions, they will increase in a bunch of stats and not even look that different. I'm totally doing it.

> Anders' Text Box: Wait, their stats get better? You never told me that, Roodg!

> Roodg's Text Box: i SAID (S) EQUIPMENT IS MORE sAWESOME!

Fournimer's new (s) equipment was almost the same as it was originally, but it was (of course) a bit more revealing. The *Emerald Helmet (s)* was even showing a bit through the avatar's hair, but it looked as if it were deliberate now.

> Mr. Max's Text Box: Studly equipment has better stats? This is the kind of plot exposition I am interested in! Let me use it next, Fourni!

Without a single shred of shame, the beefy avatar stripped down and was completely naked while throwing his gear into the *Portable Anvil*. Anders sneaked a very noticeable peek. Fournimer sneaked a much less noticeable peek.

> Lissa's Text Box: Maybe don't change the pants! You can barely contain that thing as it is. With only a codpiece to hold it in, you are going to be unintentionally slapping monsters with it on every attack.

Mr. Max ignored Lissa and stuffed himself into a very unfortunate codpiece. Anders guessed that Mr. Max would be too interested in the boost to stats to worry about the fact that he would be slipping out every time he did his trademark *Flex Animation*. The truth was that Mr. Max simply forgot.

> Lissa's Text Box: Dear Maker, I can see it breathing!

> Palcath's Text Box: Okay, that is over. Do we have any other exposition to get out of the way, lads, lass, and Roodg?

The avatars thought for a few rounds.

> Anders' Text Box: Oh, I picked up my stuff from the *Portie Tent*!

> Fournimer's Text Box: I fixed all my decorations that had been moved in the *Portie Tent*.

This time, it was Lissa who was lucky not to get a dose of *Laser-Guided Bunny Eye Missiles*.

> Mr. Max's Text Box: I fixed my *Four-Handed Sword* by throwing it away and using a much better *Five-Handed Sword*.

> Lissa's Text Box: Damn. I can't think of anything else. There are still like 204 rounds left. So fucking #SoFuckedUp!

> Palcath's Text Box: It is a very nice view now, though, lads—you can almost see the whole map from up here.

> Fournimer's Text Box: crap!

> Palcath's Text Box: You don't agree? I think it is. Even if you never take screenshots, Fourni, I am taking one!

Palcath took a panaramic shot to upload to his Player Pager later.

> Fournimer's Text Box: no, crap as in crap. down there. I just saw that Jive Turkey warrior's name down at the bottom of the platforms. it just popped out of view now.

> Lissa's Text Box: Did you seriously just call someone a 'Jive Turkey'? Please don't make that his official nickname; I couldn't stand it.

> Anders' Text Box: Which Warrior?

> Mr. Max's Text Box: No, his name is warrier. That Jive Turkey is Breaker's head stooge.

> Palcath's Text Box: Breaker. That guy … no, uh… man … no … dude … no. Damn it, Fourni, you've taken so many things as nicknames I can barely talk anymore. Oh, wait! Breaker, that lad with the Codes? Well those lads are rounds and rounds behind us! We can still easily beat them there.

> Roodg's Text Box: hEY! wE FOUND MORE EXPOSITION BY ACCIDENT!

> Fournimer's Text Box: OMM! I forgot completely! Guy was right! Breaker was actually Buddy who we met before, that scam artist guy. when I saw him again those other two henchmen were gone, just like Roodg said! I bet the other two are dead now. Man you were really lucky because that Jive Turkey can cut avatars in half and Kill Kill them!

Palcath's eyes opened wide, and he added another checkmark to the Roodg is smart column.

> Roodg's Text Box: rEALLY! nO WAY! iF HE CAN CUT AVATARS IN HALF, i BET HE KILLED KILLED Grandiger & Hellsfight FOR REASONS! tHEY WERE PROBABLY HIS OLD FRIENDS! bE CAREFUL, DRAMATIC STUFF IS AFOOT!

Palcath added another.

> Palcath's Text Box: How could you possibly know that, Roodg?

> Roodg's Text Box: i ATE ALL THE COLD CUTS!

Palcath added another, but this time under Roodg is not smart.

> Fournimer's Text Box: no, I only saw Jive Turkey. he was much taller than Buddy though. does height come into distance to see avatar names at all?

> Lissa's Text Box: Does common sense come into your nicknames at all? #Seriously. The possibly hyper evil master of all Code creation, chief competition in our chance to succeed, is nicknamed 'Buddy'? The evil henchman 'Jive Turkey'? No more Jive Turkeys or Buddys, Scarfy!

> Mr. Max's Text Box: I don't know, fellow Bro. That is a good question about height. Probably not for horizontal distance, but maybe vertical. Perhaps you could help me experiment horizontally and vertically sometime?

Fournimer was beginning to change *Blush Shades* after that comment. He needed some kind of distraction before everyone started to notice how positively flustered the innocent question had made him. So far, only Roodg was giving him a *Smirk Animation*. Well, Fournimer assumed it was a *Smirk Animation*, since he could see a flash of Roodg's teeth.

Suddenly, the map shook violently below. The cloud platform nearly came off its pre-determined path. Far below them, a pinpoint on the starting city's geometry turned red, and transformed everything into thick black ice as it spread outward. A pulse of energy waved from a corner of the city and continued outward, completely covering the starting areas in a desaturation filter. Distant popping noises could be heard, even from this far away, as the filter crept out. With each pop came a tiny spurt of black pixels that drifted away from the city.

The pinpoint spurted a column of flames, which quickly spread until the entire start city was first burned, then melted into a black patch of no geometry. A spiral comet flew upward from the spot and began to float in place about 300 move units above the city.

> Fournimer's Text Box: I guess that works.

> Palcath's Text Box: The Flaming Pit?

> Mr. Max's Text Box: Strange, that didn't happen last time I went up these stairs.

> Roodg's Text Box: i gUESS WE DON'T NEED TO REMEMBER THE NAME OF THAT CITY ANYMORE. iT IS DEAD DEAD NOW.

The comet dropped a very small blue speck that hit the ground with a loud thud and a cascade of shattered crystal. After the crystal was released, the comet rose again and flew toward Starting Mountain Range. Once there, the comet hovered over an obvious path that ended in a dead end—a dead end with a scenic bush and a signpost.

> Palcath's Text Box: What did it just drop?

> Mr. Max's Text Box: Well, some things are visible, no matter how far away they are—Golden Chests, important bosses, and dungeon doors, to name a few. Maybe the comet dropped one of those.

> Anders' Text Box: It's right over Slime Cave now! Why? What was that thing? What is it doing!?

Before anyone could answer, the comet shot out a large beam of energy at the entire Starting Mountain Range. After a pause, the area glowed a bright white, and an instant later exploded violently. Bits of debris rained over all corners of the map. Large chunks of geometry fell from the sky and tore through the scenery below. When the smoke effect cleared, much more of that starting city was gone, the Triple Bridge now was only the Twin Bridge, and the entrance to Rockagin's cave was sealed shut with the entirety of the Lushin Jungle. The entire Starting Mountain Range where Slime Cave once stood was now a single, out-of-place black square.

A single pentagon fell lightly onto the cloud platform, and Anders felt a shiver go down his spine—and an ache bloom in his heart. The Pink Slime was certainly dead now. Probably even dead dead.

> Palcath's Text Box: That's why, I guess, lad.

Anders did a *Grim Resolve Animation*.

> Anders' Text Box: Mysterious comets ... you just made my list.

Anders' List:
1. Scenic Pillars
2. Glades
3. Status Effects
4. Constrict Bars
5. Traps
6. (s) Gear
7. Swarm Beetles
8. Combo NPC/Monsters
9. Jumping Puzzle Blocks
10. The Game Explanation Text Box
11. Mysterious Comets

The avatars continued to drift upward while silently observing the scene below. They were quiet for many rounds, simply watching the destruction.

> Roodg's Text Box: iT IS MOVING!

The comet flew up toward the platform and hovered near them. It stopped just short of crashing into the cloud. It hovered, observing them, and smirked. It was not an official *Smirk Animation*, but it was still a smirk. It flew upward to the Castle in the Sky and vanished.

> Palcath's Text Box: I repeat. What in the Flaming Pit?

A further 98 rounds crept by without anyone Text Boxing another word. They were all too stunned to act, except for Lissa and Roodg, who were searching in menus. Roodg finally broke the silence.

> Roodg's Text Box: cRAZY COMET & MAP ENDING CARNAGE SCREENSHOTS UP!

Roodg's outburst was shortly followed by Lissa, who broke the silence with something far more meaningful.

Lissa's Text Box: Are NPCs on that list by chance, Max?

Mr. Max's Text Box: Huh? What list?

Lissa's Text Box: The list of things you can see from far away, no matter what.

Mr. Max's Text Box: Yes, they would be, Fair Maiden. As would pre-set campsites, Gigases, Admin—

Lissa's Interruption Text Box: It was NPC Valisha.

Fournimer's Text Box: how could you possibly know that?

Lissa's Text Box: While you were all #CarnageGawking, I did research. There are hundreds of complaints about avatars exploding near the starting city. All their files were corrupted, but nobody can start a new avatar to continue playing.

Palcath's Text Box: Well, let's try to find out while we are up here. We are just waiting ar—

Lissa's Interruption Text Box: I already did. All those pops we saw were avatars exploding.

Fournimer's Text Box: but ... there were hundreds of them!

Lissa's Text Box: According to the WorldForums, the official count is 873 avatars dead, but the count is still rising. Level didn't matter either; at least one Level 77 exploded. What is more troubling is that the entire NPC population of ... whatever, it doesn't matter anymore ... has turned to black crystals and can no longer be interacted with. People cannot restart without the initial NPC Wizard Narbenock greeting quest, so the game is locked to newcomers. A team of high levels just reported in from there.

Fournimer's Text Box: how do you kno—

Lissa's Interruption Text Box: Let me finish, Jive Scarfy. Text Boxes can only be so long.

Palcath's Text Box: 550 characters including spaces.

Lissa's Text Box: Right, anyway … the high levels are led by someone named 'Jorthan the Male Troll Warrior.' It is likely that Jorthan is a Troll Warrior and male, I would think. Their party was just outside the blast and saw a different group nearby explode. They went to investigate and found it odd that the only NPC not turned to crystal was NPC Valisha. She was simply missing. This is why I think she was what we saw Breaker drop from the sky and shatter.

Roodg's Text Box: hE IS ONE OF THOSE! u R riGHT Lissa! a MALE TROLL wARRIOR! wE MET HIM!

Palcath's Text Box: We did, Roodg?

Roodg's Text Box: hE TOPPLED YOU OVER, CHECK YOUR NOTES.

Palcath did check his notes, and Roodg was right. He was forced to add another check to the Roodg is smart column.

Mr. Max's Text Box: Jorthan? I love that guy! Wait, Breaker? That comet was Breaker?

Anders' Text Box: Why would you know Jorthan's name and not ours?

Lissa's Text Box: It is definitely Breaker. There are several eyewitness accounts from now-exploded avatars that saw him yelling at NPC Valisha about her repetitive Green Slime dialog. They saw him explode, killing all the avatars in the area. My guess is that he didn't blow up, but turned into the comet instead. Hmm … at least one avatar began to restart but became stuck when the NPCs turned to crystal just after that.

Anders' Text Box: That is insane. Who would do that?

Mr. Max's Text Box: Breaker, apparently. Crap. His Insta-Wiki increased. His quests are at 100%, and his killed monsters are at 100%. Destroying Valisha must have eliminated the entire quest line. If he killed killed the Slimes, maybe they are gone from existence as well? Oh. His items and Combi-Fusions are still only at 99.9%. Each recipe was worth 0.2%…. That means he got rid of the *Vials of Green Goo* from existence but not all the *Suntan Lotions*.

Roodg's Text Box: hE OBLITERATED THEM?

Anders checked his Insta-Wiki. Both Pink and Green Slimes were no longer marked as monsters #124 and #125. They were not even in the monster list anymore. They were indeed dead dead.

> Anders' Text Box: That complete piehole! He killed them!

> Roodg's Text Box: pIEHOLE! nEAT.

> Palcath's Text Box: So, the lad went off the deep end?

Explosions began thundering from above. The once-fluffy white clouds were now dark and changing colour. The air became charged with energy and was unpleasantly hotter the closer they drifted toward the multi-coloured monstrosities.

> Anders' Text Box: Perfect, now there is a lunatic with no regard for the safety of avatars that has turned into a comet and is loose doing who-knows-what in the one area we desperately need to get to!

> Mr. Max's Text Box: I know! Exciting, right?

Chapter 32
THE FLOATING CASTLE IN THE SKY

Lissa's Text Box: This Floating Castle in the Sky is a total floating dump. Someone really needs to hire someone to jazz this place up. #InteriorDesignerForTheWin!

Fournimer's Text Box: where is the epicness? the monsters? the background music? there is supposed to be a Fergus Finders' song playing here!

Mr. Max's Text Box: I don't understand, fellow teammates. It wasn't like this the last time. We go left.

Lissa's Text Box: '♪♫... we insert the *Jewel of Krackatosh* (atosh), go left ...♪♫' Crap. It is still in my head! #StupidSong!

Heading left at the intersection only led to more of the same. The castle was not very impressive. It was a bombed-out shell. This was certainly not the final area to anything dramatic. Partly destroyed walls with their geometry showing were covered in haphazard burn marks and gouges. It might have been impressive if the entire distressed model had been designed like that on purpose, but the sections of pristine white stonework with antique black marble trim were too perfect.

Standing as the only point of interest in a very large, otherwise featureless room, a once-impressive stone statue of a heroic figure with a spear (not even a weapon in this game for a class) was broken completely in half. A hexagonal opening at the base of the statue was visible once Mr. Max lifted the top half of the figure out of the way.

> Mr. Max's Text Box: Insert the *Jewel of Krackatosh*. Get ready to fight!

Fournimer took the *Jewel of Krackatosh* from Mr. Max's inventory. The arcane golden stone was inserted into the base of the statue, and was twisted until it clicked. Dramatic music struck up in the background, and the party prepared for a mid-boss battle. A large section of wall descended into the floor to reveal … absolutely nothing. Only scorch marks and a path that continued further into the castle came into sight. The dramatic music ended abruptly.

> Roodg's Text Box: lAME!

> Palcath's Text Box: I have to agree. That was lacklustre, lass … er, Roodg.

> Mr. Max's Text Box: Well, that was much easier without the Fire Giant Chieftain to fight.

> Fournimer's Text Box: really? aww too bad, I wanted to see Anders take out another giant solo.

Mr. Max used the *Impressed Whistle Animation* while everyone else but Anders used the *Smirk Animation*.

Anders couldn't think of a retort, so instead he tried to change the subject.

> Anders' Text Box: Where to next? Let's hurry.

> Mr. Max's Text Box: Down the hallway and left.

> Lissa's Text Box: We all know the stupid song!

Uneventful scenery, a lack of music, and nothing to fight did little to increase the dramatic tension of the situation. Not even Fournimer's *Fancy Scarf (s)* could help. After a turn left and confirmation from Mr. Max to go up the stairs (not down the ladder), the party was in another long, boring, empty, and demolished corridor.

> Roodg's Text Box: tHIS IS so LAME!

> Palcath's Text Box: Lads, I agree with the Roodg. This is SO lame.

> Mr. Max's Text Box: The corkscrew is next, Man. I think that the monsters on that are set to spawn during the ride around and that you must kill them all to exit.

> Lissa's Text Box: You think? Don't you know everything about play

mechanics?

Mr. Max's Text Box: I only came here once, Fair Maiden. I didn't have time to retest my theory yet. I'm secretly excited that we are here. I have to get my spreadsheet open!

Palcath's Text Box: I always have my spreadsheet open, lad!

Fournimer's Text Box: that doesn't surprise me one bit Man.

Mr. Max's Text Box: Would you like to see some of my spreadsheets … Palcath Man?

Palcath was elated. Mr. Max had acknowledged him.

Palcath's Text Box: Hey, you know my name now, Mr. Lad!

Mr. Max's Text Box: Who could forget my joint leader who likes spreadsheets?

Fournimer's Text Box: hey, you must be important now!

Lissa's Text Box: We can't have three joint leaders, meathead!

Mr. Max's Text Box: Good thing I only count two, Palcath Man and myself.

Lissa's Text Box: I am a joint leader!

Mr. Max's Text Box: Who are you again?

Roodg's Text Box: gO! kILL!

Lissa's Text Box: With pleasure!

Roodg's Text Box: nO THE MONSTERS!

Chasing after the now-sprinting night elf, the party came to an out-of-place mechanical corkscrew. Even if the Floating Castle in the Sky was in tip-top shape, this section would still throw off anyone who was concerned with the game physics. Once the entire party was on the gigantic device (with plenty of room to battle), it began to rotate and lift them skyward. Intense battle music began to fill the air, and monsters fell from the sky as Mr. Max had predicted.

Anders originally stayed close to the battle, participating with his melee attacks. He was forced to change his plan after a single stray attack from a Queen Gribblet nearly took him out. He backed off and stuck to ranged attacks as instructed. He noted that the massive stat boost at Level 50 was making a noticeable difference in his teammates. Even the frail Roodg would be victorious against Anders in a bitch-slapping contest if one happened to break out.

The experience the monsters were dealing out was encouraging. By the time the mid-boss, a ProtoChimera (which was like the regular Chimera but was much smaller and much stronger, for some reason) had been killed, Anders had reached Level 49.01.

> Lissa's Text Box: How come a prototype is stronger that the normal version? #SoFuckedUp!

> Palcath's Text Box: Prototypes are always stronger, lass. It is a rule.

> Roodg's Text Box: u R JUST MAD BECAUSE IT TRI-HUMPED YOUR LEG!

> Lissa's Text Box: Only a little.

> Fournimer's Text Box: okay Bro, where to next?

> Fournimer's Text Box: ...

> Fournimer's Text Box: Bro?

> Palcath's Text Box: He is updating his guide. That is commitment to fans right there. A Mr. Lad after my own heart.

> Lissa's Text Box: I thought we were in a hurry! We don't have time for this.

> Mr. Max's Text Box: We go right next. Hurry! There isn't a round to waste!

> Lissa's Text Box: Except for the rounds we just wasted.

With more force than necessary, Mr. Max shoved open a door. Normally, it wouldn't have mattered, but the scenery crumbled around the door as it was ripped from its hinges. Despite his best efforts, the door would not allow itself to be dropped. Mr. Max had to eventually put the *Left Handed Door* into his *Ultra-Mega-Pack-Super Mark 2*, slightly embarrassed.

> Anders' Text Box: Max, is there another mandatory battle before we get there? I'm almost Level 50.

> Mr. Max's Text Box: Not that I know of. The mid-bosses all should be, but so far most of them have been missing. Maybe we will get ambushed soon, though!

> Anders' Text Box: Here's hoping!

> Mr. Max's Text Box: Down the ladder and right.

This time, the party avoided the stairs and went down the ladder. After a quick trip through a door and down a hallway, the party ended up in a room with three pillars, each with a lever.

> Mr. Max's Text Box: We need to flip the levers at the same time.

> Fournimer's Text Box: that isn't a challenging puzzle at all. I was scared it would be another *Puzzle Block* thing.

> Mr. Max's Text Box: It is. Flipping the levers all at once opens up the puzzle.

> Fournimer, Palcath, and Roodg's Simultaneous Text Boxes: fuck. Fuck. fUCK.

> Mr. Max's Text Box: Why are all of my party members upset? I love *Puzzle Blocks*!

> Lissa's Text Box: All of your party members?

> Anders' Text Box: I wasn't upset.

> Fournimer's Text Box: perfect. you can do it Bro.

> Mr. Max's Text Box: With pleasure, Fourni!

Mr. Max worked his *Puzzle Block* magic. For the rest of the party, it was impossible to figure out, but Mr. Max had it together in only a few rounds. The confusing yellow blocks exploded when they touched each other in groups of three.

> Roodg's Text Box: tHE YELLOW ONES EXPLODE?!

> Fournimer's Text Box: why didn't you tell us that Dwarfman? all those stupid puzzles were so hard!

> Palcath's Text Box: I had no idea, lad and Roodg!

> Mr. Max's Text Box: They do tell you that in the tutorial. Now we need to go left.

> Palcath's Text Box: Why tell someone that in the tutorial but not have yellow blocks show up until the tenth puzzle or so, after they have long forgotten?

> Mr. Max's Text Box: It reminds you during the intro to the Lova Min—

> Palcath's Interruption Text Box: Through the portcullis!

The portcullis was over-sized and imposing. It was normally only for dramatic effect, but with the destruction in the area, it was no longer attached to anything. All they had to do was push it over to enter.

> Mr. Max's Text Box: Almost there, we just need to go right at the next path and touch the summoning pillar.

The last junction had three paths: One led to the final boss (it was the glowing lights and big flashing arrows that gave it away). Another was a warp back to the entrance. The last path was an opening to a small cave.

> Anders' Text Box: Wait, in the cave … I think I just saw movement. What is in there?

> Mr. Max's Text Box: It is the not-very-secret optional boss. Pretty hard to beat, though.

> Anders' Text Box: Can we kill it quickly so I can get to Level 50? I'm nervous about the Plague of Shadow.

> Mr. Max's Text Box: Hmm … well, it wouldn't matter. Given your level and the experience split, you would only reach Level 49.92.

> Anders' Text Box: Doughnuts!

> Roodg's Text Box: LoL! lOVE IT. dOUGHNUTS!

> Mr. Max's Text Box: If you defeated it yourself, though, you would end up at Level 50.82.

> Fournimer's Text Box: Anders is a pro at defeating things solo!

> Lissa's Text Box: Definitely. I saw Loverboy take an absolute pounding and win in the end.

> Roodg's Text Box: yEP! hE CAN TAKE ON WHOLE GROUPS AT ONCE!

> Palcath's Text Box: He has challenged anything that rises! No matter how large!

> Mr. Max's Text Box: Well, that is a perfect plan!

Fournimer's Text Box: we will be right outside, just call us if you need help.

Lissa's Text Box: Finish it off quickly, though … okay, Loverboy?

Roodg's Text Box: whOOOOOO! gO Anders AND YOUR BUBBLE BUTT OF HOLDING!

Anders' Text Box: Wait! I never agreed to this plan! What is even in there? I think I've chang—

Roodg's Interruption Text Box: i SAID GO!

A single push from Roodg on the pacing—and therefore not currently *Steadfast*—avatar toward the cave was just enough closer to aggro the secret optional boss. With a flurry of prehensile branches, Anders was grabbed and dragged into the cave.

Roodg's Text Box: nEAT.

◈ Chapter 33 ◈

COMPLETELY OPTIONAL

> A nders' Text Box: —ed my mind.

Anders found himself hanging upside down and very tightly secured by his ankles.

> Anders' Text Box: Doughnuts!

Anders camera panned around himself. The room was covered floor to ceiling with plants, trees, and vines. There was a clearing in the centre. It was a freaking forest glade inside a cave glade. This was a double glade.

> Anders' Text Box: Doughnuts!

There was an official licensed song playing here. The fact that it was The Dread and, for some reason, Cary Roberts was singing a love ballad instead of her trademark death metal made it especially troubling. That couldn't be a good sign.

> Anders' Text Box: Doughnuts!

From this vantage point, he knew that his captor was a large tree—a large tree that spent its turn using *Bind More More More* and *Bind Most*. Anders no longer could move or act.

> Anders' Text Box: Doughnuts!

All the trees in the glade lifted their roots up, transforming themselves into walking plant monsters. They all spent their turns slowly moving closer.

> Anders' Text Box: Doughnuts!

The parting tree creatures revealed a secret area of the glade. Hundreds of monsters and dozens of bosses previously hidden came into view. They gathered together and moved toward him aggressively.

> Anders' Text Box: Doughnuts!

The squeezing vines clenched tighter around his body. Anders was nervous. None of these monsters were glitching out, nor were they particularly horny.

> Anders' Text Box: Doughnuts! Doughnuts! Doughnuts!

It was getting hard for Anders to breathe. Tighter and tighter his bindings became as the rounds progressed. His Hit Points actually began to drop. On his next turn, Anders would have to either pass out or call for help.

> The Dryad's Text Box: All right, Eugene. That is enough. It isn't him.

> Eugene's Text Box: Gruuu?

The vines loosened, and Anders was gently placed on the ground.

> The Dryad's Text Box: Back down, everyone. It isn't Breaker.

The gang of monsters and trees backed down grumpily. They took their next turn to root themselves back into the ground and rejoin the scenery. By the time Anders was on his feet again, all of the plants and monsters were either rooted or hiding.

> The Dryad's Text Box: But the question must be asked: who is it instead?

From behind the legs of the monster tree Eugene stepped a slim figure. He was slightly shorter than Anders, and his skin was a highly polished and varnished mahogany. The Dryad's body had been skillfully carved and sculpted by a master craftsman, from the muscles on his chest to the tips of his ears. He wasn't wearing clothing, but he really didn't need to be. Vines and leaves crawled over his body. Willowy branches and thin leaves were hanging from his head like dreadlocks. Another small patch of the leafy hair hid the creature's privates from view. The Dryad stopped just in front of Anders.

> The Dryad's Text Box: It is some sort of dangerous, sexy Pixie. I'll admit it: I am a fan of the wardrobe choice. Who are you, and why are you here?

> Anders' Text Box: My name is Anders. I'm just here to beat Breaker to th—

The Dryad's Interruption Text Box: To beat Breaker?!

Anders' Text Box: Yes, to beat him. My party and I came here to challenge the Plague of Shadow and defeat it before he does.

The Dryad performed a *Nodding with Understanding Animation.*

The Dryad's Text Box: Of course, and you know you must kill Breaker first to get there. That bastard is up there right now trying to summon the Plague of Shadow but cannot due to his Insta-Wiki not being complete. If he does manage to summon it, he will absorb it.

Anders' Text Box: He will ... absorb it?

The Dryad's Text Box: That is what happened here. He just showed up and started to absorb monsters and parts of the scenery into his belt. The lucky monsters ran here and hid. The trees and I saved as many as we could, but so many monsters and pieces of scenery just ... died. Not just dead, but dead dead. They haven't respawned since.

Anders' Text Box: He killed killed many avatars as well, and nearly all of the NPCs.

The Dryad's Text Box: So why are you here and not up there killing Breaker?

Anders' Text Box: Well, there were no monsters up here and I'm not Level 50 yet, but Mr. Max said that if I defeated you solo, I would gain enough experience to level up.

The Dryad gave an *Excited Look Animation.*

The Dryad's Text Box: You are with Mr. Max?

Anders' Text Box: Yes. Well ... uh ... in the same party, yes.

The Dryad performed a *Smile from Ear to Ear Animation.*

The Dryad's Text Box: It was a pleasure to die to that avatar. Such a pro. I didn't even think anyone could ever have stopped my tree army with just himself and some lagging out gnome. Wait. So, you must be the key to the plan? Mr. Max must know that, to defeat *Breaker's Belt of Awesomeness,* he needs an archer to snipe it from afar. What a genius.

Anders' Text Box: That is a great plan, but I don't think Max deserves credit for it. You do! You are a seriously smart NPC/monster!

The Dryad changed to *Blush Shade #Wood*.

> The Dryad's Text Box: Thank you. I am an optional boss. I am my own special type that is neither NPC nor monster. I am simply an Optional.

The Dryad spun around on the spot. He used the *Smile Gently Animation* at Anders.

> The Dryad's Text Box: Breaker must be stopped. You must do this. Please, shoot me with your arrow and defeat me.

Anders looked over the beautiful sculpture in front of him and used the *Frown Animation*. The Dryad had been nice thus far and had even possibly come up with a winning strategy.

> Anders' Text Box: I didn't really want to kill you.

The Dryad tilted his head playfully. With a simple flick of his wooden hand, the Optional used his control of vegetation to make the leafy layers of Anders' *Hard Leaf Armour* recede. Anders stood there in shock, left wearing only a necklace, bracelets, and a thin belt of leaves. The single leaf in his helmet stayed identical but blew gently in the breeze.

> The Dryad's Text Box: Who said anything about killing me?

The alluring plant man stepped forward to kiss Anders, pressing into his mouth with a wooden tongue. The wood could move and flex like it was made of flesh, but it was hard and had a smooth, polished surface. Anders enjoyed the new sensation of the tongue; it was strong and forceful, yet somehow gentle. This kiss was like nothing he had ever experienced before. He was quickly growing hard. A gentle wooden hand pressed against Anders' naked back, then down his thighs. The sculpted fingers massaging up and down made Anders become eager and start to leak.

The kiss ended, reluctantly on Anders' behalf. With another *Smile Animation*, the Dryad lowered himself to his knees, resting them comfortably on a large toadstool that grew under him. The Dryad gently took Anders into his wooden mouth, giving his head and shaft the same smooth wooden kisses. It was another strange sensation. The Dryad worked over the shaft with long strokes, his tongue lolling sweetly over the tip and his smooth hand cupping and massaging Anders' balls. Anders threw his head back from the intensity.

The Dryad began to hum. The breeze picked up around the two of them. Anders realized that the hum was the wind blowing through the Dryad's body. The sculpted wooden man began to vibrate with the music, as if his whole body were a wind chime. The music was beautiful, organically flowing and pure. Anders pushed against the Dryad in time with the song. Soon they were gently rocking together in the breeze.

The Dryad stood and planted another long kiss on Anders. Anders rubbed his fingers down the smooth back of the plant man. The skin was hard, but surprisingly giving under his fingertips. A soft moan from the Dryad was all the encouragement

Anders needed to continue exploring the wooden body. He slid his hands down to the Dryad's waist, slowly moving one hand to caress the creature's ass and the other to feel his twig and berries. Anders was a little surprised. Unlike all the other monsters he had met so far, the Dryad wasn't out of proportion. If anything, his member was a little on the small side, but it was just as sculpted and firm as the rest of the body.

Anders wanted to reciprocate the Dryad's attention, so he took to his own knees and began to explore the wooden shaft in front of him. The smooth surface and modest size made it very easy to work with. The Dryad had begun to rock and sigh. Two wooden hands brushed through Anders' hair. After too many blissful rounds to count, Anders rose and began to kiss the very gentle optional boss again.

They nuzzled and fondled each other, taking things slower than Anders had ever done in this game. It was passionate, it was intimate, and it was nice. Exploring his partner this way made Anders ache with anticipation. He had already begun to tingle and get slick. The wooden Dryad cock certainly wouldn't be the biggest thing Anders had ever taken, not by a long shot, but he was eager and ready to escalate. Anders broke the kiss, but the Dryad turned first.

Anders was sort of shocked when the Dryad presented a firm wooden ass toward him. Anders' cock twitched. He was so used to using his magic bubble butt of holding to get through encounters that he had completely forgotten that he could penetrate things as well. Now it was Anders' turn to *Smile Animation*. He knelt down and placed a hand on each of the Dryad's cheeks. The Dryad had an knothole that was smooth and sculpted like the rest of his body. It didn't actually have any give. Anders knew that it needed to get wet for him to get anywhere.

The Dryad gasped loudly as he felt a hot tongue plunge into his opening. He pushed back toward the sensation and shuddered as Anders pushed a slicked up finger all the way inside, making even the very deepest parts wet.

Anders stood and lined himself up. He guided his cockhead in, and gently pushed inside the very tight hole. The Dryad was exceptionally tight and warm. As Anders began to thrust, his spit lubrication quickly evaporated, but oily, slick liquid replaced it. It was drawn out by the friction, and with every thrust, Anders' member grew more and more oily. Anders pushed, aching for more, but he was taking his time. He wasn't like the Gigas; he wasn't like the Hydra, or even like Mr. Max. He was normal, and he wasn't going to rush.

He wrapped his hands firmly around the wooden waist, caressing the sculpted body. He was taking his time to feel his partner, to thrust, to give pleasure. He was so used to being, well, used in most of his encounters. His foes usually just used him to get off; he was practically a toy. This time, he wanted to prove that he was able to satisfy a partner on his own. The Dryad murmured with pleasure. Anders felt two wooden hands reach back to his thighs. The Dryad squeezed and pulled the two even closer together in appreciation.

On the Dryad's next turn, he completed four separate actions. The first was stepping forward and breaking the link between the two of them. The second was conjuring a mass of vines that hung from the treetops. The third was falling backward into the mass of vines and letting them lift him up and support him around the legs and arms. The fourth was spreading his legs wide and using the *Wink Animation* at Anders.

Anders used his next turn to capture the Dryad by the waist and find his way back into the waiting hole. The vine swing made thrusting exceptionally smooth and easy. Within only a few rounds, both sides rediscovered their rhythm. The Dryad began to hum once again.

On the Dryad's next turn, the only action he could manage beyond rolling his eyes back in his head was calling two more sets of vines. One set wrapped around the Dryad's solid member. The second entwined up Anders' legs and grabbed his ass tightly. The vines got to work and began to rub the Dryad's cock as they encouraged Anders to thrust harder.

> The Dryad's Text Box: Please! Please, harder now!

Anders wanted desperately to please the Dryad. He began to thrust with more intensity, more energy, and more power. The vines wrapped around his balls and squeezed. The Dryad was giving him permission to finish. With a final thrust and a gasp, Anders began to finish into the wooden hole.

The pulsing of his lover within him combined with the seed coating his insides was the limit for the Dryad. With a sigh and a final pull of the vines, the Dryad arched his back and shot out his thick, sappy seed in a single glob onto the soil at their feet. A purple flower sprung up where it hit.

Anders collapsed across the chest of the Dryad. The Dryad pulled him close, cuddling and nuzzling him intimately. After spending a few rounds clutching each other tenderly, Anders stepped away and removed his softening member from the Dryad. Releasing himself from the vine sling, the Dryad got up to stand before the small purple flower. Anders almost smirked when he saw his cum dripping out of the Dryad's hole when he bent over.

> Anders' Text Box: What is that colour flower for? I've never seen one before.

The Dryad just shrugged. He picked it up from the ground and twirled it around before holding it to Anders.

> The Dryad's Text Box: I'm not sure. But you need a drop item to win, so please, take it.

Once Anders took the little flower from the Dryad, he heard the short and uplifting trumpet music and knew he was now Level 50. The official name of the little flower was simply *Optional Flower*. Anders really didn't have the rounds to explore more options with the *Optional Flower* and stuck it into his *Ultra-Pack*.

> Anders' Text Box: Thank you.

> The Dryad's Text Box: It was my pleasure. Come back and visit anytime you like. I'll make you dinner, and we can talk.

> Anders' Text Box: I would like that. I'll bring wine.

The Dryad brought Anders forward for a *Tender Kiss Goodbye Dual Animation*.

> The Dryad's Text Box: Now, please. Go and defeat Breaker to end his reign of terror on this land, so you can end the Plague of Shadow's reign of terror on this land. I believe in you.

Anders nodded, blushing deeper than anyone ever had before. He had just unlocked *Blush Shade #7* for the world; now anyone could select it. With a quick kiss of his own and a squeeze of the Dryad's hand, Anders left the forest cave.

◈ Chapter 34 ◈
THE UNBREAKABLE BREAKER

Fournimer was averting his eyes and had just turned *Blush Shade #4*. Anders tilted his head, trying to catch Fournimer's eye to find out why. Anders couldn't quite figure it out and stared until Fournimer cracked.

> Fournimer's Text Box: what? well … uh … welcome back Dude! that was … longer than we expected.

> Anders' Text Box: Thanks, Fourni, where is everyone else?

> Fournimer's Text Box: …uh … they went ahead to try to think of a plan. we were going to leave Roodg behind instead butt, well you know. I meant to say but, not butt!

The human was still acting weird, and was tapping his fingers together nervously with a *Tap Your Fingers Together Nervously Animation*.

> Anders' Text Box: I already have the plan. Go tell them not to do anything while I change into my new Armour.

> Fournimer's Text Box: probably a good idea… see you in a bit, Elfdude.

It was only after the human left that Anders realized the *Hard Leaf* equipment was still in the completely exposed setting courtesy of the Dryad's plant control magic. Anders thought quickly about getting embarrassed by what happened but decided it was too late in the game to worry about modesty.

Reaching into his overfull *Ultra-Pack*, Anders found the *Slime Helmet (s)*, *Slime Gloves (s)*, *Slime Armour (s)*, *Slime Pants (s)*, and *Slime Boots (s)*. Taking off the *Hard Leaf* equipment broke the Dryad's spell, and the old equipment changed back into the regular sexy Pixie mode. After putting back the *Slime Boots (s)* (favouring his *Gigas Boots*), Anders switched into his slimey new duds.

Anders was pleasantly surprised with the *Slime* gear as he checked it over. It wasn't just a viscous layer of goo on top of him, as part of his brain was expecting. It was well-tailored, form-fitting, metallic Armour. Classy, stylish, and flattering. Anders used the *Smile Animation* when he saw that, even though a lot of this equipment had a semi-transparent sheen to it, everything that should be private finally was. No sneaky camera angles could look under his Armour and see his elf bits because, for the first time since Level 4, he no longer had his bubble butt of holding exposed for the world to see. This outfit didn't have large gaps around his waist or anything remotely (s) about it. Though form-fitting, this was a full jerkin, trimmed with deeper shiny metal around the neck, shoulders, waist, and arms. There would have been more around his legs, but he wasn't wearing the matching boots. The entire Armour set was currently set to pink.

Anders thought he could feel something initially slimey reach out and cradle his junk, in a non-threatening and form-fitting way. A quick sneak peek revealed that it was a semi-transparent *Jockstrap* with a cute little cartoon Slime smiling on the front fabric. Anders had no idea until this moment that Slimes could even be cute. Anders naturally took a round and changed it all to green. Even if Green Slimes had broken his original Armour, green was still Anders' colour, not pink. The *Jockstrap*, however, simply would not change; it enjoyed being pink.

Equipping the brand new Armour made Anders' weapons upgrade as well. While the stats were the same, they now matched the style of his Armour. Metallic, semi-transparent, and form-fitting.

The Armour had a passive ability called *Goop*. Anders couldn't find any description for what it did; plus, he really didn't have more time to experiment. He resisted using a round to take a screenshot, and hurried to meet up with the party.

> Palcath's Text Box: Lad, now that is an outfit! You are positively professional now.

> Roodg's Text Box: aWW BISCUITS! nO MORE ACCIDENTAL ELF BITS. i WILL MISS U SEXY PIXIE OUTFIT.

> Fournimer's Text Box: me, too.

> Mr. Max's Text Box: Yep, such a killer rack.

> Palcath's Text Box: Nope, not even a little, lads.

> Lissa's Text Box: Aww, but they were cute.

> Palcath's Text Box: Where did you get those snazzy new weapons as well, lad? They don't look like Fournimer's new ones. They just are so much +er!

> Roodg's Text Box: fROM THE tITAN! tHEY ARE sAWESOME aUTO uPDATING! hE SPANKED THAT BOSS GOOD i BET! gO Anders!

> Palcath's Text Box: What did you do to the Titan to get those from him, lad?

Anders didn't have time to explain; plus, he could tell by Palcath's *Revelation Animation* that he didn't need to. Anders had a plan that was much more important.

> Anders' Text Box: I will tell you later. We have more important things to do right now. Okay, so here is the plan.

> Lissa's Text Box: A plan? You?

> Fournimer's Text Box: I tried to tell them Dude. they didn't believe me.

Anders used a *Roll Your Eyes Animation* at the group. He knew that this plan would work, and he didn't have the rounds to waste to defend his honour. He simply tried to sound as professional as possible.

> Anders' Text Box: Breaker has equipped a Belt that allows him to absorb NPCs, monsters, avatars, and scenery. This has also made him part of all of those things, meaning that we can still see him from further away than we could if he was just an avatar.

> Palcath's Text Box: That makes sense, lad.... So, that is how he did it. It also explains the giant bird wing, the three extra limbs, that big horn, that small horn, the glowing black belt, and why we can see him from further away than normal viewing range.

> Anders' Text Box: I am a ranged-style Night Ranger. I have vastly increased range, much further than I could ever use to kill a monster with—which is silly, really. But from here, I could hit Breaker if I lock on. I am going to aim for his belt and try to destroy it.

> Mr. Max's Text Box: But if he absorbed a bunch of things, his stats would be through the roof, shooty person.

> Anders' Text Box: That is why I need Palcath to scope his stats. What

does he have? Any resistances?

Palcath activated his eyes and stared off into the distance.

Palcath's Text Box: I'm on it, lad. Wow, this is crazy. He has 88,789,678 Hit Points and a whole lot of Defence…. His magic Defence is much higher, though. Wait … all of his individual elemental resistances are much lower than his normal Defence or magic Defence, for some reason. You don't have elements, though.

Anders' Text Box: Yes, actually, I do. I can charge each arrow from a *6 Shot Multishot* with a different crystal. I'll need to borrow a *Fire, Ice, Light,* and *Dark Crystal.* The longer I charge the attack, the more damage I can do—and it sucks to be Breaker because I have 99,999,999 Magic Points.

Palcath's Text Box: Really? Crap, lad, you do. How do you have that many?

Anders' Text Box: Because I am awesome.

Roodg's Text Box: u MEAN sAWESOME!

After collecting the crystals, Anders added them each to his *Slimey Bow+.* He notched six arrows and charged them all. He took special care to notch them in rainbow order for extra visual appeal.

Anders' Text Box: Okay, I am going to start charging now. Palcath, I need you to monitor the damage formulas and other stats with your eyes and tell me when to fire.

Palcath's Text Box: All right, lad, I can do that.

Lissa's Text Box: Wow. Look at Loverboy, #TakingCharge. I didn't know he had it in him.

Roodg's Text Box: iT'S HOT.

Pulling into an *Arrow Charge Animation,* Anders watched as the arrows gradually filled with energy. He was determined to right the wrongs of Breaker, and his hard-earned Magic Point reserve was steadily dwindling.

Palcath's Text Box: Crap, lad. Given his much higher total magic Defence compared to your attack, even if you use all of your Magic Points, it will not be enough to kill him. Not even by a quarter.

Anders' Text Box: Brownies! Really?

> Lissa's Text Box: I know what to do!

Lissa began to cast every buffing spell she had at her disposal on Anders. He was now glowing with various special effects.

> Palcath's Text Box: That helped, but it still going to be a long way off, lass.

> Lissa's Text Box: Brownies!

> Mr. Max's Text Box: I know what to do!

Mr. Max summoned his *My Spiritual Storage Device from the Crags of Halm* and took out *a Platinum Necklace* and a *Super Duper Snazzy Belt*. He changed the accessories on Anders, taking extra care to not interfere with the trajectory.

> Anders' Text Box: Hey, thanks.

> Mr. Max's Text Box: No problem.

> Palcath's Text Box: Nope, still not even at half, lad.

> Mr. Max's Text Box: Brownies!

> Fournimer's Text Box: I know what to do!

Fournimer pulled the *Funnel* out of his *Backpack* and quickly shoved it down Anders' throat.

> Anders' Text Box: Mmmff?

> Fournimer's Text Box: quick! give me all your *Mana Potions*!

> Palcath's Text Box: Good idea, lad, I have a bunch, but they are in the *Portie Tent*.

> Mr. Max's Text Box: You can use *Portie Tents* at the tri-junction we just passed. Someone quickly go down there and get as many blue-coloured potions as they can. Oh, and get as many *Blue Flowers*, *Big Blue Flowers*, *Bigger Blue Flowers*, *Biggest Blue Flowers*, and *Bottles* as you can. I need someone to start mixing all the kinds of *Mana Potions* in a *Combi-Fusion Pot*.

> Palcath's Text Box: Use Anders' golden *Combi-Fusion Pot*! It is free.

> Lissa's Text Box: I'm on the *Portie Tent*. I'll grab everything.

> Roodg's Text Box: i MIX!

> Fournimer's Text Box: I'll pour.

> Anders' Text Box: Mfffm!

> Fournimer's Text Box: good point! get anything you can out of Anders' *Ultra-Pack* as well when you get back, Fair Maiden.

> Mr. Max's Text Box: Yes, and grab any stat-boosting items you find, Fair Maiden.

> Lissa's Text Box: Yeah, I already thought of that, meathead.

In just a few rounds of mixing, there was a steady flow of potions heading toward Anders' *Funnel*. Mr. Max was finding them, Roodg was mixing them, Lissa was transporting them, Fournimer was pouring them, Anders was trying to swallow them, and Palcath was calculating them. Anders' belly was noticeably swollen and was even becoming visibly blue under his semi-transparent Armour, but his *Absorb* ability was helping to keep the swelling down (a little).

> Palcath's Text Box: Keep at it, lads, lass, and Roodg. We just passed half.

Lissa was searching through everyone's packs now to find the last of the potions. She handed everyone's in-stock potions to Fournimer and the last of the *Flowers* and *Bottles* to Roodg.

> Lissa's Text Box: We are almost out. I've searched through everyone's stuff.

> Palcath's Text Box: We are not going to make it, lass.

> Mr. Max's Text Box: I knew it would come to this…. As soon as we started to use resources … I just knew it.

Mr. Max opened his bag. A semi-transparent menu opened in front of him.

> Mr. Max's Text Box: I can buy and sell items through a *My Spiritual Storage Device from the Crags of Halm*, but it is expensive. Everyone, I know it is hard, but give me all your gold, old gear, and junk items. I will not let Breaker win after what he's done!

> Various Text Boxes: What, lad? What, meathead? wHAT? what Bro? Mffmb?

> Mr. Max's Text Box: If we can't get rid of Breaker, fellow adventurers, we can't save our avatars!

Various Text Boxes: Fine, lad. *Sigh*. bROWNIES. all right bro. Mffmb.

Fournimer poured the last two potions into the funnel. Anders started to glow bright pink, overshadowing all the buffing glows. The pink glow began to pulse, and Anders was pulled into the air and flipped upside down for an entire round before settling back on his feet.

Anders' Text Box: Hummf??!!

Lissa's Text Box: What in the map was that?

Fournimer's Text Box: brownies! these were not *Mana Potions*. they were something called an *Allure Potion* and that crazy upside down *uoıꞈod ɐuɐɯ*. what did that do?

Mr. Max's Text Box: I haven't heard of either of those things.

Anders now realized why, so long ago his rescue party hadn't picked up the boss drop in Chapter 2—they never saw it—and why the *Allure Potion* didn't count toward his *Combi-Fusion* total. They were both broken items, and now he wasn't sure what they might do.

Palcath's Text Box: Well, no idea what the *Allure Potion* did, but Anders now has the *Allure* status effect on, making him 'hard to resist,' whatever that means. That *uoıꞈod ɐuɐɯ*, however, made Anders' Magic Points flip upside down. Luckily, he was at 1,895,826 Magic Points left when it happened, so he just gained a whole bunch. Those numbers all worked upside down and are larger when flipped. Huzzah!

Lissa's Text Box: Enough that we don't need to give up our gold and stuff?

Palcath's Text Box: I'm afraid not, lass.

Mr. Max's Text Box: It is too late, anyway. I spent it all. Here, everyone take an armful of potions and force feed them to that *Funnel* with the plan.

Roodg's Text Box: wAIT. wHAT IS THIS? i MIXED THIS *pURPLE oPTIONAL fLOWER?* wHAT IS AN *oPTIONAL pOTION?* tHE DESCRIPTION SAYS … UM….

Lissa grabbed the *Optional Potion* from Roodg but was just as dumbfounded.

Lissa's Text Box: Totally #SoFuckedUp. No, wait, I got this. Give me a round here to read…. It's in Leet, for some reason. 'Note to Self: Use this to kill Asshat Bastards.' Well, Breaker is an Asshat Bastard. I say we use it.

Mr. Max's Text Box: It couldn't hurt.

Anders' Text Box: Mmmmffffffff!!!

Anders was now getting his belly full of more potions than he could convert to archery power per turn. His belly was bloated, and he was choking back on the magical goodness. The last potion was administered by Lissa, and it was thick and tasted like heliotrope. Anders had no idea what it did, but suddenly his hair and skin began to beam bright purple.

Lissa's Text Box: Looking good!

Palcath's Text Box: Now Anders has the *Optional* status effect. He counts as an Optional, which is perfect for killing Asshat Bastards apparently. I don't have any idea what that means either, lads.

Fournimer's Text Box: is it permanent? he is sort of strange and sort of badass. the Armour needs to not be green for him to really pull off the purple though. maybe black or white might be good choices…

Palcath's Text Box: No idea on how long it will last. Wait … is that all of it? We will have enough Magic Points to do only about 13/16 of Breaker's Hit Point total.

Lissa's Text Box: Do we have anything left?

Mr. Max's Text Box: That is everything we have, fellow adventurers.

Fournimer's Text Box: so we did all that and we are still going to fail? that is so not right.

Roodg's Text Box: sTOOPID.

Palcath's Text Box: That is it. Anders is fully drained, and we are still a ways off. We have wasted all our gold, resources, and Anders' 99,999,999 Magic Points for nothing.

Anders' Text Box: Mmfum!

Fournimer's Text Box: huh Dude? what was that?

Anders' Text Box: Mmmmfffm!!!

Fournimer removed the *Funnel*. Anders belched a gigantic, mostly blue bubble, and Text Boxed while still standing in his *Charging* attack pose.

> Anders' Text Box: There is one *blue bubble* more thing we *seven blue bubbles* could do. *really big blue bubble* Well ... um ... I have *Absorb*. That is *last giant big blue bubble* how I got so many Magic Points in the first place.

After saying *Absorb*, Anders turned directly to *Blush Shade #7*. After hearing *Absorb*, Mr. Max also turned directly to *Blush Shade #7*. Both had skipped the rest of the shades entirely.

> Mr. Max's Text Box: Uh ... well ... then *Fill* would....

> Anders' Text Box: Yeah, *Fill* ... it would....

> Roodg's Text Box: i HAVE AN IDEA!

Roodg, who was standing beside Mr. Max, grabbed the avatar's big, beef arms and held them up in *Flex Animation* position. The big avatar was shocked but couldn't react in time as his poor codpiece flew to the side to escape his instantly growing erection. Roodg changed targets to the blushing Night Ranger and raced to yank down the avatar's *Slime Pants (s)*. Instead, as if reacting intuitively to the sexual situation, the *Slime* equipment automatically receded. Soon all but the *Jockstrap* was drawn quickly into the small, cute Slime button on the front of the pink *Jockstrap*. If either avatar could have blushed any more, they would have.

> Roodg's Text Box: hANDY! oKAY. nOW Mr. Max, GROW MAXED & *fILL* UP Anders.

> Mr. Max's Text Box: What? *Fill* who now?

> Palcath's Text Box: Lad, if I remember the sizing right, there might be enough when doubled from *Fill* acting with *Absorb* to push us over the damage threshold. At the very least expand so I can do some calculations.

Mr. Max complied with the request but was still a little embarrassed. It was unusual that Mr. Max was being so shy suddenly, but it was because this was some sort of nameless avatar, not just some sort of nameless monster.

> Palcath's Text Box: I am not sure.... There might be just enough....
> I don't know. The doubling is hard to factor in. It is really going to depend on how much is shot. Every drop would count.

> Anders' Text Box: I don't have any Magic Points left to cast *Stretch More* or *Stretch More More*. That is never going to fit.

The *Slime Jockstrap* reacted to that statement, and with a gushing noise it used *Goop*. A stream of gooped Armour came out from the *Jockstrap* and coated the inside of Anders' butt. The goop tingled, and a Text Box informed everyone that *Stretch More* and *Stretch More More* were now active. Anders felt very gooped up and ready, but realized that now all of his Armour was internal and would probably require a good washing.

> Anders' Text Box: Never mind.

> Mr. Max's Text Box: All right, let's just do this. I don't want to lose to Breaker after he destroyed most of the map.

Anders used the *Nod Animation*.

Mr. Max got down on the ground behind Anders and slowly shimmied his way toward the elf. There really wasn't any other way to do it under the circumstances. A direct approach would have affected the arrows, so Anders would have to ride him while standing astride Max's hips. Hardly the intimate encounter Anders had just experienced with the Dryad, but this was necessary.

Anders felt Mr. Maxum slowly enter him. As the big, beefy avatar shimmied up between his legs, Anders felt more and more wonderful pressure filling him up. Once he could see Mr. Max on the floor, he *Grin Animationed,* and let out a moan with some tingles. Anders saw Mr. Max tremble after a wave of tingles. Despite the audience, it was still very hot; Mr. Max was famous, after all.

After the very first thrust, Anders' ass twitched, as did Mr. Max's member. Both let out a loud moan and glowed yellow for a split-round. Mr. Max took a beefy breath, and started to thrust inside with some enthusiasm.

> Lissa's Text Box: What in the map was that?

> Anders' Text Box: I just gained a new ability under *Stretch*.

> Mr. Max's Text Box: Me too, but under *Fill*. It is called '*Surge.*'

> Palcath's Text Box: Well, lads, what does it do?

> Mr. Max's Text Box: A bit hard to concentrate here. Urgh. It says by linking with someone with *Absorb*, a *Surge* will happen during the *Fill* and both will experience a ten-round boost to stats and can share some abilities.

> Anders' Text Box: That didn't happen the last … um … I mean … nothing!

Anders realized the answer to his own question: *Surge* hadn't activated last time because there was someone pink and goopy in between the pair. It wasn't activated because their encounter was technically indirect.

> Palcath's Text Box: How much of a boost to the stats, lads? Which abilities?

> Anders' Text Box: It doesn't say!

> Palcath's Text Box: Crap, the math, I need to know by how much. It would be awful to miss by just a bit!

> Roodg's Text Box: i DON'T WANT TO MISS, SO i THINK i HAVE ANOTHER IDEA! Anders DOES IT MATTER WHERE YOU GET IT TO *aBSORB*?

> Anders' Text Box: Ghaaa … no, it just says inside. Why?

> Roodg's Text Box: k. Fournimer HELP ME MOVE THIS.

> Fournimer's Text Box: why, Guy?

> Lissa's Text Box: Okay, this is a Roodg plan, and I want to see what in the Flaming Pit Roodg could possibly be up to, so just do it, Scarfy!

> Fournimer's Text Box: you know what, you are right, Fair Maiden. I am beyond curious as well. let's do this Roodg!

Under Roodg's instruction, the pair moved a long piece of heavy bench from a pile of smashed scenery toward the intimate duo. After propping Mr. Max's upper body against the bench, both Fournimer and Roodg stood ontop of either side of the bench facing Anders.

> Fournimer's Text Box: okay, now I am very confused.

> Lissa's Text Box: Shhh … I want to see what happens next.

Roodg unbuttoned the *Dark Gigas Armour* and unceremoniously revealed a matching pair of his and hers genitals.

> Lissa's, Palcath's, Fournimer's, and Mr. Max's Simultaneous Text Boxes: OH! IT IS A ROODG!

> Anders' Text Box: What … what are you doing, Roodg?

A use of Roodg's *Switch* special ability later, and the female parts shimmered and disappeared.

> Lissa's, Palcath's, Fournimer's, and Mr. Max's Simultaneous Text Boxes: OH?

A new penis and pair of testicles sprang up underneath Roodg's current one.

> Lissa's, Palcath's, Fournimer's, and Mr. Max's Simultaneous Text Boxes: OH!

> Roodg's Text Box: u HEARD THE DWARF. eVERY DROP COUNTS!

> Anders' Text Box: Huh?

Roodg grabbed Anders by the pointy ears and buried the twin cocks into his confused mouth.

> Roodg's Text Box: sUCK US Anders!

Anders was so shocked he very nearly let the arrows go, but caught them at the last instant.

> Anders' Text Box: Mus?

> Roodg's Text Box: yEP! uS!

Roodg pulled down Fournimer's pants next, letting the human's very hard and heavily-leaking cock spring free. Fournimer changed to *Blush Shade #7*, happy for the new number. He was so aroused by what was going on in front of him, but he still tried to push Roodg off.

> Fournimer's Text Box: Roodg! that's not cool!

> Palcath's Text Box: The extra stores of you lads and Roodgs will increase the odds that this will work by at least 3% per set of balls. We all know you have a crush on him, Fourni. Just do him already!

Fournimer didn't take much more convincing. Once the mouth had started to work him over, he entirely relented.

> Mr. Max's Text Box: I hate to ruin the mood, but this absorbing girl here is tingling like mad. You two are never going to beat me without some help. I don't really want to … oh, screw it. I can help out a Bro once, right? That doesn't make me….

Mr. Max licked a big, beefy finger on each hand and began to feel the two nearby buttons. Without wasting much time, he thrust a finger into each hole and earned loud moans from each avatar.

> Palcath's Text Box: Okay, lads, the odds are more in our fav—huh! What? What are you doing, lass?

Palcath changed his view and saw that Lissa had deftly pulled down his Armour, revealing his shiny, self-vibrating penis.

> Lissa's Text Box: You heard yourself. Every drop counts. I know how we can easily increase the odds by 3% more.

> Palcath's Text Box: Not easily … because I just … well, I don't like guys like that. I don't think I could manage it.…

> Lissa's Text Box: Shut up. Anders is taking four for the team already. The very least you can do is give one to the team.

> Palcath's Text Box: But—

> Lissa's Text Box: Quiet! All you need to do is finish in Anders!

> Palcath's Text Box: I can't keep my eyes and helmet active and still use my hands, lass!

> Lissa's Text Box: I'll just have to get you the rest of the way; do we agree?

> Anders' Text Box: Mno.

Dragging the dwarf to the back of the encounter, Lissa bent over and leaned on Mr. Max's giant balls.

> Palcath's Text Box: But … this isn't a proper first time, lass.

> Lissa's Text Box: First time? #InYourDreams! This is just going to be a handjob.

> Palcath's Text Box: Oh.

Lissa began to work over the dwarf, who was now having a very hard time concentrating on stats.

> Lissa's Text Box: I am warning you, meathead. I want to win this. When you cum, I am going to squeeze the fuck out of your balls.

> Mr. Max's Text Box: You should concentrate on the dwarf, or he isn't going to finish at all.

> Lissa's Text Box: Don't worry. I'm pretty sure I'm good at this.

> Mr. Max's Text Box: You don't have time to find out! Urgh! This pussy is getting all magic and tingly. Make it slow down!

> Anders' Text Box: Mmmmfble!

> Mr. Max's Text Box: Nope. Only a few rounds left!

Mr. Max accentuated the point by pressing very hard into his avatar hand puppets, who screamed out loudly. Lissa nodded, realizing they'd have to change the plan to get things moving if they were going to contribute. Turning Palcath's vibrating penis all the way to the right, it jumped straight up to *Ultra Speed.*

> Palcath's Text Box: Whoa whoa … wait wait …Ultra? I never dared try that!

> Lissa's Text Box: We've got to step up our game. I will NOT let the meathead beat me.

> Palcath's Text Box: You have a real problem with competit—

Lissa interrupted by trying to grab onto the member, but she simply could not. So, she did what she had to do. She hiked up her *Garnet Skirt (s),* pressed her own buttons, and was both vibrating and convulsing at *Ultra Speed.* Holding herself up with Mr. Max's balls, she presented herself to Palcath.

> Palcath's Text Box: Lass… but that … *blush* That isn't exact—

> Lissa's Interruption Text Box: Just go, drama queen. We don't have the rounds to take it slow if I am going to get you to beat meathead to climax.

With a nod, the dwarf decided that he wasn't going to waste this opportunity. He blurred into the half-elf with immense speed. In just a single round, the pair had caught up with the rest and were genuinely enjoying themselves.

> Roodg's Text Box: wOW! lOOK AT THEM GO!

On the second round, Palcath and Lissa were fully into their motions, and by the third both were on the edge. The onlookers could barely see them for how fast they were moving. They had gone from nothing to the brink in a fraction of the time it was taking everyone else.

> Palcath's Text Box: Holy fuck, lass! I'm almost there!

Lissa deftly ducked out of the way, still quivering, having already been there herself. Palcath barely made it but moved forward to awkwardly enter Anders alongside Mr. Max. He shot powerfully inside. The vibrating dwarf rested right against the root of Mr. Max. This caused the entirely of Mr. Maxum to vibrate rapidly.

> Mr. Max's Text Box: My Maker!

> Anders' Text Box: Muffblins!

The vibration caused the entire inside and outside of Anders to squeeze and tingle.

It also, however, caused Mr. Max to scream out and begin to fill up the avatar.

Surge had been activated and would last for ten rounds.

Round 1: Mr. Max lent some of his powers and abilities to Anders. Anders was temporarily *Maxed*, and all sorts of stupid sword techniques and even the broken PVP abilities were made available. Max also began to convulse and gripped hard on the two avatars that were stuck on his hands. Lissa began to squeeze at the meathead's giant balls. Anders moaned.

Round 2: Fournimer and Roodg screamed out after having their places firmly pressed on by Mr. Max's fingers, and both began to release. Anders moaned.

Round 3: Mr. Max screamed while Lissa pressed firmly against his balls. With each spurt, Lissa herself released some of her aggression toward Mr. Max. Palcath finished and removed himself. He was still trembling while he tried to carry on with the math. Anders moaned.

Round 4: Fournimer and Roodg finished and withdrew, and got out of the way. Anders tried to re-establish his aim toward Breaker. And moaned.

Round 5: Mr. Max shot a last spurt into Anders but refused to move from the spot. His body trembled, still enraptured with tingles. Lissa didn't stop squeezing; she was adamant on getting every drop out. Anders finished aiming and moaning and was about to release his arrow. Fournimer stopped him. He awkwardly approached Anders with embarrassment on his face. He claimed to have an idea.

Round 6: Fournimer told Anders not to shoot until the very last round, and the human pulled down Anders' *Jockstrap* and wrapped his mouth around Anders' member. A very surprised Anders moaned.

Round 7: Anders moaned again. He was having problems keeping his aim. The human was exceptionally good at what he was doing. Anders was in such a state of euphoria that he could even see fireworks going off—little heart fireworks, and it was getting Anders ready to shoot (in both ways).

Round 8: Fournimer was now squeezing on the moaning elf's balls with a sense of urgency. Roodg Text Boxed, "nEAT."

Round 9: It was the limit for Anders. He moaned and came hard and quick into the waiting mouth of Fournimer. Fournimer drained him completely.

Round 10: Fournimer stood and kissed the shocked elf, returning to him his own release. Anders moaned and tasted the saltiness of his own seed. This *Fournimer Kiss* was the absolute best kiss he had ever experienced. Anders was in absolute paradise. Little hearts materialized around the kissing couple. When the hearts exploded into different coloured fireworks that all said "+1", the party observed, bewildered and confused. Palcath complained about math and was very curious as to what the +1s had done. Anders' *Absorb* worked on himself and he gained an extra 3% chance but completely forgot to shoot the arrows while enraptured with the Fourni kiss. After a quick spank on the ass from Mr. Max, Anders broke free from the kiss, and let the arrows fly. The purple glow faded, and Anders returned to his normal colouration (it was a very full round).

The six arrows flew toward their target, Breaker, who had been busy trying to hack the Plague of Shadow's summoning pillar, entirely unaware of the orgy-induced impending rainbow of doom.

Anders dropped his bow and returned to kiss the human. Little hearts kept emerging and exploding in colourful +1 fireworks, all of which were accompanied by sweeping romantic music.

Chapter 35
P V P

Breaker very nearly destroyed the summoning pillar, pounding on it with rage. With a *Cracking of His Claws and Dramatic Stolen Wing Spreading Animation* Breaker summoned forth lightning that struck the entire map. The Tower of Mechanis took the brunt of it due to its height and was completely destroyed.

> Breaker's Text Box: Why don't you work, you stupid summoning pillar? I hacked my Insta-Wiki and just killed all *Suntan Lotion* everywhere. I am complete. Now summon, you bastard.

He gave it one more clawe filled punch for good measure.

> Breaker's Text Box: Come on! Work, you stupid piece of crap!

Six arrows in rainbow order came into view for a split-round. They fired through his midsection with some determination. They broke through his belt, and the buckle shattered.

> Breaker's Text Box: The Flaming Pit?

Breaker didn't panic, even when his Hit Points began to fall. He had quite a few, probably more than everything else in the game combined. Nothing should be able to take him down all the way, and certainly not in one hit. Plus, he had several types of Hit Points, and there wasn't even a way to affect one of them. Whatever attacked him was wasting its time.

However, the rounds progressed, and his health was still decreasing. His buffs and other stats were falling from their elevated levels, and pieces of his pilfered body were dissolving. This wasn't supposed to be able to happen. He reached the end of his Monster Hit Points, which caused his wing to fall off, but the number still was going down.

Now that his health had entered into the avatar portion of the bar, he was more concerned. Something had hit him that was allowed to do PVP. Attempting to escape, Breaker tried to activate his *Breaker's Belt of Awesomeness* to fly out of this place, and he was relieved when it still worked. Flying upward in his comet, Breaker let out a *Laugh Animation*. He had still won for now and could come back. The *Belt* had some other ideas, though. The arrows had changed its setting to malfunctioning, and after a round it stopped working. Breaker plummeted to the ground, crashing hard. The following round, the comet activated again, and Breaker was lifted up and pummelled another move unit further into the ground.

Breaker turned off his comet, but was now under 1,000,000 Hit Points—and they were still dropping fast. He should be fine, though. He had just finished up with his NPC Hit Points, which PVP could destroy, but he still had impossible-to-destroy Administrator Hit Points from his wonderful Administrator Mode Code. Nothing could hurt those.

But, the Hit Points kept falling. What in the Annals had hit him? Was an Administrator punishing him for wrecking the map? Impossible, they couldn't hurt themselves. He'd researched this. What could hurt Admins? Nothing! There wasn't a thing on this map that could remove the almighty Optional Hit Points of an Administrator … was there? He would only have another round or two to act as his life kept falling. He desperately searched through his hacked inventory to find anything useful. He couldn't find any of the items he was searching for. He had hacked so many items into so many different things that even simple *Health Potions* no longer had the same name. He cursed his cleverness as his Hit Points fell to 9,999, the normal maximum. In a state of blind panic, he grabbed the next thing that he saw in his inventory and, out of desperation, started to eat it, hoping it was one of his potions.

With a *Stretching of His Arms and Dramatic Hand Flourish Animation,* and still with a half-eaten pair of hacked *Fritzing Gloves* sticking out of his mouth, Breaker gasped, and toppled over onto the Plague of Shadow's summoning platform face first.

~ ~ ~

The team watched as Breaker slowly fell to the ground, was blasted as a comet into the ground, tried to eat some gloves, used that overly long animation of his, and fell over. They had done it! He was no more! They still were a distance from normal visible range and used that time to sum some things up.

> Mr. Max's Text Box: We did it! It took everything we had, but we did it!

> Palcath's Text Box: I hope we can take on the Plague of Shadow with absolutely no resources, though, everylad.

> Lissa's Text Box: Hold up, hold up.

Lissa sauntered over to Fournimer, whose blush level was somewhere off the charts, possibly about to break into #8.

> Lissa's Text Box: So, let me get this straight, Scarfy. The big secret, the power that you have been hiding from us, is to give really good kisses that spawn little exploding hearts?

> Fournimer's Text Box: hey, when all you can do is make special kisses while everyone else has … enhancing powers or like … really impressive stuff. stuff that could be used offensively or is all cool. I can't do any of that … it's embarrassing. worse than only having a Code for glitter.

> Anders' Text Box: I don't even have a Code.

> Palcath's Text Box: What did those '+1's even do? They didn't change your stats or anything I noticed, lad.

Fournimer was defeated. His stupid secret move was in the open now, and being openly discussed.

> Fournimer's Text Box: The orange numbers were Gold Pieces, and the green ones were Experience Points.

> Palcath's Text Box: So, what you are saying, lad, is that when you kiss, you become stronger, and wealthier?

> Fournimer's Text Box: no, I didn't. Dude got all of that.

> Palcath's Text Box: My calculations say that, by kissing you, the lad gained +3 Experience Points, and +7 Gold Pieces.

> Mr. Max's Text Box: That isn't a very impressive amount, even for a Level 1. I still need 787,382 Experience Points to get past Level 98.

> Palcath's Text Box: That is only 262,460.6 (the 6 is continuous there) Fourni kisses to level up lad. I have no idea how many continuous cycles of kissing Fourni that would take. Let me just do some math here.

> Anders' Text Box: Aww, leave Fourni alone! The little hearts were really cute.

Fournimer couldn't blush anymore. He had done it with Anders' help. He had unleashed *Blush Shade #8* on the world. Now anyone else could get that embarrassed.

> Fournimer's Text Box: thank you Dude.

> Palcath's Text Box: Oh, sorry, Fourni, I didn't mean anything…. I was legitimately just interested in the math.

> Mr. Max's Text Box: So, how many cycles was that now?

> Anders' Text Box: We should just drop this for now and conti—

> Lissa's Interruption Text Box: Wait! We can't drop it yet! I just thought of something really important, Scarfy!

> Fournimer's Text Box: what?

> Lissa's Text Box: It is about the numbers, Palcath said!

> Fournimer's Text Box: what about them? is something wrong with them? are they like a Code or something? please say they are a Code or something cool.

> Lissa's Text Box: Nope! #BestThingEver. Those are the same numbers you get for killing a Start Rat. Kissing you is exactly the same as killing a Start Rat! You have Start Rat Kisses!

> Fournimer's Text Box: they are not called Start Rat Kisses!

> Roodg's Text Box: cOME HERE Fournimer! i'M ALMOST lEVEL 51. I JUST NEED 48 sTART rAT KISSES!

> Fournimer's Text Box: just stop it Lissa! they are called *Wonder Kisses*! besides, nobody here is making fun of your *Auto-Fuck Pussy*!

> Palcath's Text Box: Who could?

Palcath got all misty eyed.

> Lissa's Text Box: Of course they wouldn't! I finished off the dwarf in like three rounds, and I wasn't even trying hard. And, it is Fair Maiden, remember?

> Fournimer's Text Box: please, just stop it.

> Lissa's Text Box: I can't stop it because you make this way too easy, Jive Scarfy.

Anders held back Fournimer for a round, and they fell behind.

> Anders' Whisper Text Box To Just Fournimer: I need 378.3 (the 3 is continuous) *Fourni Wonder Kisses* to level up. Let me know when you are free (custom exclamation point)

Anders' custom exclamation point was a kiss on Fourni's slightly stubble-dusted cheek.

Fourni executed the *Too Stunned to Say Anything or Move Because a Cute Gay Elf Just Kissed Him on the Cheek and Completely Took Him Off Guard Animation*. He was only avatar to ever use that very situational animation, and this was his second time. He still wasn't sure why it was included in the list of *Standard Animations*, but he was again glad it was in there.

The excited group had finally reached the summoning platform smelling of victory and a few select other things.

> Lissa's Text Box: Let's all take turns with Scarfy. We can all be Level ## just before the end of time if we start now right now! Strange … Level 97. Level 98. Level ## … why did Level ## not type in properly? Hashtags are my thing Level ##, stop it!

Fournimer did not reply; he was still caught in mid-animation.

> Zal Finn II's Text Box: Sweet! It is Lissa! How could you guys possibly defeat Breaker by all standing there in a big clump for like 80 rounds hardly moving and with only one shot?

> Lissa's Text Box: Zal Finn? No way, is that you?

A group of four avatars revealed themselves from behind the summoning pillar. A troll, a light elf, a human, and a standard elf, all relieved.

There were now so many avatars around that things were bound to get confusing. It became more like a big chat room than a game, with too many conversations going on at once.

> Lissa's Text Box: Why are you here? You are dead!

> Zal Finn II's Text Box: Zal Finn I is dead. I am Zal Finn II. Well, we were all part of Breaker's party. He ditched us to chase after Mr. Max, so we came here to wait for him. When he showed up all evil and unsweet and junk we just stayed hidden.

Gliint the gnome revealed himself from behind the summoning pillar. Great, there was another one for the chat room, but Anders didn't mind. At least he already knew who Gliint was. He didn't think he had any idea who these other people were. Certainly not that NPC Zal Finn II who knew Lissa. Since when could NPCs talk like avatars?

> Gliint's Lag Text Box: OMM! *Near faint* It is Mr. Max! I love you so much! Oh, and even Anders! Hi, Anders! *Wave* Thanks for all the stuff way back when. Hey, I even know that guy! He told me 'pip pip' wasn't for me.

> Mr. Max's Text Box: Of course you love me, fellow adventurertte!

> Caëlahenãilenẇhei's Text Box: The preceding posed question is still valid. How is it possible, Lissa, that you and your companions were able to overpower and vanquish Breaker? His stats rivaled those of the Maker, and he was a combination avatar, Admin, NPC, and Monster. He had a total of four individual types of Hit Points and to destroy all four in a single hit was thought to be impossible. How did your group manage to even inflict any damage to him? As an experiment, we had Kray sneak shoot him with an arrow, and Breaker took 0 damage. Why, the villain did not even take—

> Caëlahenãilenẇhei's Text Box: notice.

> Roodg's Text Box: hI!!!

Wait, Anders knew who that was. It was the starting city! He was glad that it wasn't dead after all. No, wait, that was wrong. It was that long-winded avatar he had read a post from once; maybe it was under Golden Chests. It was a long time ago; Anders wasn't sure anymore.

> Anders' Text Box: We did it through teamwork!

> Kray's Text Box: It was an awesome shot, Kay. You give gay elves everywhere someone to look up to!

> Anders' Text Box: Well, thank you, Kay. I guess. But ... um, how would you even know if I was gay?

> Kray's Text Box: It's Kray, not Kay, kay? See, you are an elf and a guy. Therefore, you are a gay elf. That is just how things work. It is a rule or something. Boy elf = gay! By the way, that wasn't a compliment. You are way too tall for a gay elf, which is why us better gay elves need to look up to you. Also, you are, like, really, really fat for a gay elf. Like, mega fat. Just look at your ass, kay, it is sized for an avatar at least twice your size. How much *Bacon* are you eating? Maybe you should cut back, just trying to help.

> Anders' Text Box: Oh, kay....

Anders did not know who that elf was with the near-blinding mismatched accent colours and flippy red *#4 Hairstyle*, but he was instantly not a fan.

> Gliint's Lag Text Box: Mr. Max! It's been forever! *More waves* Will you sign something for me?

> Mr. Max's Text Box: Sure thing, little adventurette! Let me just grab my pen. Do you want me to sign your boobs or your ass?

> Palcath's Text Box: We won through math, too, lads! Don't forget about math. I'm going to go over the numbers. I want to know what the total damage was. I want to write it down on my Player Pager.

> Caëlahenâilenŵhei's Text Box: Now mathematics is something I can get interested in. Mind sharing your formulas?

> Roodg's Text Box: hI!

> Caëlahenâilenŵhei's Text Box: Do I know you, my good ... uh...?

> Roodg's Text Box: hI i'M Roodg!

> Caëlahenâilenŵhei's Text Box: As I see.

> Gliint's Lag Text Box: *Confused* Beg pardon?

> Palcath's Text Box: Come, elf lass. See, with these numbers here....

> Caëlahenâilenŵhei's Text Box: Interesting idea there, this is a marvelous spreadsheet....

> Zal Finn II's Text Box: Lissa, I'm so sorry my party forced you to give up the Hair Colour Code. I know you got reported for it and eventually even broken because of it. I'm really sorry. It was so unsweet of us.

> Lissa's Text Box: #WaterUnderTheBridge now. I notice you all have *(s) Armour* over there. How did you manage to break your new avatar, Zal?

> Zal Finn II's Text Box: Breaker found some Codes a few cycles ago, and we tested them out. They were supposed to be different than the Hair Code.

After hearing the word "Codes", Fournimer finally broke out of his elf-induced trance.

> Fournimer's Text Box: Buddy WROTE those Codes quite a few cycles ago.

Yallundy used the *Point Animation* at Zal Finn II.

> Yallundy's Text Box: You see? Breaker was always evil. That is what I was trying to say all along. I really tried to tell you, but everyone kept interrupting me. You see, my power is *Em—*

> Zal Finn II's Interruption Text Box: Sorry, Yallundy, that wasn't very sweet of us either.

Anders had no idea who that was. He knew that troll women were beautiful when compared to the men, but he had never seen one before now. This one was so beautiful and lovely that she radiated an accent colour of undeterminable origin somehow. Anders was convinced she might even be a Goddess and (just for one split-round) he fell in love with her.

> Palcath's Text Box: ... and once you factor in the odds for the...

> Caëlahenåilenẁhei's Text Box: ...of course, and the fractional variants of...

> Roodg's Text Box: hI!

> Zal Finn II's Text Box: So he let us break ourselves just because? He is a jerk.

> Fournimer's Text Box: if he is evil, it makes sense now. his stupid Codes broke some of us as well ... uh ... The Finnster.

> Zal Finn II's Text Box: The Finnster? Sweet! Love it! Where did you find this guy, Lissa? He is so rad!

> Lissa's Text Box: Seriously, Scarfy? The best you could come up for me on the spot was Chick.

> Fournimer's Text Box: whoa Chick, calm down there!

> Palcath's Text Box: ... percentages based on volume of ... uh ... additional magic power...

> Caëlahenåilenẁhei's Text Box: ...interesting. Why did you need to use percentages there? What was the variable...

> Roodg's Text Box: hI. Roodg HERE!

Kray's Text Box: Kay, but why are you so huge, man? You are by far the chubbiest gay elf ever.

Anders' Text Box: Excuse me? I only picked *Body Style #2* and *Average*. That is the fifth skinniest avatar available!

Kray's Text Box: Exactly. I'm *Body Style #1* and *Average*, and I still feel fat. You're just gigantic, kay? Really, it is time for you to back off more than just *Bacon*, I think. I can write you out an eating schedule if you want.

Anders' Text Box: You are really short!

Palcath's Text Box: …it was simply a matter of calculating…

Caëlahenâilenŵhei's Text Box: …of course with that fraction and the sharing of the…

Roodg's Text Box: i'M Roodg!!!

Gliint's Lag Text Box: Mr. Max, *Frown* where did you go after Stronghold F? We were going to go to the Marshes of the Frangolds together after that.

Mr. Max's Text Box: Oh! The little Hero of the Cycle! Sorry, I went to get a sandwich.

Palcath's Text Box: … for this value here. So the total damage was 92,829,978/88,789,678! We beat him by 4,040,300! We totally rocked it, lads!

Caëlahenâilenŵhei's Text Box: …actually you forgot to carry the 1 there.

Roodg's Text Box: hI AGAIN!

Palcath's Text Box: Oh … blast. I did. You're right, lass. I was really distracted at that moment. So, if I redo this bit the total damage was…

Kray's Text Box: Elves are supposed to be short, kay?

Anders' Text Box: No, elves are supposed to be tall, kay!

Kray's Text Box: Well yes, kay, but gay elf boys are not supposed to be tall. They are supposed to be URK!

Anders' Text Box: Supposed to be URK?

Palcath's Text Box: ...88,789,677/88,789,678. Oh, crap.

Breaker's Text Box: Bwahahahahahahahahahaha! Oh, maniacal villain laugh, you are much too fun! My *Breaker's Belt of Awesomeness* might be damaged, but it is still powerful enough to absorb this pathetic gay elf double twink.

Breaker stood up from his previously collapsed form. With a *Stretching of His Arms and Dramatic Hand Flourish Animation* he had wrapped his hand around Kray's neck and was lifting the short elf into the air. Had the elf picked a heavier body, he might not have been so easy to hoist into the air for this dramatic reveal. He might have been saved. Kray's skin began to tighten and turn black. The more shrivelled and black Kray became, the more Breaker began to recover, to become stronger, and to resemble a gay elf twink. The *Belt* was not functioning properly, and the absorbing was going in strange jumps, but it was still turning Kray into a black elf husk.

warrier's Text Box: ...

warrier was here! Anders had heard that warrier was Breaker's stooge; it probably was a bad thing that he was in the chat room.

Breaker's Text Box: warrier! It's you. Now that everyone is here, we finally have two opposite parties that can battle each other as nature intended! One good and one evil! Bwahahahahaha!

With a *Snap of His Fingers and Flamboyant Head Shake Animation*, Breaker flung out some dramatic shards of ice, but the ice was gay, elfy, and twinky (however that was possible). The ice shattered some nearby scenery for dramatic effect.

Nearly everyone answered simultaneously.

Palcath's Text Box: How are we opposite parties? That doesn't even make sense, lad. I don't even know who mine is. Maybe one of the Warriors, but there are two of those.

Zal Finn II's Text Box: Am I Lissa's opposite? We know each other already, but we are not opposites. Besides, we are square now, I think.

Lissa's Text Box: How would we fight each other? Most of us can't even do PVP. You are totally #SoFuckedUp.

Mr. Max's Text Box: Who is my opposite? Is it warrier because he can also do PVP? Or is it you because you are famous like me? I don't know who to fight.

Caëlahenãilenŵhei's Text Box: Your logic is flawed. I clearly have no opposite here that I can see.

Roodg's Text Box: hI! i'M Roodg!

Anders' Text Box: I'm pretty sure you just killed my opposite! Plus he wasn't that opposite. He was pretty much exactly the same as me except mean.

Yallundy's Text Box: I can see only two evil people here. Obviously this is the last desperate ploy of a madman.

Fournimer's Text Box: bring it on Lissa! wait. that's not right.

warrier's Text Box: …

Kray simply said nothing. For the chatterbox, it was a new personal best.

Breaker was furious. Not only had the idiots not just started to fight amongst themselves as he had planned, but one of them even had the gall to talk with a hashtag. With a *Snap of His Fingers and Flamboyant Head Shake Animation*, he summoned some twink fireballs that shot into the air and destroyed all the clouds, forever deleting them from the Castle in the Sky.

Breaker's Text Box: I can't believe I need to clarify this for you idiots. Okay, see Mr. Max and warrier are both PVP broken. Mr. Max took *Warrior (Skill Style)*, while warrier took *Warrior (Strength Style)*. So they are opposites. One is muscular and short, the other tall and thin.

Mr. Max's Text Box: Well, I guess, but how does being almost the same make us opposites?

warrier's Text Box: …

Gliint's Lag Text Box: Is my opposite Mr. Max? If not … can it be *Plead*?

Breaker's Text Box: That 'C' word light elf and that whatever it is night elf are both attack magic classes, but the different ones. They are opposites for both race and class!

Caëlahenãilenŵhei's Text Box: I find it hard to believe that I would have anything in common with that illiterate cur.

Roodg's Text Box: hI! wE OPPOSITES.

Breaker's Text Box: Both Palcath and Zal Finn II are different melee classes, and I know that they both used Codes of mine that broke their eyes.

Palcath's Text Box: Well, I guess, the first two were better opposites though, lad.

Zal Finn II's Text Box: Sweet. What can you do with your eyes?

Breaker's Text Box: Yallundy and the horribly named Lissa are opposites because they are both healing classes but the opposite ones. Yallundy is also a timid pacifist, and Lissa is clearly the opposite of that. Lissa also has a stupid name that I dislike.

Yallundy's Text Box: I guess that makes sense.

Lissa's Text Box: Hey, you don't know me, you bastard! My name is awesome!

Breaker's Text Box: Fournimer clearly spent hundreds of turns making his avatar, just like Kray. Plus they are both Night Rangers but the opposite versions.

Fournimer's Text Box: well yes that is true Buddy, I did do that … but I don't think he'll be ready to fight me any time soon.

Kray said nothing. His non-speaking record continued!

Breaker's Text Box: Finally Anders is opposites with Gliint. You are opposite ranged classes and both obviously have lag if it took Anders 80 rounds to fire one fucking arrow.

Anders' Text Box: I don't have lag. Hey, what about you, Breaker? There are seven of you guys and six of us. I almost believed your whole opposites thing, but you can't even figure it out, Breaker. So, why would we even do this thing?

Lissa's Text Box: I thought max party size was six.

Palcath's Text Box: Max *Portie Tent* bed size is six, I don't know what max party size is, lass.

Mr. Max's Text Box: I thought it was one until you all joined me.

Breaker's Text Box: Shut up! I did not forget about me. I simply do not

> have an opposite, for I am the end all and be all.

> warrier's Text Box: …

> Gliint's Text Box: But Anders is nice. *Confused* I don't want to fight him.

> Breaker's Text Box: Whatever. Just stuff it. You losers just fight amongst yourselves. I am busy!

With a *Snap of His Fingers and Flamboyant Head Shake Animation* Breaker summoned some happy gay rainbows that caused localized destruction with their multicoloured madness. They were devastatingly powerful, but they were still rainbows and super cute.

> Fournimer's Text Box: his attacks are so cute! he is almost cuter than Ni Hao Bunny©!

> Breaker's Text Box: These stupid gay bunny attacks are not dramatic enough!

> Fournimer's Text Box: have you tried a scarf Buddy? they add so much drama.

> Breaker's Text Box: Scarves have the worst stats! They are more useless than all of you stupid lackeys combined!

warrier used the *Change of Heart Animation*. Nobody made fun of lackeys or scarves. Most importantly of all, nobody was ever allowed to make fun of *Ni Hao Bunny*©!

> warrier's Text Box: !!!

After his poignant speech (the most warrier had ever said, to anyone's knowledge), warrier rushed at Breaker. With a mighty slash from the *Katana* in his *Earth Gauntleted* hand, he struck at the inflated windbag. The *Katana* cut deep, and Breaker was in such shock that, with a *Stretching of His Arms and Dramatic Hand Flourish Animation* he dropped the shriveled skeletal husk of Kray and fell backward toward the summoning pillar. It had knocked the gay elfishness right off of Breaker's face, and the avatar looked like Breaker again.

> Breaker's Text Box: You bastard!

Breaker struck back at warrier with one of his daggers. It sent the avatar flying backward into some scenic stacked crates.

> The Plague of Shadow's Text Box: You have completed the Insta-Wiki, Breaker, and came with a party with a full set of Gigas Gear. Your challenge has been accepted.

> Breaker's Text Box: Huh, why is it working now? Oh, fuck you, warrier, with your *Earth Gauntlet*! I forgot I didn't have that one.

A swirling vortex opened up behind Breaker, and a very large set of claws shrouded in a thick black mist came out. Just a single one of the four claws was bigger than Breaker. The size of the full creature would be enormous. The claws hovered for a bit too long and became shrouded with a different kind of black mist. The entire thing felt strange and glitchy.

> The Plague of Shadow's Text Box: However, Breaker, you have not yet encountered a true boss monster since you have been broken, and I will very much enjoy breaking you in.

The claws grasped Breaker and pulled him screaming into the vortex, which began to close up after them.

> Palcath's Text Box: Crap! Breaker is going to get a first-time monster power from the Plague of Shadow!

> Lissa's Text Box: He is going to win this stupid contest with his free sex thing and get a sex power from the final boss? That's fucking #SoFuckedUp!

> Anders' Text Box: Not in my game, he isn't!

Anders, who had been standing right beside the whole sequence of events, used the special ability that he learned at Level 1. While it had ultimately led to the breaking of his avatar, it was still his trademark move, and he knew it. He *Double Jumped* on top of the slightly askew scenic summoning pillar, even though he shouldn't have been able to. He jumped onto a miscoloured pixel that he saw nearby. With an unnecessary flourish, he *Double Jumped* off the pixel and was just high enough to enter the Vortex. With a blip, both Anders and the Vortex had vanished.

> Palcath's Text Box: Lad!

> Fournimer's Text Box: Dude!

> Roodg's Text Box: sAWESOME!

> Lissa's Text Box: Loverboy!

> Mr. Max's Text Box: What's her name?

◈ Chapter 36 ◈
THE PLAGUE OF
SHADOW

That was Caution Step's song playing in the background, "The Plague of Shadow"! Anders had wanted to hear that song so bad when he found out it was in the game. Anders couldn't even attempt to pay attention right now, which was upsetting.

He knew that this area had to be very dangerous and couldn't let a song, no matter how cool it was, distract him. Try as he might, the only thing Anders could see through the thick black mist that filled this area was himself, and he could see that only if he held his hand right up to his face.

There was no ground, which was slightly unsettling. Anders wasn't falling but instead floating. Controlling the floating wasn't as difficult as he had thought it would be, although he might have just been really good at it because he couldn't see where he was going. Anders knew that this floating was a special thing programmed for just this area and that it was pretty amazing.

Before heading blindly into battle, Anders rummaged through his *Ultra-Pack* for anything that could help. They had really picked through his supplies when they super-buffed him earlier. One of the only things he had left was something he *Combi-Fused* way back in Chapter 3. Anders had no idea what a *Lightning Shard* did, but maybe it would at least provide some lighting effects with the animation that happened when it was used. It was a long shot, but Anders threw it in the air and activated it anyway.

A small ball of lightning blinked on with a sound effect of distant thunder. It lit the area around it with a slight glow, which was helpful. It instantly informed Anders that it would attack the nearest available target and took off straight downward toward something Anders couldn't see, which was likely going to be less helpful. The ball of light illuminated the forehead of something very large and very scaly. It smacked the scaly object right between the eyes for an unimpressive 1 point of damage. Just before the lighting and lightning were gone, Anders saw the huge, yellow, slit-pupil eyes change their focus and look directly at him.

> Anders' Text Box: Oh. That was so bad I can't even think of a fake swear; I'll have to use a real one. So, here goes … oh, crud!

The Plague of Shadow dispersed both the *Plague Mist* and Anders with a few loud beats of huge reptilian wings. The force caused Anders to fly backward 48 move units in a series of awkward twirls and flips. Attempting to catch his stomach, he could now see the entire area, even if it was while spinning at ultra high *Serpent Speed.*

Black was the decorator's colour of choice here. There were black crystal walls, six of them in total, forming the outside cube structure. They were textured with a honeycomb pattern, so far off in the distance that he could never hope to reach them. Large orbs of pure black energy hovered atop black crystal spires. There was a complete replica of the Castle in the Sky in the centre (although it had not been destroyed like the real one), coloured black to match the rest. There were even black lights, black clouds, and a diseased black sun high in the sky. But above all else, the most impressive black thing was the impossibly gigantic Plague of Shadow who was hovering beside a comparatively miniscule avatar. Hidden behind huge, black wings, the Plague of Shadow was staring at the elf with hungry yellow eyes (Anders was surprised that they were not black).

Anders was the only other thing in the room that hadn't gotten the all-black memo. He was still spinning away from the force of the wings. He was wearing bright green Armour and was still shimmering an unnatural and alluring pink colour from the use of the *Allure Potion*. With every spin in the air, he let out a flash of pink light and a strange windy blowing sound effect. Even if he'd tried, he probably couldn't have brought more attention to himself.

The Plague of Shadow waited patiently as Anders slowed and stabilized. Once he was hovering steadily, the creature whipped open the scaly black wings in a show of power and ultimateness. Anders knew that this was a dragon. A massive dragon. He had also sort of guessed a while ago that the Plague of Shadow was going to be a dragon, so it was a victory of sorts (hey, there was a gigantic broken sex-dragon down there; Anders took whatever slight bit of victory he could find). With three forceful beats of the black wings, the Dragon of Shadow had abandoned Breaker and was face-to-face with Anders. "Face-to-face" was a bit of an understatement; the correct assessment was entire eyeball to avatar as Anders was just about as tall as the great dragon's eye.

The Dragon of Shadow was staring slightly cross-eyed at the elf hovering over its giant nostrils. Great, heavy breaths caused Anders to wobble while the giant eyes continued to stare. Anders had absolutely no idea what to do. This thing could easily just inhale him through a nostril or flick out a tongue and swallow him up. Heck, even a giant eyelid blink could probably crush Anders. While he should be floating away for his life, he was frozen in fear. All Anders could do was stare right back in complete awe.

Round after round passed in awkward silence, the intensity of the breathing increasing with each exhale. It was getting harder and harder for Anders to float in place, and *Steadfast* refused to activate while in the air. It felt as if, with each breath, the tension in the area increased, the wing beats got louder, the lights became dimmer, Caution Step louder, and the diseased sun brighter.

With the next inhale, Anders noted that his pink glowing *Allure* aura was sucked away into the dragon's huge nostrils. Imagining where this would go, Anders almost panicked. He was surprised to see it didn't affect the Plague like he had feared it would. The big dragon's face started to twist strangely, and the Anders-sized yellow eyes began to water. Anders could only stare dumbfounded as the gargantuan monstrosity started to thrash about in a comical fashion. The yellow eyes were covered in tears but stayed locked on Anders until the very last instant when the Plague of Shadow convulsed a final time and let forth a huge sneeze of green fire. After a few turns of regaining its composure and "pttuh"ing nose rubbing, the dragon opened the huge yellow eyes and scoffed.

> The Plague of Shadow's Text Box: No fair! You can't keep your eyes open when you sneeze!

Anders finally snapped out of the trance and reminded his heart to start beating again, his lungs to start breathing again, and his eyes to start blinking again.

> Anders' Text Box: Huh?

> The Plague of Shadow's Text Box: Making me sneeze like that with your magic aura.

> Anders' Text Box: Uh. Sorry?

> The Plague of Shadow's Text Box: Well, I guess it is my fault as well for getting so close. I guess that means you win.

> Anders' Text Box: What? I win? What?

> The Plague of Shadow's Text Box: The staring contest, dummy. I guess that means you win the entire game as well since you just defeated me.

> Anders' Text Box: You're not serious. That was the epic final boss battle?

> The Plague of Shadow's Text Box: We can battle for real as well, if

you'd prefer a full test of strength.

Anders' Text Box: No, that is okay, really! I accept the win! That was the most epic staring contest ever, honest!

The Plague of Shadow's Text Box: Promise? What was that aura I sneezed? It was so alluring. I think it is starting to hit me now or something. It is making everything … so pink.

The huge, yellow, slit-pupil eyes turned into huge, pink, slit-pupil eyes with a slight glaze on them.

Anders' Text Box: Oh, ultimate crud.

With a single beat of the black scaled wings, the Plague of Shadow backed off. Staring at Anders with pink-hazed eyes, it began to lick its lips with a long, forked serpentine tongue.

Anders' Text Box: I repeat. Oh, ultimate boss crud.

Now that it had backed off, Anders could finally get a good measure of the size of the beast. It was definitely bigger than the entire starting city whose name was no longer important since it had been destroyed. Far more troubling was the tremendously giant set of testicles the thing possessed. They were tightly compressed and hidden under the skin, but Anders could tell that they were beyond measure. Even more troubling still was the size of the member that was rapidly coming out of the Plague of Shadow's sheath. The thing wasn't even fully out yet, and it was already bigger than the Frost Gigas—and not as in the Frost Gigas' penis, but as in the entire Frost Gigas. It was impossibly, impractically, stupidly huge.

With a tooth-filled, wicked grin, the Plague of Shadow smiled ravenously at the floating elf.

The Plague of Shadow's Text Box: You're that Elfboy. I've heard all about you. You've taken on the best, but there is no way you can handle this.

Anders' Text Box: I agree.

A powerful roar filled the arena with black sparkles in a cloud of black mist. Anders didn't realize at the time, but it was a kind of magical effect, based on a Constitution save. Anders failed the save miserably and was now held fast in some black mist with his legs spread wide open. Sensing the sexual situation, his Armour withdrew into the cute little Slime on his *Jockstrap*, and with a nice *Goop* lubed him right up.

Anders' Text Box: Well, thanks for that, Armour.

Flying up, the dragon positioned himself and aimed the impossible dick in the general vicinity of Anders.

> Anders' Text Box: I wonder if I should go with Anders II or something brand new. I sort of like the name Lawrence for an avatar.

The dragon began to push forward; somehow, the giant thing was lined up correctly. Anders felt the monstrosity start to press against his hole. The flared tip was starting to enter him, and Anders was surprised by how much he was stretching. It was far more than he had ever thought possible, far surpassing the girth of anything else he had taken. Maybe the Armour was stretching him more, or maybe it was because of the additional dropped *Pink Goo*, but Anders suddenly had a ray of hope. A single big drop of dragon precum flooded his insides and further lubed up Anders. It also replenished an impressive 643,718 Magic Points.

A very small fraction of the tip was all that would fit; there was definite final resistance now, and the dragon's dick was only in about a hundredth of its final girth. The sudden hope that had lifted the avatar's spirits dwindled away. It really didn't make sense that he could take a dragon penis the size of a skyscraper up his ass, even if it was magic. Strange game logic or not, there was no way that would fit.

> The Plague of Shadow's Text Box: I'm going to enjoy this, little Elfboy. Now take my gargantuan dragon Urk!

> Anders' Text Box: Your gargantuan dragon Urk?

Anders didn't understand what was going on at first. The Plague of Shadow was screaming out in horrible pain. The black scales were withering, and the very flesh of the dragon was becoming sunken and even blacker. Suddenly, it hit Anders: this is what had happened to his gay elf rival Kray earlier. Anders saw the source. With a *Stretching of His Arms and Dramatic Hand Flourish Animation*, a furious Breaker had grabbed the Plague of Shadow's tail. His now-broken *Belt* was flickering, but with each round the Dragon dwindled more and more, and Breaker became more and more draconic.

The misty binds holding Anders dissolved, and he snapped back into a regulation floating position. For the second time this encounter, Anders was at a loss of what to do.

On the same round that Breaker's Armour broke off permanently, he sprouted large black dragon wings from his now scaled back. His emo *#8 Hairstyle* fell away, revealing an emo *#8 Spikestyle*. The Plague of Shadow's eyes cleared and turned back to the original yellow colour. Anders could see the blind panic flashing in its huge yellow eyes. Breaker was going to kill kill the final boss—and even worse, it would mean that he would win the contest!

Anders had to take action, mostly since it was his turn. Pulling back another *6 Shot Multishot* in rainbow formation, he began charging with his newly gained Mana Points. Taking careful aim as the attack finished charging, the nearly naked elf in a *Slime*

Jockstrap released the string. Six colourful arrows flew across the darkened area and mercifully struck the withering husk of the Plague of Shadow right between the eyes. It was a killing blow and caused the Plague of Shadow to perform a fantastic *Death Blow Animation*. The Plague of Shadow would die, but only normally die and not die die, to live another cycle.

> The Plague of Shadow's Text Box: Thank you, Anders....

A half-dragon/half-Breaker looked over at Anders with his brand new yellow, slit-pupil eyes. *With a Folding Out of His Wings and Dramatic Tail Flick Animation*, Breaker flew over with his brand new black scaled dragon wings (and brand new animation). Breaker came face-to-face with Anders and began to stare at him. Intently.

> Anders' Text Box: Please, not another staring contest.

> Breaker's Text Box: That is twice you and your rainbow arrows have ruined my plans, you damn elf. I will not forgive you for this.

> Anders' Text Box: That's okay. I think I can live with myself for it.

> Breaker's Text Box: You, Mr. Max, and your damn party ruined my avatar!

> Anders' Text Box: What are you talking about, Breaker? You released Codes that broke hundreds of avatars, permanently killed monsters and avatars all over the map, and absorbed the powers of the final boss. You should be permanently banned for what you did, but no! All that happened is that you are a custom badass half-dragon now!

> Breaker's Text Box: Shut up, bitch boy!

After a burst of green *Dragon Fire* (*With a Folding Out of His Wings and Dramatic Tail Flick Animation* thrown in for good measure) and a swipe of half-dragon claws, Anders was hurled backward and was now right before the *Critical* status, missing it by only 3 Hit Points. Breaker not only had most of the Plague of Shadow's strength, but he also had gained boss status. Boss status had even granted him multiple attacks per round.

Anders knew that he was no match for a final boss alone; he was no over-levelled Mr. Max, nor was he skilled with game math like Palcath. He couldn't out-nickname like Fourni, nor out-sex like Roodg. He couldn't even begin to out-compete someone like Lissa. It would be okay. Anders wasn't planning on fighting a last boss. Anders was going to fight what he had been fighting since the start of the game. Fashion.

Notching another six arrows into the *Slimey Bow+*, Anders pulled back and let fly. The *Broken Belt of Awesomeness* was struck right in the broken buckle. The arrow easily dislodged the belt that was floating in the space around Breaker's waist and carried it off into the distance. That was his one and only action this turn. The rainbow carried the belt off strong and true, much further than Anders expected due to the low gravity. He was more than surprised when the belt and arrows flew in a continued rainbow arc outward and eventually into the very heart of the black, diseased sun. With a terrible burst of energy, the sickly sun and the *Broken Belt of Awesomeness* imploded, forever destroying them both. A wave of rainbow energy, sparkles of broken code, and a cloud of magic residue filled the cube, the castle, the cavern, and everything in it. Six small balls of rainbow light emerged where the sun once had been, created by Anders' attack.

Once the dust settled, Anders smugly looked back at Breaker expectantly. The half-dragon was scowling, brushing rainbow off himself, but remained unchanged.

> Anders' Text Box: Well, snap! I was hoping that would have removed your half-dragon powers or something.

> Breaker's Text Box: Guess not, Elfbitch! You did break my *Belt* in half, though, so now Breaker is going to break you in half.

The newly made half-dragon used the *Smirk Animation.*

> Anders' Text Box: Wait. You are not a pervert, too, are you? You're not going to get all rapey, are you?

Breaker used the *Oh Sweet Maker No Animation.*

> Breaker's Text Box: What? Huh? Oh, Flaming Pit, no. Oh, yuck. I was being literal. I meant I was going use my half-dragon claws to break you in half. Literally. What in the map is wrong with you?

> Anders' Text Box: Oh, thank the Maker. That would be so much worse if a controlled avatar was going to rape someone as opposed to just some programmed creature doing it.

> Breaker's Text Box: Stop flattering yourself. I'm not into that sex with monsters crap.

> Anders' Text Box: Then why would you release Codes that broke avatars and made monsters get all sexy with them?

> Breaker's Text Box: I didn't. Getting yourself broken by cheating does that. It is funny, really. You, of all elves, should know that already. I track all the Code users and know you never used one. Is the result hilarious? Yes. But did I have anything to do with it? No.

Anders considered this, and he quickly considered something else.

> Anders' Text Box: I guess that makes sense. Now, tell me why you hate Mr. Max so much.

Breaker's Text Box: That is a stupid question. I hate him because I want to win. I never get to win; bad things always happen to me.

Anders' Text Box: What do you want to win so badly?

Breaker's Text Box: The Insta-Wiki Contest, you idiot.

Anders' Text Box: So, how did you figure out the Codes? Are you a programmer or something?

Breaker's Text Box: Maybe a little, I mean, I dabble.... Wait, why would I tell you that?

Anders' Text Box: It is okay. You don't need to tell me. Um ... so ... if you are not a real programmer, what do you do? Do you like movies or things besides epic high fantasy? I like movies about epic high fantasy myself.

Breaker's Text Box: What is wrong with you? Seriously.

Anders' Text Box: I am just curious! I like plot. Like the plot of the game. Did you figure out all the plot? I thought it was interesting, and I didn't even know what it was. You did all the quests, so tell me what your favourite bit was!

Breaker's Text Box: What are you doing!?

Anders' Text Box: Sorry, I guess I'm just nervous. I talk when I get nervous—yes, that's it. So, how did you post the Codes? Oh, and where did you post them?

Breaker's Text Box: I typed them in, you dolt and posted them on the WorldForums. Seriously, you are with avatars that used the damn things. You should know where the Codes were. You definitely do not qualify to be a Rocket Sorcerer.

Anders' Text Box: Yes, your stats are clearly much better than mine now. How much of the dragon did you absorb? Can I get a percentage, maybe? I know a guy that just loves stats. I mean, what are your stats now, anyway?

Breaker's Text Box: Better than yours, obviously. At least in Intelligence.

Anders' Text Box: Very true. Very true ... so ... uh ... I noticed that you had black accents. Now that you can no longer have Armour on, how nice was it for you that your skin is all scaly and black? Is black your favourite colour, or did you pick black because it is badass and menacing?

Breaker's Text Box: What? That has nothing to do with anything.

Anders' Text Box: Yes, it does. Oh, wait, black isn't a colour. It is a shade, isn't it? But if black isn't your favourite 'colour,' which one is? I am a big fan of green myself. You probably noticed that, but I thought just in case you hadn't, I wou—

Breaker's Interruption Text Box: Shut up. You are clearly insane. I was going to tear you apart, remember?

Anders' Text Box: That's okay. I am finished now, anyway.

Breaker's Text Box: Finished what? You never started anything. You weren't charging shit, and you don't have any magic attacks….

Anders' Text Box: I've finished stalling.

Breaker's Text Box: What?

The Plague of Shadow Phase II's Multiple Text Boxes: I believe we have unfinished business, Breaker.

Six sets of different coloured arms each grabbed Breaker tightly. During the stall Anders had watched them and delayed Breaker as the spots of rainbow energy from the destroyed sun had twisted and morphed. The residual dragon energy from the *Breaker's Belt of Awesomeness* had combined with the elemental energy of Anders' shots. Each little ball had turned into a glowing egg of a different colour. As Anders stalled, the eggs grew and eventually hatched out six different dragons. Smaller than the Plague of Shadow by a long shot, but also much bigger than Breaker, the dragons honed in on Breaker once they reached physical maturity. These creations were not from this game. They had been made from a combination of Anders and the stolen essence of the Plague of Shadow being shot into the diseased sun. It had functioned as a womb for the combination. Essentially, Anders, a belt, and the Plague of Shadow were now the proud parents of six baby dragons.

Like the elemental crystals in his bow, each of these coloured dragons was tied to a different element. A red Fire Dragon sheathed in flames. An orange Light Dragon shining bright. A yellow Wind Dragon glowing with sparks. A green Earth Dragon with leaves hovering by. A blue Ice Dragon covered in crystals. A purple Dark Dragon that absorbed the light inward. The six Rainbow Dragons were all now holding tight onto the shocked half-Breaker, and they knew how to do it in rainbow order. Anders was so proud.

> Anders' Text Box: Who doesn't qualify to be a Rocket Sorcerer now, Breaker?

> Breaker's Text Box: Mrrph!

> The Plague of Shadow Phase II Red's Text Box: Time.

> The Plague of Shadow Phase II Orange's Text Box: To.

> The Plague of Shadow Phase II Yellow's Text Box: Deal.

> The Plague of Shadow Phase II Green's Text Box: With.

> The Plague of Shadow Phase II Blue's Text Box: This.

> The Plague of Shadow Phase II Purple's Text Box: Filth.

With a Stretching Out of Their Wings and a Dramatic Movement of Their Claws Animation, The Plague of Shadow Phase II's vengeance was swift. The Multi Dragons flew off with the very stunned Breaker. While Anders could no longer see what was going on within just a few rounds, Breaker was yelling loudly and calling out for the Maker.

Justice, in the form of a rainbow.

A black robed humanoid in a cowl zapped out of thin air with a glorious *Reveal Animation.* It had glowing red eyes under its hood and a dragon tail. It was holding a wicked, curved dagger. Anders was startled and confused.

> Narbenock's Text Box: Bwahahahaha! You must be surprised to see me, adventurer!

> Anders' Text Box: Yes! Yes I am. Who are you?

> Narbenock's Text Box: It is I, Narbenock! Lord of the Dragons! Summoner and controller of the Plague of Shadow.

> Anders' Text Box: That is cool, I guess? Why are you here?

> Narbenock's Text Box: Seriously? You should be surprised and in shock from my big reveal. How could you ever see it coming? That I was the ultimate lord of darkness all along! For I am the Dragon Cultist!

> Anders' Text Box: I have no idea who you are.

Narbenock's Text Box: But didn't you think it was NPC Quivillis the Queen and not me?

Anders' Text Box: I don't know who that is either.

Narbenock's Text Box: I sent you on all those quests to gather quest items. Now I am revealing that I used those items to summon the Plague of Shadow and that the original Plague was just me in disguise to fool that idiotic royal family. I tricked you to think it was that foolish NPC Quivillis the Queen! Now with the items you brought me, I can rule the entire world of Gentalia by summoning a new, more powerful dragon with the help of my summoned star of evil!

Anders' Text Box: I didn't do any of the quests for you. I seriously have no idea who you are.

Narbenock used the *Confused Blink Animation*. This was simply unheard of.

Narbenock's Text Box: Really? Not even one quest?

Anders' Text Box: I completed the Teardrop Returned quest, but I skipped steps one through four, step six, and step seven. That is the only quest I did, and I only have two parts listed.

Narbenock's Text Box: You are facing the final version of the final boss and have only completed a quarter of a quest. There should be rules against that.

Anders used the *Shrug Animation*.

Narbenock's Text Box: I guess you really don't know who I am. Honestly, it sort of takes the wind out of my sails. I barely even want to take over the entire map now.

Anders' Text Box: That's okay. I think you can have it anyways. Breaker killed pretty much every NPC on the map. He even killed that Queen you were mumbling about and that starting Wizard guy so now no one can even start playing.

Narbenock's Text Box: What? But I am that starting Wizard guy!

Anders' Text Box: Oh! That's where I have seen you before! That would have been a cool reveal if I remembered that.

Narbenock's Text Box: I know it would have been. It was very well scripted.

Anders' Text Box: You are dead dead, though. How are you here?

Narbenock's Text Box: There must be two versions of me—Normal Narbenock and me, Dragon Cultist Narbenock.

Anders' Text Box: Well, nobody can make avatars because you are dead dead!

Narbenock's Text Box: I know all the other Narbenock's dialog. I have his abilities as well as mine, like my Dragon Birth Reveal from the ... hey, where did my diseased sun go?

Anders' Text Box: You could start new avatars? Can you do that?

Looking deep into his Code, Narbenock discovered that he not only had the Starting Narbenock's scripts, but also the scripts for Holiday Fun Narbenock.

Narbenock's Text Box: Yes, I can. There is the script right there.

Anders' Text Box: So if you reverted back to before your plans were just realized, you could help everyone start again. Sort of like turning over an old leaf!

Narbenock's Text Box: It would be only a temporary fix, but I could. It is strange that the Administrators didn't just reset the map.

Anders' Text Box: They can reset things?

Narbenock's Text Box: Well, they should have been able to.

Anders' Text Box: Strange.

Narbenock's Text Box: It is. Very strange. I have a question as well. Why are you wearing only a *Jockstrap*?

Anders changed to *Blush Shade #1*. He had forgotten that he was still mostly naked.

Anders' Text Box: Oh, uh, it is just custom Anderses only Armour. No big deal.

Narbenock's Text Box: I've heard of that Anderses only stuff, so that makes sense. Okay, now that everything is all settled up, it is time to fight to the death!

Anders' Text Box: Beg pardon?

Narbenock began to glow in multicoloured beams of light, and he rose up while brandishing his wicked curved dagger. The six dragons returned from their task and glared menacingly at Anders.

> Narbenock's Text Box: How nice, the dragons listen to my commands!

> Anders' Text Box: Eep!

Without doing anything, Narbenock cancelled his effects and floated back down. The dragons stopped being aggressive, and took out a deck of cards to start playing *Crazy Eights*.

> Narbenock's Text Box: You know what? I'm really not into it anymore. The moment has passed. Do you want to just stab me or something and get it over with? Then you can just win this whole game thing.

With a genuine smirk on his face (not an Animation one), Anders beckoned Narbenock over and whispered into his ear.

> Anders' Whisper Text Box: That's okay. I have far more interesting ways of defeating you at my disposal.

◈ Chapter 37 ◈
THE INSTA-WIKI CONTEST

It had been many boring yet tense rounds near the Summoning Pillar. Everyone had run out of off camera activities to do. All Player Pagers had been updated, all conversations finished, and all available board games played.

Fournimer's Text Box: I wish we knew what was going on in there! it has been almost a half cycle since they left.

Contest Announcement Text Box: The Insta-Wiki Contest is over. Congratulations to all who tried! The winners will be announced after a long, dramatic pause.

Palcath's Text Box: So, now we have to wait even longer lads, lasses, and Roodgs?

Lissa's Text Box: #Figures.

Mr. Max's Text Box: So, with a mighty blow, I cleaved the Flork Demon in half!

Zal Finn II's Text Box: Lissa, you look pretty tense. Would you maybe like a back rub?

Lissa's Text Box: Who would say no to that?

Zal Finn II's Text Box: Sweet!

Gliint's Lag Text Box: Golly. *Amazed* That's amazing, Mr. Max! I was there and already remembered that! But, still amazing!

Caëlahenãilenŵhei's Text Box: All this needless drama is beyond my comprehension. Why can they not just tell us who won?

Roodg's Text Box: hI.

Caëlahenãilenŵhei's Text Box: Can someone please take this thing away from me?

Roodg's Text Box: hI!

Caëlahenãilenŵhei's Text Box: Okay, fine, that is it, weirdo. Yes, hello, Roodg! We have established that already! You said hello. So HELLO! HELLO!! HELLO!!! HELLO!!!! HELLO!!!!!

Roodg's Text Box: Caëlahenãilenŵhei SAID HELLO 2 ME! dID YOU SEE?!

Caëlahenãilenŵhei's Text Box: What? You actually used my full name? With all the special characters and everything. Nobody has ever done that—or gotten past the first five letters, for that matter. There is no cut and paste option for that! OMM! You typed that all in yourself!

Roodg's Text Box: hI!

Caëlahenãilenŵhei's Text Box: Hi!

Yallundy's Text Box: Something is coming out of that … portal-thing that was left behind.

Palcath's Text Box: You mean that big vagina in the sky, lass?

Yallundy changed to *Blush Shade #B*; it was her unique female troll blue *Blush Shade*.

Yallundy's Text Box: Yes, that.

Out of the portal slunked a nearly naked elf covered in only his *Pink Slime Jockstrap* and copious amounts of portal goop.

Palcath's Text Box: Lad!

Fournimer's Text Box: Dude!

Roodg's Text Box: sAWESOME!

Lissa's Text Box: Loverboy!

Mr. Max's Text Box: What's her name?

Anders' Text Box: Ewww!

Standing up and shaking most of the goop off, Anders waved awkwardly at his friends. Unlike all the other goop the avatar had experienced, this goop was just gross. His belly was still slightly swollen with what hadn't been *Absorbed* yet from Narbenock. For a human-sized creature, Narbenock had shot *so* much into Anders. He pressed the button on the *Slime Jockstrap* and the *Slime Armour* emerged from inside his bottom, none the worse for wear.

Contest Announcement Text Box: Congratulations to the avatar Anders! Winner of the first to defeat the Dragon Cultist Contest! Enjoy your ultimate prize!

Mr. Max's Text Box: The Dragon Cultist! Exciting. I wonder who it turned out to be. I am pretty sure it was NPC Quivillis the Queen. She really seemed suspicious. Damn! I wish I knew this Anders to ask.

Anders' Text Box: Max, it is me.

Mr. Max's Text Box: You are the Dragon Cultist? I never would have guessed! Nice to meet you, Dragon Cultist!

Palcath's Text Box: So, you won? Good show! What is your prize, lad?

Anders' Text Box: I don't know. I can't see it anywhere. I'll need to search in my *Ultra-Pack*.

Yallundy's Text Box: Something else is coming out of the … thing.

With a wet splortch, a black scaled half-dragon glooped out of the portal. It was not unconscious or conscious, dead or alive. It simply was.

Palcath's Text Box: What the lad is that thing?

Anders' Text Box: Breaker?

Fournimer's Text Box: that's Buddy?

warrier's Text Box: …

warrier used the *Silent Gasp Animation*.

Lissa's Text Box: #SoFuckedUp.

Anders' Text Box: No way, I thought he was ripped apart by my dragons.

Zal Finn II's Text Box: He is a total badass half-dragon now. How fair is that?

Caëlahenâilenẇhei's Text Box: Most unfair, that is my personal opinion. For his crimes, he did deserve to be ripped apart.

Roodg's Text Box: hI!

Caëlahenâilenẇhei's Text Box: Hi!

Gliint's Lag Text Box: *Gasp* No way! Breaker?

Contest Announcement Text Box: The Insta-Wiki Contest has ended in a tie. The winning avatars are: Party One – Anders, Fournimer, Lissa, Mr. Max, Palcath, and Roodg. Party Two – Breaker, Caela... lots of other letters there; whatever, you know who you are, Gliint, Kray, warrier, Yallundy, and Zal Finn II. Congratulations to all the winners, and have fun in your special reward—two hundred cycles in the expansion before it is released to the public!

Anders' Text Box: Wait! What is my Ultimate Prize? I don't see it anywhere!

Fournimer's Text Box: really?

Lissa's Text Box: A tie? That is #SoFuckedUp!

Mr. Max's Text Box: Who the heck are all those avatars? I don't see hardly any of them here! How did they win! They are not even in the area.

Palcath's Text Box: All of us, lads, lasses, and Roodgs?

Roodg's Text Box: nEAT.

Caëlahenâilenẇhei's Text Box: Unexpected.

warrier's Text Box: ???

Yallundy's Text Box: I guess we have all won.

Zal Finn II's Text Box: That is sort of exciting!

Breaker and Kray said nothing.

A glimmering portal opened up in the middle of the area. Traces of the large island-based expansion map could be seen through the swaying gateway. It was with a slight hesitation that Anders stepped inside. As a brand new loading screen appeared, he thought while the progress bar filled, and he was just full of questions.

What would the new expansion be like? Would their avatars be fixed? Would this island be just as full of broken monsters as the continent he had just left? Would going there solve their problems or only create new ones? What was this Ultimate Prize he had won but couldn't seem to find in his inventory? Why hadn't the Administrators fixed any of the problems or answered any questions? Why was this game even broken in the first place?

The progress bar was nearly completely filled, which caused Anders to swallow hard. Was going into the expansion really the right decision after all? The bar was at 100%, and there was only one way to find out the answers to his questions. With a mix of determination and apprehension, Anders stepped into the Island of Islana.

◊ END PART ONE ◊

Gliint's Lag Text Box: *Gasp* Really? No way! Everyone?

www.ingramcontent.com/pod-product-compliance
Lightning Source LLC
Chambersburg PA
CBHW020322180626
46812CB00001B/8